A

Part 3 of the Song of Suspense series
A Novel by

HALLEE BRIDGEMAN

Published by
Olivia Kimbrell Press™

Olivia Kimbrell Press™

PUBLISHED BY: Olivia Kimbrell Press™*, P.O. Box 4393, Winchester, KY 40392-4393 The *Olivia Kimbrell Press*™ colophon and open book logo are trademarks of Olivia Kimbrell Press™.

Olivia Kimbrell Press™ is a publisher offering true to life, meaningful fiction from a Christian worldview intended to uplift the heart and engage the mind.

Some scripture quotations courtesy of the King James Version of the Holy Bible.

Some scripture quotations courtesy of the New King James Version of the Holy Bible, Copyright © 1979, 1980, 1982 by Thomas-Nelson, Inc. Used by permission. All rights reserved.

Excerpted lyrics from "It Is Well with My Soul" by hymnist Horatio G. Spafford with music composed by Philip P. Bliss composed 1873 from the public domain.

Original Cover Art and Graphics by Romance Cover Creations (www.romance-covers.com)

Library Cataloging Data

Bridgeman, Hallee (Hallee A. Bridgeman) 1972-
 A Carol for Kent; Part 3 of the Song of Suspense series/ Hallee Bridgeman
  300. 23cm × 15cm (9 in × 6 in)
Summary: A Ruthless Serial Killer Seeks to End a Love Song Eight Years in the Making.
  ISBN: 978-1-939603-43-2 (trade perfect) ISBN-10: 1-939603-43-9
  ISBN: 978-1939603265 (ebook)
1. Christian fiction 2. man-woman relationships 3. suspenseful romance 4. romantic thriller 5. serial killer 6. family relationships

 PS3558.B7534 C537 2014

 [Fic.] 813.6 (DDC 23)

A Carol for Kent

Part 3 of the Song of Suspense series

A Novel by

HALLEE BRIDGEMAN

DEDICATION

LOVINGLY DEDICATED TO …

Carol and Rob.

When I was writing *An Aria for Nick*, I needed a "best friend". As I searched my mind for "best friend for high school Aria", I immediately came up with Carol – one of my best friends from my high school years and someone whom I continue to adore and admire today.

And in the mind of high school friends, when naming my serial killer I couldn't help but choose "Rob," named after my other best friend – the first friend I made after a military relocation to Ft. Benning, Georgia, when I was 15.

This book is dedicated to you, Carol Smith and Rob Tesdahl. Thank you for the two-and-a-half decades of friendship. Here's to many more…

♫ ♫ ♫ ♫

TABLE OF CONTENTS

A CAROL FOR KENT 1
   COPYRIGHT NOTICE 2
   DEDICATION 5
   TABLE OF CONTENTS 7
   ACKNOWLEDGEMENT 9
CHAPTER 1 11
CHAPTER 2 14
CHAPTER 3 21
CHAPTER 4 34
CHAPTER 5 40
CHAPTER 6 48
CHAPTER 7 54
CHAPTER 8 59
CHAPTER 9 64
CHAPTER 10 72
CHAPTER 11 84
CHAPTER 12 91
CHAPTER 13 101
CHAPTER 14 107
CHAPTER 15 114
CHAPTER 16 120
CHAPTER 17 128
CHAPTER 18 134
CHAPTER 19 143
CHAPTER 20 150
CHAPTER 21 155
CHAPTER 22 162
CHAPTER 23 171
CHAPTER 24 174

CHAPTER 25 183
CHAPTER 26 188
CHAPTER 27 193
CHAPTER 28 200
CHAPTER 29 209
CHAPTER 30 214
CHAPTER 31 220
CHAPTER 32 224
CHAPTER 33 229
CHAPTER 34 236
CHAPTER 35 243
TRANSLATION KEY 248
READER'S GUIDE 249
    READER'S GUIDE: SUGGESTED MENU 249
    READER'S GUIDE: DISCUSSION QUESTIONS 255
SONG OF SUSPENSE SERIES 258
    EXCERPT: A MELODY FOR JAMES 261
    EXCERPT: AN ARIA FOR NICK 266
    EXCERPT: A HARMONY FOR STEVE 270
VIRTUES AND VALOR SERIES 274
    EXCERPT: TEMPERANCE'S TRIAL 275
THE JEWEL SERIES 284
    EXCERPT: SAPPHIRE ICE 286
    EXCERPT: GREATER THAN RUBIES 291
    EXCERPT: EMERALD FIRE 296
    EXCERPT: TOPAZ HEAT 299
ABOUT THE AUTHOR 304
    HALLEE ONLINE 305
    HALLEE NEWSLETTER 306

♫ ♫ ♫ ♫

ACKNOWLEDGEMENT

I'D LIKE ACKNOWLEDGE ...

... the Office of Virginia's Commonwealth's Attorney and, in particular, Elizabeth Hobbs, Assistant Commonwealth's Attorney in Richmond, who does Carol Mabry's very important job in real life. She patiently took time out of her incredibly busy day to show me aspects of her work and allowed me the opportunity to bombard her with dozens of questions.

She was very gracious with her time and incredibly helpful, for which I am sincerely grateful and appreciative. I don't want to come off as cliché, but I couldn't have written this book without the information I gleaned from her.

Thank you, Elizabeth!

♫ ♫ ♫ ♫

Personal journal entry.

April 16

He won't leave me alone about her. She consumes his every waking thought, he says. It's been years since I last gave in to his demands, but he scares me, now. If I gave in and just let him do whatever he wanted he would go on a killing spree and burn the world down. I have to appease him.

The day to day contact drains me. He saps my energy and threatens and cajoles and promises and won't just SHUT UP! I've lost the strength to fight.

We got in so much trouble last time. I don't want to move again. Maybe if I give in just once, maybe I can make him pretend to be normal, again. Throw him a bone so he'll just let me have some peace. I just want peace.

♪ ♪ ♪ ♪

DARLA Cody shifted aside to keep the big guy in the smelly flannel shirt from bumping into her arm and spilling the drinks she carried. He drunkenly shouted an apology in her direction as she shifted through the crowd.

As she approached the table in the corner, she grinned at her friends. Melissa, Rachel, and Saundra took up three of the four chairs, and Melissa had her foot on the seat of the fourth. As crowded as this place was, Darla was surprised no one had tried to wrestle away the chair from her by now. Maybe someone had?

"What a madhouse," she exclaimed over the percussive music.

"I'm sure not everyone here are CPA's like us, but it's nice to be in this kind of celebratory atmosphere in the wake of the most recent tax season," Saundra declared.

Darla snorted. "You couldn't possibly be a bigger nerd, could you?"

They laughed, because blonde and beautiful Saundra's exterior revealed nothing of the computer-like brain in her stunning head.

"What did I say?" Saundra asked.

As her friends laughed, Darla rolled her head on her shoulders. She felt drained, on the edge of complete exhaustion. She'd thought this night out would be just the ticket after 15-hour days over the last three months, but what she really wanted was a hot bath and maybe a good book. Unfortunately, she couldn't abandon her friends ten minutes after getting here, so she'd give it another hour, tops, then make a graceful exit.

"Ooh, hot guy at your six o'clock," Melissa said, gesturing with her head.

Trying her best to be casual, Darla turned and looked, immediately spotting the man in the shirt and tie. He had dark hair, a goatee, and black framed glasses. He was looking right at her.

As soon as their eyes met, he looked away, as if scanning the crowd. But it didn't take long for him to look back at her again.

"He looks like a younger and better shaved Trent Scott," Rachel said. Trent Scott was the latest Hollywood heartthrob, thin and lean with a slender, wiry build and hollow cheeks that framed deep blue soulful eyes. In addition to securing a role opposite Julianne McNeill in the latest blockbuster, he had just been nominated as *People* magazine's Sexiest Man Alive.

"You think any thin guy with dark hair looks like Trent Scott," Melissa accused.

Darla looked away. She wasn't here to pick up some random guy, no matter how good looking. She took a sip of her Cosmopolitan, flinching a bit at the strong alcohol taste. "He's shorter than me," she said.

"Most are, love," Rachel said. She grinned at the guy, and Darla thought she'd groan out loud when her friend said, "Here he comes."

He came up to their table and put his hand on the back of Melissa's chair. Darla wished she'd sat down when she'd had the chance, because now she stood next to him.

"Evening, ladies," he said, looking at each one of them. When he looked at her, she thought that she'd never seen eyes so shockingly blue before. "I'm Rob."

Melissa took it upon herself to introduce all of them. When she finished, he turned to Darla and held his hand out. "It's a pleasure to meet you," he said, looking into her eyes.

"Likewise," she said, rather breathlessly. She felt her heart flutter at his flirting.

"I noticed you from over by the bar. Would you like to dance?"

Feeling pulled into his eyes, she shook her head and said, "I –"

"She'd love to," Rachel said enthusiastically.

"Darla is our dancing queen," Saundra added.

"Well –"

Rob grinned and stepped backward, tugging on her hand. "Come on. Dance with me. I promise I won't bite. What can it hurt?"

Helpless, Darla looked at her friends, then back to him. "Okay, one dance." She took three long pulls of her drink and set the nearly empty glass on the table. Feeling the heat from the alcohol spread down her chest, she tossed a wave at her friends. "See ya!"

CHAPTER 2

♫ ♫ ♫ ♫

Tuesday, April 17th

CAROL Mabry stared down at the beautiful corpse carefully arranged on the floor of apartment 3A. The dead woman wore a gray silk pantsuit and pink silk blouse. Her hair was perfectly coifed into a French twist, and her makeup looked like it had been applied professionally. Pink beads adorned her neck, hanging loosely against her breasts. Clip-on pink ball earrings clung to each ear.

She lay spread eagle on the ground, her eyes a blank stare in the direction of the ceiling. Her limbs had been arranged in near perfect symmetry as if she were caught in the very act of making a snow angel. Some sort of wire around her neck had cut into her skin, making it look like she had on a red necklace.

At her head, at each of her hands, and at her feet, fat red candles burned, forming flickering lights at the points of the pentagram of her body. The crimson colored wax had run down the candles and pooled into the beige carpet.

Horrible, Carol thought.

She hated senseless death. After her years as an Assistant Commonwealth Attorney for Richmond, Virginia, she kept expecting to become immune to it, but so far, every time was just as horrible as the last.

Pushing aside those personal thoughts, needing to run on logic and not emotion right now, Carol knelt near the head of the body and inspected the wire without touching it. She recognized the marked tip on one end.

Detective Mitchell "Mitch" Carpenter knelt beside her and looked on, rubbing his chin with his large hand. His father had been American, but he'd inherited all of his features from his Italian mother. He was in his mid forties and about her height. His face showed the lines of strain that came from being a homicide detective in one of the largest cities in the state.

He wore a cheap suit today and she could smell the lingering odor of cigarette smoke mixed in with the scent of Old Spice clinging to the polyester blend.

"Darla Cody," he said by way of introduction. "Twenty-five, CPA at the Grayson firm. Single, straight."

"Doesn't look like she fought at all, does it?"

"No. She looks almost relaxed." He used the tip of his pen to touch the tip of the wire on her neck. "What do you think?" he asked.

"Violin string." She gestured to the marker. "G."

"G?"

"Yes. See?" She brought her finger closer. "I can guess at the brand, but that's probably unimportant. This is definitely violin string."

"So our victim was strangled with a G-string? Is that supposed to be funny?" Even years of hardening his heart to the things he saw every day could not disguise all of the disgust in his voice.

Carol raised her eyebrows. "Check her underwear?"

Mitch shook his head. "Way, way outside of my lane. I'll wait on the medical examiner for the lingerie report."

"Could have swapped for a trophy. Check her underwear drawer?"

Mitch just shook his head. "Could just be nothing. Could just be a rather interesting choice of weapon."

"Indeed." Carol stood and looked down at the body. "What's with the candles?"

"Cult?"

"Perhaps." She checked her watch. "Who found her?"

Mitch gestured with his chin to the blonde woman standing next to two uniformed officers. "Friend from work. She said they were out last night, and that this one left with a guy named Rob. She didn't show up for work, so at lunch, she came over here to make sure she was okay."

"Anything else on this Rob?"

"Nada." He stepped back as the crime scene unit arrived. "I'm canvassing now. We have people in this apartment and at the bar. We'll pull security footage, too."

"I saw the cameras coming in here. Hopefully we have something." She looked back down at the body. "Something's not right here."

"You mean other than the strangled dead girl?"

"Yeah," she said absently, staring at the gray jacket and pink blouse. "Something."

"Carol, this girl could be your sister," Mitch said in his careless and almost callous way.

Carol tilted her head and looked at the girl again. They had the same shade of auburn hair, and both were tall and thin, but there weren't too many other features they shared. Carol's eyes were tawny colored, and this girl's were green.

Unfazed at Mitch's manner, she shook her head. "Not if you took her out of her suit." She pulled her vibrating phone out of her pocket. "There's something here we're supposed to see. I think the killer is telling us something. I just can't get it right now." She checked the incoming text and put her phone back into her pocket. "I have to run."

"I'll send over witness interviews as soon as I have them."

"And the photos. I want to try to see what I'm not seeing right now."

"You got it."

♫ ♫ ♫ ♫

BECAUSE she was already out and about, Carol stopped at her favorite coffee shop on her way back to her office. The drive-through line looked really long, so she parked in the tiny parking lot and dashed inside.

She nearly groaned out loud when she saw Jack Gordon sitting in one of the leather chairs by the gas fireplace. The bell on the door had jingled when she entered and he glanced her way over the screen of his laptop. As soon as he recognized her, he set the machine aside and stood with a smile.

Carol had met Jack here three weeks ago. He'd just relocated to the Richmond area from Alexandria. He looked incredibly fit at about 220 pounds of solid muscle. With his dark hair and blue eyes, he was both handsome and very charming. Carol agreed to meet him for lunch the next day. She thoroughly enjoyed herself right up to the moment she found out he was a detective about to start work in Richmond. Unfortunately, she had a personal rule about dating lawyers or law enforcement.

She thought he'd understand, but he hadn't taken it well. He'd crushed a cup of coffee in his hand, swearing out loud when the hot liquid burned him. His angry reaction put her off of him completely. The next time she'd seen him, he'd acted utterly charming and once more perfectly poised and polite. She couldn't forget how quickly he'd gotten violently angry. Even if his looks and charm had tempted her to compromise on her personal rule, nothing would convince her to do so after that display.

"Hello, Jack," she greeted coolly.

"Carol." He approached, but didn't hold his hand out or try to touch her. "I've missed seeing you here in the mornings."

"It's been really busy at work. I'm lucky if I have time to hit the drive through." She turned her attention to the barista behind the counter. "*Café au lait*, please. Whole milk."

When Jack spoke again, he was a little too close for her comfort level. "Look Carol. We got off on the wrong foot. You're an Army brat. You know how it is when you move to a new town. I could really use a friend. I was hoping we could go out again," he gently conveyed.

Carol turned her head to look at him, but not her body. "I already told you, Jack. No lawyers. No cops. I'm afraid I really can't make an exception. It interferes with my job."

"And what's your job?"

She smiled. "If our paths ever cross, then you'll know." The barista set her coffee in front of her and collected her cash. Carol tossed the change into the tip jar, picked up the cardboard cup, and turned to leave. "Hopefully, we won't ever have to meet on the job. Wouldn't that be nice?"

As she turned away, she saw two things. In her peripheral vision, she saw Jack Gordon's entire body tense up and his jaw clench, and she knew in that moment that her instincts were spot on. Simultaneously, she saw her friend and fellow attorney, Rhonda Regalman, come in through the front door. Rhonda spotted Carol standing next to Jack Gordon and momentarily looked surprised, nearly shocked to see her there. Then, in the blink of an eye, the shocked look vanished and she grinned a hello. "Hi, Carol! Do you want to have a cup of coffee with me?"

Relieved to have a handy excuse to end the conversation, Carol waved a greeting to Rhonda and hastened over to where the other attorney stood. Still bristling over the confrontation with Jack, she gave Rhonda a curt shake of her head. "I can't stay for coffee. Sorry. Gotta' go. But thank you. I'll see you later on."

Keeping her back toward Jack, she walked past Rhonda and out the door back to her car.

♪ ♪ ♪ ♪

YOU nearly missed her solo. It's up next," Harriet Kent whispered as Carol slid into the auditorium seat next to her.

"I know. How's she doing so far?" Carol whispered back.

Harriet smiled at the stage. "She's the best one up there."

They watched the stage full of seven and eight-year-olds do their best to follow the steps they'd been taught, while parents sat in the audience dreaming of prima ballerinas, occasionally wiping at tears of pride or joy. Carol laughed when she caught herself thinking the same thoughts and wiping same tears, and she clapped just as enthusiastically as the rest of the parents and grandparents when it was over and the little bumblebees gave their bows.

At the reception immediately following, she picked up her daughter, Lisa, and gave her a smacking kiss on little lips which proudly sported a red punch mustache. "You are getting better every time I see you," she told her.

"I missed a step toward the end," Lisa said, sadness pushing through the pride.

"I didn't even notice," Carol said, then set her down and straightened the bumblebee wing on her outfit. "Did you have a good time up there?"

Lisa shrugged. "It's a little scary, but fun at the same time." She looked around. "Where's grandpa?"

Carol eyed Harriet, Lisa's grandmother. "He's not feeling too well this evening, Lisa. He decided to lie down and rest while I came here," she said.

Carol felt a twinge of nervousness. Robert Kent had been staying home more and more often lately. She waited until Lisa ran to a group of friends before speaking to Harriet about it. "Has he been to the doctor yet?" she asked.

Harriet pursed her lips and shook her head. "I can't get that man to admit anything is wrong with him. Carol, I'm about near my wit's end. Do you think your friend, Dr. Suarez, would come out to the house and talk to him?"

"I'm sure he would, Harriet, but I don't see what good it would do. He's not going to let Henry examine him, and without an examination, he wouldn't be able to tell what's wrong with him."

"I'm sure you're right," the older woman said. She looked at her watch. "I'm going to go tell Lisa good-bye, then go on home." She looked around and said almost absently, "What time will the birthday party start Saturday?"

"Four. We'll be out around three."

"Why don't you just let Lisa spend the night Friday? We can make it a special birthday treat," Harriet suggested.

Carol had seen that coming. Harriet had offered nearly every weekend for about a year now, but so far Carol only let Lisa sleep over there when her work kept her overnight.

"We have plans for just the two of us Friday night, Harriet. But we'll see you about three," Carol said with a forced smile.

Harriet frowned, then walked off to find Lisa. Carol sighed at the woman's back. When Lisa was a baby and Carol struggled just to get through law school, working nearly full time and still trying to be a mommy, the Kents had offered to take Lisa full time and let Carol visit her whenever she was free. The notion had appalled her and she had refused, almost considering relocating to a school farther away from them.

A year later, the child support checks slowly got bigger until she didn't have to work anymore, but the offer had continued to bother Carol considerably. Perhaps if they had never offered that, she would feel more comfortable letting Lisa go out to their ranch and spend more nights. As it was, she didn't completely trust their motives. They were good grandparents and truly loved Lisa, their only grandchild, but their opinion of Carol had room for improvement.

Carol watched the little bumblebees weave their way through the crowd of fans while she chuckled to herself. If their opinion of her was low, it was her own fault. She showed up in their town not only five months pregnant with their son's child, but asking for their assistance to help her find him. She remembered standing on their doorstep and explaining that she didn't even know how to start looking for him.

Her heart wept a little, as it always did when she thought of him, and she frowned at the memory. They'd contacted him for her, but he told them he wanted nothing to do with Carol or the baby she carried.

In all fairness, he had supported them financially, but in the time she carried her and the nearly eight years since Lisa had been born, he had never once called nor written, and Lisa had never met him. Lately, Carol's daughter had started expressing curiosity about her father.

Carol decided that she would tell her one day. For now, she and the

Kents both agreed that it was best she not be told just yet. They removed pictures of him from the house, and Lisa had yet to ask to see one. Once she did, she would immediately know who he was.

She shrugged off her dark mood, deciding it was probably a reaction to the afternoon she'd endured, and went in search of her little bumblebee. They were going out for dinner to celebrate the recital with Lisa's best friend and her parents. Carol always enjoyed the time spent with the Bradfords, and looked forward to shedding the tragedy of the day and the stress of Harriet Kent with tortilla chips dunked in spicy salsa and cheese enchiladas at their favorite Mexican restaurant.

♫ ♫ ♫ ♫

Friday, April 20th

"**BAH-BEE!** Bah-bee! Bah-bee!" The roar of the crowd vibrated the steel I-beams supporting the arena.

Robert "Bobby" Jason Kent was currently the hottest young male star in country music. He stood tall, a few inches over six feet even before he donned his cowboy boots, and lanky. His eyes were a bright blue with laugh lines in the corners, set in an angular face the cameras loved. Wearing a cowboy hat and a pair of jeans, he looked like anyone's iconic epitome of a modern American cowboy. His rugged, striking handsomeness made him a favorite of both the magazines and tabloids.

Even without his wholesome good looks, his voice would have been enough to push him up through the ranks of stardom. Between his trained tenor and his natural baritone, he could effortlessly belt out the fast dance tunes his fans loved so much. With his powerful tenor, he could sing a slow song that had women sighing to themselves, feeling as if he sang only for them. He answered interview questions in a thoughtfully slow, refined southern drawl honed on the whetstone of central Virginia. His responses always held a hint of dry humor that gave his spoken voice a velvety sound and female interviewers always felt relaxed and flirtatious in his presence.

The crowd continued to chant his name. "Bah-bee! Bah-bee! Bah-bee!"

He smiled as his band reset after the opening act. The trappings of modern day stardom often included things like drugs and alcohol. Early in his career, Bobby had wisely realized the reason they were called "trappings" and carefully and consciously avoided them ever since. Standing back stage in this moment, he realized once more that nothing could equal the euphoria of thousands of fans screaming his name. That feeling had no equal in this world.

"Ready?" Gary yelled. Bobby threw him a thumbs-up to cue his band, and they started the opening music to their signature song, *The Amarillo Swing*. The crowd roared. Smoke billowed from the wings as the platform Bobby stood on shot upward through the floor of the stage. He began to sing.

He could actually feel the sound waves from the crowds' voices and wondered if they could even hear his voice as they joined him for every chorus. After he finished the song, the band quieted and he held his hands up, motioning for quiet.

"Good evening, Raleigh," he said with a sideways smile. Another wave of ovation swept through the room. As it started to quiet, he said, "All right. All right, now. If y'all will just bow your heads, we'll really get this party started."

As intoxicating as the sound of the ovation of the crowd felt, there was nothing on earth like the silence of thousands of fans as they, as one, bowed their heads. Bobby prayed in a loud, clear voice, "Father God, we are so thankful to be here tonight."

He went on, praying over the concert, over hearts and minds, and ended with thanking God for his talent. Then he said, "And Father, please bless Harmony Harper tonight as she sings her new hit song, *Even if it Were Only You*!"

As soon as he said, "Amen," four spotlights bathed contemporary Christian newcomer Harmony Harper in pure white light. Her sequined lavender gown dazzled the audience even more than her bright smile and blonde curls. Bobby's band instantly began the intro of her latest hit single that had met with such unexpected crossover appeal.

The crowd went completely wild.

Harmony had a young voice and a fresh outlook and, if Bobby knew anything about the business, he had a strong feeling she had a bright future ahead in music. Her brother, Franklin, acted as her manager and he had made some savvy decisions with her career so far. Earlier in the year, Bobby and superstar Melody Montgomery had invited Harmony to add a few tracks to their annual charity Christmas Album, and Harmony had enthusiastically agreed to meet with him and discuss it further. A few weeks ago, he had contacted her about Raleigh since she had a concert scheduled at one of the largest churches in the Triangle the evening after his show, and she had agreed to surprise Bobby's audience.

The crowd was on their feet singing along with her at the top of their lungs. She finished her song with Bobby Kent singing backup. More than forty thousand voices sang the closing chorus along with them. "Even if it were only me! Just me! He would do it all for me. He would do it all for you! Just you! Even if it were only you."

It took over a minute for the shouts, whistles, and applause to die down enough for Harmony to be heard when she spoke. In her sweet, soprano voice she said, "Hey there, Raleigh! Thanks for letting me sing for you tonight!"

The crowd roared. When they settled down again, Bobby grinned and said, "I'll sing backup for you anytime." Applause. "Hey folks, we're gonna let Harmony go now, but remember she's playing her full show right here in town tomorrow night…"

The crowd's reaction was deafening. Harmony covered her mouth with her hands and laughed out loud. She reached out and put a hand on Bobby's forearm and he quickly snatched off his hat and fanned himself as if heated by her touch. She laughed even harder. The crowd ate it up.

When the audience noise faded to merely a roar, Bobby said, "I take it some of y'all already have tickets."

Laughter and applause. Bobby's band started strumming and drumming the opening chords and rhythm to *Cowboys Don't Cry*. They could keep the bridge going for as long as necessary until Bobby sang the opening lyrics.

Harmony bowed and waved and said, "Bobby, thanks so much for letting me share your stage tonight. I was really nervous, but it was great. Thank you so much for your hospitality. And thank you, North Carolina. I'll see you tomorrow night!"

"Harmony Harper, ladies and gentlemen!" Bobby declared as she left the stage and he got back to his own program.

This was the last concert of the tour so he gave the crowd all he had. He played his guitar and his fiddle, sang for two hours without a break, then returned to the stage three times to perform three "final" encore numbers. He and his band members soaked up the crowd's energy. It wasn't until much later, they sat backstage in the early morning hours after the last fan left and technicians and support crew packed up the equipment and gear that belonged to his show that they all realized how exhausted they felt.

There would be no loading onto the bus or the plane tonight to head for yet another venue. Instead, they took a limousine to the five star hotel that towered over the Research Triangle Park and went to their rooms to sleep, ready for the six-month break in touring that they'd earned. It had been eight years since they'd taken more than a few weeks off at a time.

After a steaming hot shower, and a rapid surf of cable channels that lasted less than 5 minutes before he powered off the flat screen television, Bobby settled into the king size bed. Sleep refused to claim him. He rose and paced his suite, going from one room to the next, while the remaining adrenaline from the night's show hummed through his system and kept his body from relaxing and getting some rest. He wasn't concerned or bothered by it as he would be the night before another show, because there would be no concert the next night. Nevertheless, he felt restless and couldn't stand the thought of waiting for the sun to rise before he left.

He wanted to go home.

Bobby Kent wondered why he found himself all alone in a posh hotel room at the age of twenty-nine. He didn't even have someone he could call and talk to at this hour. When or where had his life gone so far off the planned path he had laid out in his youth? By now he fully expected to be married and settled on his family's horse farm. He figured he'd have at least one and hopefully a few children by this age.

The idea of superstardom had never even crossed his mind, never become a hope or a dream, until college. He started picking guitar with a couple other guys in his dorm room, they got a drummer, a keyboard player, and somehow made a demo tape. Now, here he was. Adored by millions, but privately alone and feeling so lonesome.

Bobby Kent had the blood of his Savior. The gift of eternal life awaited him one day. He had fame, fortune, and the adoration of hundreds of thousands of loyal fans. In the dark quiet of his hotel room, he wondered, had God made a woman especially for him? Had God made Bobby to be the perfect mate for his future wife? When would he meet her? Had he already met her and blown it?

After finishing a concert tour like this one, he should be able to celebrate with someone, confide in someone, talk with someone, relax and laugh and tease someone. He couldn't celebrate like that with his fans because they didn't really see the man he was, only the singing icon they imagined him to be. Women he had never met in his life often proposed marriage within minutes of conversation. His fan mail averaged 40 marriage proposals per week. The letters that made his heart ache started with, "When I get out of prison..." But in spite of that, he still didn't have what he wanted most in this life, what he needed.

Bobby Kent was alone.

That feeling of lonesomeness led to nearly overwhelming homesickness.

Making a quick decision, he called down to the concierge and asked her to secure him a rental car right away. He had just played a full house in Raleigh, North Carolina, less than a three hour drive from Richmond, Virginia. He and his parents hadn't planned on him visiting until later this summer, but he suddenly felt a strong desire to see them. He wanted to get back to his roots, to relax on the ranch while he worked the horses, watched some sunsets, and ate his mother's cooking.

Within a few minutes, the telephone in his room rang and the clerk told him that his car would be delivered by five in the morning. He thanked her, then laid back down and shut his eyes. His mind made up, he could finally relax. He set an alarm on his phone, said a quick prayer, and closed his eyes.

♫ ♫ ♫ ♫

BOBBY Kent left a message for his manager, Gary, to let him know where he'd gone, grabbed his already packed overnight bag and his guitar and fiddle cases, then headed downstairs. Room service had delivered his breakfast earlier and he had shoveled it down and topped it with three cups of coffee. It was a little past five o'clock, and no one was in the lobby except for the clerk and a bored bellman, so he was out of the hotel and driving away into the Carolina predawn darkness within seconds.

He passed an occasional semi-truck, but other than that, he had the road to himself for the first half of the trip. He stuck to State Road One, heading north toward Interstate 85, and drove through rural northern North Carolina where his songs dominated the airwaves. As his rental car ate up the miles, the tension – and what others had diagnosed as fatigue – started to fade into the background. The predawn countryside revealed by the high beams started becoming more and more familiar. He rolled down the window as he crossed the Virginia state line on Interstate 85 and breathed in the smells of the countryside.

In the nearly nine years since he'd started recording, and in the six years since he'd made it to the top, he'd never been home even once. There had been only a few breaks in all those years, and his parents had always wanted to come to wherever he was at the time. Somehow, his tour schedule had never allowed him any extended time in Richmond. Usually, he had to back-to-back double book Richmond and the nearby Army base at Fort Lee south of Petersburg, then double book the naval base at Norfolk followed immediately by a Washington D. C. show before heading on up into New England. By the time he played two double back-to-back shows, he was utterly exhausted and would just sleep in his hotel with the rest of his crew before leaving for the next show.

His parents always visited him at the hotel or backstage at his Richmond concert, but he never even so much as saw the ranch in all that time. Perhaps that's why his longing for home was so strong right now. He'd been gone too long. Way too long.

Before he even knew it, he found himself turning onto the ranch road and drove through the gates just as the sun fully rose. He noticed the improvements that had been made over the years. While he hadn't been there in person to actually work the horses, he felt a sense of pride that at least the money he had earned and sent to his parents had helped support this ranch where he grew up. It had been so near bankruptcy when he recorded his first album.

He knew that was the number one reason why his parents had encouraged him so much when he told them he wanted to drop out of college after a recording company had responded to one of his demos. He left the University of Georgia in between his sophomore and junior year and drove his old pickup truck to Nashville, Tennessee. The first album had done nothing spectacular in the charts, but the money it made helped save the ranch.

By then he'd caught the fever and stayed in Nashville, and a little over a year later, *The Amarillo Swing* came out with a bullet on the charts, climbed a few hops to number one, and stayed there for five straight months, nearly setting a record for the longest run in the number one spot. It helped that a line dance choreographed for the song became the latest fad, and his album of the same name went double platinum.

He spotted the house through the trees and in the faint morning dusk he could see the lights on in the kitchen. Even on a Saturday, his mother would have risen before the sun, preparing coffee and breakfast, letting the smells slowly wake his father. Bobby smiled as he stopped the car and got out, leaving his bags for later. His mother was going to be really surprised to see him.

♫ ♫ ♫ ♫

Saturday, April 21st

AS Carol gathered her purse and car keys, her work cell phone rang. She glanced at the number as she answered it. "Mitch," Carol greeted as Lisa ran past her and through the front door.

"Afternoon, counselor. Wanted to let you know we got the lab results back. I know you'll have the original in your office Monday morning."

"Yeah. I have Lisa's party this afternoon, so I very definitely will not be working today."

"Well, just so you know, she was drugged. She had enough sedative in her that it wouldn't have mattered if the guy strangled her or not. She would have probably suffocated from the date-rape drug cocktail."

Carol shut the door behind her. As she was stepping down off the top step she heard her personal cell phone ringing inside the house. She almost went back inside to answer it, but then changed her mind. She was already running late, and she had her work cell since she was on call.

"Anything similar in any open cases that you know of?"

"Not this particular combination. But we are definitely checking."

"Okay. Thanks for calling."

"Sure thing. Enjoy the princess's party. Send her the wife's love."

Carol grinned. "I will." She made sure Lisa was strapped in, then got into the front seat and started her car. She had fifteen little eight and nine year olds showing up at Lisa's grandparents' ranch in less than three hours and had Lisa's birthday lunch in the meantime.

The birthday girl had selected her favorite pizza parlor for her eighth birthday lunch, just as she had every year since she could pronounce the word. She brought Amy Bradford, best friend since kindergarten, along with her just as she also always had since the day they met. The two little girls giggled and whispered as they ate green olive pizza with extra cheese, and Assistant Commonwealth Attorney Carol Mabry intentionally let go of all thoughts concerning the strangled Certified Public Accountant.

She forced herself to focus entirely on her daughter while they were in the restaurant. By the time they piled back into her Jeep, she had mentally left murder and autopsy reports behind, and transformed from A. C. A. Carol Mabry into just Carol, just Ms. Mabry, just Lisa's mom.

The drive to the ranch took twenty minutes, and the girls sat in the back seat, continuing their whispered conversation. The whispers got louder until they were full-fledged yells, and Carol finally interrupted them. "Girls! What are you two arguing about?"

"Ms. Mabry, who do you think is cuter? Trevor West or Bobby Kent?" Amy asked. Carol felt her stomach tighten.

"I told you, Bobby Kent is way cuter than Trevor West. Besides, Trevor West is married and has like a dozen kids. Bobby Kent isn't married, so that makes him even more cute," Lisa said. "Plus, he has the same name as my grandma and grandpa. That's even more extra points."

"What do you think, Ms. Mabry?" Amy asked again.

Carol refused to get a headache on Lisa's birthday. Sometimes, tension and stress built up so badly that she would get headaches that made her have to lie down in a darkened room and fight back tears of pain. She had already decided it wasn't going to happen to her today, despite the pain she felt creeping into her temples. She would will it away. "I think you two should play rock-paper-scissors, and whoever wins is right," she said, turning into the drive that led to the ranch house.

The game brought on another bout of arguing, but by then, Carol enjoyed the beautiful flowering dogwoods that lined the stretch of lane leading to the ranch house. On either side, rolling hills with green grass stretched out beyond black fences, peppered with grazing horses.

As they pulled up in front of the house, she noticed the extra vehicle but thought nothing of it. This time of the year, the Kents often hired extra hands to help with planting the hay fields and prepping the kitchen garden.

As they got out of the vehicle, she looked around and realized nothing had been done to prepare for Lisa's party. Harriet was so efficient that Carol usually had nothing to do by the time she came over. She remembered her phone ringing right before lunch and immediately worried that something had happened to Robert. She turned to the girls as they got out of the Jeep. "Lisa, go look in on the new foal Lightning dropped last week. I'm going inside to see what grandma's up to."

"Okay, Mommy. Come on, Amy," Lisa urged. They took off at a run toward the horse barn.

"Don't go inside the stall without a grown-up. Just look if Daniel isn't in the barn!" Carol called to them, then turned to go in the house. She had her hand on the door when Harriet opened it and stepped out onto the porch. With the older woman's red rimmed eyes, pale skin, and scraggly hair, Carol immediately knew something was very wrong.

"Carol," Harriet greeted with a hitched breath, then she stopped.

"What's the matter, Harriet?" Carol asked, taking the older woman's arm and guiding her back to the door. "What happened? Is Robert all right?"

Harriet put her hand over her face and burst into tears. "Oh Carol. I'm so sorry." Carol steered her through the door and into the kitchen. Harriet collapsed into a chair at the table and buried her face in her hands, her body wracking with sobs. Carol looked over and saw Robert seated at the table.

He looked so frail, like a strong wind might just break him to pieces. He reached out to take his wife's hand.

"Robert, what is it? What happened?" she asked. She started feeling really frightened.

"Carol," he whispered, then cleared his throat and stopped. He cleared his throat again, then said in a stronger voice, "Whatever happens, whatever gets said, you have to know that we are truly sorry. Don't let this spoil Lisa's birthday."

"What's going on?" Carol demanded, her teeth set. "Tell me right now. Right this second."

♫ ♫ ♫ ♫

UNOBSERVED until this moment, international Country Music superstar Bobby Kent studied Carol Mabry from the doorway of his parents' kitchen. His parents had finally decided to tell him about two hours ago having exhausted every ploy in their arsenal in an attempt to convince him to leave. The anger at his parents burned through his system slow and low, like an underground lava flow.

To the casual observer, Bobby Kent had an even temper. Some might even describe him as mild-mannered, unflappable, or cool headed. In reality, Bobby had his father's temper, which is to say, he was a hot head with a short fuse. He could instantly go from feeling annoyance to full blown anger and all the way to wrath. He had recognized his anger problem early in life and taken steps to contain his emotions. He had taught himself coping skills and went to great pains never show his anger, which he perceived as weakness, to the world at large. It was the single aspect of his father's personality he specifically wanted to prune from the family tree.

Even a lifetime of coping with feelings of anger had not sufficiently prepared Bobby for what his parents had confessed earlier. His mind rejected the fact that he had a daughter; an eight-year-old daughter. It was too much to fathom at one time. How could two people who professed to love him have kept that information from him? He hadn't been able to get an explanation out of them yet. Both of them had been too upset to make any sense, but he assumed it had something to do with money. It nearly always did.

He figured the woman standing over them at the table could shed some light on the subject. For obvious reasons, he'd known who they were talking about before they'd even said her name. The moment she spoke, the moment he heard her voice, every recollection of her became vividly pronounced in his memory. They'd met in a classical violin class during a summer semester at the University of Georgia just four weeks before he received the call about his demo and packed his bags to leave. He had been amazed with her musical skill and impressed with her in general. He had asked her out and they had shared some lunches, a dinner, and gone to a movie together on a double date.

The night he got the call, they had celebrated. They'd sat on the tailgate of his truck and eaten too many cheeseburger sliders, washed down with way too much celebratory champagne. The celebration had gone until dawn. Bobby assumed Lisa arrived a scant nine months later.

He wanted to turn his anger on someone other than his parents, but he couldn't find it in him to force it onto her. The one thing his father, Robert, had been very clear about was that they had misled Carol all this time. All these years.

Years!

All that time, all these years, Carol believed Bobby knew all about his daughter, Lisa. Taking a deep breath, Bobby ran his hand through his hair and prepared himself to face her righteous wrath. He had a feeling it would take some time to convince her that he wasn't the bad guy here.

He stepped into the kitchen, his boot hitting the linoleum, causing a sound that reverberated through the room. Carol stiffened, as if she knew whom she was about to see, and turned to face him. He watched the recognition come instantly, and suddenly her hazel eyes filled with burning rage, so powerful he almost wished he hadn't made his presence known.

"Oh, of course! Should have known," she bit out through gritted teeth. "Exactly what are you doing here? Today of all days?"

He had no idea how to even begin so he decided to start with his defense. From the look on her face, though, he wasn't sure she would even hear his words. "I didn't know, Carol."

Carol put a hand to her temple as if warding off a headache. "What are you doing here, Bobby? Why are you here?" she repeated in a weak voice.

He took a step toward her. "I swear to you, Carol, they never told me. They lied to you. They lied to both of us."

He heard the sound of two pairs of feet running across the porch. A look of panic flashed across Carol's face. She spun around as the screen door flew open. "We have fifteen kids and their parents showing up in less than an hour. I can't deal with this right now," she declared over her shoulder through gritted teeth.

He watched as she kept her back to them and intercepted Lisa before she made it completely into the kitchen. Bobby had a chance to see a flash of hair and the toe of pink sneakers, but Carol blocked the rest of his view. It took every single ounce of willpower in him to keep from shoving her out of the way to look at his daughter for the first time in his life.

His daughter.

"Mom. You should see the baby horse!" Lisa yelled, her voice rising in excitement with every word.

Carol opened the door and guided Lisa outside. Bobby could hear her speaking as she said, "Come show me, babe. Then we need to set up the tables. Grandpa isn't feeling well."

Bobby walked over to his parents and looked down at them. He felt no sympathy at the sight of their ragged faces. "It is absolutely unacceptable that you did this to her," he said. He put his palms flat on the table and leaned closer. "It is absolutely unacceptable that you did this to me. But most of all, it is absolutely unacceptable that you did this to your own granddaughter, my daughter."

Bobby waited until both of them looked away from his face. Then he straightened and walked slowly outside. He was going to have to bank his rage until the party was over. He wasn't going to disappoint Lisa any further.

"Bobby," his father said from the doorway. Bobby stiffened, but didn't turn around.

"You know what, Dad? Fire up the grill. We have a birthday party to host today."

Robert stepped out onto the porch. "Bobby, we can't have a party right now. Your mother isn't up to it and we need to sit down with Carol and talk about all this."

Bobby swung around and advanced on his father. "I could not care less whether my mother is 'feeling up to it' or not. There's a little girl in that barn who's waiting for all her friends to come over and celebrate her birthday, and as sure as the sun is shining, you aren't going to spoil that for her or her mother. Nor are you about to spoil my little girl's birthday for me. I've already missed seven of them, and I'm not going to miss the eighth." Robert's back was against the door, and Bobby was almost nose-to-nose with him, his fists clenched.

"We had our reasons, son."

"I'm sure you think you did and I'm prepared to hear you out on some later date. But in my opinion, there isn't a reason good enough for what you've done. Not one reason under God's blue heaven could *possibly* be good enough." He turned and walked away before he actually let his temper get the best of him and punched his own father.

Bobby headed to the storage shed to pull out the tables that needed to be set up in the yard. He carried the first one out and nearly ran into Carol. She had her arms crossed over her chest, rubbing them as if she felt cold, and her eyes stood out from her pale face, dark circles shadowing the skin under them. If he thought it would have done any good, he would have given her a hug, but he didn't think she would welcome that right now.

"I don't want to tell her yet," she said. Her voice sounded very strained.

It took a few heartbeats for him to process what she meant. Then the meaning of the words tore through him and he felt his jaw tighten and his eyes slit. He set the table down and faced her. "Are you telling me she doesn't even know who I am?" he demanded.

"She knows your parents are her grandparents. But, she doesn't know that your parents are *your* parents. I didn't want to tell her who you were, and it wasn't until this year that she realized that her father's parents didn't come with a face for a father."

"Oh? May I ask why?" He kept his voice low, calm, and steady despite the fact that he felt his heart rate increase and heard his pulse roar in his ears like ocean surf. He thought he might just explode with all of the emotions rushing through him.

Carol ran a hand through her hair with jerky movements. "Because everyone knows you. You wouldn't have been some faceless man that never came back. She could have turned on any radio in America and heard you or looked through any magazine and seen a picture of you alongside Melody Mason or some other starlet."

"Melody Montgomery," he corrected automatically, as if it mattered. He tasted something sour in his mouth. He didn't like it, but she made sense. "Then tell her. Then she'll know and I won't be some faceless man, and I won't stay away anymore now that I know she exists."

Carol's eyes filled with tears, and Bobby felt certain that she wasn't a woman who gave in to tears very often. "I wasn't prepared for this. Give me some time to work out what to do."

He relented, but wouldn't give up everything. "I want to get to know her," he stated. "Carol? Hey. I want to know my daughter."

He watched emotions play across her face; anger, mistrust, and eventually acceptance. She finally nodded. "I'll tell her when the time is right. Until then, please don't say a word."

Relief poured through him, then he turned to go back to the shed. "You better see what my mother hasn't done yet. She's been in the shape she's in now all morning."

"Bobby," she said. His heart skipped in anticipation of the softness of her tone. He turned and looked at her, and she shifted her eyes away, as if uncomfortable. "Lisa's spending tonight at her friend's house. If you want to come over tonight, I'll tell you about her. Show you some pictures. I don't know. Maybe the right way to tell her is to tell her together."

He nodded, and had to force the words past the lump in his throat. "Thank you."

♫ ♫ ♫ ♫

Personal Journal Entry

April 21

I'm so angry. I can't even express how angry.

Who does she think she is to turn me down? Red haired tart! I wasn't asking for a lifetime commitment. I just wanted a few stinking minutes of her time and her oh-so-precious presence.

She never even sat down? Thanks, but no thanks?

I'm beginning to think my life would be less complicated if I just let him kill her. I know the world would be a simpler place without her in it. I can't argue with him on that point.

Why is this hunger gnawing at him again so soon? Last time it was years in-between. Now it's less than a week? Why can't he control it? Why am I, even now, scouting another target for him?

Decompensating. That's what the experts would call it. That's how she would label his actions. She thinks she knows everything. But, it's because she's so close. Not like the others. She's so close and I can't do anything about it.

♫ ♫ ♫ ♫

BARBARA Daniels rolled her head on her shoulders. She'd just worked third shift, then helped Danny by picking up the breakfast shift too. All she wanted to do was crawl under some covers and hide away for the next 12 hours before her next shift.

She closed her eyes and leaned her head against the side of the bus. She worried a bit that she'd fall asleep and miss her stop, but it was so noisy she doubted she would. When she felt someone sit beside her, she barely opened her eyes to see who it was, then closed them again.

The cute guy wearing the black glasses with the jet black hair and goatee looked and smelled a whole lot better than anyone she'd ever met on this bus. He kind of looked like her favorite movie star, Trent Scott. She straightened and put her hand to the side of her hair, worried about what she might look like after fifteen straight hours in the diner.

She spared another glance at him and gave half a smile. "Hi."

When he looked at her, she thought he had the most striking blue eyes she'd ever seen in her life. He captured her gaze and just simply would not let go. "Well, good morning," he said in a slow southern drawl. "How are you today?"

♫ ♫ ♫ ♫

CAROL made it through the party without speaking to Harriet or Robert, which was a chore, and effectively ignored the fact that Bobby was there, which proved even harder. Everyone there recognized him, of course, and by the end of the festivities, he'd pulled his guitar out and sang for the guests. She tried to ignore that, too, but his voice sent her heart fluttering the same as it had nine years ago.

She endured the knowing glances from the adults who pieced together Bobby's role in Lisa's life, and wondered about the relatives there who already knew. Bobby had no siblings and Lisa openly called the Kents her grandparents. That meant every single person at the party who knew Bobby was Harriet and Robert's son played a part in the ongoing deception. What kind of planning and engineering did that take?

By the time the last guest left and she had packed the Jeep with Lisa's presents, she was an emotional wreck and almost told him not to come over that night after all. She could not bring herself to do it, though. He'd already missed eight years, and it wasn't going to be on her shoulders if he missed any more.

She dropped Lisa and Amy off at Amy's house, thankful to get away from the talk about Bobby Kent being the star of the party, then turned to go home to wait. It was ridiculous for her to feel so nervous, but for some reason, she couldn't help it. She'd loved him with a strength that had frightened her when she was in college, then despised him with an equal passion ever since. Now she didn't know how she ought to feel, or how to act.

Carol glanced at the clock on the dash as she pulled into her driveway and saw she only had a few minutes to prepare herself for his arrival. She laid her head on her steering wheel and prayed for some strength to get through the next few hours. The headache was nearly blinding her by now, and she couldn't stop the nervous tightening of her stomach. She took a deep breath and sat up, then went into the house to lie on the couch until he arrived. She would unload the presents later.

♫ ♫ ♫ ♫

THE doorbell's ring woke Carol about an hour later and, as she sat up, she realized she felt a little better. She moved through the house and opened the door. Bobby stood there, his white Stetson in his hands, and once again she felt compassion for this man because of what had been taken from him… and what had been taken from Lisa.

"Bobby," she greeted, stepping aside so he could enter.

"I really appreciate this, Carol," he said. He stepped through the doorway, then stopped just inside the threshold, letting Carol lead the way in her home.

"Have any trouble finding the place?" she asked.

He waved his hat in the direction of her driveway. "Rental's got a GPS. You have a really nice home, Carol."

She led the way and they moved through the foyer with the formal dining room to their right. They walked past the carpeted stairwell, beyond the formal living room on their left and the entrance to the kitchen on the right, and into the den at the end of the house. She turned on a lamp near the couch and waved a hand in the direction of the room.

"Have a seat, Bobby. Do you want some water or a coffee or something?"

"No, but thank you." He set his hat down on a side table and folded his long body into a chair. He cleared his throat. "I don't know why I'm so nervous," he admitted with a smile. His smile came to his lips more to set himself at ease in his emotional discomfort than to soothe her.

Carol laughed, recognizing that they shared that feeling in common. She sat down on the couch facing him. Looking into his eyes for the first time in almost nine years, she felt a lot of tension suddenly fade away. "I was thinking the same thing," she confessed, then she sobered. "I'm sorry, Bobby. You've missed so much, and it's not your fault."

"It's not yours, either."

She shrugged. "In a way it is. I went to your parents because I didn't know how to find you. But later, you weren't exactly hidden. I just never pushed."

He leaned forward and she could see sparks of anger smoldering in his eyes, though she detected no other sign of emotion. She decided he would make a tough witness if she ever had him on the stand. "They said they told you I wanted nothing to do with you or my child. Is that right?"

"Yes, but I just let it go." She ran a hand through her hair. "I thought about trying a few times, especially lately, but I didn't want to seem like I was needy or begging."

He looked around the room and she tried to see her home through his eyes. She saw an elegant, tastefully furnished house in a prestigious neighborhood. "You seem to be doing fine without having to beg."

"Yeah, well, not really. Your parents give me money every month. I thought it was from you."

"Oh, I bet it was. Their deception went pretty deep, it would seem. Carol, you have to believe me. If they ever mentioned you or our daughter, it would have been so different. I didn't know. The thought of them handing you money like an allowance..." Bobby's voice trailed off in disgust.

"I needed it when I was still in school. The bigger you got, the bigger the checks got, until I didn't have to work anymore while I was taking classes. Then, after I passed the bar, I thought about going into private practice so I wouldn't need your money anymore. But I wanted to work for the Commonwealth Attorney so badly that I kept accepting the money. I've had dozens of offers from local law firms, and I thought that if you ever pulled your support away, I could take one of them up on their offer and still be able to maintain. Lately, I've just been putting most of it in a trust account for Lisa."

She stood. "I'm really thirsty. I'm going to get myself an iced tea. Are you sure you don't want anything?"

"I'll take one, too, since you're having one. If you don't mind," he agreed.

She had already set glasses out in the kitchen. It took seconds to add ice and tea to each one. When she returned to the room, she found him looking at the sea of photographs that lined the top of her piano. He reached out with a finger and ran it over a photo of Lisa grinning around her second birthday cake. He turned when she came into the room and took the glass from her with a smile.

"I've spent all afternoon feeling miserable and angry. I'm not going to let myself get down about this," he asserted as he tipped his tea to her in a salute. "I have to trust God's timing, or I'll be consumed with bitterness. I'm happy I'm Lisa's dad. You've had to do it on your own so far, and you seem to have done a wonderful job. But, I want to have a role in her life now, in some way. I want to know all that you can tell me about her. We'll mark today as a new beginning."

Her headache receded further. "Good. Come on and sit down."

They sat at each end of the couch. "Tell me about her," he said.

"She's so smart." Carol smiled. "She takes piano lessons and seems to be a natural. She's in ballet, but only because her best friend, Amy, is in it. She loves Jesus and church. That's a huge part of our social life."

As Carol talked, she relaxed even more. She told him stories as they came to her, not in any particular order, and had him laughing more than a few times at the pictures she created with her words.

Around ten, she asked, "Are you hungry? Do you want something to eat?"

She stood to lead the way to the kitchen when she heard her work cell phone ring from her purse by the door. The real world came back suddenly.

"I have to get that," she said. She rushed to the foyer and grabbed the phone out of the purse she'd hung on the coat rack. As she answered it, she headed back to the living room. "Carol Mabry."

"I'm at Lake Reba. You're going to need to get here," Mitch said by way of greeting. He gave her directions and told her they'd wait on her.

She grimaced and looked at Bobby as she hung up the phone. "I have to go to work. I'm sorry."

"At ten o'clock on a Saturday?"

"I'm on call, and there's been a murder." She unplugged her personal cell, shot Amy's mom a quick text to let her know she was out of the house, and turned to him. "I really need to leave, Bobby. You're welcome to stay until I get back."

"I need to go check into a hotel. I'd planned on staying at the ranch, but clearly, that's not going to work."

It didn't take her half a millisecond to wage an internal debate with herself. "It's late. I have two guest rooms. Why don't you stay here tonight?"

He walked toward her and stared down at her as if studying her face. Finally, he smiled and drawled, "I really appreciate the hospitality, Carol. I'll wait right here."

She stepped away from him and nodded, already shedding the persona of Carol Mabry, mommy, and slipping on the Carol Mabry, A.C.A.

♫ ♫ ♫ ♫

"BARBARA Daniels, 22, waitress at a diner about three miles from here. Engaged to one Antoine Berkley." Mitch looked up from his notepad and looked at Carol.

"Is Antoine a person of interest?"

Miss Daniels' corpse lay spread eagle on an island of manicured grass in the otherwise black asphalt parking lot of Lake Reba Park. Her frame was illuminated by the street light above her and also by flickering candles. At her head, at each hand, and at each foot, red candles burned, pooling wax at their bases like spilled blood. She wore a black pantsuit with a bright yellow top, black heels adorned with yellow bows on the toes, and a yellow beaded bracelet. Her auburn hair had been pulled back and styled in an intricate twist.

Mitch shook his head. "Of course, but I really don't like him for it. Too much detail here to be a copycat. Feels like the same guy who did Darla Cody."

Carol took a few steps closer to the body and Mitch unconsciously stepped up alongside her, as if shielding her. When she looked up from the corpse and met his eyes, he continued, "Besides, he has a decent alibi. He was on his way back from DC when we got a hold of him on the phone."

"So, two hundred miles away in front of a thousand witnesses?"

Mitch nodded. "Something like that."

Carol could see the shine of subtle yet elegant makeup reflected in the street light. She carefully knelt and inspected the wire around the victim's neck.

"Violin?" Mitch asked.

"Think so, but I can't tell. The fret end isn't visible without moving her head." She used a penlight from her keychain to shine on the wire. "Looks like it, though."

Mitch nodded. "No one knows it was violin string. And the candles are a perfect match. That, and she's gussied up like the Cody girl was."

She sat back on the heels of her tennis shoes and looked up at Mitch. "Why would a waitress at a diner be wearing a business suit in a park?"

"Maybe she had a date?"

"With a fiancé out of town? Besides, not exactly date clothes. More like business clothes. Expensive business clothes at that."

"Maybe she had a job interview?"

Carol nodded. "Maybe." She rose to her feet. She eyeballed Mitch as if evaluating whether to say what was on her mind before she spoke again. "Mitch, I know the report's probably on my desk. But, do you know if the autopsy showed any sexual assault to Darla Cody?"

"None. Absolutely no sexual activity. Nor was there any bruising anywhere on her body other than the obvious strangulation."

She waved a hand at Barbara's body. "Doesn't this scream sex crime to you?"

Mitch slipped his hands into the pockets of his jacket. "How? Victims are fully clothed. Nothing is violated in any way."

"I don't think she owned these clothes. I think our killer dressed her like a paper doll after she was dead. I think the body was carefully dressed and arranged. Even if he didn't violate her, it still feels sexual."

He grinned. "Oh. It *feels* that way." He stressed the word and made Carol laugh.

"You hush. You know what I mean."

"I do. I'm not entirely convinced, but I do know what you mean." He looked at his watch. "Want to get together Monday and go over reports?"

"Absolutely. Nine?"

He grimaced. "Better make it ten. I have to break in a new partner starting Monday."

"Oh? Someone get promoted? Was it Johnson from Fourth Precinct?"

"Nah. He's coming here from DC. Apparently, he has friends in high places in this town."

Raising her eyebrow Carol asked, "From DC?"

"Yeah. Rumor has it that there was a he-said-she-said dispute that didn't go his way. I don't know any details and have been ordered not to let it cloud my judgment. You know me, Carol. I'll give everyone a fair shake. And I never did cotton to gossip, especially coming from that town."

She nodded and stepped backward. "Let me know what the fiancé says. Call me any time about it."

"I will. I have a uniform there now with him. I'm on my way. Want to come?"

She shook her head. "No. I have some things left undone at home. I'll just talk to you about it later."

♪ ♪ ♪ ♪

SHE found Bobby in the living room, asleep on the couch, his head pillowed on his arm at one end, and his feet hanging over the side on the other end. She thought about waking him and telling him to go to one of the bedrooms, but she didn't have the heart. He'd been through a lot of emotional turmoil in the last few hours, and even in sleep, she could see the fatigue on his face. She went upstairs and grabbed a blanket, then took it back down and covered him with it.

Before she turned off the lamp, she took a good half a minute to really look at the man who shared so many features with her daughter. He was remarkably handsome and his face looked relaxed and peaceful in slumber. Oddly, she felt like giving him a soothing pat on the cheek just as she often did with Lisa. She resisted the urge and turned out the light.

She went upstairs, but felt too restless to sleep. It wasn't quite midnight, so she decided to call her best friend, Aria Williams.

"You're up late," Aria said by way of greeting.

"How did the MTV awards thing go?" Aria, an accomplished pianist, collaborated on soundtracks for her brother Adam's motion pictures.

"The whole song award was a ruse. Adam was actually getting honored as sexiest director or something. He was horribly embarrassed and it was absolutely hysterical. My sides are still hurting from laughing so hard."

Knowing how serious Adam was, Carol grinned. "I'm sorry I missed that. I remember his mortification at being named one of *People* magazine's Sexiest Men of the year. You remember when he was ranked higher than Trent Scott a few years back? He actually called me about my opinion on suing them for slander. I had to talk him down and convince him that they were complimenting him and that any press was good press."

"I remember that," Aria said with a giggle. "Don't make me laugh anymore. My sides actually hurt. My poor brother. I think he will retire after this one. He's not happy."

"Maybe he just needs to grow a really unattractive beard and gain fifty pounds."

"In Hollywood, that would just become the new fashion." Carol heard Aria's husband, Nick, in the background. "Nick is telling me to quit making fun of my brother."

Feeling her smile fade, Carol said, "I need to talk to you."

She could tell Aria heard the seriousness of her voice when she asked, "What's wrong?"

"Remember last year when I said you'd know who Lisa's dad was if I told you his name?"

"I do. And I remember you not telling me his name."

Taking a deep breath, Carol said, "Does the name Bobby Kent ring any bells?"

There was a bit of a pause before Aria said, "Wow. I can see it."

"Yeah. Me, too. I don't know how everyone in the world can't see it."

"You have to give me a second. I'm just putting you and Bobby Kent together in my mind right now."

"Aria!"

"Oh, no. That's not what I meant."

Aria Suarez was a savant with an intellect that exceeded genius. Carol had known her since they were high school Army brats in Columbus, Georgia. Sometimes, conversations with Aria didn't go as planned, so she just waited her friend out.

Aria said, "I thought Bobby Kent was supposed to be with Melody Mason for a long time. Since she got married, they keep putting him with Harmony Harper."

Carol snorted. "Yeah, right. Like Adam Suarez is supposed to be with Julianne McNeill."

"Ah, got it." There was another pause and Carol knew that her brilliant scientist best friend was making mental connections and drawing logical conclusions that would dazzle normal human beings. Just a few heart beats passed before she spoke again. "So, why are you calling me at midnight on Lisa's birthday? What happened?"

Carol took a deep breath, then launched forward, telling her about the moment she got to the ranch and ending with finding him asleep on her couch. When she finished speaking, she let Aria digest what she'd said.

"Okay. What now?"

Carol lay back on her bed and stared at the ceiling. "Now, I have to introduce my 8-year-old to her father. And, somehow, I have to forgive his parents."

"You've held onto some pretty intense anger toward Bobby for a long time. Have you let it all go?"

Examining her heart, she took a moment before answering. "I hope so. Honestly? Welcoming him into my home and telling him all about Lisa was kind of the exact opposite of how I envisioned our reunion going down, I can tell you that. Like night and day. I've thought all kinds of terrible things over the years, but never that Harriet and Robert had lied to me. Lied right to my face. And Lisa's! It's unfathomable."

Aria took a deep breath and released it. "It is. I'm so sorry."

Something occurred to Carol when her thoughts wandered to the man sleeping on her couch. "You want to know something? I feel worse for Bobby. They're his parents, after all. I can tell he's seething inside, like completely furious, but he totally hides it."

Aria asked, "Is that healthy?"

Carol snickered, "Not sure I know him well enough to answer that question accurately."

"Oh, Carol," Aria uttered.

"I mean, I know him. At least, I know who he used to be. I know who he was in college. He was calm, cool, and collected at all times. I've known his parents since Lisa was born. He's really different from his father, but eerily similar, if you know what I mean. But I don't know anything about what he's done for the last eight years anymore than he knows about me or Lisa."

"So what's next?"

Carol ran through all the obvious scenarios in her imagination and answered, "I have no idea."

"Is there anything we can do?"

"Keep us in your prayers."

"Always. I'm going to call you at work every day and pester you now, you know."

Carol barked a laugh and they talked for another half hour. She bounced between laughter and tears as she and Aria shared the news of events of the last week. When she hung up, she felt better, just knowing her friend would listen anytime and pray. She thought it would take her a while to fall asleep with the thoughts and concerns that swirled through her mind, but after the emotional roller coaster she'd ridden for most of the day, she fell fast asleep almost the very second her head hit the pillow.

♫ ♫ ♫ ♫

Sunday, April 22nd

THE sound of the telephone jarred Bobby out of a deep sleep. He opened his eyes and, for a moment, couldn't remember where he was. As memory dawned he slowly sat up, feeling the soreness in his back and neck from sleeping on a couch that was too small for his long frame. He could hear Carol's voice as she spoke on the phone in the next room.

He stood and groaned, stretching his back muscles as he did, and limped to the bathroom. He almost groaned again when he saw his reflection in the mirror. Last night was the first time he'd slept more than a few hours since Thursday night and his reflected red-rimmed eyes stared back from an unshaven face. He splashed his cheeks with cold water, trying to wash away the last vestiges of sleep, and while his reflection didn't look any better, he definitely felt better. He rubbed his palm over the coarse whiskers on his jaw, wishing that he had a razor with him when he remembered that he never took his suitcase out of his car yesterday morning.

He went back through the house and out the front door. When he got to his car, he saw Carol standing at the end of the driveway, looking down the road. "Good morning. What are you doing?" he asked.

She turned around and saw him, then smiled. "Waiting on Lisa. Her friend Amy lives down that street," she said, pointing. "Amy's mom can see to our street, and she watches until she gets to where I can see her."

Little things. There were so many little things he'd missed out on. "Who would have watched her if she'd been home last night when you got that call?"

Carol gestured at the house next door. "I've been doing the job I do now for about two years. My next door neighbors are a retired couple. They have always loved Lisa. When she found out I was looking for someone to be a live-in *au pair*, she volunteered to just come over whenever I get a call during nonworking hours. She's been a gem."

Bobby looked at the house and nodded. "It's good you have them."

He walked up to within a few feet of her and lowered his voice. "Carol, I don't want to impose, but do you mind if I help myself to a shower?"

Carol looked at him, a bit surprised. "That would be fine. Make yourself at home."

He saw Lisa as she rounded the corner of the street, holding hands with her friend. Amy turned and waved behind them, then the two came toward them at a run.

"Hi mom!" Lisa yelled before she even reached the corner of the yard. "Amy's going to go to church with us!" When she reached Carol she threw her arms around her mom's waist. "Amy's mom said something about midnight feedings and dirty diapers and then she threw up a lot. So she isn't going to be able to make it today."

Carol hugged her back then ran a gentle hand down the back of Amy's head with a smile and a touch of wistfulness on her face that made Bobby wonder why she'd never married and had more children. "That's fine. Go upstairs and change clothes. I laid your dress and stockings out on your bed."

The two girls stopped in their tracks when they saw Bobby. "Good morning, ladies. Did you have fun last night?" he flirted, making them giggle to themselves.

"Thanks for singing at my party yesterday, Bobby. All my friends thought it was the coolest thing ever!" Lisa declared.

"My pleasure, Lisa." One of the things that had served as both a blessing and a curse over the course of his lifetime was that he came into the world with the ability to charm women. Age didn't matter. He'd seen it happen to females aged newborn baby up to a ninety-year-old great-great grandma. There were times when it frustrated him, but he was glad his daughter apparently had no natural immunity. He knelt down to her eye level. "Do you like to sing, Sugar?"

She shook her head. "I like to play the piano. And dance," she said, executing a pirouette. "You should come see one of my recitals. I usually get to have a solo."

"I'd really love to see that. Thank you so much for the invitation. And you know what? It's a date." He stuck his hand out and she shook it in a very official way. He nodded and stood, then shoved his hands in his pockets to keep from touching her again. He wanted to hug her as naturally and casually as Carol had. "Now I reckon you'd best go on and get changed like your mama said."

The girls giggled again, then dashed past him into the house. He whistled a tune as he pulled his bag from the trunk of his car and winked at Carol before going inside.

♫ ♫ ♫ ♫

"LISA Ann Mabry, I am leaving this house in thirty seconds. If you know what's good for you, you and Amy will both be in the car and strapped in before then," Carol yelled from the base of the stairs.

It would forever remain a mystery to her how she could get herself and Lisa dressed, fed, and packed to go for the day by seven every weekday morning, but on Sunday mornings it took every ounce of her will to get them out the door by nine-fifteen. Lisa still hadn't shown up, and Carol yelled back up the stairs. "You're going on ten seconds. Nine. Eight."

It took full power "mother control" not to smile as the two little girls came barreling down the stairs and through the front door. Once they were out of sight, she let the giggle escape as she picked up her purse, violin case, and Bible off the side table by the door.

"Mind if I go with you this morning?" Bobby asked from behind her. She turned and saw him dressed in slacks and a button down shirt, freshly shaved.

"Course not," she agreed, and let him lead the way. She stopped to lock the door and when she turned back around, he was getting in his car. "You can ride with us if you want," she offered.

He looked at her car, then back at her. "I don't want to impose on your hospitality any more, Carol. Besides, I'll probably go back to the ranch instead of coming back here. I have to straighten out a few things with my folks."

She grimaced as she walked past him, then stopped in shock. "Oh, no. What will they think since you spent the night here last night?"

"We're all grown up, Carol. We're parents, even. You and I know what did and didn't happen here last night and I know for a fact it's none of their business."

She let that sink in, then shrugged and kept heading to the car. "Good luck," she said. "I wouldn't want to have to have that conversation with you."

♫ ♫ ♫ ♫

WHEN Carol first moved to Richmond, she did not attend the Kents' small home church near the ranch, but found her own. She wanted a large, young church, and fell in love with the first one she attended.

As soon as Lisa was old enough for Carol to put her in the church's nursery, she started playing in the orchestra. It was one of the biggest blessings of her week, to be able to play her violin in worship to God. The time for practice and rehearsal was definitely a sacrifice, especially with her work schedule, but she managed it with joy.

This morning, as she sat with the other two violinists and tuned her instrument, she couldn't help but feel a little bit nervous, knowing Bobby Kent sat in the congregation. Classical violin class is what brought them together in the first place. They shared a love for the instrument. His musical talent lay in the larger stringed instrument, the guitar, but he'd wanted to expand his abilities. He never took classical music very seriously though, and he would often disrupt the class by sawing away on his violin like a fiddle. She imagined his fans enjoyed the fact he could play both instruments with equal expertise.

For some reason, though, as she prepared to play in what should be worship of Almighty God, she found herself wondering if Bobby would be impressed with her continued playing after all this time, and whether he would enjoy the music of the church orchestra. Then she wondered why she cared what he did or did not think about, outside of some aspect of her parenting.

It hadn't even been 24 hours since she discovered him at the ranch, and already it felt right to have him in their lives. It surprised her, really, how quickly she let go of the dislike and mistrust she'd held for him for so long. It didn't make sense that she should hold onto such bad feelings when he had absolutely nothing to do with the deception. Why harbor a grudge against an innocent man?

What fascinated Carol, though, was the sheer amount of work it took to contain a secret like Lisa. Robert and Harriet had family and friends. They all knew Bobby was their only son, so any grandchild must be his. How did they do it? How did they keep people from mentioning Lisa to Bobby? How deep did their lying and misleading go?

Carol knew – she knew it was her duty as a follower of Christ to forgive them. She also knew that she was still reeling from it all, and prayed that forgiveness could come when it was time.

She didn't envy Bobby the conversation he had to have this afternoon. A part of her thought maybe she should go with him, to provide some form of moral support. But she already had such a tenuous relationship with Harriet that it probably wouldn't be a good idea to be there and add to the hostility.

Instead, she would pray for him – for strength and patience. Because if it were her, she'd need both of those virtues in droves.

At the orchestra conductor's signal, she queued her bow. Now was not the time to dwell on such things. Rather, she forced herself to play the notes in front of her with a mind to more heavenly things. She knew it wasn't an accident that the first song she played was all about forgiveness. Accepting the conviction of the Holy Spirit, she prayed while she played, and hoped Bobby felt something similar.

♪ ♪ ♪ ♪

THE house was so quiet when Bobby stepped into the kitchen that he wondered if his parents were even there. His mother always made a big Sunday dinner, but there were no lingering smells to greet him. He looked in the refrigerator for something to eat, but found nothing prepared, so he grabbed an orange and peeled it at the sink, then worked his way through the house. Both trucks were outside, so someone had to be around.

He found them in the living room, seated side by side on an expensive leather sofa that played no role in any of his childhood memories. They didn't look at him when he walked into the room, but his mother started crying, wiping her eyes with a tired looking handkerchief, and his father put his arm around his mother's shoulders and hugged her to him. Bobby was still angry enough not to care about her current emotional state, so he just sat in a matching leather chair near the couch and ate his orange, waiting for one of them to be the first to speak.

"Where have you been, son? We've been a little worried about you," Robert said, finally breaking the silence.

"I went to church with my daughter. Her Sunday School class put on a little skit."

Harriet sniffled and looked at her husband. "Oh, Robert. She's going to be so disappointed that we weren't there. I forgot all about it."

Robert patted her shoulder, and Bobby pulled the reins in on his temper. "You go see all of her little things, then?" he asked in a dangerously soft voice. Harriet nodded. "Must be really nice to have had the opportunity."

"We thought we were doing the right thing," Harriet countered in a wail, covering her mouth with the cloth.

"The right thing?" He did not even attempt to mask the incredulity he felt. "No sane person would think that what you did was the right thing. So, are you crazy mother? Have you finally just flipped your pancake?"

"Son, don't speak to your mother like that," his father corrected.

Bobby took a bite of an orange slice and chewed. His face remained calm. "Well, gosh, Dad. Given the circumstances, I think you're just going to have to cut me a little slack."

His father sat straighter. "Son, you need to understand that every time we started to tell you, it just seemed like the wrong time, then it just, well, it just seemed too late. This thing just kind of happened. It wasn't planned."

Bobby nodded. "That is just the kind of clumsy explanation I think I needed. So, let's take me out of the picture for a moment. Even without me or my feelings, you robbed that little girl of her father for eight years. There isn't a big enough excuse in the history of mankind to pardon that."

He took a deep breath and let it out slowly, as if warming up for a show. "I would have been a good dad all this time." It was hard to say those words out loud and keep his voice from breaking with the emotions he felt. He stayed calm. There were too many words he was holding back to let his temper go.

"Be reasonable, son. At the time, we didn't know if Carol was even telling the truth. That kid could have been anyone's," Robert said.

"I see. Did it never occur to you at the time to, I don't know, ask me? I would have known, don't you think?" He nearly yelled that time, very close to losing the precious threads of control. He rubbed his face with his hands.

Harriet seemed to gain some control back. "Any girl who ends up unmarried and pregnant..." she started to say.

"Oh, no, mom. Don't. Do not go there." He raised his finger in the air to stop her words. "First off, you're talking about the mother of your grandchild, the mother of *my* little girl. Second, you've been around Carol Mabry for over eight years. You should know better yourself by now."

He leaned forward and rested his elbows on his knees. "You may not be aware of this, but I'm a reasonably intelligent person. I don't know how that happened. I obviously can no longer attribute it to good parents. Anyway, I've been doing some figuring for the last twenty hours or so. She came to you in January. I think that was right about the time I finished putting together the songs and signed the contract for my first album with Patterson Records. If memory serves, that February I finished recording the album and got my first bonus check, about three days before foreclosure on the ranch.

"A year-and-a-half later, the wolf was back at the door, threatening to foreclose again, but that was after the CMA awards when *Swing* was moving up the charts. So once again a check from me saved you. Then I started sending you money every month. I told my accountant to send you thirty percent of what I made, and your paychecks just kept getting bigger."

By now, Harriet's sniffles were full-fledged sobs and Robert wouldn't meet his eyes. Bobby hadn't wanted to believe that money was the reason he'd been robbed of his daughter, but he could see now that his suspicions were confirmed. He wanted to finish what he had to say before he left, so he continued. "Obviously, I hit it right on the mark. How much of that money went to Carol and Lisa?"

Bobby didn't like the sick look that crossed Robert's face. "Ten percent," his father whispered.

"Ten percent?" Bobby saw the edges of his vision blur to red. "You kept ninety percent and gave the mother of my child just ten percent?" he asked in a raised voice.

Bobby suddenly realized he had stood and was towering over his seated parents. He had to leave the room before he broke something. Or someone. He felt the tight control he maintained over his anger slipping away and he had to leave before he did or said something he could never take back.

He slammed through the house and out to his rental car, where he placed his hands on the hood and drew in deep, slow breaths. After he felt the skin on his face begin to cool, he opened the door and grabbed his checkbook out of his bag. On the way back into the house, he did some math in his head. He'd already calculated how much money he'd sent them over the years, so the final figuring in his formula fell into place easily. He didn't sit back down, but stood over them while he wrote. He ripped the check out of the book and threw it at his father. "That should be close to what you gave her over the years. You better spend that wisely, because that's the very last dime you will ever see from me in this lifetime."

He turned to leave, but his father stood and grabbed his arm. "This ranch has been in our family for four generations, and I was about to lose it," he said with tears streaming down his face.

"Well, golly-gee, Dad. How was that Lisa's fault? How was that Carol's fault? For that matter, how was it mine?" Bobby yelled.

"It was mine! It was my fault! I know you, son. You would have come back here. You would have given up on your dreams," Robert pleaded.

Bobby ripped his arm from his father's grasp. "Maybe so. And maybe you would have lost your golden goose. But maybe my daughter would have had a father."

"But we would have lost everything," his father said.

His eyes coldly took in his fretting mother sitting silently on the couch before coming back to rest on his father. "Yeah, well, enjoy it, dad. Enjoy every last inch of this land inside your property line. Enjoy every blade of grass and every grain of dirt.

"I hope and pray it was worth it. You've gained every last acre, but you lost your only son, and you will never see your grandchild again if I have my way. I will make you this promise, though. I'll spend the rest of my life on this earth being a better father than you."

He couldn't look at the man anymore. Bobby turned his back on them and stormed out of the house.

CHAPTER 7

♫ ♫ ♫ ♫

THE voice on the other end of the phone was probably one of the most recognized female voices on the planet. Country music superstar Melody Mason Montgomery accepted the charges for the collect call and then asked with a laugh, "Money problems, Bobby? Why are you calling me collect?"

"Hey, girl." Bobby greeted. "I'm on a payphone."

"What are you doing on a payphone in Virginia?" Melody asked. "Where did you even find a payphone in Virginia? Are you in a museum?"

Melody and Bobby had both signed with the now defunct Patterson Records early in their careers and their artistic paths in the industry had paralleled many times on the road from Nashville to stardom. They had both been awarded many prestigious industry honors when they were newcomers and the gossip rags continuously tried to put them together as a couple, christening them "Meloby" and "Bobbody" and such.

The truth was more interesting. Bobby and Melody were friends. They had a great deal of respect for each other professionally and they shared a love for Christ and a common interest in supporting charity, especially with their annual Christmas albums, but neither of them had ever seriously considered a relationship that went beyond that respectful friendship even before she married James Montgomery.

"I actually called to talk to James. Is he free?"

"I think so." Melody dropped the teasing tone. "You okay, Bobby? Everything all right?"

"Not really, Darlin'. But I hope I can handle it. I just need some advice and James is the smartest guy I know."

Melody said, "I can't argue with that. Hang on, hon."

Bobby took a few deep breaths while he held the line, then he heard James Montgomery pick up. "This is James."

"Hey, it's Bobby."

"Bobby! How are you? What's up?" James Montgomery was the M in M & L Electronics, an undisputed genius, and Melody's adoring husband. When he and Melody were newlyweds, James might have perceived Bobby as a threat until he met him backstage at a concert in Jacksonville. At that moment, James had realized the kind of close relationship Bobby shared with his wife and, since that day, he had called Bobby Kent his brother in Christ.

"Well, I think I just did something stupid," Bobby admitted.

"If that's true, I would find it astonishing. What happened?" James asked.

Bobby Kent then told James about how his parents, family, and friends of the family, had deceived him for the last eight years or more. He told him about his beautiful daughter. He told him about Carol Mabry. Then he told him about the confrontation he had with his parents.

James said, "Well, Bobby, some of that sounds amazing and wonderful and some of it sounds just awful."

"Uh, I'm not quite done. After I left my parent's house I did something really stupid."

"Go on," James urged.

"Well, I sat here in this park in my rental car and polished off the better part of a six pack of beer."

The line was silent and then James said, "Okay. You got me. I find that astonishing."

"Pretty stupid, huh?" Bobby confessed.

James sighed. "Well, yes, but let's not focus on that. To tell the truth, after my first wife was murdered, I could have become a raging alcoholic, myself. Let's talk a little bit about something else. You said you did something stupid, but, really, I think you didn't do one stupid thing. Not one."

"Really?" Bobby asked. "Now I'm astonished."

"Nope. I counted. I think you did about five stupid things."

"Oh."

"That I know of," James clarified.

"I appreciate your candor." Bobby asserted, his tone droll.

"I think the first thing you need to do is throw away any remaining beer or alcohol you have access to because God knows drinking is not going to solve anything. Would you agree?"

"Already done."

He could almost hear James nodding. "Good. Now, do you have a safe place to stay to sleep it off? Can you get a cab?"

"I have a place in mind."

"Good," James said in an analytical tone. "Now, tomorrow morning you need to get down on your knees or all the way down on your face and you need to talk to God, Bobby. You told your father you were going to be a better dad than he ever was? I don't think getting drunk and keeping your child from her grandparents is starting off right. Do you?"

"I was so angry, man."

He could hear the understanding in James' voice. "You know what, Bobby? Even though I've never once seen you lose your temper, you should know that I understand. And you should know that you had every right to be angry. But they're your parents, Bobby. You have to honor them. You have to. Even when they mess up. It's the first earthly commandment and the first commandment with a promise."

That got him in the gut. The verse echoed in his mind, *Honor your father and your mother.* "I really do, don't I?"

James rhetorically elaborated, "At least you have your parents here on earth to honor. That's more than either Melody or I can say."

"I knew calling you was a bad idea."

James chuckled. "I love you, brother. Can we pray?"

"Oh, heavens yes. Please pray with me."

"Let me get Melody."

James briefly brought Melody up to date on the current situation and the three of them prayed together. Melody disconnected and James said, "I want you to promise to call me tomorrow. I'll leave word with my office to put your call through. Promise?"

Bobby nodded, then remembered to speak. "I promise. Thanks, James."

"Don't mention it. Just call me tomorrow."

"Okay, bye for now."

"Good night, Bobby." James hung up.

♫ ♫ ♫ ♫

CAROL walked into Lisa's room and looked down at her sleeping child. She untangled the covers from her legs and pulled them up over her prone daughter, smoothing them down. In the dim light, Lisa looked a lot like her father, but softer somehow. Carol leaned over and kissed the tiny freshly scrubbed cheek, then left the room.

She massaged the tense muscles in the back of her neck on the way down the stairs, picking up pieces of dress up and baby doll paraphernalia as she went. She had court at nine in the morning and she'd planned to work the night before. She had a lot she needed to do to finish preparing, so she went into her office and powered up her laptop.

The doorbell startled her an hour later. She looked through the peephole and saw Bobby Kent, so she opened the door for him. As soon as she saw him, she could guess he'd been drinking. Then she smelled him and knew it.

"What's wrong, Bobby?"

He stumbled into the house and leaned against the wall. "I'm sorry to barge in on you like this, but I've been at a park down the street, and I realized I really shouldn't drive anywhere. I tried to call a cab from the payphone but I didn't have any cash. Can I use your phone?"

"Ever heard of a cell phone, Bobby?"

He blinked. "I've had seven. The tabloids always get the number and then somehow it gets published. Got tired of buying new phones and suing the carriers."

"Come with me." She took his arm and steered him to the kitchen. "What happened at your parents'?"

He sat down at the table and rested his head in his arms. "Money. They wanted me to stay in Nashville so they could have my money."

She was on her way to make coffee, but, at his words, sat down with him. "I'm sorry. I think I guessed as much."

"I shouldn't be here in this condition." He raised his head and rubbed his face. "I don't like to get drunk, normally. I don't even drink, really. But it seemed like a good idea at the time."

"I remember in college you didn't drink at all except that one time when we, uh, celebrated." She felt her cheeks fuse with heat. "Champagne as I recall."

"Very funny." Bobby grinned. His sleepy eyes and crooked grin did funny things to the rhythm of her heart.

"Why don't you go to the spare room upstairs and sleep it off?" she suggested, taking his hand to help him up. He stood, a bit unsteadily, and let her lead him up the staircase. She stopped at the door at the very end of the upstairs hallway and opened it. "This is the farthest from the noise that will explode around here about six in the morning," she said.

Bobby leaned against the door and looked at her with hooded eyes. "You should hate me, Carol," he observed quietly.

"For many, many years, you were my least favorite person. Yesterday afternoon, I let it all go," she told him. "Sleep well, Bobby. We'll try to be as quiet as possible in the morning." She moved to go past him.

"Carol," he said, taking her arm and pulling her against him. He held her like that for several seconds, his eyes on hers, then he started to lower his head, but she put her index finger on the dimple in his chin to stop him.

"Bobby, you've been drinking and I have court in about ten hours." She pushed against him, knocking him a little off balance, enough for him to release her. "Go to sleep."

She turned from him and went back downstairs, wondering why she had a silly grin on her face.

♫ ♫ ♫ ♫

Personal journal entry

April 23

I wish she could have been alive to see how beautiful I made her. She had done herself no justice with her choice of clothes and with her hair pulled back so carelessly. Brushing her hair, cutting it to the proper length, and styling it gave me such momentary joy. If she hadn't been so physically weak when it came to the drugs she would have agreed with me.

I remember the smell of her hair. I can still smell the shampoo I used to wash it. The scent engulfs my every thought and torments me with thoughts of her. The real her, not the imitation.

This need in me is unsatiated. Try as I might to dilute it, it's growing. I want her. I want to watch her die. I need to watch her die. I need her to breathe her very last breath and then suck that air into my lungs. I do not want anymore cheap, sorry substitutes. She doesn't want to lose her. She keeps threatening to hurt herself if I kill her but I will only tolerate that for so long before I do the hurting for her.

She will continue to feed me any way she can. Just trying to assuage me. I'll bide my time for now.

♫ ♫ ♫ ♫

Monday, April 23rd

BELLS rang in Bobby's head and his mouth felt like someone had lined it with felt and steel wool. It took all the willpower his body possessed to open his eyes and, as soon as the sunlight streaming through the white curtains hit his pupils, he groaned and wished he hadn't wasted the energy.

He hadn't gotten drunk in years. When he went on his first tour, he'd caught himself drinking after the concerts to help wind down, and as soon as he realized what he was doing, he flat out quit. It was during that time that he recommitted himself to following Christ, and to ministry for Him, and never again felt a desire to drink. Until last night.

Last night he felt the pang of guilt and regret with every drink he swallowed, but for some reason just kept on. Now he felt shame. To come here, to his daughter's home in that state…

He rolled out of the bed and stayed on his knees, burying his face in the mattress. His prayer was almost wordless, wrenched from his gut and coming out in inaudible sounds. He begged for forgiveness, for grace, and for wisdom in how to go forward from here.

When he felt spent, he forced himself to stand up, holding onto his head with one hand and the bedpost with the other. Fully dressed except for his boots, he still wore the clothes he'd worn to church the day before. He realized he slept in his clothes for two nights straight now. Rectifying his living arrangements just shot up to near the top of his to-do list, following a handful of aspirin, two tall glasses of water, a cup of coffee, and a shower. Preferably in that order.

The house was quiet as he moved through it and, judging by the brightness of the sunlight penetrating all the way to his brain at every window he passed, it was late morning. That meant Carol and Lisa were already gone. Good. He didn't want either one of them to see him in this condition. The last two days had been bad enough.

He was a confident person, something that had helped him rise through the ranks in the music business with such ease. He knew what he wanted from life, had succeeded in achieving most of it, and now ran an empire that operated under his name and existed because of his talent with all the skills he learned in college. The last two days had thrown him for a loop and had set him a little off kilter. High time to find his balance again and regain some control over his life.

The time spent on his knees that morning was a good beginning.

He went into Carol's bathroom and searched her medicine cabinet until he found a nearly empty bottle of aspirin. He dumped what was left in it into his hand, then swallowed them down with water from the faucet. Knowing the drug was in his system and would do some good already made him feel better, so he went down to the kitchen to find the second and third items on his list. Water and coffee.

He pushed open the door to the kitchen. Carol Mabry was a beautiful woman. If he hadn't already thought that before this moment, the full pot of coffee on the counter would definitely have convinced him. There was even a cup sitting on the counter for him, along with a note telling him where to find the aspirin he'd already swallowed, and where to find clean towels.

Bobby opened a few cupboard doors until he found drinking glasses and downed two tall glasses of water before he poured his first cup of coffee. He drank his second cup of the life saving brew while standing under a massaging shower head in the guest bathroom that delivered a steady stream of steaming hot water. It seemed to further ease the ache in his head.

After his shower, as he dressed, his mind started clicking full force. He remembered his priorities and began to make plans. The first item on his agenda was to buy a house in this very neighborhood. He would prefer it to be on this street, but he would settle for something within a one-block radius. The house itself didn't matter as much as the location. He'd tear down what was there and build a new one if he had to.

This morning he had to find a hotel room so he had a place to stay while he searched for a house, and he needed to call his offices in Nashville and get his secretary and accountant working on a few things. He also needed to brief his attorney. Then there was the matter of what to say to the press once word got out.

Because word would get out. It always did.

He'd caught more than a few smart phones in the hands of teenage girls at church yesterday, cameras quite obviously pointed in his direction. If there wasn't already buzz, it would start happening very soon. The paparazzo were going to have a field day over Bobby Kent's long-lost love child. As chilling as that thought was, he knew he needed to make sure everyone was prepared for that, too.

He left the house, turning in the direction of the park where he'd left his rental car. As he walked down the driveway, he saw an elderly man watering a flower bed next door. The man nodded to him and stuck an unlit pipe in his mouth, and Bobby decided to amble on over to speak with the man. He would know about any houses for sale in the area.

"Howdy," he greeted.

The old man nodded, removed his pipe and asked, "Howdy yourself. Anyone ever tell you you are the spittin' image of that singer, Bobby Kent?"

Wearing his best album cover smile, Bobby nodded and reached out to shake the man's hand. "My parents do all the time."

♫ ♫ ♫ ♫

RHONDA knocked once on Carol's door, opened it, and stuck her head through. "Carol, are you free after lunch today?"

Carol nodded and saved the work on her computer. "I am now. Just got word the jury's on their way back in on the Latsbaugh trial."

Rhonda carefully wedged herself all the way inside carrying a stack of poster-sized white foam boards with pictures of a gruesome drug related slaying printed on them. "Timothy asked me to bring these to you. Where do you want them?"

Carol's small office housed her desk and two credenzas full of books. Along various portions of the wall and credenza space, she stored the photo boards she used for presentations in court. She walked toward Rhonda and held out her hands. "I'll take them. Thanks." She found the appropriate stack and set them against it.

From under the window, she grabbed up her briefcase and purse and started walking around her desk. Rhonda said, "I'll walk up with you. I have court in ten."

The two walked along the corridor, offices on one side, a sea of cubicles manned by paralegals and clerks on the other. "Did you get the exhibits finished on the Kennedy case?" Carol asked.

Rhonda stuck a strand of black hair back into the bun at the base of her neck and pushed her black framed glasses further up her nose. She looked at her watch as they left the office of the Commonwealth Attorney and entered the lobby of the building. While they waited for the elevator, the two attorneys watched in apathy as a woman with a really bad dye job over by the metal detectors at the entrance to the building argued with the security guard about some contraband item in her purse.

"Timothy printed some pictures for me today. I'll finish getting the exhibits ready this evening."

"As complicated as this case looks on the outside, I think in the end, it's going to be cut and dry." Most of the time, attorneys tried cases alone.

Whenever big cases came, they would pair up so there would be help in the courtroom to ensure a conviction.

They stepped into the elevator. Carol looked at their reflections and noticed how different they looked. Rhonda, medium height with a dancer's body in her perpetual black and gray, and Carol, tall, red-haired, in a light green pantsuit and bright gold jewelry.

Rhonda's lips thinned. "I hope it's cut and dry. I'd hate to see defense pull some magic rabbit out of a hat."

"Nothing to pull. You and I both know how solid this case is."

Rhonda nodded as they stepped off the elevator onto the third floor and looked up at the big monitor that displayed the day's docket. It always reminded Carol of an airport flight status monitor. Rhonda glanced at her phone and fielded an incoming text. Almost absently, she said to Carol, "Let me know where you want to eat lunch."

♫ ♫ ♫ ♫

CHAPTER 9

Tuesday, April 24th

GARY Lindin sat perfectly still while Bobby spoke. When the star finished, he stayed silent for about thirty seconds, clearly letting it all digest before he whistled through his teeth. "Unbelievable, man." He stood and paced in front of the couch upon which Bobby sat, his mind working in a thousand different directions. "So what do you plan to do now?"

They flew in a chartered jet, en-route from Nassau, where Bobby had interrupted Gary's first vacation in eight years. He had hugged Bobby when he saw him and told him he was glad for the diversion. Lying on a beach watching the tanned or sunburned bikini clad bodies had lost its appeal after the first day, and he told Bobby he had begun to wonder how he was going to make it through the rest of the week.

Bobby took a sip of his tea and crossed his long legs in front of him. "I need to get with Jerry and Harry first," he said, referring to Jarrod Marcum his accountant, and Harrison Dunbar his attorney. "Jerry's meeting me tomorrow morning at the office, but Harry isn't going to be back from wherever he is until tomorrow or the next day. This happening during our first mass vacation wasn't the best timing. I'll come back to Nashville on Monday."

"Does the kid know?"

Bobby felt a quick tug in his chest, then relaxed again. "Not yet. Her mom wants to give it a little time. She probably wants to make sure I'm not about to bail."

Gary was the only manager Bobby ever had. As Bobby's star status grew, Gary's personal clientele list shrank, until he worked exclusively for

Bobby and had a staff of agents for other rising stars. Because of him, Gary could take boring vacations in Nassau, or travel by chartered jet, or host parties for sixty intimate friends and their plus ones. His one and only goal when he moved to Nashville and set up shop a decade ago had been to make a lot of money. Without Bobby, he'd still be peddling demo tapes on Music Row, and he knew where his loyalties should lie.

Bobby watched swift dislike and anger cross his manager's face. It was a look directed at a faceless woman who claimed she didn't know how to get a hold of Bobby Kent when all she had to do was pick up a tabloid to find out. Bobby knew in a few moments he'd be defending the honor of a woman even he barely knew.

"That's the biggest bunch of baloney I've ever heard. She doesn't have the right to keep that kind of news from *your* kid," he said, emphasizing the word "your."

Bobby shrugged. "She doesn't have any malicious intent. I think she's just letting it all sink in for a while. I threw her for a pretty big loop on Saturday."

"So she says." He sat back down on the couch. "Are you going to request a paternity test?"

Bobby grinned, remembering how much his daughter resembled him. "Don't need to. I have no doubts."

"Look, man. Do you have any idea about the deluge of phone calls we get weeks after you do a show in a town from the groupies there who claim to be carrying your child? You're hot, man, and any woman would give her right arm to have you as the father of her child."

Bobby put his head back and laughed. "Gary, you know as well as I do that all of those phone calls are bogus because I don't sleep with my fans and I never have. Not once. This is an entirely different situation. I know this girl. I know how innocent we both were when we were together. Plus, when you look at Lisa, if there was even the smallest doubt, it's gone in a second. She's mine, all right, and I don't need to do anything else to further prove that very obvious fact."

Gary shrugged. "Your call, man." He rubbed his face. "So, what time is it?"

"Where?"

Gary laughed. "Nashville, baby. The only place that matters."

Bobby smiled, glancing at his watch. "Six-thirty. You should be there in the next hour. We're dropping me off in Virginia first. Listen, keep this from the press as long as you can. I don't want them descending on Carol until we just can't help it anymore."

"I'll do what I can, but as soon as you buy that house you're talking about, some of the more slimy ones are going to do their homework."

"I know, but nothing's going into effect for that until Saturday. Besides, my parents live like fifteen miles from that house. Maybe throw them off the scent that way?"

"Maybe. Doubtful. Where are you staying in the meantime? Nashville?"

He shook his head. "Shelly's working on securing me a hotel in Richmond. I'll stay there until the weekend when I can move into my new place." Shelly was Bobby's secretary.

Rebecca, the flight attendant who always worked on this particular charter, came from the galley into the main room. "Mr. Kent, we're just about to start our descent into Richmond. If you two would just hand me your glasses and get yourselves buckled in, please?"

Bobby winked at her as he handed her the glass and watched pink tinge her cheeks. She was fifty years old and the mother of two grown children, and he liked the way she could still blush like a schoolgirl. "Have you started divorce proceedings yet, Rebecca?"

She laughed and shook her head. "Not yet, Mr. Kent. But you'll be the first one I tell when I do." Gary rolled his eyes, never understanding Bobby's need to flirt with the nearest woman.

"You better," he said, then reached behind him for the seat belts. "Don't forget me, now. But let's not tell your husband until after he lands this bird."

♫ ♫ ♫ ♫

Wednesday, April 25th

CAROL stood outside the choir room door at her church and listened absently while three of her closest friends made plans to go to the latest Julianne McNeill movie. She wanted to partake in the jovial fun, and on any other week, she would have, but instead, her mind kept drifting off to the 6'3" singing cowboy with the deep blue eyes.

"Earth to Carol," Georgia Lambert teased, snapping a finger in front of her eyes.

Carol shook her head as if to clear it. "Sorry. What did you say?"

"I said," Georgia conspired, looking around as if to ensure they were alone in the hallway, "what's with you sitting next to Bobby Kent on Sunday? You're killing us here."

Carol felt her cheeks fuse with color. "What do you want to know? We went to college together."

"Hmm," April Harris sagely observed, tossing her blonde hair over her shoulder and grinning a wide grin, "remarkable how many years that's been. Would you say eight? Nine?"

Carol put a hand over her eyes. "Oh heavens," she whispered, "how obvious is it?"

"Without a DNA test, we can only be about 99 percent certain." Sherry Young laughed. She put her arm over Carol's shoulder. "Why in the world would you keep something like that from us?"

"Because I thought he didn't want anything to do with us." The emotions from the last several days caught up with her and swamped her. Suddenly, she could barely breathe and hot tears stung her eyes. "We were both lied to for years. He's missed half of her childhood on the basis of lies."

"Whose lies?" Sherry asked.

Carol shook her head. "It's not important. I used to hate him. Now I'm so sad for him."

"Honey," Georgia said, "you can't undo what was. You can only fix what is and what will be."

April's eyes widened as she looked over Carol's shoulder. "Might want to dry those tears, girlfriend." Carol watched her friend's face flood with color before she smiled.

Carol knew who was approaching before she even turned around. She closed her eyes and took a deep, calming breath, smiled slightly, and turned her body. When she saw Bobby walking toward her, she felt a nervous leap of her heart.

"Hi, Bobby," she said as he drew closer.

"Evening, Carol." He smiled at her friends and spoke in a soft, flirtatious tone. "Ladies."

She couldn't decide if their nervous giggles annoyed her more than they amused her or not. "What are you doing here?"

"Why, I've come to worship," he drawled. "You?"

"Choir slash band practice," Carol replied.

Bobby smiled a slow, heart-stopping grin. "That so? You know I always did enjoy the choir."

Sherry slipped her arm off Carol's shoulder. "Well, let's get in there, then, and get you a song book."

"Really, we probably shouldn't –" Carol said, but Bobby cut her off.

"That would be really great. Thank you so much."

♫ ♫ ♫ ♫

Thursday, April 26th

"LISTEN, Bobby, the old man isn't going to sign anything until he's spoken with her, and I can't force him to go over there and do it. Everything's ready down to that son who is a contractor meeting you at the house on Tuesday, but until we have a signed contract, nothing can happen," Harrison said through the phone.

"Don't worry about it, Harry. I'm not. He said he'd do it and I don't think she'll have a problem with it," Bobby opined, hoping he was right.

"I don't like things being done at the last minute. Leaves too much room for mistakes," Harrison hedged.

"You don't have a choice," Bobby announced, impatient with the conversation. "If it doesn't work, then I'll get the other place. It won't be as ideal, but it'll work."

"You'd save about three million dollars if you went with the other place."

"So?"

He heard Harrison give a big sigh. "Okay, Bobby. I'll have the contract ready to sign for the other place, too. There's a title company that will work late Friday, whichever place it ends up being, and my assistant will be there with both sets of contracts whatever time the pilot delivers her."

"Good. I'll be back in Nashville on Monday."

"Do you want me to have any documents drawn up for child support and visitation?"

Bobby rubbed his eyes. "I'll let you know. I'll call you from the plane on Monday." He hung up the phone before Harrison could complain about having to do that paperwork at the last minute too, then went into the bedroom of his hotel suite and stretched out on the bed.

He lay there, with his hands behind his head, staring at the ceiling, thinking about all the outstanding details still up in the air. He had renovations in mind for the house he was going to buy. With the walk-through he'd had on Monday, he could see all the work he wanted to do to it, and was anxious to get started. He'd been majoring in architecture when he left college, and had designed his house in Tennessee. He had specific things he wanted in his house, and while the one he was buying would take some minor renovations, it had the basics, and he could work with the rooms' sizes.

He wanted to call Lisa and explain things to her, get her excited about it, ask her what color paint he needed for her room, but he held himself in check. That would come soon enough. He trusted Carol. He knew a good portion of that trust came from her obvious faith and the faith centered home in which she was raising their daughter.

He thought of watching her practice with the orchestra last night at church while he sang tenor in the choir. He pondered why his thoughts turned to Carol as often as Lisa. He was here to establish a relationship with Lisa, not Carol, but he was having a hard time figuring out why he thought of his daughter's mother as often as he thought of his little girl.

He had found Carol strikingly attractive in college. In fact, once he met her it was difficult not to let thoughts of her distract him throughout the day. He admired her lovely looks, of course; the way she moved with such grace for someone of her height and the way she tossed her hair or smiled. But her talent and her drive coupled with her faith impressed him even more. They had started somewhat of a courtship in college, but it had been very brief and very informal. He had certainly hoped for more back then. Who knew what could have happened between them if Bobby hadn't received the call of a lifetime.

When he'd gotten the call he felt as if he'd been drawn to her door, looking for someone with whom to share the amazing news. The excitement she had shown was sincere and he dragged her out of the dorm to celebrate with him, buying two bottles of champagne and heading for a spot he knew about along the banks of the Oconee River.

He dropped her off at her room as the sun started to rise, and when he came out of the building carrying the box of stuff he'd quickly packed, she stood at his truck, holding a bouquet of flowers she picked from the flower bed in front of the school sign. She handed them to him with a laugh, wished him luck, and had given him the most memorable goodbye-and-good-luck kiss he'd ever experienced before or since. He remembered looking in the rear view mirror as he drove away, wanting to turn around and convince her to get in the truck with him.

She'd slowly become a shadow of a memory, just someone he thought of in conjunction with his college days, or of his impulsive life before fully committing his life to Christ. He had always regretfully assumed he had missed an opportunity. He just knew someone as special as Carol had certainly married and gone on with her life, perhaps thinking of him as fondly as the years passed.

He suddenly felt very lonely, so he picked up the phone and dialed a number from memory, wanting to talk with someone who didn't work for him about what was currently going on in his life.

The second he heard Melody's voice, he smiled. "Hello, Darlin'," he greeted with a drawl, and as soon as he heard her answering laugh, he felt himself relax. "Is James free? I don't want to bother him if he's busy."

♪ ♪ ♪ ♪

HEIDI Conried sat in the corner of the piano bar and nursed her white wine. She was bored out of her mind. She leaned toward her friend Wanda and said, "Let's get out of here. This place is just not happening."

Wanda brushed her red hair off her forehead and rolled her eyes. "I know. How did I let Howie talk us into this dump?"

"Howie could talk you into anything," Heidi said with a snicker. She watched as an attractive man with a black goatee and black framed glasses walked up to their table. She put on her best winning smile and twirled a blonde curl around her finger. "Well, hello there, handsome," she purred.

He glanced her way and nodded, but spoke directly to Wanda. "Excuse me. May I buy you a drink?"

"Wanda!" Howie yelled from at the bar.

Heidi watched Wanda look from the stranger to her latest crush before she slid out of her chair and stood. At five-one, she barely came up to this guy's shoulder. "Excuse me," she said before looking at Heidi. "Come on. Let's get out of here."

Annoyed at the stranger for ignoring her, Heidi stood, teetering a bit on her high heels. Why she wore them, when they put her over six feet tall, she could never remember. But high heels always called her name.

The stranger looked her up and down and stepped between her and Wanda. "You are very beautiful," he said, his bright blue eyes almost glowing from behind the glasses.

Not ready to forgive him – yet – for ignoring her in favor of Wanda, she countered with, "And you're very short."

He winked. "Only when I'm standing."

She felt her cheeks fuse with heat, then laughed and held out her hand. "I'm Heidi."

When he took her hand, she felt like the breath was knocked out of her body. He kept her eyes locked with his gaze and squeezed her hand gently. "It is an absolute pleasure to meet you, Heidi. I am Rob."

♫ ♫ ♫ ♫

Friday, April 27th

THE sweet sounds of the Irish tune, *Danny Boy*, flowed through the spring night. Carol inhaled the scent of her tree's cherry blossoms while she sat in a chair on her front porch and mindlessly played her violin, watching Lisa ride her bicycle up and down the driveway. The instrument had always been a way for her to wind down and relax and, while she knew she'd never have been good enough to take it anywhere professionally, she played well. Lately, Lisa would ask her to play if it had been a few weeks since she pulled it out at home instead of just at church, and Carol was happy that she'd been able to give her daughter a memory she would always carry with her from childhood: a memory of her mother sitting on the front porch playing her violin in the springtime evening.

She watched her neighbor, Ed Westbury, walk across the lawn separating the two houses. He was a sweet old man, retired from his own construction business for about ten years, with a wife who made the best oatmeal cookies Carol had ever eaten. Over the last few years, the families had grown very close. Carol knew their relationship with Lisa was almost a grandparent to granddaughter relationship, and she loved that she'd found that in neighbors.

She made as if to stop playing, but Ed waved his hand at her and sat in the chair next to her, pulling out his pipe and watching Lisa. Ed quit lighting the tobacco years ago, but he still enjoyed the feel of his old pipe and relished the fragrance of his chocolate or cherry pipe tobacco. Carol finished the song, then set the instrument and the bow in their case on the ground next to her. "Hi, Ed. How are you?" she asked.

"Doing better than ever, Carol." He puffed for a moment on his unlit pipe, then set it down. "You know how the wife and I have been thinking about getting a pool put in?" Carol nodded and waited. He always took a while to get around to his actual point. "Well, the house about three doors down from us that's for sale already has a pool. It also has two more bedrooms, which is a big thing to consider when you have twelve grandchildren."

Carol raised an eyebrow and looked at him. "I thought you were going to have one of your sons build an addition to this house."

"That's a lot of racket to put up with if we could just scoot down about three doors." He put the pipe back into his mouth and chewed on the stem.

"You're going to sell your house and move down three doors?" she asked. "You built that house yourself twenty years ago."

"I already sold it," he told her with a wink.

Carol shook her head, trying to glean some sense from the conversation. "What?"

"Yep. This guy came over couple a days ago and offered us more than the market value, and even offered to buy the other house for us. Nice young man. Gloria just preened over him. A moving company is coming tomorrow morning, and me and the wife just have to sit back and let them just shift us over."

"Did you recognize the guy?" Carol asked, suspicious.

"Well," Ed stretched the word out. "He reminded me a lot of your little girl to be honest with you. And he was real persistent."

Carol started laughing with that confirmation as to just who bought the house. "Yeah, I bet." She put a hand on his arm. "Thank you."

"Well, now, it isn't up to me to come between a man and his baby girl. Especially one that's as sweet as that little thing over there. I just thought I'd stop on over and see how you felt about the whole thing." He stood and slipped his pipe into his shirt pocket. "You just tell her to come on over as often as she does now, and all of this will be okay. Can she swim?"

"Like a fish. And I'll tell her. Do you need any help tomorrow?"

"I would appreciate it if we could come sit on your porch and watch them do all the work."

"It's a deal. I'll even have a pitcher of tea waiting for you," she said.

He patted her shoulder and stepped off the porch, stopping to talk to Lisa on his way back to his house. She shook her head, amazed at the turn of events. She hadn't seen Bobby since he showed up at the church

Wednesday. That had been the first time she'd seen him since Sunday night, and she didn't get much of an opportunity to speak with him then. After choir practice, he just had a few quick words for her – telling her that he had a room at the downtown Viscolli Hotel and giving her the room number – then turned his attention to Lisa. She chuckled again when she thought of him buying the house next door to them. It crossed her mind that she should, at the very least, feel just a little upset that he hadn't even thought to mention it to her, but she didn't. She thought it was an incredibly positive statement about his intended role in Lisa's life.

Carol's phone rang and she answered it absently. "Hello?"

"Carol, this is Harriet." Carol's stomach tightened with nerves.

"I don't really feel like talking with you right now, Harriet," she said.

"That's fine, Carol. I was actually calling to talk to Lisa."

Carol almost laughed out loud, but stopped herself in time. It was possible to be firm without coming off as mean. "Umm, no. I don't think that's a very good idea just yet," she said casually.

"But I haven't seen her or spoken to her in nearly a week."

"Really? That's too bad, Harriet. A whole week. Not eight years?"

"You can't keep me from my only grandchild! My life has revolved around her since the day that child was born," Harriet said, a tinge of hysteria coloring her voice.

"I don't intend to keep Lisa from you. When she asks about you, I'll have her call you." Carol thought that was as fair as she was willing to be right at that moment in time. "Good-bye, Harriet."

She hung up the phone and sat back in her chair, crossing her ankles. She let Lisa ride her bike until it started to get dark, then called her to come sit on the porch with her. They sat there in the warm evening and talked about the little things going on in life until it was time to go inside and pop popcorn and watch the movie Lisa had picked out.

♫ ♫ ♫ ♫

THE telephone rang again as the credits rolled. For some reason, she wasn't surprised to hear Bobby's voice.

"I'm hoping your neighbor spoke with you by now," he verified.

Carol laughed softly. "He did, just a couple of hours ago."

"He wouldn't sign the papers until he cleared it with you, and since the movers are showing up tomorrow, I thought I'd better check."

"Ed moves at his own pace. Hang on a sec, Bobby." She put her hand over the receiver. "Lisa, go get ready for bed. You can skip your bath. It's already late."

"Aw, mom, just ten more minutes, please," Lisa begged.

"It will take you ten minutes to get ready. I let you stay up to see the end of the movie. Go now." She smiled as her daughter ducked her head and dragged her feet as she left the room. "Sorry about that," she said back into the phone.

"Why would you ever feel the need to apologize for being such a great mom?"

That stopped Carol. "I don't know."

Bobby said, "For me, it's a delight."

"You wouldn't say that if you were here. I don't know why bed time is such a chore."

His voice sounded very serious when he responded, "Don't underestimate me. I'd like to give it a try sometime."

"Well then you've got a deal," Carol said, then jumped a little when her work cell phone rang. "Hang on again. I can't ignore this." She set the phone in her lap and dug her other phone out of her pocket. "Hello?"

"Carol? It's Mitch."

Not again. "What have you got?"

"Two things. The autopsy labs finally came back on Daniels. I was about to take up arms against the lab, they were taking so long. They arrived via special messenger about an hour ago and confirm that the same sedative used on Cody was also used on Daniels."

"So no surprise, really. What's the second thing?"

"I'm at the townhouse of one Heidi Conried. You'd better get over here."

"Is it the same guy?"

"Looks like it. How long before you can get here?"

Carol sighed and ran a hand through her hair. "At least half an hour. I need to get Lisa taken care of."

He rattled off the address. "I'll see you as soon as you get here."

Carol put away her phone, then remembered the other one in her lap.

She picked it up and thought about pretending nothing was wrong, but she knew he'd heard the whole thing. "Sorry about that, Bobby."

"My hotel is ten minutes from there. I can come right over if you don't mind my staying with Lisa."

She didn't have to think about it for long. "Of course I don't mind."

"I have an appointment with a title agent to come to my hotel room and sign the papers for the purchase of the house. I'll have to call him and have him come over there instead. Do you mind?"

"That's fine."

"Then I'm on my way. See you soon," he said and hung up before she could reply or have any second thoughts.

Carol put the phone down, then went upstairs to make sure Lisa had gotten ready for bed. She found her in the corner of her room, already dressed in her pajamas and playing with her tea set, her long hair down and brushed.

"Hey, kiddo. You brushed your hair already," she declared, sitting next to her daughter on the floor.

"Uh-huh. Who was that on the phone?" Lisa asked, stealing a glance from under her lashes.

"Country music superstar Bobby Kent. Well, and detective Mitch." Carol ran a hand through Lisa's hair. It was slightly redder than hers, and had more blonde streaks in it. She loved Lisa's hair.

Lisa frowned. Her entire face reflected immediate displeasure in the way that only an eight year old's features can do. "You have to go to work now?"

Carol nodded. "Here in a few minutes, and only for a little while. What's up, kiddo."

She poured herself an imaginary cup of tea. "Mom?"

"Yeah, babe."

"I've been thinking. Figuring a few things out," Lisa began.

Carol lay back on the floor and propped herself up on her elbows. "About what?"

"Well, we talked about grandparents a few weeks ago in school, about how some kids don't have grandparents, and how some kids live with their grandparents. How grandparents are your mom and dad's parents. And I know Grandma and Grandpa Mabry are your parents."

Carol nearly groaned out loud, but she just lifted an eyebrow. "Go on," she said.

"So I heard Bobby Kent call Grandma Kent his mom last week. And later, I asked him if he had any brothers, and he told me no."

Her daughter had way too many active brain cells. "That's right."

"I was wondering if Bobby Kent is my dad." Lisa stopped fiddling with her tea set and looked at Carol with such a need in her blue eyes that Carol couldn't put off answering her, even if she had wanted to do.

"Yes, he is, Baby. He's your father."

Lisa looked down, but not before Carol could see the hope spring in her eyes. "Well, like I said, I was just doing some figuring in my head."

Carol sat up and pulled Lisa into her lap. "There's a lot to this story, Lisa. A bunch of stuff that I can't explain to you right now, but I want you to understand that your father didn't even know he was your dad until the day of your birthday party."

"Why didn't you tell him?" The tears in her voice broke a little corner of Carol's heart.

"I relied on someone else to do that, baby, and they lied to me. They lied to him, too. It was partly my fault, too. Important things like this shouldn't be left for someone else to handle. But he's here now, and he wants to be your daddy more than anything in the world."

Lisa stilled, tense in Carol's lap. "Really?" she asked.

"He wants that so much that he bought the house next door. Mr. and Mrs. Westbury are moving down the street to the house with the pool, and your daddy is going to move in tomorrow."

"He's moving next door?" she asked excitedly.

"He is. And I bet if you ask him, he'll let you decorate a bedroom any way you want for your very own room at his house."

Lisa jumped off her lap and turned to look at her. "Do you think we could call him now and ask him?"

Carol hid a smile. "Well, we could, but why don't you just wait until he comes over?"

"But mom, I can't wait all night for something that important. Can't we call him right now?"

"He's on his way over to sit with you, baby girl. I have to go to work for a little while." Carol stood and put her hand on her daughter's head. "You can stay up while he's here, but when he tells you to go to bed, you have to listen."

"Oh, okay. I will." Lisa did a quick pirouette just as the doorbell rang. "I'll get it!" she cried, then took off to answer the door. Carol put her hand to her stomach and took a deep breath. She didn't realize the strain she'd been under keeping information of such import from Lisa. She felt like such a weight had been lifted from her shoulders. She smiled and left the room, stopping halfway down the stairs with her hand to her mouth to keep from crying while she watched Bobby kneel and embrace Lisa. She squeezed his neck with every last ounce of strength in her eight year old arms.

♪ ♪ ♪ ♪

"TWENTY-THREE-YEAR-OLD registered nurse. Heidi Conried. Single. Straight. Roommate found her. She's on the couch in the front room."

Carol stared at the body on the bed. Heidi wore a navy skirt and blazer with a white and navy striped shirt and matching navy heels. Her auburn hair was perfectly brushed and smooth, and her makeup cleverly applied. Five fat red extinguished candles sat at her head, hands, and feet. Carol walked closer to the bed to look at the violin string around her neck. "These candles are barely burned. Do we have a time of death?"

"Guessing about 24 hours." Mitch slipped his hands into his pockets and rocked back on his heels. "Doc thinks she was dead before he strangled her."

Carol raised an eyebrow. "Too much drug?"

"Likely. He'll know more, of course. But look at her hair line."

She leaned in and caught the wafting smell of the corpse's shampoo. When she recognized her own brand, she felt a little skitter of fear. Trying to brush it aside, she accepted a rubber glove from Mitch and parted the hair at Heather's temple. "Dye," she said.

"Yep. About 24-hours ago, Miss Conried here was a blonde with long curly hair."

Carol frowned. "He dyed and straightened her hair?"

"To look like the other victims."

"So, who is our killer killing?"

"That's the question, isn't it?" The voice came from behind her, but she recognized it. Startled, she turned around and saw Jack Gordon. He inclined his head in a greeting. "Good to see you, Carol. Now I know what you meant by you hoped you never saw me on the job."

Mitch frowned. "You two know each other?"

Carol slipped the glove off and straightened. "We met in a coffee shop a few weeks ago. We very much enjoyed a lunch until I found out Jack was a cop."

Mitch's lips thinned in an amused line. "Carol has an aversion to dating cops. My wife admires her intelligence," he joked.

"So I gathered," Jack said, clearly not amused. "In point of fact, she made that abundantly clear."

"Jack's my new partner," Mitch clarified. "Been breaking him in all week."

"Dandy," Carol muttered. Uncomfortable, she turned her back on Jack. "Where were the women when they last saw each other?"

"At a piano bar named Baby Blues a few blocks away. I have uniforms there now doing interviews."

"She leave with anyone?"

"Unknown. She was talking to a man when the roommate left with her boyfriend. She didn't come back here until her shift at the hospital ended tonight."

"She an RN, too?" Carol opened the flap on the blazer to look at the label, recognizing the expensive designer.

"PA." Jack looked at his phone, scrolling through what looked like notes. "Worked three to seven today. Texted Heidi here at midnight last night and told her she'd see her tonight."

Carol nodded. "So if our guy was with her, he'd have known."

"And would have taken time to dye her hair," Mitch replied.

Carol gestured at the body. "Does the roommate know if these are her clothes?"

Jack answered. "Looking through the case files this week, the clothes are standing out to me, too. So, I asked. Roommate has never seen them. They don't seem to match the styles in her closet."

"Same with the other victims," Mitch said.

"Which brings us to the original question," Carol said.

Jack continued for her. "Who is he killing?"

Carol turned to walk back to the front of the house. She glanced at the couch, where a redheaded woman in light blue scrubs sat, legs drawn up, slowly ripping a tissue into little pieces. Her tear-filled eyes met Carol's. "It coulda been me," she said.

"What do you mean?"

She took a shaky breath and waved in the direction of the bedroom. "That guy, he ignored her at first. He was flirting with me until I stood up. Then it was as if I hadn't existed in the first place."

Carol looked at her, mentally taking in the size of her legs pulled up to her chest, and the small hands. "How tall are you? Five feet?"

The young woman shrugged. "Five-one."

Turning to Mitch, Carol gestured with her chin. After expressing her sympathy at the loss of her friend, she led the way out of the apartment. In the hall, she looked at Mitch and Jack. "She's too short."

"He honed in on her because of her hair. The blonde was an afterthought."

Feeling a sense of urgency, she replied, "Yes. Which means the hair dye was also an afterthought. You might want to check 24-hour places around here for a man who came in sometime in the last 24 hours and purchased a box of red hair dye."

Mitch nodded, pulling out his phone. "We might even get some surveillance."

"Exactly."

♫ ♫ ♫ ♫

IT was closer to midnight than she wanted when she pulled into her driveway, and she was glad to see the lights upstairs were turned off. Hopefully, that meant Lisa was in bed and asleep. Not only was it several hours past her bedtime, Carol hadn't been able to leave it all behind her this time, and she didn't want Lisa exposed to even the slightest bit of the darkness she faced at work.

She didn't realize Bobby sat on the porch until she had her key in the lock and he spoke. She nearly jumped out of her skin when she heard his voice coming from her right. "How bad was it?" he asked.

She put a hand to her chest and weakly walked over to the chair next to him, sitting down. "You scared me half to death," she vented.

"I'm so sorry. You looked right at me. I thought you saw me."

She set her purse next to her chair and ran her hands through her hair.

"When did she go to bed?"

She could see his teeth flash in the dark when he smiled. "Well, I told her we wouldn't have to tell you, but she informed me very seriously that you knew everything and it's best if we don't lie. So, Carol, the truth is she's been in bed for about half an hour."

Despite her mood when she walked up, she smiled and leaned back. "You'd best remember that, dad. The mom always knows."

"I'll be sure to keep that in mind. Not that I would ever lie to you anyway. I think we've both endured enough lies for a lifetime." She heard ice rattle as he took a sip from the glass he held in his hand. "Thanks for telling her, Carol. It's been heavy on my heart and mind."

She tilted her head back and closed her eyes. "I wish I could say that I did, but I didn't. She figured it out on her own."

They sat quietly for a while and her eyes adjusted to the low light. Before she could capture the thought, she found herself admiring his handsome profile in the silver moonlight.

"I helped myself to your tea. I love a good Darjeeling. Pour you a glass?" Bobby offered.

Carol shook her head. "The caffeine would keep me up."

Bobby nodded. "I hope you don't mind I borrowed your instrument," he confided, then took another sip.

"What?" she asked, lost in thoughts of the night. She turned her head to look at him.

"Your fiddle," he elaborated. "I played her a few songs."

"Oh, my violin. Do you ever do any classical work anymore or is it all *Red River Mud*?" she teased, naming one of his biggest hit songs.

His teeth flashed white against the dark night, and she heard him try to choke back a laugh, then finally let it out. She smiled at the sound. "I fiddle, mostly. Sometimes, secretly, I play a few pages from Bach or Weinberg or even that old Bartók thing you used to torture. I think it would destroy my image if I was ever overheard playing classical violin. I'm a closet violinist," he answered. "Anyway, I prefer the guitar, now."

She laughed with him, then said softly, "You have the gift I always wished I had." She felt a wave of exhaustion wash over her, so she stood and stretched, then said, "I need to go to bed. What time are the movers supposed to come?"

Bobby stood next to her and drained his glass. "Nine." He pulled his keys out of his pocket. "I'd like to pick Lisa up in the morning and take her with me while I go shopping for furniture. Would that be okay with you, Carol?" he asked, handing her his empty glass.

"She has a birthday party to go to at two. As long as she's back here in time to eat lunch and get ready to go, I don't mind."

He started to turn, but stopped himself. "By the way, thanks for everything. I want to say something to you right now."

He put his hands in his pockets and leaned back on his heels a little bit. "I've been thinking about how to say this so don't take it wrong if it doesn't come out right, okay? What I want to say is that I know this is all new for you. It's new for me, too. But I just want you to know that I don't have any expectations or preconceived notions. I don't. I'm not here to complicate your life or hers. I just want to get to know her. I want to let her get to know me. But that will only happen with your blessing and your permission, Carol."

He stepped off the porch and started to leave, but turned back. "So that's all informal and that's how I really feel. But I have to go to Nashville on Monday to meet with my accountant and lawyer about taking my parents off some things. So I'm asking you. Do you want me to do anything official about when I get to see Lisa and that sort of thing?"

"Bobby, I'm exhausted." Carol rubbed the back of her neck. "This really is neither the time nor place. I don't have any intention of standing between you two. I never have. And obviously, neither did you. That was all your folks." She turned to go inside, but he stopped her by speaking quickly.

"I know you had a long day, but please don't misjudge me. I was only asking because I know my attorney well enough to know he's having a litter of kittens and will want to create six inches of paperwork. You know how lawyers are."

Despite her fatigue, she laughed at his teasing tone. "Present company excluded, of course."

Carol agreed, "Oh, of course."

Bobby cleared his throat. "Anyhow, I want to go into that office Monday afternoon prepared to head that off. I never wanted to deal with the court system, either. I never would have wanted to be away from you or my child. Like you said, that was all my folks. I would have done the right thing by you, Carol. I hope you believe that."

"I'm sorry," Carol said. She rubbed her eyes. "In my professional opinion, it's always best to have some sort of protection, especially when dealing with a child as it pertains to visitation and child support. However, personally, I have every intention of working with you, and since we aren't dealing with hostile and or bitter feelings between the two of us, the paperwork will probably be unnecessary."

"And what about child support? Do you want something in writing?"

"For everyone's protection, it should be legal. The amount is something we can agree upon. I can tell you how much I need to be able to stay in this house and to pay for Lisa's school. Any excess money I've gotten has been put into a trust for Lisa. Truly, all I want from you is that little extra to make my mortgage and her tuition. Anything more you want to give, I would prefer it to go into the trust account or that you set up one for her on your own."

"That sounds fair. Thanks." He stepped back onto the steps and walked up two until they were eye level. "Now, how bad is it, this case you're working on?"

With the sharp sting of tears in her eyes, she stepped backward so that she couldn't actually feel his body heat. "I can't discuss it."

"You've had three murders in just a few weeks, Carol. The news is saying words like 'serial killer.' Is that what's happening, here?"

Rubbing her eyes, she shook her head. "I can't talk about it, Bobby. This doesn't concern you. Go back to your hotel, now. I'm tired."

His eyes flared, but he grinned and nodded. "Sorry I brought it up."

He turned and walked back down the steps and down the driveway. He had his hand on the door handle of his car when he looked back at her. "I'll pick Lisa up at eight tomorrow morning," he said, then slid behind the wheel and started the car without waiting for a response from her.

CHAPTER 11

♫ ♫ ♫ ♫

Personal Journal Entry

April 28

Her overdose ruined everything. I tolerated the fact that I had to fix the hair. I knew I'd have time. I had no idea that she'd be dead even before the first rinse. Thankfully, we were in her apartment so I didn't have to try to transport her empty headed blonde dead weight around.

I made her look pretty but it just didn't work for me. The need in me is nearly overwhelming now. It's agonizing to constantly battle this clawing need. I don't know how much longer I can keep it at bay. I keep telling her these cheap tawdry weak substitutes aren't going to work. She says they have to be enough because she's in love.

In love in love in love.

As if she knows what love is. "Oh, I love her. Oh, she's so precious to me. She is too precious to me." Stupid cow.

♫ ♫ ♫ ♫

Saturday, April 28th

BOBBY pulled into Carol's driveway and saw Carol and Lisa sitting on the porch. A wave of love washed over him at the sight of Lisa waving frantically at him, and he felt as excited as she looked for the day they would spend together.

Carol smiled at him as he walked up the drive. He started to return the smile when he heard her cell phone ring and watched her frown as she answered it.

"Hey, Sugar," he said, bending down to catch Lisa as she ran toward him. He walked up to the porch and sat in the chair next to Carol, keeping Lisa on his lap.

"I don't have an official comment, Larry, you know that," Carol said into her phone.

Bobby cupped his hand around Lisa's ear and whispered, "Who's your mama talking to?"

Lisa shrugged. "Work."

"I can't help you with information you have from unnamed sources, Larry. I can't comment. This is an ongoing investigation. Call Mitch Carpenter and he'll give you what information he can."

Bobby watched Carol pinch the bridge of her nose, and filed the gesture away for future hints of frustration. "Then use what he gave you and run with it." She paused for a moment, then smiled and added, "Well, if he gave you Jack, run with Jack. Or Jill. Don't care. I can give you unofficial, but it will have to be Monday at my office." She hung up, put away the phone, then smiled and looked at him. "You guys ready to go?"

"Yep," Lisa said. She snuggled herself closer to his chest, and he put an arm around her.

Bobby watched Carol's face for some sign that might reveal some better clue about her emotional state, but she had apparently placed the phone call in the background. He marveled at her ability to deal with what she dealt with on a daily basis and still come home and provide a normal life for her child. Or rather, their child.

"We'll be back around lunch," he said. "I'll bring something back with us."

"You don't have to worry about that, Bobby," Carol said. "I'm making lunch for the Westbury's." She looked up when she heard another car pulling into the drive, and Bobby saw surprise and pleasure flash in her eyes. He turned to see who was in the car, lifting his eyebrow at the sight of the new Mercedes-Benz, just as Lisa jumped off his lap and ran in the direction of the car.

"Henry! Henry!" she yelled, and he watched as Lisa threw herself into the man's arms before he even had time to get his car door shut. He kissed Lisa then set her down and pulled a wrapped package out of his back seat and handed it to her. He followed her back to the porch, bending his head down so he could hear what she said. He stood tall and was well dressed with strong Hispanic features. The dislike for this man passed swiftly through Bobby, surprising him. He wondered if it was because Lisa had greeted Henry with the same enthusiasm she'd shown for him, or if it was because Carol looked so happy to see him.

"Mom! Look what Henry brought me!" she said, running the last few feet to the porch. "Can I open it now?"

"Sure, babe," Carol answered. She stood to greet Henry while Lisa ran into the house. "We missed you last week at the party," she said as she took his hand. Bobby watched Henry's lips graze Carol's cheek, and felt another surge of dislike for him.

"That plane crash at the airport last Friday tied me up for a couple of days," he said.

"Henry, this is Bobby Kent, Lisa's father. Bobby, Dr. Henry Suarez, a dear friend of the family," Carol introduced. "Henry and I went to high school together. His sister is my best friend."

Bobby stood and saw a mirror of his own feelings of dislike and mistrust in Henry's eyes.

"Lisa's dad?" Henry asked. Bobby nodded, then had to grit his teeth when the other man added, "Nice of you to show up."

"I would have been here sooner if someone would have had the courtesy of telling me the happy news," Bobby bit out, surprised by the level of resentment and anger he still felt. He knew he had to get a grip on this. He resolved that he would not let it affect him for at least the rest of the day.

"What are you talking about?" Henry asked, leaning against the railing of the porch and crossing his arms over his chest.

"Henry, Harriet lied to me. Robert, too. They never told Bobby," Carol said. She hadn't sat back down yet, and it amused Bobby when he realized that she could read their feelings and was probably going to step between the two of them if it proved necessary.

Henry stared Bobby down for a moment, then straightened and held out his hand. "Nice to meet you. I never listen to your music."

From his new perspective of calm detachment, Bobby didn't rise to take the bait. He knew he wouldn't have acted any differently if the situation were reversed. He took the offered hand, still feeling a twinge of jealousy at the love and acceptance Carol and Lisa seemed to naturally have for Henry. He had missed so much. Bitterness rolled in his stomach.

"Mom! Look what Henry got me," Lisa announced as she threw open the door and ran across the porch. She had on a pair of black leather cowboy boots with girly hot pink swirls running through the design. "Look! They have the Melody Montgomery logo on the side!"

"How exciting!" Carol smiled.

"I can wear them when I'm at grandma's riding horses," she declared.

"Sure you can," her mother agreed. "Make sure you tell Henry thank you."

"Thank you, Henry," she said, throwing her arms around him, then turned to Bobby. "Can I wear them today when we go shopping?" Lisa asked, gripping his leg.

Bobby knelt down to eye level with her. "Not today, sugar. Brand new boots will hurt your feet if you have to walk in them too much and we have a lot of walking ahead of us today. Put your sandals back on and, next time, you can wear them when they're more broke in."

"You're wearing boots," Lisa accused with a pout, her head bowed. Carol rolled her eyes behind her back, and Bobby had to bite the inside of his lip to keep from smiling. He could see Lisa was learning feminine wiles early.

"Mine aren't brand spankin' new, Darlin'. They're good and broke in. Now go change, or I'll have to find some other little girl to help me decorate your room." Lisa looked like she wanted to resist, but the threat of not being able to go was enough to dissuade her, so she ran back into the house, her boots stomping on the wooden floor of the porch. Bobby stood back up and rubbed the back of his neck. "She's hard to resist," he admitted to Carol.

Carol laughed and sat down. "You remember that when you're out shopping today. Lisa knows how to play people." She looked at Henry. "Last week, Jen told me she was stopping here to visit on her way down to Atlanta to see your brother. Have you heard from her?"

Bobby watched Henry's lips thin. "She's in DC. They broke up again."

"What happened this time?" Carol asked. Bobby pulled a list out of his pocket and reviewed it, looking at store names and purchase items, only listening with half an ear to a conversation about people he didn't know.

Henry shrugged. "Pretty simple. She doesn't want to get married and have kids. He does."

"I hate that. How's John dealing with it?" Carol asked.

"Yeah, well, she's not exactly an easy person to love. John will be okay." He leaned back against the railing.

"I was hoping I'd get a chance to talk with her and see if she could help me with a profile," Carol said.

"I've seen the speculation in the papers," Henry began, but Lisa threw open the door and ran back on the porch.

"I'm ready to go now," she said.

Bobby stood and held out his hand. "Well then, let's hit the road." Lisa grabbed his hand and the two stepped off the porch. "We'll be back around lunch time, Carol. It was nice to meet you, Henry," he said for Lisa's sake, then the two walked to his car where he helped Lisa get strapped in.

Bobby looked back at the porch as he got into his car, and definitely didn't like the feeling that went through him at the sight of Henry Suarez sitting down in the place he had vacated and turning his chair to face Carol. He was going to have to explore that feeling later, figure out what it was exactly.

He started the car and backed out of the driveway. "Have any ideas for your room, Sugar?' he asked Lisa.

"Oh, yes, I do. I know exactly everything I want," she said enthusiastically, making Bobby laugh as they drove away.

♫ ♫ ♫ ♫

"I can't comment on it. You know that," Carol said as she came out of the house carrying two cups of coffee.

"Then listen to me without feeling like you need to share the details of the case. I'm merely concerned that the lead attorney on this case looks enough like all three of the victims to make me worry that you'll become a target simply because of your high exposure. You're all Lisa has besides Bibbity-Bobbity Kent, there," Henry said, nodding his thanks for the drink.

She wondered about defending Bobby's honor, but let it slide. Henry felt protective of Lisa and Carol, and the words were born out of love and not malice. She had a feeling that Bobby would prove himself in time, and Henry would come to accept him. "That isn't something I'm allowing myself to think about right now." She sat back down in the chair she'd left a few moments before. "I'll become very paranoid and go out of my mind with worry and fear before I ship Lisa off to California to my parents or something."

The telephone beside her on the chair rang, and she answered it. "Hello?"

"Hi, Carol," Lori Bradford, Amy's mom, greeted.

"Hello, Lori. I heard you were saying something about midnight feedings and dirty diapers, then rumor had it you threw up," Carol offered in an ironic tone.

"Heaven help me. There is a reason I waited so long between children," Lori said. "Listen. I was wondering if Amy could spend the morning over there. I can't even get out of bed."

"She's welcome to come over, but Lisa isn't here." Carol bit her lip and decided that Lisa would tell the second she had the opportunity. "She's out shopping with her dad."

There was a long pause. "I see."

"Do you remember last weekend Lisa and Amy babbling excitedly about Bobby Kent?" Carol asked.

There was another long pause. "Well, honey, you just shattered the hopes and dreams of about fifty million women," Lori observed. "I think I may be one of them."

Carol laughed, glad she had good friends. "I didn't know you were a country music fan."

"Honey, one need not be a fan of country music to appreciate everything about that man. So do you mind if she comes over?"

"Of course not. I'll go watch for her now."

"Thank you. By the way, I'm a little upset with you for not telling me, but I'll get over it quickly if you tell me the whole story and then let me meet him."

"You're about to throw up again from the second pregnancy in your ten year marriage," Carol observed.

"Don't take the fun out of it." Carol could hear Lori talk to Amy. "She's on her way down. Thanks, Carol. I owe you one."

"Not a problem, Lori," Carol said, and hung up the phone.

"I'm going to go. I have to be at the hospital by nine," Henry said. He set his coffee cup on the ground next to his chair and stood. "You let me know if you need anything, Carol. I'm going to worry about this until it's over with."

"Just don't tell your sister anything," Carol said, referring to her best friend, Aria. She walked down the driveway with him so she could watch for Amy. "Hopefully, the national news will stay out of it."

"You probably want to tell her about Bobby Kent. That's rather friend-worthy news. You don't want her reading about it in a tabloid."

"I called her last weekend."

He grinned. "Did she tell you about Adam's award?"

Carol chuckled. "Yes. I wish I'd been there to see that."

"I recorded it. I cracked up when I watched it. It's on the internet. Check it out." He kissed her cheek, then walked to his car. "Go ahead and call Jen, Carol. She probably wouldn't mind helping you out."

"I'll think about it. Thanks, Henry," Carol said as she saw Amy turn the corner.

♫ ♫ ♫ ♫

"YOU know, dear, this whole time Ed has been talking about getting a pool, he's said it was for the grandchildren. But he was on the phone all morning with pool services trying to get someone who would come out this afternoon to clean it and what have you," Gloria Westbury said. "I wouldn't be surprised if he took himself a little swim tonight."

"And you?" Carol asked with a smile.

"Well, now, I can't just sit back and let him have all the fun, can I?" the older woman chuckled, causing Carol to grin. She was going to miss having them next door. They'd been good neighbors the past three years. "But, Carol, there is one thing I worry about with this move," she added.

"What, Gloria?" Carol asked. "Don't do this unless you really want to."

"It's not that. I just worry that we won't be able to hear your music at night anymore. We might be too far down to hear it. It's been such a blessing to us."

Carol felt touched and reached over and patted her hand. "I'll play loudly at first, then you can just mosey on over," she said. They laughed together, and Carol watched Ed cut across the yards.

"They kicked me out. Actually told me I was in the way," he complained as he sat down and mopped his forehead with a handkerchief.

"You probably were, dear," Gloria asserted, pouring her husband a glass of water from the pitcher on the small table next to her. Carol watched them and hoped that she would have that kind of close relationship with someone one day. She ignored the fact that Bobby popped into her head at the thought.

"Ms. Mabry?" Amy called from the screen door.

"What, babe?" Carol answered her.

"May I play up in Lisa's room? The movie's over."

"Of course you may," Carol confirmed. "Do you want a snack first?"

"No, ma'am," Amy hollered over her shoulder as she ran through the house.

Gloria snickered. "That kind of energy is wasted on the young."

At that moment, Carol groaned out loud when Robert and Harriet Kent's pickup pulled into her driveway. She pinched the bridge of her nose and prayed for patience.

"What do you want, Robert?" she called out before they even reached the porch.

"What's all this?" he asked, waving his hand toward the two moving vans occupying the street and taking up the driveway next door.

"My neighbors are moving," she said. "What do you want?"

"We just came to visit Lisa," Harriet explained. The two stood at the base of the porch, not stepping up.

"Lisa isn't here. She's out shopping with her *father*," Carol replied, emphasizing the last word.

"Ms. Mabry!" Amy exclaimed in a panicked voice. She ran out of the house and dashed onto the front porch.

"What happened?" Carol was up and out of her chair before she finished speaking.

"There's a spider in Lisa's room!" the little girl squealed.

Ed Westbury stood and held out his hand. "Well, this is a job for a grandpa. Come with me, Amy, and I'll see if I can save you from the wild animal," he said, making Amy giggle. The two went inside the house.

Robert's face turned a dangerous looking red. He stabbed his finger at Carol and put a boot on the first step. "You're lying. Her little friend is here playing with her. You're just trying to keep her from us to punish us."

"I'm not lying, Robert. Lying is your thing, not mine. Lisa left with Bobby this morning to go shopping. Amy's mom is sick, so she's over here playing while I babysit." Carol did not like the fact that she suddenly found herself on the defensive.

"We'll see about that," Harriet said, stepping onto the porch and moving toward the door.

Carol felt her temper snap, and placed her body in the older woman's path. "If you touch that door, I will call the police and charge you with criminal trespass so fast it will make your head spin," she announced.

Harriet must have believed her, because she stepped back. Carol continued, "I told you on the phone last night that I have no intention of keeping Lisa from you, even though, as far as I'm concerned, you've lost your rights as grandparents. So, if and when she asks to see you, I'll make sure it's arranged."

"How do we know she hasn't been asking about us all week?" Robert asked.

"Because she didn't call you. And, I'll tell you one more thing. Lisa's an intelligent child, and she's probably already put two and two together. Don't be surprised if it takes her a while to decide she even wants to see you," Carol said.

Lisa had never gone this long without wanting to see her grandparents, and if she figured out that Bobby was her dad on her own, it was entirely possible that she'd figured out a simple version of the entire story, including her grandparents' deception.

"How dare you soil us in her mind!" Harriet wailed.

Carol sighed and spoke in a weary voice. "I'm going to ask you both to leave now. I don't want to call the Sheriff so, please, just get off of my property. I don't care where you go, but you can't stay here."

"You can't poison that child's mind and heart against us!" Harriet declared.

"I haven't said a word, and I don't intend to," Carol stated. "But, right now, her focus is where it should be, on her father. I suggest you just stay out of it for now. Give them time, because the time they should have had was stolen from them... by you."

Harriet marched off the porch and grabbed her husband's arm, as if for support. Suddenly and inexplicably, she screamed in a voice that made Carol's hair stand up on the back of her neck. "You slept around and then got stuck with the consequences! You're an unfit mother and have always been an unfit mother! More concerned with your career than your own daughter. Just you wait and see, Carol Mabry! You'll pay for every foul word that's come out of your mouth about us to our little angel!"

Carol felt her stomach knot and a burning anger boil up her chest. Instead of reacting, she took a deep breath and pulled her cell phone out of the pocket of her shorts. "Please don't make me call the Sheriff. He's a friend and it would embarrass me."

Robert put his arm around his wife's shoulders, and led the sobbing woman to their truck. Carol didn't sit back down until they had driven away. She looked at Gloria, worried she would find revulsion in the woman's eyes, but instead found indignation. "I'm sorry you had to witness that," Carol said, a tinge of embarrassment coloring her tone.

"Don't be, dear," Gloria said, patting Carol's hand. "Oftentimes, extreme circumstances bring out extreme emotions. I'll be praying for this to resolve itself soon."

♫ ♫ ♫ ♫

THEY hit furniture stores, department stores, electronic stores, then the grocery store, all within four hours. Bobby knew exactly what he wanted, and if he hadn't needed it in such a short time, he would have just had his secretary order everything from a catalog. But as it was, he arranged for it all to be delivered on Tuesday morning, and paid twice as much as he should have for the furniture store to give him two men to help set everything up.

Lisa's enthusiasm barely dimmed during the shopping spree. Initially, he'd wondered how an 8-year-old would choose to decorate a room, having no personal experience with little girls' taste in interior design. She impressed him with her choices. The colors were bright, the patterns matched, and the furniture would convert easily as she grew up.

He wanted to keep her with him for the entire day, but she expressed excitement about the party she planned to attend, so instead of calling Carol and begging for a few more hours, he drove her home. He looked at her as they turned onto her street and was glad he'd made that decision. After going to bed so late the night before, and walking for miles while they shopped today, she looked exhausted. She would need a nap if she planned to enjoy the party this afternoon.

But the second they pulled into her driveway, she perked up and ran into the house, excitedly yelling to her mom about the morning they'd had. Carol met them at the door with a smile, and Bobby watched her nod and respond to what Lisa had to say, leading her into the kitchen where the neighbors made sandwiches from the offerings Carol had spread out.

"So I decided to go with the yellow and blue colors like we talked about this morning," Lisa chattered, appearing not to even take a breath while she grabbed a plate and started dishing up. "I even got a new laptop that's yellow to match, and the curtains are blue with yellow stripes to match the bedspread and the carpet that is going in on Tuesday is going to be light blue."

She finished dishing up her plate and pulled up a chair next to Ed Westbury. "Hi Mr. and Mrs. Westbury. Can I come swim in your pool when you get settled?"

Carol looked up at Bobby with a sparkle in her eye while Ed entertained Lisa. "Has she been this hyped up all morning?" she asked with a laugh.

Bobby smiled and leaned against the counter. "No. She's actually calmed down considerably."

She looked over her shoulder to make sure Lisa was still occupied, and when she looked back at Bobby, the sparkle was gone. "Can you come with me a moment? I need to speak with you."

He straightened and followed her out of the room. She led him down the hall to her office. He briefly wondered if she'd started some legal paperwork or something.

"Your parents came over this morning unannounced," she said without preamble. "I'm afraid there was a bit of a scene."

Bobby felt a rush of anger, but put a damper on it. "How bad of a scene?"

Carol cleared her throat and pushed her hair out of her eyes. "I had to threaten to call the police if they wouldn't leave." She spoke in a rush, clearly embarrassed.

He frowned, concerned. "What exactly happened?"

Carol smiled, but it didn't light up her eyes. "Apparently, I'm a loose woman who slept around and got myself knocked up," she explained.

He stilled, a cold anger seeping through him. "Say that again." His voice came out in an icy rasp.

Carol held a hand up. "It's okay, Bobby. I just thought you should know."

He advanced on her until she had to crane her neck to keep eye contact. "What else did they say to you?"

She put a hand on his chest to stop him. "Never mind. Really. Never mind. I handled it."

He placed his hands on her shoulders. "Tell me what else was said, Carol," he demanded through clenched teeth.

She looked at the button on his shirt, her cheeks flushed red. "That I'm an unfit mother who's more concerned about my career than my daughter."

Bobby felt horror at what his parents thought about the mother of his child. His heart hurt and his stomach clenched. He released her shoulders and stepped back. "Thank you for telling me. I promise you I'll take care of it," he quietly vowed.

A worried look crossed her face and she grabbed his arm. "I already did, Bobby. Just leave it alone. There's enough hurt feelings flying around right now to last a lifetime."

He looked her up and down. "No. They can't say that kind of thing to you and get away with it. I won't stand for it."

"They already did say those things, and I sent them packing. I never would have told you if I thought this was how you'd react."

Bobby forced himself to calm down. He stepped away from her and went to look out the window into the backyard. "Have they said things like that to you in the past?"

He heard the hesitation in her voice. "No. They've always been... polite, sometimes even friendly."

He turned back around and stared at her for a long time. "Why did you even move to Richmond?"

She ran a hand through her hair. "Lisa needed a family. My dad was in the Army, and my parents were in Germany. They didn't know where they'd retire, and I wanted to go to a good law school in a state where I would enjoy practicing. I was accepted into the University of Richmond Law School and halfway through my first semester before I found out about your lack of interest." She waved her hand to stall his interruption. "I mean, before they told me you weren't interested. I couldn't change anything at that point."

He approached her again, but this time she didn't back away. He lifted a hand and brushed her hair off her shoulder. "I'm sorry, Carol. As little as that means at this point, I really am sorry."

She put a hand on his cheek. "I have a good life, Bobby. I have good friends in a good church, and Lisa goes to a good school. Don't kick yourself over this whole thing. Let's just enjoy what we have from now on."

♫ ♫ ♫ ♫

Sunday, April 29th

"**LISA,** if you continue to argue with me, you won't be able to go over there Tuesday after school," Carol declared.

"But mom, it's just next door," Lisa whined. She took her fork and played with a green bean on her plate.

"We've all already discussed it. I have to leave early in the morning and you have school," Bobby proclaimed, backing Carol's play.

Carol had to admire the way he'd managed to keep Lisa from manipulating him. She imagined he would try to do anything to make Lisa like him, but he held his own pretty well.

"Your dad can come get you day after tomorrow once school is out. One more word about it and you'll go to bed right now and have to go to the after school program on Tuesday," Carol threatened. She watched Lisa bite her lip and could see dozens of arguments swirling around in that little head, but even Lisa knew when she'd pushed too far.

"Why can't you pick me up tomorrow and bring me home?" she asked, minus the whine.

"Sorry, Sugar. I have to go out of town tomorrow," Bobby addressed her by looking her frankly in the eye.

"Like Amy's dad?"

Bobby glanced at Carol, who nodded. "Yep, kind of like Amy's dad."

"Are you going to have to be gone all the time like him?"

Carol watched Bobby take a deep breath and slowly release it, obviously trying to find the words. "Sometimes I will. I have several months off right now, through the summer and part of the fall, but then I have to go back to work full time. I'll come home as often as I can, though," he said. "The good thing about what I do is that when I'm not on tour, I can take big chunks of time off if I want to take them, or work from here."

"Then why do you have to go away tomorrow?" Lisa whined again.

"Lisa," Carol cautioned, and her daughter ducked her head and let the subject drop for the rest of the meal.

After dinner, Carol just tried to relax while Bobby helped Lisa get ready for bed. She sat on a recliner willing the aspirin she'd taken to work. She rubbed her temples, trying hard to beat back the headache that had threatened ever since her confrontation with the Kents yesterday. She must have dozed off, because she jerked awake when Bobby gently touched her shoulder.

"She's ready for you to tuck her in," he announced. Carol stood and pressed hard against her temples.

"Thanks, Bobby," she acknowledged, walking out of the room. She went upstairs to Lisa's room and found her lying in bed with her favorite teddy bear in the crook of her arm. "Hey there, kiddo," Carol greeted, sitting on the side of the bed.

"Mommy?" Lisa asked, plucking at the fabric of her bedspread.

"What, babe?" she asked.

"Were you and daddy ever married?"

Carol pulled the covers tighter over her and smoothed them out. "No, honey. I didn't even know I was pregnant with you until he was already gone to Nashville to become a big star."

"Are you going to marry daddy?"

The question was simple and innocent but Carol felt her heart skip a beat.

"Lisa Mabry, that is a grown up decision and it is between me and your father. You will not bring it up again. Understand?"

With her eyes wide, Lisa said, "Okay."

"All right. Ready for prayers?"

Lisa's eyes filled with tears, and her lower lip quivered. "Am I unwanted?"

"What?" Carol's head suddenly throbbed. "Where did you even hear that?"

Lisa answered, "There was a TV show on the other day and the mom told the little girl she was stuck being a single mom without a husband because the little girl was unwanted."

Carol sighed and wondered if all children's brains worked with the efficiency of Lisa's, or if she just had a very special little girl. "You were wanted from the moment I found out about you. Don't you ever doubt that. You know what? Your daddy loves you and wants you, too. I can tell he is really sad that he didn't know about you. Can't you? Sometimes, God gives us gifts we aren't expecting. You are a gift to me and your dad."

The tears disappeared and Lisa sat up quickly, throwing her arms around her mom. Carol held her close for a minute, then squeezed her tight and kissed the top of her head. "Time to sleep now. You have school tomorrow."

Lisa lay back down and Carol helped her say her bedtime prayers. Then she rearranged the covers and kissed her one more time. "Good-night, Mommy," Lisa said.

"'Night, Kiddo," Carol answered, and turned out the light. She went back downstairs, but Bobby had already left, so she locked the doors and loaded the dishes into the dishwasher. As she was finishing up cleaning the kitchen, her doorbell rang.

"Hi Rhonda. Thanks for meeting me here," she said. She opened the door and let the young attorney come inside.

"I don't mind," Rhonda said. "Besides, 9 a.m. Monday court kind of interferes with Sunday nights. I really like your house, though. I feel like we get more work done in your office than anywhere else."

"Thanks. I just put Lisa to bed, but I think she's probably asleep already. She was pretty tired. Would you like some coffee or tea? Water?"

Rhonda shook her head and brushed her black curls off her shoulder. "No thanks. I grabbed dinner on the way." Then she lifted the files in her hand. "Ready to get to work?"

"Let me grab a cup of coffee and I'll meet you in my office." As they walked through the foyer, Rhonda, who had been here many times over the course of the preparations for the trial, turned toward the office. "Give me just a few minutes."

"Take your time. I need to get organized anyway," Rhonda said, and the two separated in the hall.

♫ ♫ ♫ ♫

BOBBY sat on his front porch and watched the woman pull up in the little sports car. He knew Carol planned to work tonight, and assumed this was the attorney, Rhonda, she'd mentioned. While he watched lights going off and on in the house next door, he idly plucked at his guitar with the song that had nagged at him in the back of his mind for the past week. He saw a light go on in her office. His fingers kept playing while he watched the light, imagining her sitting at her computer or at her desk bent over and writing something. The woman worked like a draft horse, as far as he could tell, and got less sleep that anyone he knew. How she remained standing after the weekend she'd just had, much less focused her mind on her work, was something that continued to amaze him.

Gloria Westbury had given him the replay of Carol's confrontation with his parents, and he fought back another wave of anger that he felt too relaxed to deal with. He knew that something like that couldn't be overlooked, but he was new at this sort of thing and didn't know how to deal with it. Would another screaming match do any good? Or should he just ignore it and hope they went away?

With a sigh, he closed his eyes and put his head back. What he really needed to do was pray. This anger he felt had to go away, no matter how righteous he could make himself feel about it.

As he prayed, his fingers absently played a new tune. He didn't recognize it, but the words to the song came eventually, and he filed them away, not wanting to move from his spot to find a pen and paper to write them down, not wanting to disturb his communion with God. He realized at some point it was a love song, and then, further into it, he realized it was a really good love song.

Bobby stopped praying, stopped paying so much attention to the light across the lawn from him and started paying attention to the song currently unfolding. He started getting excited. He closed his eyes and heard the musical accompaniment in his head as it reached full culmination. Then, as naturally as a leaf falls in autumn, the music paused for two beats and the song softly ended.

This song was going to be a huge hit. There was no doubt about that. He let the last of the notes fade into the night, then set his guitar down and stretched his legs out in front of him, focusing once again on the light in Carol's window. He wasn't ready to dissect his feelings for her yet, so he emptied his mind and allowed his body to relax. He sat that way until he saw the attorney, Rhonda, leave with an arm full of files and watched the lights inside go off downstairs then another one turn on upstairs. Instead of letting himself sit there imagining Carol getting ready for bed, he got up and went inside his house.

♫ ♫ ♫ ♫

Monday, April 30th

"HARRISON, I neither want nor need a mound of paperwork. I already told you we have things worked out," Bobby said with very real annoyance.

"I heard you, Bobby. And as I explained to you, right now she holds all the cards. Sure, she wants to keep things on an even keel right now. Everything's informal. Just simple written agreements. What happens when she sues you for back child support and you have absolutely no record of ever paying her a dime? What happens when she decides she's not getting enough money from you and suddenly wants more? What then?"

Bobby grit his teeth until he felt sure that one of them might crack. "Then, when she asks, which she won't, I'll write her a check for more money. That isn't an issue for either one of us."

"Money is an issue for everyone at some point or another."

"Do I need to remind you that it isn't your money, Harry?" Bobby asked.

Harrison blinked, perhaps realizing that Bobby Kent's patience was at an end. "No, Bobby. You don't need to remind me. But you pay me to protect your interests and this is how I do that. I'm just doing my due diligence. She's an attorney, Bobby. I've seen these kinds of things go places you wouldn't believe."

"Carol Mabry has more than eight years of one opportunity after another to come to me for whatever she wanted, and she did nothing. If anything, I owe her more."

Harrison's voice came out even, sounding reasonable and confident, as if testifying in court. He obviously spoke in his role as the devil's advocate. "Well, of course. What guy wants to deal with a rampant toddler or potty training? But now some woman's got you over a barrel, now that the kid's all broken in and can talk, and it looks like parenting is just going to be one big fun game."

Bobby's emotions had been through the wringer in the last few weeks. He knew it, and he knew he was reacting right now instead of thinking. That knowledge didn't stop him from standing up. He stood and very softly said, "That's the last time, Harrison. We aren't talking about 'the kid.' We're talking about my daughter. My little girl. Her name is Lisa. And we aren't talking about 'some woman.' We're talking about my child's mother. Her name is Carol."

Realizing that Bobby would never sign any of the paperwork he had so carefully prepared, Harrison removed the pen from his blotter and deposited it into the top of his desk drawer. He straightened the corners of the blotter so that they were perfectly even with the edge of his desk. "I didn't mean to offend you, Bobby. I'm just trying to look out for your best interests."

Bobby laid his hands on the desk and leaned forward. "I'm tired of all of the people around me looking out for my best interests as if I'm incapable of rational or logical thought. I'll speak with you later when, hopefully, you'll be prepared to respect my decisions."

He retrieved his hat, put it on his head, and turned to leave the office. Harrison coughed and sat up straight, putting his hands up as if surrendering. The attorney's voice followed him out the door. "Bobby! Please wait a few…"

Bobby slammed the door behind him and walked away, not bothering to look at the secretary who stared at him in shock.

♫ ♫ ♫ ♫

BOBBY still felt angry with his attorney, but he was even more angry with himself for losing his temper. As he waited for the other attendees at this lunch meeting to arrive, he sipped his ice water and considered what Harrison had said in spite of his feelings.

As a young man, Bobby Kent had realized that he had a quick temper. All his life, he had taken steps to overcome it. As an adult, it wasn't a completely unheard of event for him to lose his temper, it simply had not happened in years. Even when he felt greatly annoyed, usually no one ever knew it. People who knew him best, like Melody for example, might claim

Bobby never got angry.

The fact that he had lost his temper, that both Harry and his secretary had witnessed it, embarrassed him. He owed them an apology for his rudeness if nothing else.

As far as what Harrison said, Bobby decided he would have to talk with Carol. He trusted Carol instinctively, and he didn't think that was a mistake. He felt like she trusted him, too. He wanted nothing more than to prove himself trustworthy after the deception his parents had orchestrated. He would talk with Carol and the two of them, together, would figure it out. They would have to put legal protections in place to protect themselves, and Lisa, from all the well-intentioned people in their lives if nothing else.

Things would be so much simpler if we were married, he thought.

That thought stopped him for a long minute. How much did he trust Carol? How much did she trust him? They couldn't have gotten off to a rockier start. Could they overcome all that? Could they seriously talk about a lifelong covenant of love in a state of holy matrimony?

He intentionally set all his inner thoughts aside when his lunch meeting arrived. Bobby stood as Harmony Harper crossed the dining room behind the hostess. When he saw her, he could not help but grin. Without her heels, he stood taller than her by a good foot. She was small framed, with long, curly blonde hair and vivid blue eyes. She had such a fragile appearance that she always looked like a strong wind could knock her down.

But her voice. Her voice could silence fifty thousand people. Bobby had seen it happen. He'd never heard anything like it. She topped chart after chart in contemporary Christian music, and was a driving force in bringing thousands upon thousands of teenagers to Christian concerts and events who might otherwise never have come. Even more exciting, her latest single had crossed over and was finding air time on every pop station in North America.

Harmony grinned and walked right into his open arms, hugging him with enthusiasm. "It is so good to see you again!" She stepped back and took his hands, looking him up and down. "Something's new. What is it?"

He gestured at the seat and nodded his thanks to the hostess who set the menu next to her plate. Harmony slid into the chair and looked over her shoulder. "Quick. Franklin's due here any time. You're practically glowing."

Bobby snickered and shook his head as he sat down. "How do you know this stuff?"

"Intuition." She grinned and picked up her menu. "But you're not denying anything, so you better spill."

"Seems that I'm a daddy."

Her smile faded and she set her menu down. He could almost see the change come over her countenance as she emotionally distanced herself from him. "Oh?" For two heartbeats, she stared at him, then spoke again. "I thought you didn't play games like that."

"I don't." He saw her brother, Franklin, step toward the hostess stand, so he spoke quickly. "I dated a girl in college, before I fully gave my life to Christ. Seems I have an eight-year-old, perfectly brilliant and beautiful daughter named Lisa. I can't wait to introduce you two."

He watched her face as she processed the information, then she grinned again, all coolness gone, all warmth returned. "Oh, Bobby. What a surprise! Is this good or bad?"

He smiled. "It is very good." As Franklin approached, Bobby stood again and held out his hand. "Frank, good to see you."

Bobby only called Franklin Frank because no one else dared. Harmony laughed every time. Franklin bristled, but he never reacted. Instead, he took it with as good a spirit as someone as stodgy as he could manage.

Franklin Harper was probably the only person in Nashville, Tennessee, to wear a three-piece silk suit so late in the spring. Yet, despite what must be a suffocating outfit, he never appeared affected by the heat. He was a little taller than his sister, but very thin, with long pianist's fingers and a deep receding hairline.

Bobby knew he adored his sister, but he protected her much like a hawk. When it came to matters of business, Harmony did not speak. Franklin handled it all. But in meetings with Bobby, she always came along. They'd been friends for three years, since she was 19 and trying to release her second album.

"I thought you were on a sabbatical," Franklin said, shaking Bobby's hand.

"From performing. Still doing a little business here and there." The two men sat and Harmony picked up her menu again.

The waitress came over and took Bobby's steak order. Her cheeks flushed starting the first time he called her "Darlin'." She took Franklin and Harmony's salad orders and rushed to the back. After she left, Franklin said, "I appreciate that you offered some promotion for Harmony's Raleigh concert, Bobby. But I didn't greatly appreciate you following her song with fanning yourself. The tabloids are already claiming that my sister is carrying your love child."

Bobby shrugged. "That right, Frank? But I heard your concert the following night sold out. So..."

Franklin said, "That is really beside my point."

Harmony interjected with, "We've already talked about this, Franklin. Let it go. It was fun and I got to sing a song with a very clear gospel message to a secular audience."

The waitress brought their salads and the conversation halted until she retreated from earshot. Then Franklin said, "Tell me about this Christmas album."

"Harmony, Melody Mason Montgomery, Carson Bridgewater, and me; a quartet. Some solos, some duets, some quartets. It will be amazing. We already have twenty songs picked out to choose from."

Franklin pursed his lips. "What about proceeds?"

"Every dime will go to Montgomery's Children's Home Association. They're building an orphanage in Kenya next year. This project should sufficiently fund the property and building and hire security for the construction."

Franklin looked at his sister. "As you know, I'm not crazy about you partnering with secular musicians."

Raising her eyebrow, she said, "Of that you have been abundantly clear. However, like I told you before, every one of these artists are proclaiming, practicing Christians. And, not one of them has a song with objectionable lyrics."

"Well," Bobby drawled, "unless you object to dancing. Then you have quite a number of objectionable lyrics."

"Bobby!" Harmony laughed.

Turning serious, he sat forward. "This isn't secular Christmas, Franklin. You should know me by now. Every song glorifies Christ and celebrates His birth. This album will touch millions. We believe God led us to Harmony to be a part of it with us. I urge you to pray about it before making any firm decisions."

As the waitress brought them fresh drinks, their conversation halted. As soon as she was gone, Franklin placed his elbows on the arms of his chair and leaned back, steepling his fingers. "I have prayed about it ever since Harmony discussed it with me. I don't like it. And if it were anyone but that group you named, or if it were for profit, the answer would be a resounding no. But, as long as we have final say in the songs, then it is a hesitant yes."

Relieved, Bobby grinned. "I'll accept that, Frank." He winked at Harmony. "Warm up your pipes, girl."

"When do we record?"

"After Melody has the babies. We're looking at July, which will be pushing the envelope with production, but it's the best we can do." He took a long pull of his iced tea.

Harmony frowned. "Should we just wait until next year?"

"We may have to, but for now, Mel's insisting." He leaned back in his chair when a sizzling steak was placed in front of him. As he shook his head at the siblings' plates, he laughed. "How do you live on rabbit food?"

"Very healthily," Franklin said, accepting the fresh ground pepper from the waiter. "You should give it a go."

Harmony sprinkled shaved Parmesan onto her lettuce leaves. "I eat fish. You can't grow up in the Cascades and not eat fish."

Bobby reached out his hands and the Harpers each laid a hand in his so that the three of them formed a circle of prayer. "Frank, would you bless the meal?"

♫ ♫ ♫ ♫

Personal Journal Entry

April 30

The empty talking heads somehow connected the dots on the women. They're calling me Richmond Red. It's disgusting. They're disgusting. They are stupid, shallow, entitled Philistines, and frankly death is too good for them.

The surveillance photo they are oh so proud of is grainy and indistinct. Clearly, I need to be more cautious with spontaneous moves.

To make matters worse, she's calling me Richmond RED. It makes my blood boil. I vow that before she dies, my name will be the last word on her lips.

♫ ♫ ♫ ♫

"BOBBY Kent, it's been too long," Pastor Douglas Brown said, coming from behind his desk and shaking Bobby's hand. The handshake turned into a hug, and the two men moved to a pair of chairs near a low table at the other end of the office. "Cassandra will be pleased that you're back in town," he added, referring to the choir director of the Nashville megachurch.

"It's been a long time, but it's been a long road, too, Pastor." Bobby leaned back in the chair and hooked his boot on his knee, then draped his hat on his bent knee. "I've had a rather serious – what's the slang? – a serious life event happen recently."

The pastor raised an eyebrow. "Would you like to talk about it?"

Bobby took a deep breath and felt his eyes burn. "I don't even know where to begin."

The pastor stood and put a hand on Bobby's shoulder as he walked by him. He cracked open his office door and said to his secretary, "Mary, go ahead and free me up for the rest of the afternoon." He returned to his seat. "I find that the best way to start is usually in the beginning."

Where would the beginning be? He contemplated for a moment before replying, "When my grandfather died, my family's horse farm was in serious financial jeopardy. He mismanaged it nearly into the ground, and my father didn't know how to fix it. I was a senior in high school at the time, and between us and God, I was able to go to college. My dad thought that maybe a formal education would help us save our legacy.

"In college, I met a girl named Carol." He paused, thinking back to the first time he'd seen her sitting on that hard metal chair in the classical violin class. She'd already mastered the instrument and sat in first chair almost as soon as the teacher assigned them. Bobby learned right away that he could make her giggle if he'd pop out a jaunty Irish tune or a boot-stompin' country tune in what he considered a hoity-toity environment. He'd liked the way she laughed.

He continued, "We started dating. I was rather enamored with her. But before things got serious, or even official between the two of us, I got called to Nashville. The night I got the call, I sought her out and convinced her to celebrate with me. I bought some champagne, because that seemed to be what one did during such a moment, and we took my truck out by the river and, well," he coughed and felt his cheeks burn, "one thing led to another."

Pastor Douglas did not look shocked, nor did he demand Bobby pick up his hat and leave. He simply said, in a gentle voice, "Go on."

"I kissed her good-bye the next morning, and that was the last time I saw her. I signed a record deal, recorded my album, and started touring. About midway through my first tour, I realized that while I'd grown up in a churchgoing home, I'd never actually been committed to Christ before. I was doing things I shouldn't have been, and drinking…"

He let his voice trail off. "Until one night on our bus, I was reading a devotional that someone had sent me and went to my knees before God. I was different after that, and from then on, the places my music took me became my mission field."

Douglas smiled. "That's a good story. You should share it one morning for the congregation."

"That's just what you call the beginning." He cleared his throat. "So, I started sending as much money back home as I could spare. The family farm was saved. I was there this past week and it's a beautiful place. My father truly brought it back."

"You did."

He nodded. "Right. I brought it back, financially. But my father put in the physical improvements."

The older man waved a dismissive hand. "I'm not going to split hairs with you. Go on."

"Well, it seems that night with Carol..." Again, he let his voice trail off, then took a big, unsteady breath. "That night with Carol was her beginning as well. Basically, we, ah, have a daughter. An eight-year-old."

He waited. Again, no shock came from his church leader. Just encouragement. "Go on."

"She went to my parents, pregnant, alone, asking for a contact number for me. They lied to her, pastor. They told her I wasn't interested in anything to do with her or my little girl. All the while they were giving Carol a few dollars here and there and keeping what I sent them." He felt his jaw clench, felt anger fuse his cheeks with heat. And, finally, he saw shock on his pastor's face. "For eight years, they've lied to her, to me, and to my little girl, Lisa, while they pocketed the majority of the money I sent home."

The pastor's eyes widened. "What?"

"They knew I'd leave Nashville and come home, and they'd lose that paycheck. So, they've hid her, convinced family members that I didn't want..." His breath hitched and he bowed his head, praying for strength. Douglas leaned forward and put a hand on his shoulder. "I am so angry," he whispered harshly.

They were silent for several long moments before Douglas spoke. "Your anger is understandable. But, there is soon going to come a time when you have to forgive, and you have to let it go."

"I really don't want to." He realized he'd fisted his hands. He intentionally relaxed them and flexed his fingers.

The pastor nodded and folded his hands. "Not wanting to is going to eat at you, and open you up to all sorts of bad and worse. The truth is you don't have to accept them. You don't have to pretend they were right, and you don't have to condone their sin. But you have to forgive, and you have to honor. The price for their sin should not be your soul."

Bobby snatched his hat off his knee and surged to his feet. "How can I? What they took from me…"

"Can never be replaced. You can't go back, Bobby. You can only go forward. Our Lord Himself said, 'But I say to you, love your enemies, bless those who curse you, do good to those who hate you, and pray for those who spitefully use you.'"

"You're asking the impossible."

"No, son. I'm not the one asking." Douglas stood and approached him. "Their sin in lying to you, in deceiving you, and selfishly taking your money – their sin is no worse than your sin of drunkenness and fornication. But you have a daughter, now. You have a little girl because God makes beautiful things out of even the most sinful things we do. The Lord has forgiven you for your sin, and more, without a fight or any hard feelings. What do you think He's about to do with your parents? What part must you play in His plan? Let me pray about it with you."

Bobby looked at his watch. "Can't. Have to go." He put his hat on his head, desperate to remove himself from this feeling of conviction. "Thank you for meeting with me."

Before he put his hand on the doorknob, Douglas spoke again. "I love you, Bobby, and so does your heavenly Father. If you need me, call me. And if you need Him, you know how to find Him."

Bobby cleared his throat. "Thank you, Pastor." He pulled open the door and walked out without a backward glance.

♫ ♫ ♫ ♫

"RHONDA, I can't believe you lost your temper like that," Carol admitted, taking a bite of her sandwich, her teeth audibly crunching through the grilled pumpernickel bread as the flavor of corned beef and sauerkraut filled her mouth. She didn't know how Rhonda had managed to convince one of the file clerks to have the deli lunch waiting for them when they got in from court, but she was so thankful for whatever powers of persuasion she used.

"I can't believe it took me two hours to do it," Rhonda offered. "I'm just lucky Judge Williams was as fed up as I was or else I could be in serious trouble."

"I know. He must have hit your last nerve. I've never seen you even impatient in traffic." Carol declared.

Rhonda smiled a small smile. "He let me ramble a bit. He should have stopped me before I even got going."

Carol's phone vibrated with an incoming text message. "Jury's back in," she confirmed, taking one last bite of her sandwich before she stood. "They were out all of about, what, fifteen minutes?"

"Surprised?" Rhonda asked almost rhetorically.

"Not really," Carol answered, picking up her briefcase. "No one in their right minds would let him go since the entire crime was committed on camera. I think the judge should have the state sue him for legal fees, honestly."

They exited the office and entered the lobby of the building. As they waited for the elevator, she heard her name. "Ms. Mabry!"

Carol turned. She didn't recognize the woman wearing a bronze colored pantsuit and shockingly high heels awkwardly rushing toward them. She hesitated, because she knew, somehow instinctively, that this woman was a reporter.

"Yes? Can I help you?"

The woman stopped and pushed her silvery blonde curls behind her shoulder. "I thought we could talk about your new next door neighbor."

With an inward sigh, Carol pointedly looked at her watch. "I have nothing to say and I have a jury coming back in on a felony trial. Have a nice day."

As she and Rhonda stepped into the elevator, Rhonda looked at her with a raised eyebrow. "What was that all about?"

"Just gossip." She tugged on her suit jacket and brushed at the sides of her hair, making sure all strands still stayed tucked inside the stylish bun on the back of her head. "I hate gossip." Unfortunately, she knew that was just the beginning of what would most certainly be a storm.

♫ ♫ ♫ ♫

"THANK you for taking the time to meet with me today." Richmond's Commonwealth Attorney Maurice Davidson returned his telephone to the cradle and formally greeted Carol and Mitch. He sat behind his large desk in a leather chair, elbows on the arms of the chair, long fingers steepled. He wore his white hair closely cropped to his head. His light brown eyes stood out from skin the color of dark caramel. Despite the political savvy his job required, he rarely ever played politics on the job. Carol had nothing but respect for him and enjoyed working for him.

"What did you need specifically?" Carol asked, knowing Maurice rarely wasted time or words.

"The mayor called this afternoon. We're desperately trying to put a lid on this, but it's going to blow at any time. Do we have anything the press can use?" Maurice asked, slanting his eyes toward Mitch, who busied himself by checking the screen on his vibrating smart phone.

"I'm already fielding calls," Carol said. "Young women being murdered in a ritualistic manner is going to attract attention. One of the crime scenes would have been enough to cause mass speculation. Three go beyond our ability to contain."

"I agree. What do you have at this point?"

"We only have test results back from the first two victims. Both were drugged with the same cocktail. The DEA stepped up. They're trying to identify the street source."

Maurice nodded. "What else?"

"We believe the latest victim wasn't the original target, and she was a blonde the last time her roommate saw her. We're questioning drug stores, beauty supply, and grocery stores in the area to see if anyone bought it that night. We might get lucky and get a better image from security cameras or ATMs in the area," Carol said.

Maurice sat forward a bit and placed his steepled fingers atop his desk. "Found any correlation between the victims besides their appearance?"

Mitch shrugged. "He's clearly killing someone else; replaying something over and over. I have profiles being created. The clothing is always professional and so far hasn't been owned by the victims, including the first one who was a professional herself. Dying the hair to closely match the first two victims... it's clear he's killing a tall, red haired, professional woman."

Maurice pursed his lips. "Any cold cases fit that?"

"Not in Virginia in the last fifteen or so years, best we can tell," Mitch said. "We're branching out as far as we can, but prior to recent years, in many cases, those kind of things require a manual search. With our available resources, it's too daunting of a task to pursue beyond what we've done."

"Understood." Maurice glanced at his watch. "Thanks, Detective. I appreciate your time."

Mitch nodded and stood. He reached over and shook the older man's hand. "I'll let you know if anything breaks."

With half a smile, Maurice resteepled his fingers. "My ear's to the ground with this one. I'll let you know if I need anything else." As Carol started to stand, he met her eyes. "Give me just a second, Carol."

When the door shut behind Mitch, he looked at her. "Got an interesting call today from a reporter out of Nashville asking all kinds of questions about your relationship with 'country music superstar' Bobby Kent." Maurice actually made air quotes with his fingers when pronouncing Bobby's title.

Carol licked her lips and tried not to jump to any kind of defensive posture. "I'm sure it won't be the last call you get," she said after clearing her throat.

"Doesn't sound like it." He paused, as if giving her time to elaborate, but she didn't. "Care to explain?"

"Not particularly," she said, shifting. "But I will confirm that Bobby Kent is Lisa's father and ask that this remain between you and I. I know it will get out. He said it always does."

"Consider it between us, then." He sat up suddenly, his chair squeaking as he moved from a near reclining position. "Okay. I heard Rhonda lost her temper in court today."

Carol smiled. "About a millisecond before Judge Williams blew up."

Despite his nod, he said, "That would have been up to him. The judge isn't my concern. My attorneys are my concern. What's your opinion?"

"That I'm glad I wasn't the one questioning the witness. The way we divvied up the duties in court today, it could have just as easily been me."

"Okay," he said, his tone sounding mollified. He opened a file on the center of his desk blotter. "Thanks, Carol. Have a good one."

Clearly being dismissed, Carol stood. "You, too," she said. On her way out of his office, she glanced at her watch and mentally calculated how much time she could spare before she had to pick up Lisa from dance practice.

CHAPTER 15

♫ ♫ ♫ ♫

HIS eyes burned and his neck felt sore from driving for so long, but he was almost home. The drive from his house in Nashville all the way back to his home in Richmond took the better part of 10 hours and three interstate highways on a good day. He had been driving for at least eleven hours with only a ten minute stop to fill his fuel tank. He continued to hit knots of slow moving traffic that frustrated him tremendously.

Common sense told Bobby he should have stopped hours before and rested for at least a little while, maybe eaten a meal. Then, as he left Tennessee behind and crossed the North Carolina state line, he listened to a talk radio host taking calls about the serial killer they were calling Richmond Red who was slaying women in Virginia's capital. He knew he needed to keep driving. Carol was going to need him, going to need an extra hand with Lisa due to the extra hours she would have to put in at work.

Or did he need her?

His entire life had shifted underneath his feet in such a way that he was still reeling from the blow. He'd lost his parents. Deep inside his soul, he felt himself mourning that loss underneath the anger. And he'd gained a daughter.

A daughter.

How had she existed for over eight years and he'd not known about it? How could something so profound have been so obscured from him?

And Carol.

What did he mean, and Carol? Why did so many of his thoughts about Lisa end up about Carol? Why did his mind keep going there?

For the last week, he'd been replaying every interaction they had together before he left for Nashville. They'd both known that something would potentially bloom between them. Just as she'd known that what he had to do that moment was go chase his dream. Why had he never followed up with her? Why had he spent nearly nine years never even trying to track her down?

Now she found her way into so many of his waking thoughts. Why? Could they recapture what they shared nearly a decade ago? Dare they even try?

It ate at him, because he didn't want to confuse his feelings for his daughter with any feelings for Carol, but as the days went on, he felt certain that there was no conflict there. Carol was a special person. He recognized it when he was in college, and he recognized it now.

A green highway sign informed him that Richmond lay just twenty miles ahead. He sat up straighter, feeling a sudden burst of energy. It was nearly two o'clock in the morning, and he wouldn't see her until early evening, but he would be near. Then, in about fourteen hours, he would pick his daughter up from school and spend the afternoon with her.

♫ ♫ ♫ ♫

CAROL leaned her head back and rested it on the wall behind her, listening to the night sounds all around her. The neighborhood had long since closed down for the night and the lights from the houses on the street had extinguished one by one.

She knew she should go inside and go to bed, too. She didn't think she could sleep even if she tried, so she stayed where she was and tried to make the image of the burning candles leave her mind.

Her mother had called a few hours ago. The murders in Richmond had made the national news. The cable news networks had gotten wind of the candles. There were more red candles on the news stations right now than on any church altar on Christmas Eve. Carol spent nearly twenty minutes convincing her mother that she and Lisa were perfectly safe. Then she spent another twenty minutes convincing her mother that Lisa was perfectly safe learning to love Bobby Kent.

The glare of headlights crossed her face as they pulled into the driveway next door, and she opened her eyes to watch Bobby get out of what looked like a brand new full-sized pickup truck. She guessed he must have seen her sitting there because he didn't head into his house. He crossed the lawn toward her instead.

"You're up late," he observed in a quiet voice, slowly sitting down in the chair next to hers and angling it so that he could prop his feet on the porch railing. His voice came out deep, so baritone it nearly sounded bass, and mellow. She could hear the fatigue in his speech. She wondered when the last time he had spoken to anyone that day was.

"I'm having a hard time winding down tonight," she asserted. Carol knew she should offer him something to drink, but she really didn't feel like getting up. "It's been a busy day."

"I imagine."

He must have driven for at least twelve hours. "I didn't know you were driving back. I figured you'd fly."

Bobby shrugged. "I was sick of that rental car. I wanted my truck and some stuff from my house." He rolled his head in a slow circle on his neck. She heard his neck bones pop like cracked knuckles. "You wouldn't mind if I got some water, would you? I'm thirsty and still wired from the drive."

Carol sat up. "Yeah. Sure," she said, but Bobby put a hand on her shoulder to stop her.

"I can help myself, Carol. Stay put." She leaned back and closed her eyes again while he was gone, and a few moments later, jumped a little when she felt something cold being pressed into her hand. "I grabbed you one, too," he said. He sat back down while she took a sip of her water and propped his feet back on the railing. "You want to talk about it?"

"Talk about what?"

"Richmond Red."

Carol shrugged. "What is there to say that I can even talk about?" She took another sip, feeling the cold liquid slide down her throat. "I just wish he'd make one mistake so I could actually do something," she said. "All I do now is sit back and observe."

She stood, nervous energy keeping her from being able to sit still. "The press started showing up today. By the time I left this afternoon, they were camped out on the outside steps. I'm probably lucky they haven't decided to come here yet."

She suddenly realized something, and turned to look at Bobby. "Some reporter wanted to talk about my new next door neighbor yesterday," she asserted with her eyes narrowed.

Bobby held his hands up. "I can't do anything about that, except keep it quiet as long as possible."

She didn't listen to him, her mind raced too fast for that. "Oh Lord above," she said, running her hands through her hair, "how could I not have thought of that before? You're like this big superstar. They'll eventually track you down. Lisa probably told everyone she knows at school today, and the kids from her party already know you were there."

The ice in Bobby's glass rattled as he took a sip. "I think you're concentrating on the wrong thing here, Darlin'. Lisa and I are a separate issue from the murders."

"No, no. You're wrong. It all has to do with the press hounding me. You'll just be an added incentive." She sat back down in a huff. "Why in the world, with all of the years behind us, did you pick now to come back, Bobby?"

"God's timing is perfect, Darlin'." Bobby sat up and his voice lost the teasing tone. "Look, Carol. What time is it right now? Two? You've been up for what, twenty hours? Why don't you go inside and get some sleep? Turn your mind off for a while."

Carol set her water down and stood back up. "No. Bobby, you and I need to discuss this. How in the world are we going to prevent the storm?"

He sat up straighter. "I hate to tell you this, beautiful, but there is no way to prevent the storm. It's one of the sacrifices I make for fame. Comes with stardom. Unfortunately, it's a price we all will have to pay, now."

Carol rubbed her temples. "That is just not acceptable. There has to be something we can do." She dropped her hands and sat on the second step of the porch. "How can you be so nonchalant about all of it?"

"I used to thrive on it. Now I simply live with it. Comes with the job. Comes with yours, too. You've been on TV more than I have recently." He moved so that he sat next to her, and took her hand. "No one's looking to you for the blame, hon. They're just looking to anyone for the answers. After the Sunday talk shows, the whole country's worried about this, and the cameras have chosen you. It could just as easily have been the detective or your boss, but you make better print. More... photogenic."

Carol turned her head to look at him, smiling despite the conversation topic. "That's rather sexist, isn't it?"

Bobby shrugged. "Sexist or not, it's the truth."

His hand felt cool from his glass of iced water. Within a few heartbeats, his hand had warmed again.

"I don't think that's it. Or at least, I don't think that's everything," she asserted.

He raised his eyebrows. "What do you mean?"

She said, "Since the late 1960s, there have been more than ten thousand murders every year in the United States. Some years there are more than twenty thousand. The talking heads seem to focus on cases that are rare enough to be interesting while reinforcing whatever agenda they're peddling that week."

Bobby nodded. "I can see that."

"It's just an agenda. They push a controversial agenda, they sell more advertisements, because they have higher ratings. These murders involve strangulation. Of all murders in the US, strangulation has historically accounted for less than 1 percent. That makes it pretty rare. The killer has strangled only women. No one has a handle on his motive yet. That makes it interesting. Then there are the candles. They're nothing but camera fodder. That the killer lays them out in a pentagram plays like a media script. The alleged ties to the occult are endless."

Bobby took a sip of his water. "Carol, what do you think the candles mean?"

Carol shivered. "It could mean the killer regrets killing. It could mean he wants to shed light on his crimes. What scares me a little is that it honestly could have some kind of Satanic significance, and that would mean this is cult activity. But I have a different theory."

He peered at her face in the dim light. "What's your theory?"

She returned his gaze, wondering if Bobby would understand the context of her answer. "I believe the killer is simply insane."

Bobby pursed his lips and nodded. "That fact is probably often overlooked."

"Doesn't play well as a six o'clock sound bite."

He let go of her hand and moved up until he occupied the top step, and shifted so that he sat directly behind her, then he began rubbing the muscles in her neck and shoulders. Carol practically melted into the porch and rested her head on her knees to give him better access. "Maybe just ignore them, give them the 'I can't comment on an ongoing case' comment, then turn on the news every night and watch yourself walk by the cameras looking like a million bucks."

"Mmmm," Carol said, not even trying to comprehend the words he said while his fingers were doing such magical things to her muscles. She turned her head to one side and almost moaned out loud when he found a particularly good spot. She felt the rest of the world wash away with the tension, felt her threatening headache slip into the background. She let her body drift until the pressure ceased and he simply caressed her skin. It felt so right when he pressed his lips to her neck, that she tilted her head to one side and shifted her body until the back of her head rested on his knee.

It had been so long since she had been touched this way, and it felt like her whole body was suddenly one large nerve ending centered in her neck. He slowly kissed his way up across her jaw and to the corner of her mouth while one of his hands resumed its caresses, and he wrapped an arm around her and pulled her closer to him so that she was practically cradled in his arms.

When his lips covered hers, she felt every pore in her body vibrate as if they were the strings on her violin. Every touch, every stroke, seemed to hum through her until she felt like she was about to explode.

She shifted to turn her body to get closer to him when her knee hit her glass. It tumbled down the steps, and the sound of the glass striking the pavement and shattering broke through the moment.

What was she doing? She broke the kiss and pushed away from him, scrambling to her feet and putting a hand over her mouth. Bobby rubbed his face with his hands and stood. "Sorry about that," he said, sticking his hands in his pockets. "I meant to take it a lot slower."

She slowly shook her head. Her voice sounded hoarse when she said, "I don't have time for this."

"I know that, Darlin'. No pressure. No rush." He pulled his keys out of his pocket, jingling them in his hand while he ambled back to his house. "We've got the rest of our lives," he threw over his shoulder with a grin.

She finally found her voice. "Bobby, do you remember what got us into trouble the first time?" she asked, loudly enough so that he could hear. He stopped in the middle of the lawn and turned to look at her.

"Darlin'," he said, "there aren't a whole lot of nights in my life I remember more vividly." He winked as he turned his back on her again, and she could hear him whistling a tune as he unlocked his front door.

CHAPTER 16

♪ ♪ ♪ ♪

Tuesday, May 1st

CAROL opened the glass door and stepped into the chaos of the elementary school office at seven-thirty in the morning. She wove her way through children and teachers, who were going in every direction getting ready for the day, and finally made her way to the desk. It wasn't even eight yet, but the school secretary looked like she'd just worked a national disaster. It took several minutes before she noticed Carol, and she had to answer the phone twice before she could finish her greeting.

"Sorry about that, ma'am. We're a hand short this morning." Her voice evidenced a cultured Richmond, Virginia southern twang.

"I'm Carol Mabry. I have an appointment with Doctor Sessions," Carol said.

"Yes, of course Ms. Mabry. Doctor Sessions is waiting for you right now. Just go on into that door right there," she replied, pointing and nodding while answering the phone again. Carol smiled her thanks then went through the gate separating the lobby with the reception area, and knocked on the door bearing the hand painted sign reading, "Principal", entering after she heard, "Come in."

Doctor Nancy Sessions sat behind her desk reading something on her tablet. When she looked up and saw Carol, she shut off the screen and stood, holding her hand out. "Ms. Mabry. It's a pleasure to see you again," she said.

Carol shook the other woman's hand and sat in the chair across from the desk. "I appreciate you seeing me this morning. From the looks of your outer office, you're already having a busy day."

Nancy sighed. "We begin standardized testing today. Since we're private, we don't rely on state funding, but the results help keep us rated as a top school in the commonwealth. I think the teachers panic right before they begin, worried they will somehow fail us if the students don't score as high as they usually do." While she spoke she cleared her desk until the area in front of her was clean, then found her coffee cup under a file folder. "What can I do for you?"

Carol crossed her legs and laced her hands in front of her, refusing to fidget. "I need to adjust some of Lisa's paperwork and, basically, add her father to it. I also need to sign something that will allow him to have access to her at any time for any reason; pick her up whenever he wants to, that sort of thing."

Nancy raised an eyebrow and said, "You really didn't need to see me privately about that."

Carol brushed an imaginary piece of lint from her thigh. "No, but I need to warn you about the uproar this may cause."

Dr. Sessions leaned back in her chair. "Oh?"

"Her father is Bobby Kent." Carol watched the other woman's eyes widen, but she didn't offer a comment. "I expect the fallout from the press may be a bit extreme for a while."

Nancy nodded. "I'm afraid you're probably right. We can keep them off the grounds, of course. We have certain rights under the law when it comes to the privacy of children and we can exercise them, but they know the law, too. In my experience, they are expert at skirting the edges of those laws. There isn't going to be much I can do about them hanging out at the gate waiting for you or any other adult they can harass."

"I understand. I just wanted you to be forewarned. I have a feeling the eruption is coming soon. There's also the matter of a case I'm working on that is getting its own share of the news. I worry about the repercussions on Lisa."

"Yes. I watched the news last night along with the rest of the free world." Nancy leaned forward. "You don't need to be overly concerned, Ms. Mabry. I can see the strain this is causing on you. You're not alone. We have more than a few students with parents who attract a fair amount of reporters, but once the initial storm passes, Lisa should be left alone."

Carol stood. "I just wish there was a way to prevent it in the first place." She held out her hand and the other woman took it. "Thank you for seeing me this morning, Doctor Sessions. I'll go out front and fill out the forms I need."

"It was good to see you again, Ms. Mabry. Please, don't worry about Lisa while she's here. We take good care of her as always."

Carol gave a small smile. "I know," she said, and left the office.

♫ ♫ ♫ ♫

"CAN you tell us if you have any suspects?"

"Ms. Mabry! Can you give us a statement about any further developments on the case?"

"Can you tell us what the mayor and governor are meeting about this morning?"

Carol held her cell phone to her ear and put her hand up to cover her other ear. "Hang on a sec, Maurice. I can't hear you for the locusts," she said, then finally pushed through the doors of her building and entered the quiet of the lobby. Locusts came out about every seven years in Virginia and, when they were chirping, it wasn't uncommon for Virginians to have to raise their voices to be heard at the dinner table. Carol found the swarm of reporters outside very reminiscent. "Okay, sorry, go ahead."

"I said, come straight to my office, before you even go to yours," Maurice repeated, then hung up without waiting for a response. Carol glared at her cell phone before she put it in her pocket. She removed her sunglasses and stopped at the security area.

"Morning, Ms. Mabry," the uniformed woman at the guard station said, gesturing with her hand to have her step forward through the metal detector.

"Good morning. How are you?"

"Bit busy today. Reporters think they get a pass on the no recording equipment here. You can always tell the folks that aren't local." As the equipment read her cell phone and metal badge, it sounded an alarm, but she just handed her identification to the guard, waited for confirmation, then headed for the offices.

"Good luck with it today," she said.

"Oh, you know us, Ms. Mabry," the woman said, turning her attention to the next person in line.

Carol looked at her reflection in the glass doors as she approached, automatically straightening the red jacket that she wore over the blue pantsuit. She had on red heels and a red, white, and blue scarf to tie it all together.

She moved through the office, nodding hello to greetings she received, and trying to ignore any behind-the-hand whispers she caught. Why did someone who sang into a microphone for a living garner so much attention? She headed straight for Maurice's office, and saw Janice, his secretary, sitting at her desk.

"Go on in, Carol. He's been waiting for you," Janice announced.

"Could you please find me a cup of coffee? I haven't had time yet this morning," Carol begged. Janice nodded, and Carol entered the office without knocking.

Carol acknowledged Mitch Carpenter and Paul Taylor, the Mayor of Richmond, while she set her briefcase and purse down near a chair and sat down. "It is a madhouse out there," she said.

"Lots of news happening around this building recently," Paul remarked sarcastically. He sat in the chair to her immediate right.

"Where've you been?" Maurice asked pointedly.

"The same place I'm at every morning before nine. *En route* to or from Lisa's school," she answered.

"It doesn't look good for this department to have you show up late for work, Ms. Mabry," Paul said. "If your house is burning down are you going to shuttle your kid to school or put the fire out?"

"Is my house on fire Mr. Mayor? Do I need to further the impression the press is peddling that we are at a complete loss and running around in a panic?"

He actually harumphed. "They need to know that we are taking the matter seriously and working the hours it deserves."

"Then they can come and report on the four or five hours of work I do every single day from my house in the evenings, Mayor Taylor," Carol answered. She'd gone to law school with Paul, had been his partner on the debate team. They'd been casual friends until he made a pass at her one evening about a year after his wedding. She never spoke to him on friendly terms again, and he'd started calling her Ms. Mabry when he'd been elected mayor.

"That's enough," Maurice said. "Mayor Taylor, last time I checked, I'm in charge of the hours my people work in my office. And Carol, we need the lab reports back from the last victim." He stopped speaking and she realized he was waiting for some sort of response.

She had never fallen asleep the night before, and her temper was on a very short leash. She waited for about five long seconds of silence while he kept her gaze, then asked, "I'm sorry, Maurice. Is that a question?"

He ignored her, and looked at Mitch. "Bring me up to date since yesterday. The governor is calling here inside of ten minutes."

Mitch stepped forward, clearly uncomfortable with the mayor in the room. "We might have him on video. I have our tech people working on that right now and intend to release it to the media as soon as we have clear footage. It might be more useful than the grainy photo we released two days ago."

"Wonderful," Carol said, feeling like maybe the tide had turned. The feeling was short lived, though. When the door opened and Jack Gordon entered.

"Sorry I'm late," he said by way of preamble. "Stayed at the ME's office hoping they'd have something more for us this morning. No luck." He sat next to Carol on her left hand side and she had to keep herself from shifting away from him.

"There's one thing we should be concerned about," Carol offered. "All three murders were five days apart."

"We're on day 5, right?" Maurice asked Mitch.

"Yes," Mitch said, drawing the word out. "Richmond Red needs to kill. That's the driving need of every serial killer. If he can only compensate for 5 days between each kill, then he has likely already planned the next one."

Jack stared frankly at Carol and asked, "How about it, Carol? Know any women about your age and height with red hair like yours? Maybe we could narrow down the field a little."

At his words and his look, Carol felt anger rising inside her like magma in a volcano. She quickly discarded the emotional reply she had started to form when Janice entered on a knock. Carol nearly wept at the sight of the steaming hot cup of coffee she carried. She smiled her thanks and took the first heavenly sip. Jack could take a long walk off a short pier as far as she cared.

"Are we holding anything back from the press?" Maurice prompted.

Carol swallowed her coffee and said, "The violin string is being kept out of anything official. I've told a couple of trusted sources, but they've all promised to keep it under wraps."

"Here's the thing." Maurice stood and pounded his desk for emphasis. "I cannot stand the thought that we're just all waiting for the next victim."

Jack cleared his throat. "Sir, we have our best people working around the clock on this case. It's just a matter of time before he makes a mistake."

"Let me tell you something. Waiting for him to screw up isn't good police work. It's wishful thinking. How many more women in my city have to die before he makes that mistake you're hanging your hopes and dreams on?"

Paul Taylor interjected, "I don't think it's fair to blame the detectives working this case – or any member of our esteemed police force – for not finding any meaningful evidence so far."

"Oh, save it for the microphones, Mr. Mayor," Carol uttered between her teeth.

"Hey. I have an idea. How about the two of you set aside any unrelated personal animosities so the rest of us can focus on what's important?" Maurice suggested. "What about the profile you received. Anything there we can work with?"

Jack answered. "That profile read just like a textbook example. Probably Caucasian. Choice of victims indicates the killer is male. Age of victims suggests the killer is also age thirty to thirty-five. Strangulation is personal so he's got a lot of repressed anger. Arranging the bodies indicates a mother complex. Mother issues. Blah, blah, blah. Nothing we hadn't already surmised and nothing substantially useful. The only new thing is this; the profile suggests the unlikely possibility of multiple actors with occult ties."

"I'm not entirely convinced of an Oedipus complex with this one," Carol offered thoughtfully. "Something's off about it."

"I tend to agree. Same with the occult." Mitch turned to speak directly to Carol. "I'd bet my pension this is just one guy and has nothing to do with the occult."

"What makes you say that?" Maurice demanded, clearly hoping for anything he could tell the governor.

Mitch turned back to the CA. "If this were occult, we would have hard evidence of more than one actor. The times and places the killings took place, just one killer slipping in and out is barely possible. More than one actor would have been seen. Also, occult killings are all about human sacrifice. The killers would have severed fingers or toes for use in cannibalistic ceremonies. They likely would have dismembered the bodies and written incantations using the blood of the victims. The crime scenes are way too clean. The bodies are fully intact."

Maurice nodded. "Got it. Good. Any of that in the profile?"

Mitch shook his head.

"Anything else?" Maurice asked.

Carol said, "I have a contact in Washington who isn't with the Bureau who I think might be able to give us an in-depth profile, one that doesn't contain the standard boilerplate or last minute nonsense."

Maurice checked the time, then nodded. "Then get it, Carol."

"I'll have to send her all the files," Carol said.

Maurice raised an eyebrow. "Send her whatever you have to send her. Whatever it takes."

After a quick knock, Rhonda poked her head inside and her eyes sought out Carol. Finding her sitting between Mitch and Jack, her eyebrows knotted in apparent confusion. She said, "Carol, there's a new development in the Kennedy case. You need to hear this."

Carol closed her files, picked up her coffee, and said, "I'll be right there."

Maurice waved them all off like shooing flies off a picnic lunch. "All of you, get back to work. The boss is calling any second." Just then, his intercom buzzed and he wiped his forehead with a handkerchief. He picked up the phone and greeted the governor while waving them all out of the office.

♫ ♫ ♫ ♫

"I want this room stripped and completely redone. I drew up some plans for the walls and floors. It needs to meet with all of my acoustical specs," Bobby said, stepping into what used to be the den.

The contractor, Ed Westbury, Jr., followed with a notebook, silently cringing at the memories in the room. He wasn't a sentimental kind of guy, and he was pleased as punch that his parents seemed to be happy about the situation, but tearing down the walls that had to be repainted when he and his brothers decided to create a mural with magic markers sent a little twinge through his stomach.

"Got it, Mr. Kent. Anything else?" he asked with a smile.

"I bet you think that's enough for now. You can get started right away?"

"Yes, sir. Dad let me know you were in a hurry to get settled in, so as soon as I finish writing up the list of supplies we need, I'll send Joe on over to the lumber yard while me and the rest of the boys get started on the demolition."

Bobby narrowed his eyes at him. "You run a multimillion dollar construction company, right?"

Ed, Jr., grinned. "Yep."

"So why are you joining the boys in the demolition?"

"Well, dad was also pretty specific about that. I'm supposed to be on hand to make sure it's done and done right, and since he still sits on the board of directors, I really don't have a whole lot of choice."

Bobby stuck his hands in his pockets and rocked back on his heels. "I don't want to come between you and your father, but won't your company suffer from your absence?"

Ed, Jr., said, "My company would suffer more from my father's wrath than me being away for a few days to mind a job, Mr. Kent. He may come across as a sweet and somewhat addled old man, but there's a reason his company grew to one of the largest in the state."

"Did you grow up in this house?" Bobby asked.

Ed Jr. grinned. "Dad built this house when I was eight. It was the second one he built for us. I lived here for more than ten years."

Bobby looked around, perhaps trying to see small children gathered around a television or a dining room table or a Christmas tree. Then he turned back and asked, "How do you feel about gutting it?"

His contractor grinned a bittersweet grin. "To be honest, Mr. Kent, I have mixed feelings. But at the end of the day, she's your house now and the old girl could use a few updates."

Bobby smiled, then nodded. "Then I'm in good hands. Allow me to get out of your way."

"We'll be done before the end of the week. We have crews and subcontractors that we'll pull off some of the bigger jobs to help knock this one out."

Bobby walked through the doorway and into the entrance hall, opening the door to let some fresh air inside. "If you can see what you can do about getting the bedroom upstairs done first, I'd be grateful."

Ed, Jr., appeared next to him in the doorway and gave a sharp whistle to a man standing by a truck. "Already know about that one, Mr. Kent," he said, handing Joe the list of supplies. "The bonnie blue carpet and paint should be here any minute."

♫ ♫ ♫ ♫

Personal Journal Entry

May 1

He hides his intentions so well. He's like a chameleon. But I know him. The need is gnawing through his chest, consuming him like a fire. She has no idea he's right beside her, toying with her like a cat with a baby bird. He was right there in the same room when she met with Maurice and the Governor called. He's right in front of her face and she can't see him for what he is. Maybe she just finds him a nuisance. She doesn't see his power and his rage. She ignores his power. That only makes it worse. It incenses him.

I thought he could wait. I can't fight him anymore. I thought the last girl had appeased him, but she hadn't. It's all he can think about. Killing her is all he can think about.

And she's all I can think about. I'm trying to protect her, but I'm losing the battle. It's like he knows my moves and thoughts ahead of time and he's just wearing me down.

♫ ♫ ♫ ♫

RHONDA Regalman walked out of a courtroom at the same time Carol came out of hers. They met in the center of the shared waiting area, entrances to courtrooms on both sides all around them. Rhonda raised an eyebrow as Carol yawned so hard she thought her jaw might pop.

"Rough night?"

"This Richmond Red thing's going to be the death of me."

Rhonda shuddered. "I don't think I'd want to be that literal."

"You're probably right."

It was after three and she was practically stumbling by the time they arrived back at the office. As they went through the glass doors and into the reception area, Carol nodded to the receptionist before going through the next set of doors. As they walked down the corridor, Carol said, "I think I'm going to try to cut out of here early, Rhonda. I'm not feeling well."

Rhonda narrowed her dark brown eyes at Carol. "You look exhausted. Did you sleep at all last night?"

Carol rubbed the back of her neck. "Not even a little."

"That makes for a long day." She gestured at Carol's office. "I think I left my file on your desk after lunch."

Carol opened the office door. When she turned on the light and looked at her desk, she stopped short. The largest bouquet of flowers she'd ever seen sat right in the center. Every color in the spectrum had to be represented, and she knew it would take a horticulture expert to name all the blooms. She enjoyed the smell of the sweet fragrance while she searched for the card. Finding it nestled in the center, she felt the first genuine smile of the day when she read, "Happy Mother's Day Month. Love, Bobby and Lisa."

"Oh, how very sweet," she said, moving the vase from her desk to her credenza.

"Who are they from?" Rhonda asked.

"My daughter." She felt a renewed sense of energy, and sat in her chair. "For an early Mother's Day."

"Rather elaborate for an 8-year-old, isn't it? Seems like she'd get more joy out of picking some flowers."

Carol quickly estimated the approximate cost of the bouquet and realized that it amounted to an extravagant gift. She grinned and said, "I don't even care right now. These flowers made my day."

Rhonda picked up her file. "Get some rest tonight."

"Congratulations on the guilty verdict today."

"Well, he was guilty." Rhonda paused at the doorway. "Hope you manage to get out of here."

With a laugh, Carol answered the ringing phone. "Yeah, here's hoping." As she pressed the button to engage the call, she said, "Carol Mabry."

♫ ♫ ♫ ♫

CINDY Brooks sat at the table in the corner of the coffee shop and felt her eyes blur a bit behind her reading glasses. She'd been in the same spot for about four hours, and thought maybe it was time to pack up and go home.

As a freelance writer, she enjoyed getting out of the apartment and people watching while she fulfilled various commitments, but today just dragged on and on. The words weren't coming, and evening approached. Cindy decided she'd grab some coconut soup from her favorite Thai place and move to the pool side of her apartment complex. Maybe inspiration would strike then.

"Hello," a warm voice said. She paused in the middle of packing up her laptop and looked up into the bluest eyes she'd ever seen. Her writer's mind immediately started compiling all the different descriptions of blue she could come up with: cerulean, sapphire, cobalt.

"Mind if I sit here? The rest of the good seats seem to be taken."

She felt nervous, flustered, excited. As she felt sweat bead on her upper lip and her cheeks flush, she gestured to the chair across from her. The pool could wait. "Of course. Please. I was about to leave anyway."

"Oh, please don't leave," he said. "You're the best looking view in this place."

Unsure of what to do, feeling clumsy and silly, she held out her hand. "I'm Cindy."

The hand that gripped hers felt warm, strong. "Rob," the man said. He had dark lashes that framed his blue eyes, a black goatee, and black hair. He was perfectly dressed in a dark gray suit and royal blue shirt that made his eyes glow. She felt herself getting lost in their depths.

"It's a pleasure, Rob," she whispered.

♫ ♫ ♫ ♫

"SO the trick is not to use any salt. No water on your meat, make sure it's completely defrosted, and absolutely no salt. You can use butter or some olive oil, and you can use some pepper and other seasonings. No problem. But water and salt will just ruin an otherwise good steak. So, what are the two most important things?" Bobby Kent turned the steak on the grill and added some more seasoning to it.

"Start with a defrosted steak, and don't use water or salt," Lisa answered.

Bobby grinned. "That's my girl."

Lisa sat in the swing on the back porch playing with a pair of dolls. The beautiful voice of Melody Mason Montgomery on the radio filled the air. "Where'd you learn that?"

He frowned a little bit. "From my dad."

Lisa looked up, her dolls momentarily forgotten. "Grandpa Kent?"

Bobby nodded and felt his shoulders tense and his jaw clench. "Yeah. Your grandpa. He knows his way around a grill. Always has. I'll give him that."

Bobby felt the tension in his shoulders relax a bit when Lisa went back to her dolls. He closed the lid on the grill and took a deep breath. He picked up his glass of ice cold tea and took a long swallow, thinking the picturesque scene lacked only one ingredient. Then he smiled when he heard a vehicle pulling into the driveway next door.

He lifted the lid on the grill long enough to toss on three ears of fresh corn smothered in butter and wrapped in foil, then closed the lid and waited. He knew she would walk over to get Lisa, and the two of them would convince her to eat dinner at his house. They'd both already conspired about it. The only downside was that he would have to watch them leave at the end of the evening, but that would eventually change. He felt confident of that.

After last night, and then the afternoon he spent with Lisa, he no longer thought the feelings that had begun to bloom for Carol were a backwash of his feelings for Lisa. He loved Lisa as if he had been there since the very day she was born and nothing would change that. His feelings for Carol, though, were another matter.

He found Carol, well, intriguing. That was the only word his artist's mind composed that adequately described her. She intrigued him, with her ability to shoulder so much responsibility and make it look easy, and for the love she so obviously had for her heavenly Father, her friends, and their daughter.

There was a reason he'd knocked on the door of her dorm room the night before he left college, a reason why he'd chosen to celebrate such a momentous night in his life with her. There had already been something in the makings there that a simple telephone call had interrupted, and Bobby intended to continue on with that regardless of the near decade interruption they'd endured.

Logically, he wanted to take it slowly with Carol. Her life was packed as full as it could get, and he wanted nothing to throw her off balance, especially if he could prevent it. Intellectually, he knew there was nothing but time in front of them now.

Emotionally, he wanted to make up for lost time. Spiritually, he knew with a certainty that went much deeper than knowledge or something as fallible as the human heart that he and Carol belonged together as husband and wife; that God wanted them to be the married parents He intended all along. Bobby determined that for now he would keep praying, biding his time, loving his daughter, and honoring Carol until she reached the same inevitable conclusion.

In the meantime, he flipped the corn and watched her cut across the lawn. She'd obviously taken the time to change clothes before heading over, because she now wore a pair of Capri pants and a T-shirt for which Bobby felt silently grateful. Convincing her to stay would be that much easier since she didn't have to change out of her work clothes. He watched his daughter run to meet her mother, then started to whistle a tune he had been working on lately.

She reached him, her arm around Lisa's shoulders. First, he noticed how tired she looked, then the wary look in her eyes. He gave an inward sigh, prepared to use whatever charm necessary to put her at ease.

"Hello, Bobby. Thank you for the beautiful flowers," Carol conveyed.

"That was entirely your daughter's idea. She wanted to make sure I understood that Mother's Day was one of my duties as a dad," he explained, walking over to the umbrella-covered table and pouring her a glass of iced tea. "But you're welcome, Carol. Hope they cheered you up."

"They did," Carol confessed.

He handed her the glass and waited until Lisa was back on the porch. "How was your day?"

Carol shrugged. "It was a productive day."

"Productive is good," he replied with a grin. He could see the fatigue under her eyes.

She walked over to the grill and sniffed. "I am really hoping that this extra food is for us. I am not anywhere near being in the mood to cook. I had planned on taking Lisa out for pizza or something."

"Well, I aim to please, Darlin'," Bobby said. He frowned when Carol's cell phone rang from her pocket, and wished he didn't know that she had to answer it.

"Carol Mabry," she answered. He watched her face light up and, when he heard her acknowledge the person on the other end, felt an unfamiliar tug of jealousy. "Henry! How are you?"

She drew in a sharp breath after a few moments, and reached behind her for one of the chairs set around the table. Bobby tried to hear what was being said on the other end, but couldn't, and decided to just wait for the call to end. "Thank you for calling. How much longer will you be on duty?" There was another short pause, then Carol whispered good-bye and put her phone away.

"Something wrong?" Bobby asked.

Carol rubbed her forehead, obviously trying to find her voice. "Bobby, your father had a major heart attack today and has been rushed to the hospital. He's hanging on but it's really bad. They don't think he'll make it through the night."

He expected to feel nothing, so he was unprepared for the wave of panic that overtook him. Carol stood and touched his arm. "We can go right now, if you want."

Bobby nodded. Most of him didn't want to care, but the small part that did started taking over. He would regret it for the rest of his life if he didn't go say good-bye. "Let me get this food off the grill. We can eat on the way."

CHAPTER 18

♫ ♫ ♫ ♫

CAROL took hold of Lisa's hand just outside of the emergency room doors and knelt down to eye level with her. "Henry said he'd try to sneak you in, babe, but you need to remember that grandpa might look a little scary to you. He'll probably have all sorts of tubes and wires in him that are helping him feel better."

Lisa nodded, her eyes wide. "Is grandpa going to get better?"

"We have to wait and see. It might be that God is ready for him to go to heaven, but maybe He plans to keep him here for a little while longer."

Lisa pressed her lips together and took Carol's hand, and then the two followed Bobby into the emergency room. At the front desk, a young man answered the phone, took charts from doctors, and signed patients in all at the same time.

As soon as the man freed a fraction of his attention, she asked to see Dr. Henry Suarez. Carol noticed that she received his entire attention after that request. Henry had recently been promoted to the director of emergency services. She waited for Henry to receive the page.

In less than a minute, Henry entered the waiting room. He walked to where they stood and put his hands in his pockets, then spoke directly to Bobby. "Your mother told me not to call you. I'm not sure what her reaction will be when she sees you. There are some people here you may not want to expose to that kind of confrontation, so if you want to come with me alone, I can come back and get Carol and Lisa later."

Bobby swallowed and nodded, then knelt down to Lisa. "Henry will be right back to get you. Stay with your mama, okay, baby girl?" Lisa nodded. Bobby stood and ran a hand down her hair, then followed Henry. Carol took Lisa's hand and found a place for the two of them to sit.

Ten minutes later, the doors to the waiting room burst open, and Harriet Kent dashed into the room. "You!" she screamed at Carol, who stood up as soon as she saw Lisa's grandmother. "This is all your fault!"

Carol wasn't sure if Harriet intended to physically attack her or not, so she was thankful when she saw Henry come back into the room. But Henry or no Henry, she could not let this continue.

"Stay there, Lisa," she ordered over her shoulder. She took a struggling Harriet by the arm and moved her away from Lisa. Out of the corner of her eye, she saw Henry sit in the chair she'd vacated. She pulled Harriet to a quiet corner and whipped her around until she backed her into the corner and they faced each other.

"Never speak to me that way in front of my child again, or you will never see her again for the rest of your life. Not ever. Do you understand me?" Carol demanded, shaking her arm for emphasis.

"You've had Robert so upset for the last two weeks that he had a heart attack. If you hadn't gone and gotten yourself pregnant all those years ago, this never would have happened," she said, spittle flying out of her mouth.

Carol hadn't let go of her arm yet and gave her another shake. "Baloney. If you had encouraged Robert to go to the doctor six months ago when he started feeling sick this never would have happened."

She let go and took a step back, drawing in a deep breath and consciously trying to calm down. "I brought Lisa here to tell him good-bye. I can just as easily leave with her if you want me to."

Harriet looked over Carol's shoulder to where Lisa sat next to Henry, and Carol saw a trace of sanity return. "I'll take her in," she said.

"No. I will take her in or we will leave. That decision is yours, just as any consequences of your choice are yours to live with."

Harriet studied Lisa for several moments, a calculating look in her eyes. Carol said, "Whatever you need to do and still sleep at night, Harriet."

Finally, Harriet said, "All right, then. I'm sure your little boyfriend here will break the rules and allow a child into his room for you. Far be it from me to stand in the way."

Carol stepped closer, close enough to Harriet's face that she could feel her breath. "This thing between you and me and Bobby has absolutely nothing to do with that little girl sitting over there. Do you hear me? Don't punish your only grandchild for our mistakes."

Harriet rubbed her face with her hands and nodded. "You're right, Carol.

I apologize. Please, bring Lisa in for as long as Doctor Suarez will allow it."

Carol let go of her arm and stepped out of the way, allowing Harriet to lead them out. Henry saw them and picked Lisa up, then followed behind them. Harriet led the way to Robert's room, and stepped back so Carol and Lisa could go inside. Henry set Lisa down in the doorway of the room, then put an arm over Harriet's shoulders and guided her away.

Carol took Lisa's hand and they walked into the room, shutting the door behind them. Robert lay on the bed hooked to various medical appliances. Wires ran from under his blanket to a computerized device that monitored his heart. He was asleep. Bobby stood at the window with his hands in his pockets.

Carol pulled a chair close to the bed and set Lisa in it. "You may hold grandpa's hand, Lisa, but you must be very gentle," she said. "If you feel like you might want to say something, I'm sure he'd like that."

Lisa gingerly took her grandfather's hand in one hand and stroked it with her other one. Carol went to where Bobby stood at the window and laid her fingers gently over his shoulder. Her heart broke for him when she saw the ragged expression on his face. She could tell he struggled with anger and sorrow, and from the look he wore, she couldn't tell which one might win.

"It's okay if you want to let it go, Bobby. Sometimes, the anger is no longer important," she said, giving his shoulder a gentle squeeze.

Bobby pulled her into his arms, and she went without protest. "What he did was unforgivable," he said. "Why do I feel like I should feel guilty?"

"Because he's your dad and you love him," she said.

Bobby nodded against her neck, and held her tighter.

Henry let Lisa stay for fifteen minutes, then he came back into the room and whispered to Carol that they needed to return to the waiting room. Carol considered the prospect of confronting Harriet yet again, and the look on her face must have informed Henry of the direction of her thoughts.

"Why don't you go to my office?" He suggested. "Lisa might even be able to get some sleep in there."

Robert had still not roused and Carol gently look Lisa's hand and helped her down from the chair. Lisa took one last look at him, and tearfully said, "I love you, grandpa."

As she turned around, Robert partially opened his eyes. "I love you too, pumpkin," he said in a hoarse whisper, then drifted off again.

Carol had to carry a hysterical Lisa from the room to Henry's office.

They walked by Henry and Bobby while the men were talking. She overheard Henry saying, "I got the latest cardiology report. I have to tell you, it doesn't look good, Bobby."

♫ ♫ ♫ ♫

BOBBY stood next to his father's bed. His throat ached with unshed tears, and he realized his hands had balled into fists in the pockets of his jeans.

The frail man on the bed looked nothing like the rancher Bobby remembered as a child and a teen. In Bobby's youth, his father had appeared larger than life. Over six feet tall, with wide, broad shoulders and large hands, he was perfectly suited to his profession as a horse breeder. Year after year, his farm produced champion thoroughbreds, and Robert Kent worked side by side with his staff of breeders and trainers, never stopping to consider that the owner of the farm shouldn't have his turn at mucking out a stall or two.

"You couldn't have done more to hurt me if you'd tried," Bobby asserted. He found himself jumping at the sound of his own voice, unaware of the fact that he'd spoken out loud.

So many memories from his childhood crowded Bobby's mind as he turned to look at his father. He remembered everything from birthdays to Christmas mornings. He remembered reaching up to hold his father's hand as he crossed the street in downtown Richmond when he was five. He remembered holding his father's calloused hand to bless their evening meals.

"You...," his voice hitched and he swallowed hard. "You took something from me that will never come back. You took Carol's trust and crushed it under your boot. You robbed me and my daughter and the mother of my child."

The man he remembered was strong, honorable, hard but fair. His father always played by the rules. He was kind to animals and children and a loving husband to his wife. He was firm when animals or hands got out of line. He was giving when children in the community were hungry.

"You robbed me of years that I can never get back. And you did it for something as common as money."

He remembered the first time his father had let him ride the stud horse all the way to the edge of their property by himself. He remembered how his father had savored Bobby's first perfectly grilled and seasoned steak. He remembered spending hours alongside his father in the workshed, working late into the evenings rebuilding the engine block on a used pickup truck that would become his first car.

Bobby leaned down, situating his lips close to his father's ear. "Christ said the love of money is the root of all kinds of evil. I believe that. I believe I've witnessed that. What you did was evil."

His father had bought him his first six string guitar and they sat on the porch on Saturday nights while the crickets chirped and the frogs bellowed and the horses whinnied. Robert Jason Kent, Senior had taught his son how to strum chords and how to pick melodies. They played everything from rockabilly to country western to theme songs from classic spaghetti westerns. Some nights, his dad would just strum chords and Bobby would pick melodies right out of his imagination.

Straightening, Bobby walked to the glass door and looked out into the busy ICU ward. "Most people would consider it unforgivable, and most would understand my desire to hate you for the rest of my life. But Christ isn't most men, is He? Our Lord said I have to forgive you."

He turned and looked at the man hooked up to the monitors, at the washed out pale skin blending into the white sheets. "Not just once. I have to forgive you over and over again."

As a child – that is to say by Bobby's childish understanding – his father was more heroic than the Lone Ranger, more musically gifted than anyone on the radio, smarter than any scientist, wiser than Solomon, and a more devout man of God than any Saint. By his teen years, his father had convinced Bobby that there was absolutely nothing out of his reach, and constantly encouraged him to aim for the stars. As a grown man, he could not reconcile the man of his childhood memories, the man who had loved him and protected him as a child, the man he loved and trusted, with the Judas he had become.

"I have no idea how or why you would do this thing you've done. It doesn't matter. Because, as I stand here in this world knowing you face eternity, and understand that we are all fragile humans who are just a drop in the bucket of time, I will not let you rob me of my eternity, too."

He walked to the bed and gingerly sat down in the chair next to it. Then he slowly bowed his head. "Father God, I pray that You help me release the anger clutching my heart and taking over my mind. Help me to be Christ-like in all things, including this thing. Amen."

As he raised his head, he met his father's gaze. He had no idea that tears streaked his cheeks. "I forgive you, dad. I forgive you for your lies and your deceit. I forgive you. It doesn't make a single thing you did for all this time right. But you need to know that I really do forgive you. You can take that with you where you're going if you've asked for forgiveness yourself."

Robert lifted a shaking hand and Bobby took it in his strong one. Weakly, Robert said, "Son…,"

"No words needed, dad." He shook his head.

His father gasped and tried again. "I never…"

"Save your breath. Just save your breath."

♫ ♫ ♫ ♫

CAROL spent an hour trying to calm her daughter down. She finally got her to lie down on the couch long enough to rest, and Lisa drifted in and out of sleep. Bobby came and went as the night wore on, his face appearing more and more haggard as the hours passed.

At one point while Lisa napped, Henry came into the office and sat with her, explaining how Harriet had found Robert in the horse barn, but that he had already been down for too long. The damage to his heart had been substantial. Barring a miracle, they were just waiting now.

Harriet came into the office around four in the morning with coffee, and treated Carol as she had in the past. Carol couldn't help wondering how much of her civility had been feigned all these years, then decided she didn't really care. Harriet treated Lisa well, and as long as she kept her act up in front of the child, that was what truly mattered.

Carol didn't allow Lisa back into the room, not wanting her there when Robert's heart stopped. She knew his death might frighten the child, so she stayed in Henry's office with her and, whenever Lisa wanted to, she helped her pray for her grandpa.

At five-thirty in the morning, the door to Henry's office opened and Bobby walked in, his hands in his pockets, his shoulders hunched. She could tell from his expression that the wait was over. She shifted a sleeping Lisa onto the couch, and met him halfway across the room, letting him gather her into his arms. She cried for him, feeling his heart pounding in his chest as she pressed her ear against him. He released her and his gaze fell on Lisa. She left him alone with his daughter so he could tell her.

As she left the room, she saw Henry walking down the hall and intercepted him. "Thank you, Henry. Thank you for letting Lisa see him."

Henry reached a hand out and wiped a tear from her cheek. "Sorry I couldn't do more, Carol," he said.

"You've done so much for us, Henry. You've risked…"

Henry held up a hand. "Don't."

Carol nodded, knowing she could never speak about that time not so long ago when Henry had treated a man with a life threatening gunshot wound in her guest bedroom. Not ever. Instead, she turned around and saw Bobby standing in the doorway of the office holding a sobbing Lisa, watching them, and she went to soothe her daughter.

♫ ♫ ♫ ♫

"MOMMY?" Lisa asked from her bed back home.

Carol turned from the doorway, thinking Lisa still slept, and softly replied, "What, babe?"

Lisa started crying again. "I didn't want grandpa to die."

Carol went back to the room and sat on the side of the bed. "I know you didn't, honey, but we can't usually control that kind of thing."

Lisa sat up and put her arms around Carol's neck. "Why couldn't God have let him stay just a little bit longer?"

"Maybe God was ready for him to live in heaven. Grandpa will have so much fun up there, sweetie. We don't have to worry about him not feeling good anymore." Carol felt tears in the back of her throat.

"What if God wants you or daddy to come live with Him, too?" Lisa demanded. The panic in her voice was real, and Carol thought very carefully before she answered the question.

"I think God knows it takes both of us to take care of you right now, babe."

Lisa leaned back on her elbows. "But one day, you're going to die just like grandpa, aren't you?"

Carol ran a hand down Lisa's hair, wishing that at least this once she thought like a normal eight-year-old. "The Bible says there's a time to live and a time to die. Everyone does, honey. Everyone lives and everyone dies. So I will too, one day. So will your dad. I hope it's a long time from now, when you're all grown up like me."

Lisa's lower lip quivered. "I hope so, too."

Carol leaned over and kissed her. "Now, lie back down and try to sleep. We had a really long night."

She sat there until Lisa fell asleep, then tiptoed out of the room and went down to her office. She was supposed to be in court in three hours and had to make arrangements with Maurice. Rhonda hadn't returned her texts, and she didn't want to risk not having someone cover for her.

She found his home number and dialed, hoping that he'd be awake. When his wife answered, she identified herself and asked to speak with him.

"What's wrong, Carol?" he asked as soon as he came on the line.

"Lisa's grandfather passed away early this morning. I've been at the hospital all night and I have court at ten."

"With what judge?"

"Adams. Can you help me out?"

"I can give you his number. Call him and explain your situation. He won't want to hear it from me."

Carol took the number down and hung up the phone, then rested her head in her hands, feeling a wave of exhaustion wash over her. She heard a movement behind her and turned to see Bobby standing in the doorway.

"What's the matter?" he asked.

Carol picked up the phone and punched out the number just given to her. "My whole little organized world is crumbling around me," she said. "A year ago I told my best friend that maybe my life needed a little disrupting. I've changed my mind." She listened to the other end ring three times, then someone finally answered. She asked for Judge Adams, and had to wait three minutes before he picked up the phone.

She explained her situation to him in full detail, and asked that the case be moved to the next day. "This is your father-in-law?" he asked.

"He would have been if I'd been married to his son," Carol said.

"So, you aren't married to the father of your child?"

"No, sir," Carol said, her teeth gritted.

"Well, your daughter doesn't know the difference, does she? And a grieving child needs her mama. You have your continuance. Tell you what, call my office later today, and we'll try to find a place in the docket where we can fit this case in, Counselor. "

"Thank you, sir. I'll do that," Carol said, and hung up the phone.

"Now, go to bed," Bobby said.

"Nothing can stop me." She walked by him, but paused just inside the doorway. "I'm sorry, Bobby. I wish there was something that could have been done."

"Me too," he said. "Go lie down. I'll stay here in case Lisa wakes up, then take her over to my house."

"You haven't slept either," Carol challenged.

"No, but I'm okay. I don't have court in the morning." He brushed her cheek, mimicking Henry's earlier action, then nudged her shoulder. "Go to bed. Set your alarm for whatever time you want to wake up."

Carol closed her bedroom door, stripped down to her underwear, and collapsed on her bed. She fell asleep almost instantly.

♫ ♫ ♫ ♫

Personal Journal Entry

May 2

It was wrong. Wrong. Wrong. Wrong.

I had to kill her. She knew, so I couldn't go back.

She realized my power of persuasion and started fighting it. Something triggered an instinct in her, and I had to force the drug into her. After that, after the physical struggle, it just didn't feel right anymore.

Why did she have to mess it up so completely? She deserved to die. She didn't deserve the death I gave her. She deserved far worse.

But nothing about it was right. It was wrong. I wish I could kill her again and again. She didn't suffer enough for how badly she messed up my plans.

♫ ♫ ♫ ♫

Wednesday, May 2nd

"CINDY Brooks, twenty-seven years old. Single. Straight. Freelance journalist and blogger. Last seen yesterday evening at a coffee shop a block from here. She works there every day from two until eight, but the barista on duty yesterday said she clocked out and left with a guy around six." Jack held his notebook, but did not read from it. Instead, he stared intently at Carol until she shifted and turned to try to block it.

Carol studied the redhead with the open, staring green eyes. A violin string, the G chord, cut into her neck, going deep. Her hands were clawed and, caught up in a topaz ring, Carol spotted black strands of hair. She wore a Kelly green and white chevron striped skirt and a green blouse, a white belt cinching her waist. Around her neck lay a silver necklace made out of several strands of silver chains. Green shoes completed what would be the perfect look if the stockings weren't ripped and run. Her makeup looked clownish, and her hair brushed but not styled. The candles had been carefully placed, but not lit.

"Think it's the same guy?" Jack stood off to her side. She could feel him staring at her even though she couldn't see it anymore.

"Yes. But something's different. I feel like he's angry."

Jack raised an eyebrow. "Oh? You feel like that?" He leaned toward her and whispered conspiratorially. "Do tell."

"Are you actually flirting with me over a dead body?" She demanded, turning to face him.

"I'd flirt with you anywhere I could, Carol Mabry." He looked her up and down. "You're beautiful, and you dress like you know it. If a crime scene's the only place I get to see you, then this is where I guess I have to flirt with you."

With a snarl, she replied, "No, you won't."

She left him standing there and marched up to Mitch. "Your new partner is a jerk, Mitchell."

He raised an eyebrow. "I haven't really seen that. He's quite observant."

"Trust me. And tell him I'm seeing someone."

Mitch cocked his head. "You're seeing someone?"

Carol felt her eyes close and let out a huge sigh. "Let's not go there right now."

Mitch shrugged. "Okay."

Shaking her head, she gestured at the body. "Brooks made our killer angry."

"Yes, she did," Mitch said, sounding hopeful. "There's no telling what we'll find on her body. Did you see the hair in the ring?"

"I did. Any physical marks?"

"Yeah. He really violently struck her with the hypodermic needle. Don't yet know if that's where the drug went in, or if there's another spot. He also punched her in the face more than once. "

Carol crossed her arms and watched the crime scene technician assigned to photograph the scene as he zoomed in for a close-up of the hair on the ring. "This may cause him to decompensate."

"We can only pray it won't," Mitch said, agreeing with her.

♫ ♫ ♫ ♫

Friday, May 4

"I'M waiting on the rest of the reports, but from what I saw this morning, the hair on the ring is definitely from a wig," Carol explained to Maurice, holding the phone up to her ear and turning her car engine off.

"Does that mean the photo we released to the press won't be useful?"

"No, I think it just gives us that much more information." She looked at her watch.

"True. Where are you?"

"At the church waiting for Lisa and her father. The rest of the family's already here, and the two of them should be here any minute."

"I'll try to keep anyone from bothering you."

"Thanks, Maurice," Carol said. She saw Bobby's truck turn the corner and come down the street. "I appreciate it."

Maurice continued. "I need to warn you about something. About half the questions tossed at me as I passed through our throng this morning were about your daughter and Bobby Kent."

"I kind of guessed that. The police have them barricaded off here, but someone dug the story up, and they've been screaming questions to me all morning."

"You're holding up well, Carol. I'll see you Monday."

"Thanks, Maurice." Carol stepped out of her car and walked up to greet the truck. An unusually solemn Lisa got out of the passenger's side and dusted off her navy dress, then walked around and took Carol's hand.

"How are you doing, babe?" Carol asked.

Lisa shrugged. "Daddy said after some time goes by, my stomach won't hurt so much anymore. I guess I just have to wait."

"He's right, you know. Come on. Let's go inside and find grandma."

Lisa pulled on her hand. "I don't want to see grandma. She's acting weird."

"She's upset about grandpa too, babe. She just shows it in a different way." Carol sighed.

Bobby said, "Lisa, honey, you're probably the only person that can make your grandma feel better. Why don't you come in with me, and we'll go talk to her for just a minute, if that's what you want to do." He could hear the cameras going off behind the barricade, and knew that they'd just provided about sixty seconds, an eternity for the paparazzi, to take pictures of the three of them together. He took Lisa by one hand, and Carol took Lisa by the other, and the three of them walked into the church together.

The instant they stepped in the door the scent of flowers was so overwhelming Carol thought she might gag. When they entered the sanctuary, she could see why. There were so many bouquets inside, they lined the walls and covered the entire platform. She couldn't see where they were going to put another one, yet funeral home staff still carried them in.

"Where are all of those flowers coming from?" she asked, turning in a circle as the men from the funeral home started arranging them in the choir loft.

Bobby raised an eyebrow and looked at her. "Nashville, more than likely." After that sunk in, he said, "Let's go find out what we need to do and where we need to do it." She saw him look over her shoulder and say, "What in the world? That girl is plain crazy sometimes."

Carol turned, not knowing what to expect, and saw Melody Mason Montgomery holding onto her husband's arm and walking their way. Well, waddling their way. Carol knew she was more than eight months pregnant with twins and the doctors thought they could come at any time, which is why they hadn't expected her. But Carol could hear the warmth in his voice and was glad his friends came.

She watched Bobby walk up to them and pull her to him and hug her. "What are you doing here?" he asked when she finally let go of his neck.

She brushed a strand of her dark hair out of her eyes and waved a hand at him. "I'm perfectly fine, Bobby. Besides, the plane is standing ready, and the flight back is just a little over an hour."

Bobby turned to the tall, thin man standing next to her and held out his hand. "James. I'd put some blame for this on you if I didn't know better."

James laughed and shook his hand. "It was with me or without me. I figured at least if they came on the plane, I get to be there."

"Carol, this is Mr. and Mrs. Montgomery. Melody, James, this is Carol Mabry," he said, putting a hand on the small of her back and guiding her forward. Then he put a hand on top of Lisa's head. "And this is our daughter, Lisa."

Melody smiled at Lisa then bent forward. "You sure are. I can't believe how much you look like your daddy," she said. "I've heard so much about you." She stood up again and held her hand out to Carol. "It's nice to meet you."

"And you. You're the first person to say that about her," Carol said with a smile, then she shook James's hand.

"Excuse us," Melody said. She hooked an arm through Bobby's. "I'm sorry about your dad, Bobby. Come sit with me for a minute," she said as the two walked away.

"You've had a pretty busy few weeks," James said to Carol, watching his wife and Bobby.

Carol looked up at him. "They've certainly been interesting." Whether his pregnant wife was in the room with him or not, she couldn't help noticing how handsome he looked. He was as tall as Bobby, with dark hair. His glasses couldn't disguise his powerful green eyes. She finally remembered where she knew his name. "James Montgomery," she said thoughtfully. He raised an eyebrow at her, waiting for her to continue. "I knew I had heard your name someplace other than the news. You helped out some friends of mine a little over a year ago," she said.

"Who?"

"The Suarez family and a friend of theirs. Jen Thorne," she said.

James shook his head. "More like they helped me out. I owe Jen Thorne a lot, Carol. John Suarez too, for that matter."

"Oh?"

"A debt I can never repay," he began before her phone vibrated.

"What a small world." She looked at the number, recognizing Mitch's cell phone. "Please excuse me, James. I have to take this call," she said.

♫ ♫ ♫ ♫

BOBBY sat next to Melody and put an arm around her shoulders. "How ya holding up, Darlin'?" he asked with an accentuated drawl.

"I feel great. I look more uncomfortable than I really am." She turned so that she could look at him and took his face in her hands. "I'm sorry, Bobby. The last few weeks have been so hard on you."

"They have, but I'll hang in there. The up side is Lisa," he said.

Melody stared into his eyes for several seconds. "And Carol."

Bobby grinned and winked at her. "And Carol."

Melody let go of his face and shifted, putting a hand on her belly. "So, you're in love with her?"

"I don't know. Enamored, definitely. But love? Time will tell."

"I'll take that as a yes." Melody looked over her shoulder at Carol. "You've always been such a romantic. Carol is a lucky woman to be the recipient. Looks like she's getting some bad news right now, though."

Bobby followed the direction of her gaze and saw Carol's face as she spoke on her phone. "I wish she could let it go for just a day."

Melody accepted Bobby's hand as she wedged herself into a standing position. "Keep in mind the things about her that make you so enamored. I'm lucky if I see James three days a week because of our schedules, but I wouldn't ask him to slow down any more than he'd ask me." She looked back at Carol. "Some vaguely familiar looking extremely handsome man is kissing your girl, cowboy. If I were you, I'd go defend her honor."

Bobby saw Henry kiss Carol's cheek while she still held the phone to her ear, then lift Lisa into his arms. "That's another thing I wish she'd let go," he said under his breath.

Melody laughed and started to walk back toward Carol. She stopped and turned around. She held her hand out and waited until he took it. "James thought the same thing about you for about five minutes, Bobby." When she saw the words sink in, she kept walking.

"Melody, this is Doctor Henry Suarez, John's brother," James introduced with a genuine smile.

Melody stepped forward and gripped Henry's hand. "What a pleasure to finally meet you. John is always bragging about his doctor brother," she said with a grin.

Bobby froze, as memories of the night he met John Suarez assaulted him. Melody with a gun to her head, a madman, a high speed chase. He shook his head and refocused on the conversation.

"It's a pleasure to finally meet you, Melody," Henry said. "I've heard a lot about you from John."

"Your brother is John Suarez?" Bobby asked. Henry nodded, and Bobby sought further clarification. "Atlanta Detective John Suarez?" Henry smiled and nodded again, sticking his hands in his pockets. Bobby felt his opinion of Henry do a radical turn. "Your brother is one of the bravest men I've ever met."

Henry nodded and dryly offered, "Runs in the family."

James barked a laugh.

Bobby watched Carol put her phone away, then rub her temple. He noticed the lack of color in her complexion, the tightness around her lips. "Excuse us a moment please," he said as he took Carol's arm and pulled her out of easy hearing distance. He took her chin and tilted her face up, studying it. "You look like you're about to break down. What was that phone call about?"

Carol shrugged. "Work."

"Another –?"

"No. Bank robbers. A sibling team. One died during the serving of the arrest warrant. A female police officer is in the hospital with gunshot wounds." She cleared her throat. "She's a friend. We have lunch together two Thursdays a month when our schedules mesh."

Bobby pulled her close and wrapped his arms around her. "I'm sorry, Carol."

"Thank you," she said against his chest. He realized his arms felt good around her. They felt too good. He kept holding her as long as he could, drawing strength from her touch. Finally, he let her go and they rejoined the group.

Harriet Kent entered the sanctuary where they all stood, looked at the small group, then looked away. Carol touched Bobby's arm, and though he clenched his jaw, he took Lisa's hand and they walked over to see his mother.

♫ ♫ ♫ ♫

"**HOW** was it at the ranch, Bobby?" Carol asked, stepping onto his back porch. She helped herself to a chair that flanked the swing he occupied and set her cell phones on the ground next to her.

"It was hard. Every person there helped keep the secret, and then they all sat back and bragged to their friends that their son, nephew, or cousin was *the* Bobby Kent." He could hear the bitterness in his voice. When he felt his jaw clench, he took a deep breath and forced it to relax. "I've forgiven my father. Now I'm working on forgiving others."

Carol knew he was right and her heart broke for him. She had been betrayed too, but not by her own family. While she knew they'd never do that to her, she didn't know how she would respond if they ever did.

She had told her parents about Bobby Kent when she first found out she was pregnant. For a few years, her father had wanted to intervene and go speak to Bobby on her behalf. Every time, she begged him not to. Why, she wondered now, had she done that? Maybe she just couldn't stand the idea of even more rejection.

But at least she'd dealt with the issue honestly with them and now didn't have to face any lies or misdirections. Bobby's family had broken his heart, and she hated that for him.

They sat quietly as the world turned pink and orange from the setting sun.

"I'm really, really impressed with how you forgave your father." She spoke before she could talk herself out of it. "That was an amazing show of faith."

"God forgave me. How can I accept that without offering it in return?" He said it so matter-of-factly that she knew there was no doubt in his mind.

"Then, why are you working on forgiving others? Should it not just be so?"

He stared at her without speaking for several heartbeats. "Probably. You're probably right. That's clearly an area where I need to spend some time praying." He rubbed his face with his hand. "Where's Lisa?" he finally asked.

"Over at Amy's. I figured Amy would be better for her than we would be right now," she said.

"She spending the night over there?"

"I told Lori it was up to her. She's supposed to call me and let me know," Carol said as the phone rang. She smiled at Bobby as she answered. She and Lori spoke briefly, then she hung up. "I guess she is," she said.

Bobby turned until he was lying on the swing with his head cradled in his arm. His feet hung over the other side. "You know what I need right now?" he asked. Carol just raised an eyebrow and waited. "Music," he said.

"Where's that radio you had out here the other night?" she asked.

"No. I need your music." He lifted his head up. "Will you play for me?"

Carol shrugged. "I have to go get my violin."

"Mine's just inside the door," he told her with a smile.

"Well, my oh my. What kind of fiddle must Bobby Kent own? Is it a Strad?" Carol smiled and set her drink down, then went inside and found the case propped against the wall. She brought it back outside and sat back down, gasping in surprise when she opened it. "This is the exact same violin you had in college," she said, running her hands over the curves.

"Now just how do you remember that?"

She was so wrapped up in remembering, and so loose from the stress of the day, that she didn't realize that she was speaking out loud. "I think I fell in love with your violin before I fell in love with you," she said wistfully.

Bobby sat up. "Is that a fact?"

Carol gasped, put a hand to her mouth, and shook her head. "I didn't mean to say that," she said.

"But you said it."

"Pretend I didn't say it."

"I'm not so good at pretending on subjects of this consequence, Carol."

Carol shook her head again. "That was over nine years ago, Bobby. I was very young."

"What difference does that make?" he asked, leaning forward, very interested in her answer.

"There's been so much between then and now. Even if I wanted to go back, I don't think I could."

"You can't control feelings, Carol. Time doesn't necessarily change them."

"I know I can't control feelings, Bobby. I did a radical switch from loving you to loathing you back then. How am I supposed to gauge my feelings now? Do I go back to the mindset of that young virgin, or an exhausted mother of a toddler who's trying to pass the bar, or the cool professional who has her life straight? You can't take the feelings I had way back then and use them to advantage now."

Bobby stared at her, then tilted his head back and laughed. "You must be good in front of a jury," he said. "You just talked to me in a complete circle."

Carol smiled and picked up the violin and bow. "Don't ever try to win an argument with me, Bobby. I do it for a living."

"I actually wasn't arguing with you, Darlin'. You were doing the talking for both of us." He leaned forward until his face was close to hers.

"And I didn't say you won. I just said you were good," he said in his slow drawl. He kissed the tip of her nose and sat back on the swing, lying back down in his earlier position.

Carol took a shaky breath, straightened her back as she tucked the violin under her chin, and raised the bow. Then she began to play.

The sky darkened as the sweet sounds filled the air. She kept her eyes closed, picturing the notes she needed to play, then eventually just letting her hands and heart take over from her mind.

At some point, she opened her eyes and caught him sitting straight up, staring at her with such an intense expression, almost an angry look, that it took her breath away. She felt the air crackle around them and felt a bit unsteady at the energy his stare possessed. Escaping back into the song, she closed her eyes and tried to pretend she was alone.

She finally played the last song, and the notes drifted into the night air long after she put the bow down. The apprehension she'd felt about playing in front of someone who had been lauded as one of the best fiddle players on the Nashville scene had disappeared sometime in the middle of her impromptu recital. She'd always wanted the gift of music, had dreamed of it since her first lesson on the instrument, but it had never come to her the way it had manifested in Bobby. Instead, she developed a practiced skill as opposed to cultivating a natural gift.

She rolled her neck on her shoulders and straightened and stretched her arm. It had gone stiff from being held in the same position for so long. She lifted her ice tea and took a long swallow, taking her time before she faced him. Then she turned her head, catching her breath at the look on his face. The light coming from the house was shining directly on him, and his blue eyes were intense, boring straight through her.

Carol's pulse picked up, and the air crackled around them. She felt a shiver run through her that carried something she couldn't define.

The memories suddenly bombarded her, and she felt herself flush with the thoughts, felt her pulse begin to race. For years, she'd kept so many thoughts at bay, but now they collapsed forward in her mind. She thought of the first time she'd ever seen him, how giddy she felt whenever she could be near him, how listening to him play the violin in school had done strange things to her heart rate. She thought about the first time she'd kissed him. Then she thought of the last time she'd kissed him.

She stood and ran suddenly shaking hands down the sides of her skirt. "Thank you for letting me play your violin. I've always wanted to." Bobby didn't respond, but his eyes followed her every movement. "I need to go home now," she said, bending to pick up her phones from the porch. She slipped them into her pocket.

"Why?" he asked. His voice sounded low, gravelly.

Carol took a step backward. "I have to work."

Bobby stood and walked toward her. "It's Friday night, counselor. You spent all day at a funeral. Take the night off."

"I took the day off, remember?" Carol took another step back, trying to keep him from closing the distance. She felt the back of her leg hit the leaves of a bush, and knew she had reached the edge of the porch. If she took another step back, she would fall down into the bushes. Bobby took the final step toward her, closing the distance. She had to tilt her head back to maintain eye contact.

He reached out and ran a strand of her hair around one of his fingers. Carol knew hair didn't have nerve endings, but she swore she could feel the touch all the way to her toes. He leaned close, until his lips were just a whisper above hers. "Thank you for spending the evening with me."

His low voice vibrated around her and through her. She framed his face with her hands and looked straight into his eyes. "I need to say something," she said, taking a deep, steadying breath. "I have a knee-jerk reaction of not trusting you born of nearly nine years of a broken heart. But, despite that, I find myself getting swept away, much like before. But this time, I'm not the only one who will be affected if you take off and don't look back."

His arm snaked around her waist. "Quit expecting the worst of me, Carol. And understand that this," he said, squeezing her closer to him, "is good, and right, and has nothing to do with our daughter and everything to do with us."

He gave her a soft, slow kiss that she felt unfurl from her lips down to her ankles. Before she could even think of reacting, he stepped away. "Go home, beautiful Carol. I enjoyed listening to you play more than you even realize."

♫ ♫ ♫ ♫

Chapter 21

Personal Journal Entry

May 5

I've tried to placate him over and over. I've tried to mollify him. I've even tried to bargain with him and threaten him, but it does no good. Every time he speaks to me it's all about her. That intolerable voice yelling her name. The last one went so wrong. He says she doesn't count. But it was his fault. I gave her to him. I practically gift wrapped her. It was all his fault. He tries to blame me or blame her but it was all on him.

Maybe, maybe I can give him another. Maybe I can hold him off. Maybe I can distract him from her for a while. At least for a little while longer.

I'm not ready to lose her yet.

♫ ♫ ♫ ♫

Saturday, May 5

BOBBY lifted Lisa onto the saddle and adjusted the stirrups. He ran a hand down Josey's flank, then swung himself into Jupiter's saddle. As they left the corral, the door to the house opened, and Bobby clenched his jaw but turned in that direction. Josey docilely followed behind.

"Mom. How are you feeling this morning?" he inquired from horseback. His mother looked like a wreck, and she still wore the same dress she'd worn yesterday, the day of the funeral.

"Time heals, Bobby. I was hoping Carol was with you," Harriet said.

Bobby shook his head. "She had to work this morning."

"I wanted to apologize to her. I'm afraid I've been way out of line for years now. I suddenly realized about three this morning what a horrible person I've been. I would like to talk to her, Bobby."

He watched his mother swallow a few times, her eyes staring at the ground. "I need to tell her what a good job she's done," she finally said, ending on a sob. She put her hand over her mouth to try to hold her emotion back.

"I'll be sure to give her the message, mom." His voice sounded perfectly flat, utterly without emotion. He felt a tug, fought it, then gave in. He let his voice warm. "Lisa and I are going to take the back trail."

He turned Jupiter, but then quickly reigned in and waited while Lisa jumped off the horse and gave her grandmother a hug. Harriet hugged her back, then helped her granddaughter back into the saddle. She stood on the porch and watched the two of them ride way.

♫ ♫ ♫ ♫

A weekly tabloid was thrown on top of the brief Carol was trying to read, and the picture on the front was her hugging Bobby Kent outside the church the day before. The headline read, "Bobby Kent's Secret Love Child!" The subtitle read, "Love Child's Mom Chases Richmond Red!"

Carol shook her head. The print setter must have had everything ready in advance, just waiting on the picture from one of the paparazzi before going to press. She looked up and saw Rhonda standing there with her arms crossed.

"Can you believe they would invade your privacy like this?" Rhonda demanded.

Carol picked up the paper and put it in the trash can. "I have a feeling it will get worse before it gets better," she said. She would have to be more wary of presenting such easy photo opportunities in the future. "Why are you here on a Saturday?"

"It's quiet here. No phones. No paralegals. I can work and not be bothered. You?"

"Exactly," Carol agreed. "I feel like I can't get anything done during the day anymore."

"Well, you're getting harassed by the big case on top of everything else. That has to be breaking into any quiet time." Rhonda stepped out the door but paused and looked back. "Want to catch lunch later?"

Already back into her brief, Carol's brain registered the question and she looked up. "Lunch? Oh, no thanks. I have plans later. I'm just working through the morning."

Rhonda smiled. "I'll leave you to it, then. Enjoy the quiet."

"You too," said Carol.

♫ ♫ ♫ ♫

BOBBY kept Jupiter from running because Lisa rode beside him, but the horse practically vibrated with the desire to let go and fly. He almost wished he hadn't picked this horse to ride, because by the time they finished the trail, he had to fight him to keep him under control.

Lisa handled Josey well, and he felt proud of the way she sat in the saddle. She explained to him on their way back that Robert had her in a saddle before she could walk, and her mom had often let her come out to ride.

Bobby smiled. His father had put him in a saddle before he could walk, too. He felt a small tug at the thought. As they left the woods and entered the clearing, he spotted Daniel Phillips, the foreman of the ranch, coming out of the barn that held the foals and their mothers. At Bobby's shout, he waited until they reached him, then nodded to Bobby's request and took Josey's reins.

"I'll be right back, Lisa. Jupiter needs to breeze. Help Daniel brush Josey down," he said.

Then he turned Jupiter, loosened his grip on the reins, and let him go. He bent down low over the animal's thick neck as they flew across the pasture, feeling the powerful muscles under his legs working to eat up the ground as fast as he could. He was a racehorse, built and bred for speed, and would have been one of the best if Bobby had hired a trainer. But he picked Jupiter out for his personal use, not to race, and he'd turned out to be one of the best horses Bobby had ever ridden. He'd missed riding him over the last few months while he'd been on tour.

As he rode, he shed the week he'd just had. All the funeral arrangements and tears, the sounds of Lisa crying herself to sleep. Seeing his mother a while ago just made it all converge into one horrible nightmare, so he pushed Jupiter, thinking he could shed the week with every beat of the horse's hooves.

He turned him around when he lost sight of the ranch buildings, and though he wasn't ready to go back yet, Jupiter complied. He seemed to know that this was the end of the trail, so he gave it all he had and ran as fast as he could. Bobby just let him go, not reining him in until it was either jump the stable, or run into it.

He turned Jupiter and let him walk around to cool off while Daniel gave a low whistle. "That is about the finest horse I've ever seen, Bobby," he said, tilting his hat back on his head and looking up. "I thought he was good looking when he was delivered the other day, but if I'd known he could run like that, I'd have snuck him out of the stable and given him a gallop myself."

Bobby swung out of the saddle and handed the reins over to Daniel with a laugh. "He is a fine horse. Dad and I talked briefly about a month ago about breeding him with Carly. I'd still like to see that happen," he said.

"Be a good match. She's nearly ready now," he said.

Bobby nodded and spotted Lisa just inside the door, standing on a stool so she could reach Josey's back with the brush.

"About ready to go, Sugar?" he asked. She looked up with a smile and nodded.

♫ ♫ ♫ ♫

"THAT smells good," Carol said, coming around the side of Bobby's house. He stood at the grill turning chicken on the rotisserie spit while Lisa and Amy played on a swing set in the corner of the yard. Carol watched them, then turned to see Bobby watching her. "Go shopping today?" she asked, gesturing at the swing set.

"I was corralled. She begged and pleaded, and I ended up falling for the sales pitch and bought the super deluxe model. Took two men from the store two hours to put it together," he explained with a chuckle.

"You're forgiven," she said. She walked up beside him, close enough that their elbows occasionally brushed, watching his hands as they turned the chicken. "So, who's Heather Dean?"

"A friend and probably one of the best banjo players alive today." Bobby never missed a beat. Then he grinned and met her gaze. "Why do you ask?"

Carol shrugged, a smile hinting at the corner of her mouth. "A reporter asked me if you two were still seeing each other."

Bobby winked at her. "One dance at an awards party, and you're suddenly engaged and planning six kids." He brushed sauce onto the chicken. "I don't know, though."

His eyes went far away, as if pondering. Carol asked, "Don't know what?"

Bobby met her gaze. "Well, if she and I could have six kids who could play banjo like her..." He couldn't keep a straight face and broke out in a toothy smile.

Carol just raised an eyebrow but she couldn't hide her dimples at his teasing. "You already have a daughter, mister."

Bobby nodded. "I have a daughter. What a blessing." He stirred the coals and said, "That Heather story is probably mild in comparison. You should have seen what they wrote about me and Melody before she got married."

"Oh, I did," she said with a smile. "I used to sit up nights with a teething Lisa and read all about you and Melody Mason's future as the darlings of country music. I'm pretty sure I still have your photos on some dart board somewhere." She leaned over and smelled the chicken, her mouth watering from the smell. "What do you have to go with this?"

"Well, I was thinking that what would really go with this is whatever you can find in the kitchen to make."

Carol started laughing, then surprised herself by giving him a quick kiss. "Let me go to my house. I know what's there. I'll be back in about thirty minutes," she said. She started to walk away, but Bobby grabbed her arm and pulled her to him for a longer kiss, then let her go again. She stuck her hands in her pockets and walked to her house, listening to the sounds of Lisa and Amy's giggles following her.

♫ ♫ ♫ ♫

"I don't mind taking her to church tomorrow, Lori, if you don't think you'll feel up to going," Carol said. "We can walk over now and get some clothes for her."

"I sure appreciate it, Carol. I didn't think I could feel worse, then this afternoon, it hit me. Why did I get pregnant again?"

"Have you talked to your doctor yet?"

"I called him, but he told me it was just hormones, and gave me the whole spiel about how good it is to be sick, blah, blah, blah," she said. Her voice grew weaker as they talked.

"Get some rest, and we'll be over in an hour. We'll finish eating. Do you need anything else?"

"No. You're doing plenty, thanks Carol." She hung up the phone, and Carol picked her fork back up.

"Was that my mom?" Amy asked.

"Yup. She's feeling sick again," Carol said.

"Jeremy Bunford rode the bus home with me yesterday because his mom had her nail appointment, or something like that, and he threw up all over the bus. Mom had to take his temperature for him and everything," Amy said around a barbecued drumstick.

Carol looked at Amy. "So your mom has the 'flu." Amy shrugged, and Carol picked the phone back up to call Lori.

She spoke to her quickly, and told her to call her doctor. She found out that Amy's dad was due back in town Sunday night, so Carol told Lori that she would keep Amy until then, and that Amy could wear some of Lisa's clothes to church. Carol hung up the phone, hoping that Amy wasn't carrying the bug. She had a full plate at the moment, and didn't need a round of stomach 'flu to go with it.

♫ ♫ ♫ ♫

MICHELLE Lewis stretched her back and leaned against the enclosed smoking area outside of the medical center. She never smoked during her shift. She knew the patients could smell it a mile away, and didn't want to add to their distress. But, that first cigarette right after a long shift like this one – she drew deeply on the filter and held the smoke in for just a moment, then slowly let it out. That first off the clock cigarette was the best one of the day.

She looked at her watch. The bus was running late today, and that annoyed her. She longed to get home, strip out of her nurse's uniform, and slip into a hot bubble bath.

"Got a light?"

She turned her head and looked into the most intriguing blue eyes she'd ever seen. The handsome man with the black goatee and baseball cap covering his dark hair smiled flirtatiously as he held his cigarette up.

"Sure," Michelle said, pulling her lighter out of her pocket. Instead of taking it from her, he put the cigarette in his mouth and waited. She lit the lighter, and he cupped her hand in both of his while he guided the flame to the tip of his cigarette.

Even after she extinguished the flame, he didn't let go of her hands. He kept eye contact and held her hand between his two warm palms. "Thank you...?"

He left the sentence hanging, waiting for her to fill it in. "Michelle," she whispered, losing herself in his eyes.

"Michelle. Such a beautiful name for such a beautiful woman. Thank you, Michelle."

Michelle grinned and, emboldened, asked, "What's your name?"

♫ ♫ ♫ ♫

CAROL put the last plate in the dishwasher, then went through the house, following the sound of music until she found Bobby and the girls. They were in what used to be the Westbury's den, but now was some sort of a music room.

Bobby had been busy over the past week. A piano stood in the corner where a large window replaced a wall once covered in bone colored wallpaper. In various cases and shelves along three of the walls, he opted to display different stringed instruments ranging from the antique to the ultra modern. Framed photographs of Bobby with different famous people, including two presidents, intermingled with gold and platinum albums graced one wall. The carpet had been ripped out, and in its place was a gleaming hardwood floor.

He sat at the piano, silhouetted by the setting sun coming through the window, and tapped out a very happy, simple tune while the girls went through one of the bumblebee dances they had recently performed. Carol stood in the doorway and watched them, then loudly applauded their performance.

"Okay, girls, time to go back next door and take a bath," she said when they finished executing almost graceful curtseys. After some token hem-hawing, that quickly ended with a stern look from Carol, they raced out of the room to go find their shoes on the back porch. Carol barely flinched at the sound of the door slamming.

Bobby slid out from behind the piano and walked up to Carol. Grabbing her by the waist, he hummed the tune he had just played and swung her around the room, ending in a low dip. "You dance well," he said, sneaking in a quick kiss.

Carol kissed him back then stood up. "I like what you've done with the room," she said, walking around and looking at the pictures.

"The construction team worked quickly. I had a crew out here Friday moving things in. It's not perfect yet, but it will be. My ranch in Nashville already sold."

"Really?" She turned around, surprised. He was back at the piano, shutting the lid over the keys. "That fast?"

"It was a beautiful piece of property in a prime location."

She lifted her chin toward the photographs of Bobby. "Nice picture of you with the first lady."

Bobby followed her eyes for a second and teased, "Yeah. She's a surprisingly good dancer, too. Not much of a kisser though."

He waited to see if she had taken him seriously before he continued, "I'd really like one of you and Lisa up there. Maybe the three of us. See where I saved a spot?"

Carol felt her eyes widening and wondered why his simple request touched her heart so deeply. The empty space he referred to was central to everything else. He had reserved pride of place for the equivalent of a family portrait. A few weeks ago, Bobby lived hundreds of miles away behind security cameras and twelve foot walls in a mansion. Now they shared a property line in the suburbs. It felt surreal. "So this is your home now?"

He crossed his arms over his chest and, with a touch of impatience he said very slowly, "Why, yes, Carol. This is my home. My only child and the mother of my only child live right here in Richmond where I grew up. There's nowhere else I'd rather live."

Realizing she'd had a knee-jerk negative reaction to him again, she put her hands behind her back. "I'm glad. I kind of like having you close."

He opened his arms. "Why don't you come closer and say that?"

She smiled and stepped into his arms.

♫ ♫ ♫ ♫

RESTLESS, Bobby moved through his house, wandering from room to room until he finally went to his music room and sat at the piano. A song had scratched at his subconscious mind all day and he wanted to see if he could at least get the melody down on paper.

The faintest of pink highlighted the eastern horizon, itching to burst through the dawn sky when he finally finished. He rubbed his tired eyes and slowly stood up from the piano. It was a good song, a happy dance number, and he knew it would be a hit. He would make sure to schedule time with a choreographer and come up with a line dance to accompany the video when he got back to Nashville in the fall. He made a quick note on the corner of the music sheet to coordinate with Melody about it, then went up the stairs, shedding his clothes as he went. He might just be tired enough to sleep in his empty bed now.

Before he fell asleep, he remembered to set the alarm for eight. Two hours of sleep should be enough to get through church services. He could make the rest up later.

♫ ♫ ♫ ♫

"MICHELLE Lewis, twenty-eight years old, registered nurse at the medical center, transplant ward," Jack Gordon said, looking down at the carefully arranged corpse lying near the shore of Fountain Lake in Byrd Park. "Married six months. Discovered right here this morning by some Sunday morning joggers just before sunrise."

"Do we have a time of death?"

"About three in the morning," Mitch said from behind her.

"I never trusted joggers. They're always the ones who find the bodies," Jack quipped.

Carol ignored his attempted humor. She didn't think any joke that relied on an actual murder deserved a laugh. "His hand is getting better at the makeup," Carol observed.

Mitch nodded. "Jack said the same thing earlier."

Michelle wore a faint pink pantsuit with a ruffled gold top. Gold hoops hung from her ears. A gold necklace made out of thick chains lay over her chest, and gold bracelets encircled her wrists. Around her neck, a violin string cut into the skin. Pink shoes with gold heels adorned her feet. Her red hair was twisted into a stylish bun and her makeup looked flawless. Recently snuffed out by crime scene technicians, thick candles sat in pools of red wax at five perfect points around her body.

Carol sniffed the air. "I can smell shampoo. Passion fruit."

Mitch raised an eyebrow. "How can you tell passion fruit from cherries?"

Feeling the hairs on the back of her neck standing up, she answered, "Because I use the same brand."

"Ah. I thought it was a *feeling*."

Carol shook off the feeling of dread and took in the entire scene. "Speaking of feelings, he seems to be back under control. Looks less angry, more sexual again."

She stood and stepped back to stand next to Mitch. "She was last seen in her uniform at the bus stop at work," he said. "Her husband called the department this morning and reported her missing."

"She's the first victim who's been married. I wonder if that's significant. I'm guessing we don't like the husband?"

Mitch shook his head. "He started calling the hospital around ten last night and stayed up all night calling friends, family, emergency rooms, morgues. He had already called the station twice."

Carol nodded, putting her arms around herself. "You been yet?"

His lips thinned. "On my way."

"I don't envy you that job."

"Nor I." He shut his notebook and slipped it into his jacket pocket. "You might make it to church."

"Bobby took Lisa and her friend for me," Carol said.

"You mean international singing sensation Bobby Kent? That Bobby?" Mitch asked.

"Want an autograph?" Carol stole a glance at her watch. "You know what? If I leave now, I might just make church. I'll talk to you tomorrow."

♫ ♫ ♫ ♫

Monday, May 7th

THERE was a police guard outside the gates of the school. He stood there in his rain garb, frowning at the reporters who converged on Carol's vehicle while she tried to navigate to the entrance.

"What do they want, Mommy?" Lisa asked, fascinated as they yelled questions and snapped pictures. Carol finally cleared the gate, and then got stuck in the long line of cars filled with parents and students.

"They want the hot new story, Lisa. Between a case I'm working, and everyone finding out your dad is so famous, we seem to be that story." She slowly inched her way through the parent's drop-off.

"Well, they're blocking the drive there. Can't they just stand back and wait?"

Carol laughed. "They should, babe." She was nearing the covered walkway, so she leaned over. "Give me a kiss. I'll see you tonight," she said.

From the back seat, Lisa put her arms around her neck and kissed her, then grabbed her backpack. "Who's picking me up?" she asked as she put her hand on the door handle.

"Your dad. I'll be home in time to eat dinner."

"Is he taking me to dance?"

"Yes, Lisa. Now go. Other parents are waiting." She watched Lisa run into the school, then pulled out and headed toward work. Because it was Monday, and because it was raining, the traffic inched along, going slower and slower the closer she got to downtown. As the clock approached nine, her phone rang almost nonstop. She took two calls from a paralegal she had working on some research, but ignored about thirty of them that were more than likely from reporters.

She finally reached her parking lot, then had to push her way through the throng in front of the building, while holding onto her briefcase and an umbrella. She nearly started swinging one of them around to get a spot cleared for her, but then she reached the door and was able to get inside.

By the time she made it to her office, she was fuming. She threw her briefcase onto her desk, let her wet umbrella land on top of it, then stormed to Maurice's office. Janice tried to stop her, but she waved her off and threw open the door.

The governor sat in front of Maurice's desk, along with Mitch's captain. Maurice stopped in mid-sentence and glared at her for interrupting, then sat back in his chair and waited.

"Is there nothing we can do with those reporters down there?" she asked, pointing to the window.

"Well, I suppose we could have them all arrested. Oh, but wait," Governor Wilson asserted. "They're apparently protected by what some people like to call the Constitution, Ms. Mabry. Have you heard of it?"

"Why does their freedom get to interfere with mine? They had to assign a police officer to Lisa's school to keep the entrance clear enough to allow vehicles in, and the second they saw mine, they bombarded me. Then, I needed some sort of weapon to make it to the door downstairs."

Maurice cleared his throat. "I don't think the ones at the school are there because of the case, Carol. Do you?"

She put her hands on his desk and leaned forward. "My personal life wouldn't be as exciting as it is now without this case, and you know it. They would have taken a bunch of pictures of Bobby Kent's long lost daughter, then slithered back to their holes." She stood and put a hand to her hair to make sure it was still in place. "Is there any kind of court order we can get to keep them back ten feet or something?"

Governor Wilson pulled a small pad of paper out of his pocket. "I'll see what we can do to keep them from impeding entrances to buildings and schools. I won't be able to stop them from approaching you personally, but it isn't right if you have to physically push your way through them to reach a door," he said while he wrote.

"Actually, this is an active case. That's technically obstruction," Maurice offered.

The Governor nodded and raised one ironic eyebrow. "Did you know that I went to law school myself about a hundred years ago Maurice?"

"Thank you, Governor. I apologize for the interruption," Carol said, and started to leave the office.

"You might as well stay now, Carol. It will keep me from having to repeat everything you've said to me anyway," Maurice said.

"I would, but I have court in half an hour with the Kennedy case, and I still need to review my notes."

Maurice nodded. "Good luck with that one. Doesn't he have David Black representing him?"

Carol narrowed her eyes and nodded. David Black was the sneakiest, slimiest lawyer in Richmond, the kind that could find the smallest error on the state's side and get his client off with it. "Don't worry. They're shooting for insanity, and we have a stockpile of witnesses and experts who'll testify that the man is as sane as they come."

"That's why you got the case, Carol." He picked up a paper in front of him and turned back to the Governor, and Carol knew she had been dismissed. Janice glared at her from her desk, but she ignored her and went back to her office where Eunice, the paralegal assigned to this case, and Rhonda waited.

Eunice flashed a quick smile, then handed her a file folder. "This is an affidavit from Shannon Kirksey."

"Who is Shannon Kirksey?"

Eunice cleared her throat. "Shannon Kirksey is Dr. Kennedy's girlfriend. She says he came to her apartment immediately after bludgeoning his wife."

"Why is she just now coming forward?"

"Because, apparently Dr. Kennedy hasn't been all that forthcoming with the engagement ring he promised."

Carol looked at Rhonda over the rim of the open file. Their eyes met and the two attorneys shared a smile. "How very unfortunate for Dr. Kennedy. Any idea how we look with discovery?"

♫ ♫ ♫ ♫

CAROL followed Bobby while he carried a sleeping Lisa from his house to hers, then upstairs to her room. He gently laid her down on the bed, then Carol stepped forward and expertly removed shoes and clothes from her without waking her up. She pulled the covers over her, then smoothed them down and leaned over to kiss her.

Bobby followed Carol down to the kitchen, where she intended to make some coffee to get her through the next few hours of work she still had to do. He sat at the table and toyed with an apple, watching her move around the room.

"How do you do it?" he finally asked.

Carol hit the button to start the coffee and went to sit next to him while it brewed. "Do what?"

"Bounce between your two worlds without a hitch, get less sleep than most mortals, and still manage to be happy most of the time," he said. He put the apple down and grabbed her hand.

Carol shrugged. "I don't think about it, I just do it. The joy of the Lord is my strength." She propped her chin in her other hand and looked at him. "Why the psychology?"

Bobby stared at her for several moments, and the look that was in his eyes both excited her and made her nervous. Finally, he spoke. "I was analyzing all of the reasons for how I managed to fall in love with you in less than three weeks."

That was the last thing she had expected to hear, and she gasped and tried to pull her hand away, but he wouldn't let her. "You don't mean that," she said. "You're confusing your feelings for Lisa with me."

Bobby smiled and slowly shook his head. "Now that is interesting. I thought that too, at first. That isn't the case. Maybe my feelings for you started back in college, maybe not. I don't think the when really matters. I know they're here, and I know they're real."

She put a hand to his cheek, her fingers lightly grazing his lips and chin. "I've seen your face every day for eight years, you know. I can't understand why God would give us such an amazing child, but keep you and I apart."

"I believe His timing is perfect. But I also believe with every cell in my body that He wants us to be a family. He made you for me, Carol. He made me for you. In His infinite wisdom, He knew that you and I should be the parents that reared Lisa up in the way she should go."

Carol saw the sincerity in his eyes. "You really do believe that, don't you?"

Bobby nodded. "When I first started touring, I ignored God's voice. When I felt His conviction, I made a promise to Him and myself that I wouldn't do that anymore. I promised I would love God and keep His commandments and I have. Now I'll make a promise to you, Darlin'. I am going to love you until the day I die."

He stuck his hand into the watch pocket of his blue jeans and pulled something out. "I bought this today, but I didn't think I was going to do anything with it for a long while. Turns out it's been burning a hole in my pocket since I put it there. Why wait when I know my heart and I think I know yours?"

He took her hand and lowered himself to one knee, looking up at her. "Carol, will you do me the very great honor of taking me as your husband, of becoming Mrs. Bobby Kent? Will you marry me, Carol?" he asked, sliding a ring onto her finger.

Carol tried to speak around the tears that choked her throat, but she couldn't. At first she just nodded, but she knew that would not be the answer this moment deserved. She finally croaked, "Yes. Yes! I will. Yes!"

She watched the words sink in, and when he realized what she said, he gave a whoop and sprung to his feet. He grabbed her to him, whirling her around the room. Carol laughed and hung on, and was still laughing when his mouth covered hers. Just as quickly as he started the kiss, he ended it, grabbing her shoulders and pushing her back a step.

"I want Lisa's permission. I know she's eight, but I'm marrying her too. I want her to take my name, Carol, just like you. I want to give you both everything I can in this life. I want her to have everything I can give her as her father."

She started kissing him. She kissed his neck and cheeks and his wonderful warm mouth. She never wanted to stop.

♫ ♫ ♫ ♫

Chapter 23

Personal Journal Entry

May 8

I can't sleep. I can barely eat. All my thoughts are scattered. I can't get them back. She consumes me.

Her. Her. Her. Her.

I have to make it stop. I have to quiet this obsession or else I'll go mad. There's only one way to still them. The cheap substitutes just make the need greater.

I can't keep her close, like I thought. It must be her.

I must let him kill her.

♫ ♫ ♫ ♫

Tuesday, May 8th

CAROL sat at the table in the kitchen and nervously tapped her fingers. The light coming through the window reflected off the diamond on her left hand. Though the excitement hadn't dimmed, in the light of day it seemed like a hasty decision – an incredibly hasty decision.

Whenever she made up her mind to slow things down, she felt a sinking loss in the pit of her stomach. Perhaps it was time for responsible, respectable, methodical Carol Mabry to do something spontaneous and out of the ordinary. Of course, the last time she'd done something spontaneous, she'd ended up with a child.

She groaned and lowered her head to the table. Years before, she had lain in her small efficiency apartment, alone and scared, pregnant and too young, and dreamed of Bobby Kent coming through the door and going down on one knee, professing his love for her. That frightened pregnant young woman loved Bobby Kent. She had loved him desperately.

She still loved him. She always had, save the eight years or so when she thoroughly loathed him. To know that he loved her too was something she never would have anticipated, not even as recently as a mere month ago.

Now she knew she was over-analyzing, as she would the significance of a piece of evidence from a crime scene, and she worried that she would make the wrong decision. Once someone saw the ring on her finger, there would be no turning back. And the person that it would impact the most was barreling down the stairs at that moment, about to burst through the kitchen door, and Carol still hadn't decided how she was going to tell her.

Right at that moment, Bobby came in the back door, and she looked up and met his eyes, and she knew. She loved Bobby, he loved her, and they had an eight-year-old child together. Perhaps without the latter, they could slow down and get to know each other better, but it was important to Lisa that they skip the courtship and create a real family. The chemistry was right, and they would have the rest of their lives to discover each other's eccentricities and secrets.

"Mom, I need you to braid my hair!" Lisa yelled, running into the kitchen. She stopped when she saw Bobby, then made a beeline for him. "Hi, Daddy! What are you doing here?" she asked excitedly, throwing herself into his arms.

"Lisa, honey, sit down. Your daddy and I need to talk to you about something very important," Carol said. She pulled out the chair next to her and patted the seat.

♪ ♪ ♪ ♪

BEFORE the ink had dried on the first tabloid that carried a picture of Bobby and Carol, Gary called wanting to know what was going on in Richmond. Bobby had been evasive, knowing what he was planning, but wanting to keep it to himself for a while.

Now he sat in his house and dialed the phone, knowing that somehow, in the paparazzo's magical way, word would get out. Rather than deal with rumors and innuendoes, he wanted to get ahead of things for once. He would much rather face them head-on with a firm grip on the horns, starting with his own statement. It was going to be a bigger deal than most announcements of engagements from Music City, because there was a child involved, but Bobby smiled at the thought, knowing how much Gary enjoyed playing with the press. Bobby knew Gary planned to work from Bobby's offices today, working with his PR team on an upcoming album, making the timing of this call perfect.

Shelly Wright, Bobby's personal secretary, answered the phone, so Bobby bantered with her for a while, then she patched him through. "Gary, my man, how's it going?"

"All's quiet on this end. Doesn't look like it's quiet for you over there. What's new?"

"I need you to get a statement ready for me. Press release," Bobby said, pulling his coffee cup closer.

♫ ♫ ♫ ♫

"WHAT'S that I see on your finger?" Rhonda asked, staring at her hand. Carol couldn't stop the grin. She'd been at work an hour, and no one had noticed. She'd never worn anything that felt so conspicuous in her life, and had been wondering how long it would take someone to notice.

"Bobby proposed last night," Carol said, waving her hand.

"Wow. That seems... really fast." Rhonda looked thoughtful. "Are you sure it isn't too soon?"

She shrugged. "Not really. Besides, we aren't getting married tomorrow. It'll be a few months before anything can happen. We both want a real wedding, with flowers and guests, and God and witnesses – the whole nine yards."

"So, when do you think it will be?"

"Sometime in the early fall." Carol pulled her keyboard closer to her and pulled up a file. "No specific date yet."

"Well, congratulations, my friend. You've gained quite a catch."

Carol grinned a silly grin that felt too big for her face. "I really have."

CHAPTER 24

♫ ♫ ♫ ♫

CAROL leaned back in her chair and rubbed her aching eyes. She looked at her watch, but it was only three. She needed to get more sleep tonight than she'd been getting lately, or else she was going to cease to function. When she opened her eyes, she jumped a little when she saw Mitch standing in her doorway.

"Seems congratulations are in order," he said, holding up his phone to show her the news story about her engagement to Bobby.

"Wow," Carol said, "that was pretty immediate. I guess this really is the age of information."

"Seems like bad timing, don't you think?" He stepped into her office and gently closed the door.

"Will the timing ever be good?"

"I can think of months that didn't end up quite so busy," he said with a wry grin. "But, I hope you don't end up distracted with all those hearts floating around in your eyes."

Carol snorted. "There are more than 700 police officers in this city. Do you know how many attorneys do what I do?"

"Carol…"

"That's right. One. Me. I get the violent crimes. Sometimes another attorney is on the case, but not all the time."

"Meaning?"

"Meaning, I'm pretty used to my attention getting split all over the place all the time. You are getting a lot of pressure. I understand that. But, I'm not going to put my life on hold just because of some maniac out there. Say we catch this guy tomorrow. There are still seven other murder cases on my desk this month. And you and I both know the way this one is going, we may never find out who's behind this."

"God help us if that's the case." He gestured at her computer. "Autopsy reports are in for Brooks. Same cocktail. She had about twice the amount of drug in her system."

"He really was angry."

He pursed his lips. "What could she have done to make him so mad? I'm thinking the drug is to loosen them up so that they get dressed and such complacently. Do you think maybe she didn't respond well to the drug?"

"Possibly. Maybe it made her sick or something. The M.E. report show anything?"

"She'd been hit with a blunt instrument many times. Her body was not treated well, before or after death."

Carol nodded. "Until now, it's almost like he was worshiping each victim. With her, it was like he was punishing her."

Mitch stood. "I have a feeling that the psych report on this guy is going to be extreme."

"Indeed." She turned to her computer and clicked all the appropriate links to pull up the autopsy report.

"Congrats on the wedding thing, I guess," Mitch said without a smile. "Wifey will be tickled if we get invites to the wedding."

Engrossed in the report, she barely looked from it. "Of course. How could I not invite your wife?"

Mitch barked a laugh and opened the door. As Carol looked toward him to tell him good-bye, she spotted Jack Gordon, leaning against the wall across from her door, hands crossed over his chest with a very eerie smile on his face.

Just as she looked away from him, her cell phone rang. The number looked familiar, so she answered it.

"Carol Mabry," she said.

"Ms. Mabry, this is Caroline Adams at Lisa's school."

"What happened?" she asked.

"I'm afraid that Lisa has a touch of the stomach 'flu. I know that there's only a half an hour left in the day, but we need you to come pick her up," she said.

Carol sighed to herself. She'd had a feeling this was coming. "I'll be there right away. Thank you for calling." She hung up the phone and turned to Mitch. "Lisa's sick. I have to go."

"Anything I can do?"

"Yeah. You can keep your partner away from me," she said, grabbing her briefcase and purse.

He frowned. "Maybe we need to talk soon. I hope Lisa feels better."

As she stepped out of her office, she said to Jack, "Always a pleasure, Detective."

Jack Gordon actually waggled his eyebrows. "I'll remember it always."

As Carol left the office, she ignored the reporters, who followed her to her Jeep Cherokee. During the drive, she forced herself to quit puzzling through autopsy reports and discoveries and just shift to being a mom Lisa's school. Once there, she went around the line of cars filled with parents waiting to pick up their children, and parked in the parking lot. She went into the school where the receptionist handed her the forms to sign her out, then directed her to the nurse's station, where she found a very pale Lisa lying on a cot.

"Hey there, sweetie. Are you ready to go home?" she asked, then turned to the nurse. "Thank you. I admire anyone who can do your job."

"The feeling is mutual, Ms. Mabry. I hope you feel better soon, Lisa," she said, and went back to putting a Band-Aid on the knee of a little boy.

Carol held Lisa's hand, wishing she didn't have on high heels so she could carry her daughter to the car. They had to stop in the parking lot so Lisa could get sick, then Carol helped her into the Jeep and strapped her in. "We'll be home in no time, baby. Just lean back and close your eyes," Carol said. She got in on her side, started the engine, then turned the Jeep toward home.

"Did you call Daddy and tell him not to pick me up?" she asked in a weak voice.

"Argh," Carol said. She pulled her phone out and told it to call Bobby Kent's number. She put in her earpiece headset with one hand while she drove with the other. She caught Bobby just as he was headed out the door. "We need to get you a cell phone," she said after she told him about Lisa.

"You're right. I think I'll go get one right now. Do you need me to get anything else while I'm out?"

"I think I have some ginger ale at home. That's all we'll need for Lisa today. Stay away tonight, Bobby. I'm guessing your velvet voice could do without you catching this."

"I'm not worried about that. I'll bring you dinner tonight, since you won't be cooking for Lisa," he said. "I haven't had a chance to buy you dinner yet."

"Thanks, Bobby. Not many men are as brave as you are to face a little girl with the stomach 'flu."

She hung up the phone as Lisa said in a weak voice, "Mom." Carol put her phone down and reached under her seat where she kept brown paper lunch bags. Carol had learned to be prepared from carpooling the dance classes.

"Here baby, use this. We'll be home in ten minutes," she said, handing the bag back to Lisa. She watched Lisa in the rear view mirror and willed the trip home to go by just a little faster.

♪ ♫ ♫ ♪

"WHERE is she?" Bobby asked, walking in the door with some Chinese takeout containers.

"In my room on the bed, watching a movie," Carol said.

She followed him into the kitchen, where he set the food on the table and handed her a small card. "That's my cell number," he said. She turned to get some plates out of the cupboard, but Bobby stopped her and pulled her close. "How was your day?" he asked, nibbling on her neck.

Carol sighed and leaned her head back. "I did battle with a psychiatrist on the stand, received a mini-lecture from Mitch, and Lisa has thrown up on me twice," she said.

Bobby moved from her neck to her mouth, and gave her a long, exhilarating kiss. "So you basically had a normal day?" Carol laughed and pushed him away. "I'm going to go check on Lisa," he said, leaving Carol to dish up plates.

He found her nearly buried under a mound of blankets, very pale, lying still and staring at the television. "Hey, Munchkin. How ya feelin'?"

Lisa turned her head to look at him. "I'm sick," she said with a rough voice.

"That's what your mama told me," he said, sitting on the edge of the bed. "I guess you got it from that little boy who went to Amy's house."

Lisa shrugged. "Two kids threw up all over the floor right in the middle of our math lesson today. I made it to the bathroom," she said.

"I bet your teacher appreciated that, Sugar. You just lie here and rest. Call out if you need us," he said.

♫ ♫ ♫ ♫

CAROL almost purred. That was how good it felt. She shifted the pillow under her head and stretched her arms up, thinking that she'd died and gone to heaven. Then he picked up the other foot and started rubbing that one. "I've never had my feet rubbed before," she said in a dreamy voice. "You have just established a precedent for our future marriage."

Bobby laughed and looked at her. "Aw, shucks, ma'am. We're just engaged at this point. Now's the time I get to impress you."

"When does humble little-old me get a chance to impress world-renown international superstar Bobby Kent?" she asked.

"Too late," he said. "He's already duly impressed." He stared at her for a moment. "I don't think I've ever seen you relaxed. I like the way it softens your face."

She grinned, feeling a little flustered. "My face isn't normally soft?"

"Your face is often intense," he corrected, pressing on her arch and eliciting a sigh from her. "You take the troubles of the world on those shoulders of yours."

When her phone rang, she tensed up. She sat up and reached over the back of the couch, lifting the receiver from the base. "Hello?" she said.

"Hey Carol, this is Jen."

"Jen! I've been trying to get a hold of you for a week. Is everything okay?" Carol asked. She moved her feet off Bobby's lap and swung her legs around to sit upright.

"I had to clean up a mess overseas. Just got back. I just received your package. What do you need?"

Carol's mind shifted to the case. "I need a profile. As detailed of one you can get me."

"That's it? You could have gone to the Bureau for that," Jen mused.

"I did. They ripped a page out of the handbook and plagiarized it. I need a real profile. In-depth."

"Okay. It will take me a few days."

"I appreciate anything you can do. There've been two more murders since you got the package."

"I'll need that information as well."

"You should have it by tomorrow at the latest. I sent it out earlier today."

"It will still take me a few days. I want to do it myself so I need to read everything, get into the mind-set, that sort of thing. But I'll call you as soon as I have it."

"Can you e-mail it?"

"Yes, but I'd rather send it via fax."

Carol would never understand spooks. "Okay. Let me give you my home fax number. You can fax it straight to me, and don't worry about sending the hard copy anywhere." Carol gave her the number, then bit her lip. "I saw Henry the other day. He told me about John."

"I saw John last night," Jen said, then she surprised Carol by laughing. It was a sound so rarely heard from Jen. "He's trying to wear me down."

Carol smiled. "There's nothing wrong with being in love and getting married, Jen."

"Uh huh. Walk a mile in my shoes, then say that. I understand you also have some news."

Carol grinned. "I'm sitting right next to him."

Jen Thorne said, "Tell Bobby I said hello. I only met him once, but I'm sure he'll remember it. It was kind of a bad day. Tell him I look forward to meeting him again under better circumstances. I assume I'm invited to the wedding?"

"I'm afraid not, but you can come as a bridesmaid."

She heard Jen snort. "Can you imagine me in a bridesmaid dress?"

"Actually, I can't wait to see you in one."

After a long pause, Jen said, "Aria your Matron of Honor?" Jen had worked closely with Aria's husband Nick for several years.

"Haven't asked her yet, but that's the plan," Carol confirmed.

"I'm sure she'll say yes. Be good to catch up with Nick again. And that gives John a good excuse to come, too. So, sure. I'll be there for you. You going to get Melody Montgomery to sing?"

"I guess it depends. She's due soon. I'm sure he'd love it. Bobby and

Melody apparently go way back."

There was a pause and Jen said, "Yes, Carol. I know that."

Carol blinked. "What does that mean?"

"It was a bad time, Carol. For Melody. Ask Bobby."

Carol heard a tone in Jennifer Thorne's voice that she hadn't heard in over a year. It was a tone of evasiveness and stoicism that meant someone had been seriously hurt or even killed. It said without saying it that the subject was off limits. A little over a year ago, Jen Thorne had been instrumental in turning Carol's life upside down. She wondered if Bobby could tell a similar tale.

Carol said, "Will do, Jen. I'll wait on that profile. And thank you."

"Thanks for bringing it to me, Carol. Hope it helps me even up our score a little." She hung up before Carol could say anything else.

Carol lay back down and propped her feet back into Bobby's lap. "So, Jen Thorne said to tell you hello and that she looks forward to meeting you under better circumstances next time."

She watched Bobby's jaw clench. "She's a good woman. I think I'd like to meet her when she isn't shooting at someone."

Carol stared at him for a little longer, but he didn't continue. "So you don't want to talk about it?"

Bobby shrugged. "It was all in the papers. I was at Melody Mason's party when she was kidnapped."

Carol felt her eyes widen. She had read about it and heard some things from John Suarez when she had seen him months ago, but it never occurred to her that Bobby had also been present.

"What else did Jen say?" Bobby prompted, trying to change the subject.

"She's going to be a bridesmaid for me," she answered.

He grinned. "That will be something to see. Will she have John with her?"

"How do you know John Suarez?"

He finally met her eyes. He looked amused. "Same way I know Jennifer Thorne."

"It's fascinating that you know John and Jen. My best friend's Aria, John's baby sister. Henry's, too, for that matter."

At the mention of Henry's name, Bobby's eyes darkened a little bit.

Carol noticed. "You know Henry's like my brother, don't you? I've known him since I was fifteen."

"Being like a brother and being a brother are two different things."

Carol suddenly felt oddly flattered. "Bobby, are you jealous of Henry?"

Bobby shrugged. "I don't think I'm jealous of you and Henry anymore than I envy how close his relationship is with you and Lisa. But, I'll get over it."

"Yeah, well, you ought to." She turned her head so that she could see the television again.

"I have to go to Atlanta this weekend," he said a short time later.

"Why?"

"Melody was booked to sing the National Anthem at this Braves game over a year ago, but she obviously can't. I told them I'd do it. Thought I'd take Lisa if that's okay."

Carol stretched. "Who will watch her while you sing?"

"John Suarez," Bobby met her surprised look, but kept his expression blank. "He said he'd be free."

Carol thought how strange it would be to be home without Lisa. "I think that's a good idea. She'd have a lot of fun."

"Come with us," he suggested.

Carol shook her head. "I think it would be good for you and Lisa to have time alone, and I know it will be good for me to have an opportunity to focus on just work."

Bobby frowned and started to say something, but Carol held up her hand, listening to the baby monitor she'd pulled out of the closet. The other end was in her room where Lisa was, and she could hear Lisa groaning while she got out of bed. Carol jumped up off the couch and ran upstairs, reaching her just as she made it to the bathroom.

Once Lisa unburdened herself of the ice chips she'd swallowed an hour before, Carol helped her rinse out her mouth, then helped her get back into the bed. She wet a washcloth with some cold water and wiped her daughter's face, then sat next to her until she fell back asleep. She kissed her forehead, which felt hot, and hoped that she'd be able to hold down some medication soon. It wouldn't do any good to try to give her anything right now.

"Should you call Henry?" Bobby asked from the doorway with a worried look on his face.

"It's just a stomach 'flu, Bobby. She'll live." Carol went back into her bathroom and rinsed out the washcloth, hanging it up to have on hand for the next time. She walked back down the stairs and found Bobby standing at the window, staring out. "By tomorrow morning, she'll be weak, but able to hold down water. By tomorrow afternoon, she'll probably be able to eat some toast," she said coming up behind him.

"I don't like seeing her sick," he said.

Carol put a hand on his back and rubbed him through his shirt. "Neither do I, but she's a kid. Kid's get sick."

"Do you have to go to work tomorrow?"

"I've already arranged to work from home. I didn't think you were ready to deal with this."

Bobby laughed. "I don't think I am, either." He pulled her close and hugged her to him. "You're an amazing woman, Carol Mabry. I love you."

She put her arms around him and laid her head on his chest, feeling secure and at peace. "I love you, too, Bobby. I think I always have."

CHAPTER 25

♫ ♫ ♫ ♫

Personal Journal Entry

May 8

When I went home he was waiting for me. He won't leave me alone. He flew into a rage. I couldn't get him to calm down for such a long time. He bellowed and yelled. I thought the neighbors might call the cops.

When he finally ran out of energy, he just stewed, seething and so very, very angry. For the rest of the night he just taunted me, whispering her name over and over again, promising to kill her and make me watch.

I want to warn her. I want her to listen to me. Can't she see? Can't she see I don't want to have to let her die? Why won't she listen to me? If she would just look into my eyes and really listen, she would understand.

She can't be the next one. I won't allow it. I love her! I never should have given in to his demands this time. He was once my ally, my partner. I relied on his strength and his decisiveness. Now he's just my nemesis. I'll hold out as long as possible, but he'll eventually force me to do what he wants. I'll no longer be in control. I dread that day as if it were already upon me.

♫ ♫ ♫ ♫

Tuesday, May 8th

SHE felt exhausted. Her entire body ached. If her little girl had to rush to the bathroom one more time and put her young body through that again, Carol knew she would end up in tears over her daughter's suffering.

Finally, though, Lisa fell soundly asleep. Some color had even returned to her cheeks; not much, but some color. It was after three o'clock in the morning. As Carol adjusted the covers on her bed that seemed to swallow Lisa whole, she felt thankful that her daughter's breathing sounded steady and deep, and that she was no longer whimpering in her sleep. She turned her morning alarm off, then crawled into bed next to Lisa.

The stomach 'flu stunk, and she was thankful that she only had one child. She didn't know how women did this with three or four children while it moved through the house, one child at a time.

She must have dozed because the next time she opened her eyes, Bobby sat in the chair next to the bed writing something on a pad of paper. "Hi," she whispered, sitting up.

His eyes looked distracted at first when he looked up at the sound of her voice, but they cleared and he gave her a quick smile. "I didn't mean to wake you. I was just getting some lyrics down on paper."

"I don't think you woke me. I think I was only out for a few minutes." She stretched and decided she wanted a cup of tea.

"Can't you sleep?" she asked as she stood. She'd made up a bed in one of the guest rooms for him a few hours ago.

"I had to write down this song. It's been nagging at me." He followed her downstairs and into the kitchen and watched her open and shut cupboards. "What are you looking for?" he asked.

"Tea. I think I have some left, but I can't remember where I put it."

"Don't you keep it in that container?" he asked, pointing to a set on her counter.

"No, I mean herbal tea. Aria likes to drink it so I keep it around, but it's been a few months since she was here last and I can't remember what I did with it." She pushed aside a box of macaroni and spotted the box. "Aha, there it is." She filled the kettle with water and pulled down a mug. "Do you want some?" she asked.

Bobby gave a small chuckle. "You're dead set on destroying my image, aren't you? Violins and herbal tea. What is it, a nice chamomile? Or perhaps rosehip."

"Wow. You know your herbal teas. Does that mean you want some?" she asked with a smile.

He smiled at her teasing tone. "No thanks. I'm fine. Tea should have ice in it just like grits should have cheese in them."

Carol moved around the kitchen, making her tea, feeling the tension slip away. Soon she would be just tired, then maybe she would be able to sleep. She sat at the table, and Bobby pushed his pad and pen away.

"When Lisa and I went riding on Saturday, we saw my mother briefly. She had a message for you," he said after a few minutes of quiet.

Carol grimaced. "I'm not sure I want to hear it," she said.

He kicked back in his chair. "It basically boiled down to the fact that she's been a harridan where you're concerned all these years, and wanted to let you know you've done a good job."

She stopped with the cup halfway to her mouth, processing the information, then she shrugged. "I guess when you're at your lowest, you start looking for all the friends you can find."

"Ouch," he said. "Has it been that bad?"

Carol raised an eyebrow. "You mean, all the years I spent raising our daughter on my own without her father when at any moment they could have changed that?"

He tilted his head and stared at her. "Point taken, counselor. She did not mention that, just the other."

"See? She still doesn't think she did anything wrong. She will say they thought it was for the best until her last breath, and that's inexcusable."

"It would seem I'm not the only one who needs to work on forgiveness."

She took another sip of her tea. "I've done a lot of healing over the last few weeks, and having you here with me is a major catalyst for that. But right now I'm suffering from the morning after nursing a sick child all night, so I'm feeling a bit catty. I'm sorry you heard me do that."

Bobby took her hand and kissed it. "Why don't you go upstairs and try to rest a while. Take the bed you made me. I'll stay up and listen for her."

She started to decline, but then yawned so hard she was surprised she didn't unhinge her jaw. "I think that might be a good idea," she said.

♫ ♫ ♫ ♫

"HEY sweetie. Let's move you downstairs to the couch and let me change my bed," Carol suggested. Lisa was propped up on pillows watching television, but still looked a little worse for wear. She managed to hold down the ginger ale she'd sipped at for the last hour, and Carol thought that they had made some progress.

She helped Lisa to stand and take off her nightgown, then put on a new one. The two made a slow journey down to the living room where Carol already had sheets and a blanket made up for her on the couch.

"Where's daddy?" Lisa asked as soon as she was settled in. She could barely keep her eyes open, clearly done-in by the movement through the house. Carol moved the coffee table to within her reach and set the glass of soda on it.

"He ran out to handle some errands. If you take a nap, he'll probably be back by the time you wake up."

Lisa gave a half nod, then immediately fell asleep. Carol went back upstairs and stripped the bed. She'd only slept about three hours, and wanted to get as much done as she could before she lost her second wind.

She got her bed and Lisa's bed changed, then went down to the basement to put the bedding in the washing machine. She finished putting in the first load of linens, added detergent, then went back upstairs just as the doorbell rang.

She checked on Lisa on her way to the door to make sure that she was still asleep, then opened the door for Rhonda.

"I brought you the files you called me about," Rhonda said without any preliminary greetings as she handed over several manila envelopes.

Carol stepped outside and gestured at the porch. "You don't want to go in there. I don't want you catching this bug. It's a killer."

Rhonda sat in a chair. "Is she real sick, then?"

Carol nodded while she glanced over the files. "She's getting better now, but we had a pretty rough night." She looked up at her. "Do you want something to drink, Rhonda? I bleached everything so no worries."

"No, thanks. I need to get back to work, and you look like you've done enough fetching for at least a day."

"Thanks for bringing these by. I don't think anyone else would have understood my organization system."

♫ ♫ ♫ ♫

Wednesday, May 9th

CAROL walked into the coffee shop and spotted Mitch and Jack at a small table. Smiling, she walked up to them and set the pink bag on the center of the table.

Mitch looked up at her and spotted the bag. "What's this?"

"Blueberry filled doughnuts, your favorite," she said, pulling out a chair, "from Frank's."

"And this means –"

"This means that I appreciate your honesty, but the hearts floating in my eyes aren't impeding my ability to see anything." She looked at Jack. "I got you a chocolate éclair," she said.

"Are you apologizing to me, too?"

"No. I'm just not rude."

Jack laughed and opened the bag.

Mitch took a sip of his coffee and wiped his mouth with a paper napkin. "Lisa better?"

"Yes. We made it through the bout." Carol fielded an incoming text before slipping the phone back into her purse. "I've been looking at that security camera footage from our guy buying the hair dye."

"Yeah?" Mitch asked around a mouth full of blueberry filling and fried dough.

"Yeah. Something's wrong."

Jack smirked. "You mean other than the ridiculous camera angle and the lack of face shots?"

"Right. Something other than. Just not sure what."

Mitch smiled half a smile. "So it *feels* wrong."

Carol barked a short laugh. "Exactly. I've watched it a dozen times and I can't put my finger on it. Something about the way he moves."

♫ ♫ ♫ ♫

CHAPTER 26

"SO daddy said I get to ride in his plane and everything," Lisa said while she and Carol picked up her room. "And, I get to spend the night at Melody Montgomery's house! I can't wait."

"It will be lots of fun, I'm sure." Carol put the last doll on the shelf. "Okay. Hop in bed. You have to go back to school tomorrow."

"But I want to wait for daddy to come kiss me good-night," Lisa said with a whine.

"He isn't always going to be able to be around to kiss you good-night, Lisa. He's next door working. Get in bed. He'll probably come over to check on you later."

She tucked Lisa in, kissed her good-night, then turned out the light and walked downstairs. She didn't feel like working, so she grabbed a glass of tea and went out onto her porch. It wasn't quite dark yet, so she sat in a chair and watched her neighborhood slowly settle in for the night. She could faintly hear the sound of Bobby's piano next door, and leaned back in her chair and listened to him tap out a new song. Every so often, there would be a long pause, then the same refrain was repeated, with a little more added to it. He'd been over there for about two hours now, and she wondered how long this process normally took him.

"Hi Carol," Lori Bradford said, stepping onto the porch, startling her.

"Oh, hi Lori," she said, sitting up. "What brings you out?"

"Amy's getting in some quality time with her father, and I felt good, so I thought I'd go for a walk."

"How long is he in town for?" Lori's husband was a corporate lawyer, but his clients spanned the globe, and he was rarely in town for more than two or three days at a time.

"A whole week, barring some unforeseen crisis. Then he's taking his vacation as soon as school lets out. He says he'll have the entire month of June off. I'm not going to know what to do with him being around for so long."

"I have a feeling my marriage will be the same way," Carol said.

"Think you'll stay here?"

She shrugged. "I want to, but we haven't talked about it yet. Since he hasn't said anything to the contrary, probably."

"Well, that type of relationship isn't easy, but once you get into the swing of it you get used to it. I'll take having Houston sometimes rather than never." She put her hand over her mouth and laughed. "I can't believe one of my best friends is marrying Bobby Kent! It's just so unreal."

Carol smiled. "He's just Bobby to me. Always has been."

"I'm going to have to work on not swooning every time he's around."

She heard the front door across the yard open and shut. "Yeah, well, consider this practice. Here he comes," Carol said with a grin.

Lori looked panicked, as if she was about to bolt, but she moved too slowly. "Hello ladies," Bobby greeted, ambling onto the porch and leaning against the rail. He looked at Carol. "Afraid I lost track of time. She already in bed?"

"She's worn out from the last couple of days. She went down before eight."

"Well," Lori said, standing, "I have my own to get down. I'll head on home."

Bobby said, "You're Amy's mom. Bradford, right?"

Lori's eyes widened. "Yes. Lori."

Bobby straightened. "I'll walk you, Lori. It's already dark."

Lori gripped her hands nervously. "No, really, I'll be fine."

"It's no trouble at all. I'll walk you, at least to your street." He gestured with his hand, and Lori gave Carol a look of nervousness as she walked by. Carol just smiled and waved good-bye. She watched them until they were shadows that blended in with the night, then a few minutes later, a single shadow came from the night and slowly became a form walking back toward her.

Bobby stepped back up onto the porch and sat in the chair that Lori vacated, crossing his ankles. "We need to have her over as much as possible," he said.

"Why?" Carol asked, studying his profile.

"Because she still sees a superstar, and she needs to see Bobby or else you'll lose a friend. Lisa might, too."

His voice held a touch of impatience that confused her. "Does that bother you?"

He uncrossed his ankles, sat forward, put his elbows on his knees, and laced his fingers. "I've never given it much thought. I've never had reason to give it much thought, but now I do, and the more I see your friends and church members stutter or flush or bat their eyes, the more uncomfortable I get. I expect it from fans, but not from peers. With fans I can be larger than life. With peers they should be part of my life."

She didn't respond right away. Instead, she took the time she needed to form her answer. "You are a superstar, Bobby. And you've created an image for yourself of this hunky cowboy. It worked. You sold songs. It's going to happen wherever you go and whatever you do, but with the people who matter, it will slowly fade until you're just Bobby."

She reached over and took his hand. "If it really bothers you, to the point that you can't take it anymore, then quit. You don't need the money. You're just doing it now because you love it. But if it becomes something you're warring with, you can just as easily go back to working your dad's ranch."

He sat quietly for a while, and she wondered if he'd gotten her point, or if he thought she was actually giving him advice. She almost retracted what she said, then he spoke. "So, basically, you're saying I need to grin and bear it?"

"If you want the fortune cookie version, then yeah," she agreed with a smile.

He looked at her thoughtfully. "You're a wise woman, Carol Mabry."

She put her head back and laughed. "You need to keep that in mind for the next fifty years or so." He still held her hand, so he stood and pulled her up, surprising her by catching her mouth for a long kiss that she felt all the way to her toes. When he ended the kiss, she had to grip his shirt to stay standing, and he smiled down at the expression on her face.

"I wonder about something, though." His voice sounded very low and vibrated her bones.

"What's that?"

"I wonder," Bobby said, "how wise you'll be after I change your name."

Carol grinned at the idea of being Mrs. Carol Kent. "I can hardly wait to find out."

♫ ♫ ♫ ♫

Thursday, May 10th

"OH mom, I forgot to tell you! Jen called right before you got home. She said she'd call back tonight," Lisa said.

Carol sat on the couch next to Bobby, who had a laptop in his lap and was in a teleconference with his secretary and publicist. It was already after eight, and she just saw her early night disappear. "Okay. Go on and get ready for bed."

Lisa packed up her homework into her backpack and ran up the stairs. Carol watched her go, and as soon as she was out of sight, left Bobby to his meeting and left the room to call Mitch. "I'm going to get my profile tonight if you want to come over," she told him. "Unless you want to wait until tomorrow."

"You're kidding. Maybe your profile will shed some light. I'll be right over." He cleared his throat. "Should I bring Jack?" he asked with a laugh.

"Good-bye, Mitch," Carol said, then hung up the phone.

She went back to the living room in time for Bobby to close the lid of his computer. She told him about Jen agreeing to do the profile for her.

"What's so important about this profile?" he asked.

Carol shrugged. "We don't even know what kind of person we're looking for right now. There's been zero physical evidence up until this last crime, and what's there is so vague it can't be used to lead us to someone, only to confirm him when we do catch him. I'm talking vague like a horoscope. 'Today, you may experience a change of fortune.' That kind of nonsense."

"So what can a good profile do?" he asked. He helped Carol pick up empty glasses and popcorn bowls, and carry them to the kitchen. Carol put the dishes in the dishwasher, then pulled up a chair next to him at the table.

"Well, it will tell me the sex of the killer, though almost all serial killers are men. It will tell me his age range, personality traits, perhaps even ideas of some major events in his life."

"Based on what?"

"The style and method of the murders, the rituals involved in the taking of the life, that sort of thing," she said.

"So you take the profile and match it to someone?"

"There are over 200 thousand people in this city alone. Right now, in this country, there are over 100 serial killers that have never been caught and about 400 at large on any given day. Every little bit of description helps."

"How accurate can it be?"

"With Jen doing it, I am comfortable saying it will be dead-on."

♫ ♫ ♫ ♫

CHAPTER 27

Personal Journal Entry

May 10

She's been hunting. Offering up this one and that one and this completely unsatisfactory other one. Nothing. No one. They're all imperfect. Too tall. Too short. Too brunette. Wrong height. Wrong hair. Wrong eyes.

Wrong. Wrong. Wrong. Wrong! Wrong!

She knows what she must do. I've known all along. Maybe, when I take HER, maybe when I kill HER, maybe I'll leave her alone for a while. Like a little reward. Like a treat for my favorite pet. Maybe I'll give her some peace again, at least for a short time. She's always whining about wanting peace. She's so weak.

SHE is too distracting. HER very existing offends me and she knows it. Maybe I'll pretend to become a productive member of society and act normal again for more than a week at a time after I kill HER.

♫ ♫ ♫ ♫

IT took her little time to put Lisa to bed. She went with almost no protest, too tired from her first day back at school after being so sick. Mitch was seated at the couch with Bobby when she walked back downstairs, and she poured everyone iced tea while they all waited for the phone to ring.

The men made small talk about baseball while Carol paced the room, waiting. It seemed like forever, but finally the phone rang, and everyone in the room jumped, then fell silent. Carol picked up the receiver. "Hello?"

"It's Jen. I've got your profile," she said. Count on Jen Thorne to skip the pleasantries.

Carol set her glass down and reached for a pad and pencil on the table behind her. "Do you want to give it to me verbally, or fax it to me?" she asked. The two men in the room watched her, waiting.

"I'll do both. Okay, here goes. What you have is an incredibly complex person. Someone who is charming and uses a form of hypnosis, kind of like a snake does to its victims. Someone who is likely at least two personalities, if not more. And the other personalities may not know what's going on all the time. There is an incredible rage inside that is prevalent in the violence of the blows on the last victim, but despite the violence, your killer isn't necessarily physically strong, or at least not exceptionally so. The rage is something your killer contains, or if you want to look at it this way, controls. When things don't go as planned, the tight grip on the control is lost and the rage takes over. When the rage takes over, things can't be completed - like the lighting of the candles or the arranging of the hair. Something was wrong, the killer lost control, so the ritual couldn't be completed.

"Your killer is extremely methodical, detail oriented, and plans extensively with everything but the victims. The victims are random."

Carol wrote as fast as she could. It was a few moments before she realized Jen had stopped speaking. "What else?" she asked.

"The killer is in love with the woman represented by the victims. There is great love and care taken with the women before they're killed, and after. This is an act of love.

"The killer doesn't want to be caught, which is odd in serial killers. Most of them are crying for help or daring law enforcement to catch them. They send manifestos to reporters or try to insert themselves into the investigation somehow. That sort of thing.

"This one doesn't want help. This one feels there is a purpose, a higher calling for the killings, as if maybe being ordered to do it. Like I said, more than one personality. With at least a mild case of schizophrenia at work here, though I didn't put that in the written report in case it's used as a defense. I think one personality is protecting the other so they all don't get caught. If and when you catch the killer, there will be a terrible rage, perhaps even a suicide attempt over the capture, because the carefully laid plans, or if you will, mission, will have failed."

Jen paused, and Carol thought perhaps she was through. "Is that everything?" she asked.

"No. Just looking through my notes, making sure I cover everything. This is definitely not an occult killing. There are no symbols or relics at any of the crime scenes other than the candles, and they're just a stereotype. Cult killings almost prescribe them. Also, the bodies are all intact. Cults usually like to mutilate the victims. The candles are more symbolic than anything but the context lacks iconography, like a pentagram or written incantations or other symbols.

"It means something else; something personal to the killer. The light of life snuffed out or the blood colored wax dripping out though the slayings are basically bloodless. They may hold some additional significance to the killer but it's unlikely we will ever understand the rationale. Maybe just chalk it up to insanity."

She heard Jen shuffling pages. "Let's see. Your killer is between thirty and forty years old. Closer to thirty if you want my opinion. There was a trigger. A death, maybe exposure to the representative victim, a life stressor like losing a job. Something made this killer snap."

"You mean ...," Carol started to say, seeking clarification on the stressor, but she was interrupted.

"Let me finish. That brings me to my final point. I know you have eyewitnesses. I know you're looking for a man. But, I want this to be taken very seriously, some dominant personality in this killer is a female."

"What?" Carol demanded, feeling her eyes widen.

"Carol, I know from personal experience, women can be just as violent as men. I believe the primary clue to the sex of your killer is the drugging of the victims. Women are far more apt to use poisons. Men use their strength. Strangulation and smothering are also more common in female perpetrators because cutting off the air supply fits common female acts of violence. As with poisons, there's little or no blood, no mess, no fuss. Your killer drugs the victims. Then your killer always strangles them, whether they survive the drugging or not. The strangling is performed ritually.

"Also, each victim is representative. He is definitely killing someone, and he's in love with that person – whether she's alive right now or dead. I believe she's alive. I'm almost certain there's something personal on every body that belongs to the person he has fixated upon for all this. Either a piece of jewelry, some lipstick, some nail polish, or an article of clothing. Something like that."

Carol's mind was reeling. "Do you have anything else?"

"I think the other personality is male. Whether they're working together or separately, you have all the drives that fit the classic male unsub pattern, especially when you consider the time in between kills. But all of the desired outcomes are highly consistent with female spree killers. Think Lizzie Borden. "

How would they catch this guy?

"One other thing, Carol," Jen said.

She had to clear her throat twice before she could speak. "What?"

"Have you had another murder since this one on the sixth?"

"No."

"Then you need to prepare yourself for one. Tomorrow is five days, and he hasn't deviated from his pattern since the first murder."*Personal Journal Entry*

May 10

She's been hunting. Offering up this one and that one and this completely unsatisfactory other one. Nothing. No one. They're all imperfect. Too tall. Too short. Too brunette. Wrong height. Wrong hair. Wrong eyes.

Wrong. Wrong. Wrong. Wrong! Wrong!

She knows what she must do. I've known all along. Maybe, when I take HER, maybe when I kill HER, maybe I'll leave her alone for a while. Like a little reward. Like a treat for my favorite pet. Maybe I'll give her some peace again, at least for a short time. She's always whining about wanting peace. She's so weak.

SHE is too distracting. HER very existing offends me and she knows it. Maybe I'll pretend to become a productive member of society and act normal again for more than a week at a time after I kill HER.

♫ ♫ ♫ ♫

IT took her little time to put Lisa to bed. She went with almost no protest, too tired from her first day back at school after being so sick. Mitch was seated on the couch with Bobby when she walked back downstairs, and she poured everyone iced tea while they all waited for the phone to ring.

The men made small talk about baseball while Carol paced the room, waiting. It seemed like forever, but finally the phone rang, and everyone in the room jumped, then fell silent. Carol picked up the receiver. "Hello?"

"It's Jen. I've got your profile," she said. Count on Jen Thorne to skip the pleasantries.

Carol set her glass down and reached for a pad and pencil on the table behind her. "Do you want to give it to me verbally, or fax it to me?" she asked. The two men in the room watched her, waiting.

"I'll do both. Okay, here goes. What you have is an incredibly complex person. Someone who is charming and uses a form of hypnosis, kind of like a snake does to its victims. Someone who is likely at least two personalities, if not more. And the other personalities may not know what's going on all the time. There is an incredible rage inside that is prevalent in the violence of the blows on the last victim, but despite the violence, your killer isn't necessarily physically strong, or at least not exceptionally so. The rage is something your killer contains, or if you want to look at it this way, controls. When things don't go as planned, the tight grip on the control is lost and the rage takes over. When the rage takes over, things can't be completed - like the lighting of the candles or the arranging of the hair. Something was wrong, the killer lost control, so the ritual couldn't be completed.

"Your killer is extremely methodical, detail oriented, and plans extensively with everything but the victims. The victims are random."

Carol wrote as fast as she could. It was a few moments before she realized Jen had stopped speaking. "What else?" she asked.

"The killer is in love with the woman represented by the victims. There is great love and care taken with the women before they're killed, and after. This is an act of love.

"The killer doesn't want to be caught, which is odd in serial killers. Most of them are crying for help or daring law enforcement to catch them. They send manifestos to reporters or try to insert themselves into the investigation somehow. That sort of thing.

"This one doesn't want help. This one feels there is a purpose, a higher calling for the killings, as if maybe being ordered to do it. Like I said, more than one personality. With at least a mild case of schizophrenia at work here, though I didn't put that in the written report in case it's used as a defense. I think one personality is protecting the other so they all don't get caught. If and when you catch the killer, there will be a terrible rage, perhaps even a suicide attempt over the capture, because the carefully laid plans, or if you will, mission, will have failed."

Jen paused, and Carol thought perhaps she was through. "Is that everything?" she asked.

"No. Just looking through my notes, making sure I cover everything. This is definitely not an occult killing. There are no symbols or relics at any of the crime scenes other than the candles, and they're just a stereotype. Cult killings almost prescribe them. Also, the bodies are all intact. Cults usually like to mutilate the victims. The candles are more symbolic than anything but the context lacks iconography, like a pentagram or written incantations or other symbols.

"It means something else; something personal to the killer. The light of life snuffed out or the blood colored wax dripping out though the slayings are basically bloodless. They may hold some additional significance to the killer but it's unlikely we will ever understand the rationale. Maybe just chalk it up to insanity."

She heard Jen shuffling pages. "Let's see. Your killer is between thirty and forty years old. Closer to thirty if you want my opinion. There was a trigger. A death, maybe exposure to the representative victim, a life stressor like losing a job. Something made this killer snap."

"You mean…," Carol started to say, seeking clarification on the stressor, but she was interrupted.

"Let me finish. That brings me to my final point. I know you have eyewitnesses. I know you're looking for a man. But, I want this to be taken very seriously, some dominant personality in this killer is a female."

"What?" Carol demanded, feeling her eyes widen.

"Carol, I know from personal experience, women can be just as violent as men. I believe the primary clue to the sex of your killer is the drugging of the victims. Women are far more apt to use poisons. Men use their strength. Strangulation and smothering are also more common in female perpetrators because cutting off the air supply fits common female acts of violence. As with poisons, there's little or no blood, no mess, no fuss. Your killer drugs the victims. Then your killer always strangles them, whether they survive the drugging or not. The strangling is performed ritually.

"Also, each victim is representative. He is definitely killing someone, and he's in love with that person – whether she's alive right now or dead. I believe she's alive. I'm almost certain there's something personal on every body that belongs to the person he has fixated upon for all this. Either a piece of jewelry, some lipstick, some nail polish, or an article of clothing.

Something like that."

Carol's mind was reeling. "Do you have anything else?"

"I think the other personality is male. Whether they're working together or separately, you have all the drives that fit the classic male unsub pattern, especially when you consider the time in between kills. But all of the desired outcomes are highly consistent with female spree killers. Think Lizzie Borden."

How would they catch this guy?

"One other thing, Carol," Jen said.

She had to clear her throat twice before she could speak. "What?"

"Have you had another murder since this one on the sixth?"

"No."

"Then you need to prepare yourself for one. Tomorrow is five days, and he hasn't deviated from his pattern since the first murder."

♫ ♫ ♫ ♫

CHAPTER 28

Friday, May 11th

CAROL dropped Lisa off at school and turned in the direction of work. On an impulse, she dialed Maurice's cell phone before she tried his office, and caught him just as he was about to pull into the parking garage.

"It's Friday, Carol, and as long as you have no court, there shouldn't be a problem if you want to work from home today," he said.

"I have a quick plea hearing at nine-thirty. I'll just leave from there."

"Who's that on?"

"The Henley assault. Her husband's pleading guilty, so it should be an in and out type of thing."

"Go home after that. I'll call you if anything comes up."

"Thanks, Maurice," she said, then hung up her phone. It rang almost immediately, but she didn't recognize the number, so she didn't answer it. The press still hadn't given up on her, and though they'd thinned out at Lisa's school, they were still in full force outside of the office.

She was in and out of the courtroom and on her way back home in thirty minutes. Something had bothered her since the first murder scene. Something scratched and whispered at the back of her mind and she couldn't quite place it until now.

Her tires chirped as she pulled into her driveway. The engine had barely shut off when she barreled out of the driver's seat and rushed into her house, tossing her purse and keys on the foyer floor by the door. After taking the stairs two at a time, she ran into her bedroom, through the room, and into her walk-in closet.

Clothes. So many clothes and shoes. Her weakness, ever since she was a little girl. She loved pretty clothes, and she loved working a job where she could wear dressy, fashionable apparel.

A tall, thin dresser held her jewelry. Hundreds of necklaces, all different colors, shapes, sizes, materials; bracelets, rings, earrings – the drawers were full of them, organized by color and material. There, among the pink jewelry, should have been her clip-on pink fake-pearl earrings. Big pearly pink balls the size of small gumballs that matched the necklace; the store didn't have post earrings, so she bought the clip-on variety.

They weren't there. They weren't there because they'd been on the ears of Darla Cody, the 25 year-old CPA found dead in her apartment on the 17th of April. A vile taste flooded her mouth, and her hands and feet went cold.

She ran downstairs and, with shaking hands, pulled her laptop out of her briefcase. She raced back upstairs, powering up the laptop on the way, letting it boot up as she hurried back to her closet.

After three failed attempts with fingers that wouldn't connect with her brain, she finally logged in to her work site. She pulled up the file on Barbara Daniels, 22 year-old waitress, found drugged and strangled in the park on May 22nd. She'd been wearing black and yellow and had on a yellow bracelet that Carol noticed but didn't realize –

She ripped open the drawer with the yellow jewelry and dug through it, looking, searching, frantically hoping she would find the yellow beaded bracelet on the elastic string she'd bought to go with her black and yellow suit.

Not there.

No, no, no, she thought to herself. *It's not possible.*

She accessed Heidi Conried's file, the 23-year-old registered nurse who was blonde the last time her roommate saw her. Carol couldn't remember any jewelry on her. She pored through the pictures then the inventory. There it was; a pearl ring. Somehow she missed seeing that at the crime scene.

Knowing what she wouldn't find when she looked in the drawer containing her rings, she opened it anyway. She searched through all of them finding no pearl set in sterling silver ring.

By now, her vision had started to gray and her breaths came quick and shallow. *Calm down,* she said to herself. *Passing out won't fix anything.*

Michelle Lewis, 27-year-old transplant nurse, wearing gold hoop earrings. Strangely calm, Carol opened the drawer with hoop earrings and searched for the gold ovals she picked up last autumn when she was at her best friend Aria's wedding in Portland, Oregon.

They weren't there. Not that she expected them to be. She thought of Jen's profile.

I'm almost certain there's something personal on every body that belongs to the person he has fixated upon for all this. Either a piece of jewelry, some lipstick, some nail polish, or an article of clothing. Something like that.

Who could be doing this? How? How did someone come into her house and steal her jewelry? Why didn't Carol recognize the jewelry as her own this entire time?

She thought of the drug store surveillance camera photo, the one that showed their unidentified suspect buying red hair dye. There on the floor of her highly organized closet, she dug through the files on her computer until she pulled up that photo.

Dark hair, goatee, black framed glasses – nothing about him even looked familiar to Carol. No spark of recognition. No reason to believe this person had killed four women in her place. HER place.

Dear God.

She covered her face with her hands. "What now, God?" She whispered. "What do I do now?

♪ ♪ ♪ ♪

BOBBY stacked the last book on the shelf and stood back to admire his handiwork as he ripped the tape off the bottom of the box and unfolded it so that it lay flat. He set it on top of the six other boxes he'd emptied that afternoon. Floor to ceiling bookshelves in the formal living room had been the perfect thing for him. He had more books than he had time to read, but he loved them and usually spent travel time with a book in his hand.

As he gathered the empty boxes and packing material, he heard his doorbell. Unsure who would be bothering him on a Friday morning, he left the boxes behind and went to answer the door. The last thing he expected to see was a very pale, very shaky fiancée.

"Carol?" Concerned, he opened the door wider and beckoned her inside. "What's wrong? Did you catch the bug that Lisa had?"

"What?" For a moment, the eyes that looked at him were dazed, but then she shook her head as if to clear it. "Oh no. Can we talk?"

"Darlin', the very best part of my day is the time I get to talk with you."

He led the way into the kitchen. Carol pulled a bar stool out and sat at the island in the center of the room. Bobby pulled coffee cups out of the cupboard. While he prepared cups of coffee, he watched her out of the corner of his eye. She stared at the counter, immobile. Occasionally, her breath would hitch, but otherwise she could have been made of stone.

Bobby handed her a cup, then leaned on the counter facing her. After he took a sip and noticed that she hadn't even reached for her cup, he set his coffee aside and took both of her hands in his. "What did you want to talk about?"

"Can…," she started to speak, but her voice barely squeaked out, so she cleared her throat and tried again. "Can Lisa stay with you for a while?"

Bobby didn't know this Carol Mabry. He had never seen her this distraught. He realized that he didn't know her well enough to truly read her, yet. Even so, he knew something was very, very wrong. "Lisa's welcome here any time. That isn't even a question. What's going on, Carol?"

"Oh, nothing," she said, sliding her hands out from under his and picking up the coffee cup. She didn't take a drink, though. She just held it between her hands as if to warm her palms. "I just thought you might want the time to get to know her better. And work is really busy for me right now."

She refused to meet his eyes. He set his cup down and walked around the bar until he stood next to her stool. With his elbow on the counter, he draped his other arm over the back of her chair and leaned down. She stared straight ahead.

Very quietly, he said, "I've forgiven my parents and family for the secrets they kept from me – for keeping you and Lisa a secret – for the lies they told me and the way they manipulated me. It's taken a lot out of me. Don't think it's been easy."

She whipped her head around and finally looked right at him. "Why would you think that I thought it was easy?"

He allowed himself a small smile. "Because you're obviously hiding something from me and I'd really prefer we have no secrets between us." He raised a hand and ran a finger along her cheekbone. "What's going on, Carol? Tell me. Right now."

Instantly, tears filled her eyes. She looked around, as if wanting to escape, but he'd pinned her in very effectively. "It's me," she whispered, then cleared her throat and said it again. "It's me."

He felt his forehead come together in a frown. "Beg pardon?"

"Last night, Jen said the killer was fixated on someone he was in love with. I think that it's me."

Confused, he ran a hand down her arm until he could lace her fingers with his. "Why in the world would you think that?"

"Well, the obvious clues are just circumstantial," she said, waving her free hand in the air. As she spoke, he could see her gaining a little bit of control. "Every victim was tall and thin. Like me. Red hair," she said, pointing to her head in an almost accusatory fashion. "Dressed for business." She gestured up and down her body as if to draw attention to her black pantsuit with the bright blue blouse and matching silver jewelry. "He's strangling women with violin string."

"Violin string?" His voice sounded shocked to his own ears.

"We've kept that from the press. That was our little secret tidbit. But it's me. How did I not see this before?"

Bobby raised an eyebrow. "There are over 200 thousand people in this city, and you're not the only well-dressed, professional, tall, thin redhead."

She took a deep breath. "Bobby, the killer dressed every victim and finished them off with some of my jewelry."

He felt his blood run cold. Immediately. He didn't need her to clarify, but he needed to think, so he asked, "What?"

"Something had been bothering me. Something from the first crime scene. I just couldn't place it. I put the pieces together this morning. Every single victim was wearing a piece of my jewelry."

Feeling a little panicky, he shook his head. "That's not possible."

"That's what I thought, but it's true. I just checked. I'm missing a bunch of jewelry. I just went through my own jewelry, and all of my pieces that match the jewelry on the dead girls are missing. Someone stole them from my home and placed them on dead women, dressed up and made up to look like me. Bobby, he even dyed one of the girl's hair red."

He grabbed her shoulders with both hands. "Did you call Mitch?"

"I don't know what to do!" She leaned forward and wrapped her arms around his waist and rested her head on his chest. "I don't know who to call."

Bobby's arms went all the way around her and hugged her to him. "Go see your boss. He'll know what to do."

"I will." She raised her head and looked at him. "Please take Lisa away for right now. Don't wait for tonight to leave for Atlanta. Just go check her out of school right now."

"What good will that do?"

"Take her. Five days has been the cycle. This is the fifth day. There's going to come a time when he completely decompensates and comes after me. It's just a matter of time. "

"You want me to take Lisa away while you, what, make yourself bait?"

"I don't know," Carol whispered, pulling away from him and pushing herself off the bar stool. She walked to the window near the table and looked out at the darkening sky and the approaching storm. "Maybe. Maybe that's how we catch him."

Bobby walked up behind her and rested his hands on her shoulders. "I'll go pick her up now and we'll leave for Atlanta. But I'd feel better if you went with us."

Carol shook her head before leaning back and resting it against him. "I can't. One day I will. But not today."

He wanted to argue but didn't have the right words. He needed time to think about how best he could convince her. He wrapped his arms around her and let her lean against him for the time being. He determined that, no matter what, she would leave with him today.

♪ ♪ ♪ ♪

CAROL stood in the doorway of Maurice's office. He finally quit typing on his laptop and looked up at her. "Carol," he said, "I thought you were working from home today."

"Can I talk to you?" She walked in without waiting for his answer or permission and shut the door. Her stomach felt like a brick of ice, and occasionally a shudder ran through her. She lowered herself into a chair and wondered how she would begin this conversation.

"Make yourself at home, Carol," he said, staring at her quizzically.

"Something's been off to me since the first killing with this serial killer. I couldn't figure out what it was until this morning."

He frowned. "Off? How?"

Taking a shaky breath, she plunged forward. "A piece of jewelry that I own has been on every body."

Maurice's eyes drew together. He stared at her, frowning, for several seconds. "What do you mean?" He asked, enunciating each word.

"I mean," Carol said, feeling queasy, "that every single victim was wearing a piece of jewelry; a ring, earrings, bracelet, something of *mine*, something that I own. I checked my jewelry collection this morning and my items are missing. Locked away in an evidence box somewhere in Mitch's office, I'm sure."

Maurice turned away from his computer and faced her fully. Again, he stared at her for several seconds, as if digesting what she said. "I read the profile you obtained last night. Is that what prompted you to check?"

"Yes. I mean, I saw the jewelry on the victims, but I just never realized it was mine. Nothing was really extraordinary, so I didn't look too closely. It all matched other jewelry on the victims and their clothes, so looking at an individual earring or ring or something just didn't really occur to me until I heard that profile last night."

He slowly nodded. "This is going to seem like a stupid question, but do you have any idea who could be doing this?"

Carol felt her eyes sting with unwanted tears. She blinked them away. "I have been wracking my brain for the last hour, and I don't know. I have no idea. Looking at the profile, no one comes to mind. Not unless it was someone I put away who was just released. That would make sense."

"So you think this is revenge instead of –"

Interrupting him, she nodded. "Yes, instead of some romantic fantasy. Maybe it's just someone killing me over and over because he perceives me as the person who ruined his life."

Maurice leaned back in his chair and rested his elbows on the arms, steepling his fingers. "I want you under protection. I'll contact the mayor and talk to Mitch. I'll also call in a special prosecutor. As of now, no one in this office has anything to do with this case. No exceptions."

"I understand," she whispered.

"In the meantime, take a few days. Go home, under protection. Or leave town if you have somewhere safe to go that no one knows about. Maybe start talking to your friends in DC. Start looking through old case files. See if anyone matches our killer's description. If he does, call Mitch immediately." Carol stood too quickly, causing her vision to gray. She swayed a bit on her feet. "Do you want me to have someone drive you home?"

"No. I'll be okay. I'm going to go get some water, then go collect some files from my office."

Maurice stood. "Carol, I mean it. You're off of this case. From this point forward, anything you do could jeopardize the prosecution when we catch this guy."

"I understand." She had to escape. "Thank you, Maurice."

Her hand slipped off the doorknob on the first try. She finally got the door open and rushed out of his office, down the corridor, to her office. As the door closed behind her, she wrapped her arms around her stomach and slid down the wall.

Silent sobs wracked her body so violently she thought her spine might crack. She pressed the heels of her hands against her eyes and fought for, prayed for, calm. Calm. Peace.

She had to function. There was no other choice. She started humming *It is Well with My Soul*, letting the words settle around her mind.

When peace like a river, attendeth my way.

When sorrows like sea billows roll...

As the song rolled around in her mind, she felt calmer, steadier, more in control. On weak legs, she stood and went to her purse, pulling out a package of tissues. She blew her nose, wiped her eyes, and did the best hasty repair she could to her makeup with a compact mirror.

She pulled her phone out of her pocket and looked through her contacts, finally finding Nick Williams' cell phone number. She hit the button to dial it and put the phone to her ears. It immediately went to voice mail. "Nick, it's Carol. I need your help. Please call me ASAP."

Feeling steady enough to face people, she opened her door again. Just as she opened it, Rhonda was raising her hand to knock.

"Hi," Rhonda said, tilting her head to look at her. "Oh, my. What's wrong?"

Carol gestured to the interior of her office. "I can't talk about it." She gathered her briefcase and purse, and picked up two stacks of files off her desk. "But I'm going to take next week off. Work from home."

Rhonda pursed her lips and walked over to Carol's credenza, where the last of the flowers from her Mother's Day bouquet still struggled to hang on to beauty. "Anything to do with the country star?"

"What?" Carol frowned and stared at the bouquet. "Oh, no. Not at all." She fit what files she could into her briefcase and carried the rest. "This is something else entirely."

"If you're sure," Rhonda said, straightening the jacket of her black suit. "I've never seen you emotional like this before at work. Is there anything I can do?"

With a smile, Carol touched Rhonda's arm. "Thank you for offering. It's nice to know I have friends." As she walked out the door, she said, "I have my cell if anyone needs to get me."

♫ ♫ ♫ ♫

"I want you to come with us this weekend," Bobby stated.

Carol rubbed her arms and looked out into the back yard. The wind blew so hard that the swings on the swing set were swinging around like they were full of kids. "I wish I could, but I can't."

"Why not?"

Feeling scared and very brittle, she turned until she faced him. "Because this is the day. There will be another victim today."

"And?"

"And eventually he's going to decompensate and come after me."

He shook his head while he spoke. "You aren't seriously considering sitting around here acting like bait, are you?"

Unsure exactly what she was doing, she shrugged. "I don't even know who this can be, but I can't leave. Please don't ask me to."

He crossed the room in three strides and stopped in front of her. "You're out of your mind if you think I'm going to leave you alone here tonight and wait for him to try to kill you."

"I won't be alone. Jack and Mitch are guarding me until different arrangements can be made." Which meant until Aria's husband, Nick Williams, could come out here in the morning and set up her security. Nick was a former military commando who worked for a secretive branch of the US Government's Intelligence arm for a number of years, the same Agency Jen Thorne now directed. If she trusted anyone to keep her and Lisa safe, it was Nick.

Carol started to walk past Bobby but he grabbed her arm and swung her back around. "You need to stop and think about something other than your all important job, Carol. You have a daughter who relies on you," he said forcefully.

Her temper, as if made from a thin thread overloaded with too much weight, finally snapped, the ends flying in different directions. Though she fought to get it back, she couldn't stop her mouth. "Yeah, and that all important job is what fed her while you were off in Nashville picking your guitar strings for swooning teenagers. Don't try to tell me what I can and can't do. I managed for all this time without you just fine."

Bobby's eyes iced over and he gave a brief nod as he let go of her. "Is that right? Well, that's kind of interesting because for three of those years, my house was on the Nashville's Map of the Stars. For the last six years, my official website got over a million hits a month. And in addition to surrounding cities and military bases, I played right here in downtown Richmond for the last seven years because it's my hometown, Carol. Don't try to pretend you couldn't find me if you wanted to."

Needing to take the words back, but unable to forge a coherent thought, she just stood there, shocked at what had just come out of her mouth. Carol crossed her arms and stared at her shoes. She wished she could take it back the second she said it, but now it was too late. "I'm just upset, Bobby."

He took a deep breath. "No, Carol, you're not. You're really not upset. What you are is scared. And you ought to be. Know how to not feel so scared? Come with us to Atlanta. That's how."

She shook her head. "My mind's made up. I'm staying here."

He left her office without another word. She heard his boots on the stairs and guessed he was going up to Lisa's room where their daughter was busy packing for her trip to Atlanta.

The phone in her pocket rang, making her jump. Then she felt foolish for being so jumpy. Carol dug it out and answered it. "What?" she answered harshly.

A detective on the other line requested her presence at a crime scene. "I'm sorry, Detective Devore, I'm off for the next week. Let me get you the number of the attorney on call."

She hung up after providing the number, then sat at her desk and closed her eyes. She heard Lisa's feet as they ran down the stairs, so she forced herself to stand and coax a believable smile onto her face.

"I'm ready to go, mom!" Lisa yelled, running into the room. Carol knelt and held out her arms, and Lisa ran into them without hesitation.

"You be good for your dad, dollface, and have fun. I wish I could go with you," Carol said. She hugged Lisa tightly, then let her go and straightened. Bobby stood in the doorway of the room, holding Lisa's suitcase, his anger still clearly evident on his face.

"There's a bad storm coming in. I'll call you from the airport if we're delayed taking off," he informed her in a voice that carried no emotion.

"I appreciate that," Carol said. She put her hands in her pockets, and wished she could rewind the last ten minutes.

"Go on ahead and get in the truck, Lisa. I'll be right behind you with your bag," he said. Lisa gave her mom one last hug and dashed from the room. Bobby stepped closer to Carol, but didn't touch her. "I can understand that your job is important to you, and I can understand that it is more than a job. But you are stepping over a boundary here that is incomprehensible to me. Risking your life isn't part of your job description."

"I'm not intentionally risking my life. I have Mitch and Jack outside. I'm not alone. Tomorrow, Nick will be here. Once he's here, a Roman Legion couldn't get near me."

"You would be safer if you packed your bags and left. That is an option you didn't even consider. Stop being such a pillar, and let someone else take some of the weight. You can come with us right now and leave this all behind. We could go somewhere and never come back."

"I could, but the next time I read about another murder happening at his hands, I wouldn't be able to live with myself. If, and I stress the word, if I am the next target, this is the perfect opportunity. If I'm not his next intended victim, then this entire conversation is just a waste of time and energy."

He grabbed her by her shoulders and shook her. "Carol, don't do this. Please."

She tilted her head back to look at him. When she spoke her voice barely rose above a whisper. "You didn't see the bodies, Bobby. You didn't see those dead girls dressed up to look just like me."

She wrenched away from him. "You don't understand how important my job is to me, but you're the one who's leaving me alone so that you can go sing a song so a bunch of men can play a silly game. You tell me what's important and what's not."

Bobby held up a hand, his voice no longer exactly quiet. "Good Lord, Carol. It's not just a song. It's the National Anthem. And it's not just a silly game. It's the regular season, and baseball is America's pastime. I really hope you aren't being serious right now."

Realizing he was genuinely upset, Carol felt like giggling. He was such a guy. All that ridiculous fame and notoriety and at his core he was just an American guy who liked to watch the boys of summer play a few innings. In a much more calm voice, she said, "I can't conform to be what you think I should be. I'm an attorney for the city of Richmond. If you don't like that, you don't have to stick around. You can go back to Nashville or wherever you think you need to go."

She started to walk past him so he wouldn't see the tears she could no longer contain. He grabbed her and pulled her to him, wrapping his arms around her. She struggled but he was stronger, so she finally relented. He held her until she stopped crying, then stepped back and framed her face with his hands.

"I'm sorry," he said, kissing each eye. "I'll see you Sunday." He kept her head tilted back and looked into her eyes. "I love you, Carol." She wrapped her arms around his neck and kissed him back.

He stepped back and ran his hands down her arms until he gripped her hands. "Pray with me," he said, clearing his throat. "Father God, I'm asking You, I'm begging You to watch over Carol. Protect her against this madman, Lord. Guide the police in stopping him before he kills another woman, and, God, ease Carol's heart. Remind her You're with her all the time. Amen."

After he left, she sat at her desk, looking out the window as the room slowly darkened with the gathering storm. As a wind tunnel of leaves swished passed her window, she picked up her phone and called Mitch. When he answered she said, "There's no reason for you two to sit outside in this. Come inside, please."

"I got called to a crime scene," he said.

Carol frowned. "Wait. If you're there, then who's outside of my house?"

"Jack."

Carol clenched her teeth so hard she was surprised she didn't hear her jaw crack. "I'm not comfortable with that."

"Come on, Carol. Jack knows his job. You've got nothing to worry about."

"I'm hanging up now, Mitch. Get back over here as soon as you can." She hung up, then tried to call Bobby's new cell phone, hoping to catch him before his plane took off, but she got a recording from the carrier saying that there was trouble with the signal.

As she put the receiver down, she heard the distant rumble of thunder, and couldn't shake the eerie feeling in her gut.

Shaking off her mood, she walked through the house and turned on the lights. It was early still, but the dark clouds rolling in were giving the city a dusk-like appearance. She made her way into the kitchen to start a pot of coffee, pressing against her temples to ward off the headache that threatened.

She rubbed her arms to battle the chill that descended upon her house, and tried Bobby's cell again, getting the same recording. She didn't know how to get in touch with his pilot, or even where to call at the airport, knowing the security that he and his private plane would be under, so she didn't even try.

Thunder rumbled overhead, causing her to jump again. After the irritation passed, she laughed at herself. She was being ridiculous. Okay, Carol, she thought to herself, snap out of it.

She dug through the drawers and cabinets in her kitchen until she found some candles. Then she pulled out spare saucers and put the candles on them in case the power went out. She worked mechanically, wanting nothing more than to keep her hands busy. When she finished, she stepped back and looked at what she'd just done and laughed at herself, realizing she'd prepared about ten candles.

Shaking her head, she found a pack of matches and put them in her pocket, then poured herself a cup of coffee and decided to sit out on the front porch, Jack or no Jack. This was her house, nothing was going to happen tonight, and she was going to sit on her porch and watch the storm roll in.

♫ ♫ ♫ ♫

CHAPTER 30

Personal Journal Entry

May 11

What gave it away? How did she find out?

In a way, it's a good thing. I told him. Now HE knows that Carol knows. She'll be next. She has to be.

In another way, it's disastrous. This is the end. There can be no others. No more fakes. No more counterfeits.

Just her. Just Carol Mabry. Her in all her original glory.

She'll feed his need to kill and he should quiet down for a long time. He can settle into day to day life here in Richmond as a normal person and not as Richmond Red.

I even know how he'll do it. He'll just go to her house and bide his time. No one will suspect him. No one ever suspects him. He's invisible. He's like a puff of smoke. He's like a ghost. They search and search and he is right in front of them but they can't even see him.

I'll be left to mourn again, and mourn I will because I love her. Like before, I'll hope against hope she's the last one.

♫ ♫ ♫ ♫

SHE lasted half an hour. She couldn't see Jack Gordon – didn't even know if he was still out there – but she felt very conspicuous sitting out there. She felt as if she could almost feel him watching her. She gritted her teeth and forced herself to sit for fifteen minutes, then, because she felt impatient with herself for this nervousness, she forced herself to sit for fifteen more.

Finally, she allowed herself to go back inside. She wandered through her house, wondering what to do. She normally worked or played with Lisa. But Lisa wasn't there, and she couldn't think. She couldn't concentrate on work. She thought about chopping vegetables for a light supper, but didn't feel hungry.

Instead, she went upstairs and changed out of her work clothes and into jeans, a button down shirt, and a pair of hiking boots. She would go out to the ranch and take this opportunity to talk to Harriet without Lisa's presence. They had some talking to do, some forgiving to do, and some healing to do.

On her way to the front door, she grabbed her purse and keys. When she opened the door, the wind that had picked up since she'd left the porch nearly blew her backward and back inside. It was almost fully dark now, an hour earlier than usual, and the streetlights had yet to come on. She reached behind her and automatically flicked on the porch light, then walked down the driveway to her Jeep.

The more she thought about talking with Harriet, the more she felt a sense of urgency. Her fingers fumbled a few times before she finally inserted the key into the ignition. The interior of the car flashed with blinding light from the lightning that continued to battle above, transforming everything she could see to sharp shades of black or silver. At last the key found home and she gave it a hard turn.

Nothing. She tried again, but there wasn't even the sound of the motor trying to start. No clicks. No moaning complaints. No weak or dimmed lights on the dash. Nothing. She pulled the lever to pop the hood, then got out and walked around to the front, lifted the hood, and used the miniature flashlight on her key chain to look at the engine, not really knowing what she was looking for.

She didn't know anything about the inner workings of a car, but it didn't take an expert to know that there were cables that were supposed to be attached to the battery. Hers were gone. They weren't knocked loose and dangling down somewhere. They were cut off and lengths of the cable were simply missing.

She felt the hairs on the back of her neck rise before she heard the voice.

"Got a problem, Carol?" Jack asked at her ear.

She jumped and started to turn until she realized how close he stood behind and just beside her. "Yes, Jack, as a matter of fact I do. Did you see anyone messing with my Jeep?" she asked, refusing to let him see her nerves.

The first drop of rain hit the side of her temple. "It's starting to rain," he said, ignoring her question. "Go back inside, and we'll see about your car after the storm lets up."

Carol turned then, hoping he'd move out of her way, but he stood close enough that she could feel his breath on her face. She tried to step around him, but he shifted, leaving her trapped between him and the front grill.

She lifted her chin, refusing to let this man intimidate her. The rain started to fall harder now, and the wind whipped her hair out of the pins holding it in place, blowing strands around her head. "Move, Jack, so I can get out of the rain," she said.

She lifted a hand to get some hair out of her eye, but he moved faster, snatching the bothersome strand. She jerked her head away, but he still held the strand of hair. She only succeeded in causing a sharp pain to streak through her temple from the force of the hair being pulled at its roots.

"How about this? How about I go inside with you?" He grinned in a way that she felt sure was meant to come off as charming but ended up looking smarmy. "Get you out of those wet clothes. Then we could both stay warm and dry."

Her first instinct was to respond with anger, but she had a feeling that would have the wrong effect on him. Instead, she decided to deflate his ego and started laughing. "Are you serious?"

Some of the laughter left his eyes and they started to harden. Carol suddenly realized that just maybe she should have gone with anger. "Don't try to deny you want me as much as I want you, Carol. I've seen it in your eyes."

"Get over yourself, Jack. The only thing I've ever wanted from you was for you to go away." She tried to brush past him.

She wasn't expecting it. After all, he was a cop. He was one of the good guys. If she had thought it were possible, she would have been prepared for the blow, been able to block it. Instead, she found herself being knocked backward from the force of the back of his hand connecting with her cheek.

She lay there, staring at the black sky above her, feeling the raindrops hitting her face, and wondering what had just happened. Suddenly, Jack's face appeared above her. The rage in his eyes made him nearly unrecognizable.

"Some women like it rough, Carol. I really didn't think you were that type, but if you want to play it that way, I'm game." His grin slipped back into place, but it looked distorted.

Her senses returned the second his hand grabbed her arm, and she started fighting as the skies opened up and let loose their downpour. The rain helped rather than hindered, making her harder to grab onto and hold as her skin became wet. She finally broke completely free of him, knocking him down with a kick to the shin, then ran to the house. She still had her keys in her hand, and by feel found her house key just as she reached the door. She inserted it into the lock just as he reached her, grabbing her waist from behind.

It was part of his job training to learn how to restrain people who otherwise would rather not be restrained, and no matter how hard she fought him or kicked him or struggled, he was bigger and knew what he was doing. Within seconds he had her pinned against the wall of her house, her face pressing into the brick, her hands held behind her at a painful angle with only his right hand holding her wrists in a vice grip, while he unlocked the door with his left hand.

She closed her eyes and gathered her strength, not willing to let the circumstances overwhelm her, not willing to pay attention to or concentrate on the fact that this man was Mitch's partner. Right now, he was just some insane guy who was going to hurt her if she didn't do something about it.

She heard the door swing open and almost had herself under control. Her breathing was starting to even out, and she couldn't actually taste the coppery bitter panic any more. Screaming would do no good with the force of the rain pouring outside, so she tried to remember everything her father had taught her about hand-to-hand combat, Army style. One lesson that suddenly stood out was that no matter how big a guy was, if you broke his foot, or even just a toe on his foot, he'd go down.

She concentrated on that, and let her body relax, giving Jack the idea that she was now complying. She said a quiet prayer, then gave a husky laugh. "You scratch my pretty face on this brick, Jack-O, and you'll learn what it really means to play the game rough," she said in a sexy voice that hinted at promises.

Jack froze, and though he didn't let go of her hands, he did loosen his grip enough for her to step back away from the wall. She turned her head and looked at him, licking her lips, hoping the porch light wasn't strong enough for him to see that loathing, not desire, filled her eyes.

He gave her that cocky, boy-next-door grin. "I knew it," he said. "You just like to play games, don't you?"

If her arms hadn't been twisted at such an angle, she would have given a coy shrug of her shoulders. Instead, she smiled back, sure that her face would crack with the pressure, and let her eyes roam down his body, checking to see what he was wearing on his feet. Leather loafers. No match for the hiking boots she wore. She forced her eyes back up his body slowly, as if inspecting the merchandise, then made her way back up to his eyes. "Who doesn't?"

He let go of one of her hands and let her turn around, pulling her closer to him. "We are going to have us some fun tonight, baby," he said with unsavory glee, and started to lower his head to kiss her.

She stepped back from him, grabbed the wrist of the hand still holding hers, lifted his arm above her head, pivoted on one heel until her back was to him, and with all the force she could muster, she brought the heel of her other foot down on his toes. He screamed in pain and collapsed on the ground. Without waiting to see how long it would be before he got back up, Carol ran.

She flew down her steps and into her yard, undecided about where to go, when she remembered that Houston Bradford was home. She turned and started to slip on the wet grass, and just as she got her footing back, he tackled her from behind with the force of a lineman.

He screamed profanities in her ear, and while she fought, he rolled her over onto her back and straddled her, the rain continuing to beat down on them. He grabbed her hands and forced them down to the wet ground near her head, trapping her legs with his. She was completely immobile now, and couldn't see his face from the glare of the porch light behind him.

He clamped her hands above her head with his left hand. His intentional restraint brought his face close to hers. Rain ran off his nose and dripped into her eyes. "Think you're pretty smart, don't you? Pretty clever in your boots. I bet you broke my toe."

Carol tasted the coppery panic again. She didn't swallow. Instead, she spit right in his eyes.

He didn't loosen his grip. He sat up straighter and carefully struck her right on the cheek with the back of his right hand. When she didn't make a sound he hit her again, making Carol gasp.

He wiped her saliva from his face and demanded, "Exactly how do you think this is going to play out, Carol? It's just you and me here. In what universe do I not get my way tonight?"

Carol stared at the outline of his face as he towered above her, backlit by the porch light. In that very heartbeat, all the pieces finally clicked into place.

The first murder took place just three short weeks after Jack Gordon moved to Richmond from DC. Mitch had said there had been a "he-said-she-said" dispute that hadn't gone Jack's way. Carol suddenly realized there must be a lot more to the story than that. Even so, Jack's friends in high places in Richmond managed to secure him a position as a Homicide Detective.

But he was already decompensating. Probably the incident in DC had provoked him. Jack was overly Alpha, not the type of man to ever accept responsibility for whatever he did to that unnamed woman in DC. The stress of the job loss, the stress of the move, and the stress of the loss of his social or family support system... it all added up.

Then the stress of her flat rejection obviously exceeded his ability to curb his murderous desires. He had become obsessed with her. He had inserted himself into the investigation. And now he would act out his sick fantasy at the cost of her life.

She had to be sure. "How does it play out, Jack? Does it play out with me spread eagle on my living room floor surrounded by red candles with a violin string around my neck?"

Even without seeing his face, she could tell that he smiled, savoring the idea. "Well, now. Is that what you want, honey?"

Suddenly, a dark figure blocked the light from the porch. Carol opened her mouth to scream as she watched the figure raise both arms high, holding onto something big, and bring it down hard. She felt Jack's whole two hundred and twenty pound frame jerk in reaction to something crashing into the back of his skull. He fell forward, propelled by the force of the blow, and his forehead crashed into hers, sending her into darkness.

♫ ♫ ♫ ♫

THEY'D driven halfway to the airport when Bobby made-up his mind. He turned the truck around and tried to use his phone, but got a recorded message about no available signal.

"Where are we going, daddy?" Lisa asked.

He reached over and ran a hand down her hair. "This storm is too rough for me to want to take off in the airplane, sugar. I'm taking you to spend the night at your grandma's, and we'll leave first thing in the morning."

Lisa looked a little disappointed, then she got excited. "I haven't got to spend the night at grandma's in a long, long time. We've been so busy since you got here," she said. "Then she was acting so weird because she's sad about grandpa."

"She's feeling better now. You know what? You staying there with her, just the two of you girls, that will really cheer grandma up." He hoped he was right and he prayed she was home.

The airport lay on the east side of Richmond while the ranch was on the west side. He had to go back through downtown. Coupled with the fact that it was nearly five o'clock on a Friday and the fierce storm had started to hit full force, the traffic suddenly slowed to a crawl.

Under normal circumstances, Bobby Kent considered himself a pretty easygoing guy. By design, he was slow to anger. He kept a strong grip on his temper and was rarely seen out of control. With the stress and strain he'd been under for the past month, on top of the fact that he couldn't get the fear in Carol's eyes out of his mind, he finally reached the point that he'd had enough.

The only thing that kept him from bellowing at the cars around him was the fact that his daughter sat in the seat next to him. He got off the interstate at the first exit he came to and started to work his way through the back streets. He was a native Virginian, born and raised in Richmond, and had family who had lived there before the interstate highways were built. Some of his uncles refused to use them. He remembered every back street, every shortcut that he'd ever used with his cousins while they were out joy riding through the city as teenagers. When he hit a traffic snarl, he merely turned at the next road and tried an alternate route.

By the time they made it to the ranch, the wind was starting to pick up and the sky had nearly completely darkened. He parked his truck next to his mother's and helped Lisa out of the cab. They found her sitting on her back porch, nursing a cup of coffee, when the two of them walked up.

"Hello mom," Bobby said.

"Bobby. What are you two doing out on a night as bad as this?"

He sat in the chair next to her and stretched his long legs out in front of him, trying not to let the nerves show. "We were on our way to Atlanta, but the weather's too bad for flying. I was wondering if Lisa could stay here with you tonight."

Harriet looked at Lisa with a smile. "I'd love to have her. It's been a little lonely out here lately."

"Thanks, mom." He stood back up. "Lisa, be good for your grandma. Mom, I'll be by early to get her."

"Tell Carol I said hello, Bobby," Harriet said. Before Bobby stepped completely off the porch, she stood and said, "Wait. I need to talk to you."

He hid his impatience and waited for her to reach him. She left Lisa on the porch playing with a kitten that had materialized at her feet. She walked down to his truck with him. She put a hand on his arm and looked up at him as the first few raindrops began to fall. "I meant what I said after Robert's funeral, Bobby. That wasn't just a grieving woman speaking. We were wrong for what we did, and I was wrong about my opinion of her for all those years."

"Thanks, mom," he said, and brushed his lips on her cheek. "Enjoy your granddaughter. See you in the morning."

The traffic had thinned out considerably for his drive back to town, but it still took him twenty minutes. As hard as it was raining, he couldn't go too fast for fear of losing control of the truck, but the urgency he felt nearly overwhelmed him. Something was very wrong. He could feel it in his gut.

Carol needed him. He knew it as if she'd picked up the phone and called him. The strokes of the windshield wipers beat a cadence to the ticking of the clock, telling him that he needed to hurry – hurry before he was too late.

The rain had tapered off somewhat by the time he reached his neighborhood. He knew more was coming. They'd just seen the beginning of the storm.

Panic skirted on the edges of his mind when he pulled into the driveway and saw the hood of Carol's Jeep propped up and the front door to her house open. He practically tore the truck door off its hinges with the haste of his exit from the truck. As fast as he could without slipping on the wet ground, he ran up the driveway. Her keys dangled in the lock on the door. He ran past them, then through the house, looking for her.

Every room was empty. Panic gripped his chest full force now. He went back and stood in the doorway of the house and looked out into the night, wondering what to do next. Praying for inspiration.

He heard the car before he saw it, the gunning of the engine, the squealing of tires – then it pulled to a screeching stop in front of the house, directly under the street light. Bobby recognized it as the sedan Mitch was supposed to be sitting in down the street. He saw the car door open and started marching across the yard.

As soon as his boot hit the grass, lightning lit up the sky. And he saw it. He froze. Though it couldn't have lasted for more than two seconds, the world around him was plunged into slow motion, and while the silver light danced around him, and the wind whipped his hair, he stared at the body lying on the ground not ten feet in front of him.

When the world fell back into sudden darkness, his mind cleared and he could move again. His boots slipped on the grass and he landed on his knees near the body. Another flash of lightning confirmed what his hands already knew.

It wasn't her.

Relief surged through him, temporarily replacing the fear. He looked up and saw Mitch standing over him, a flashlight in his hands pointed at the face of Jack Gordon, revealing eyes that stared blankly into the sky, a look of shocked surprise on his face.

Bobby's brain finally clicked into place and he surged to his feet. Gone was the panic and fear. In its place was deep, burning fury. "Where is she?" he screamed at Mitch.

With his face reflecting the shock of seeing his partner lying on the wet grass, Mitch took a step back from the man in front of him. "I don't know. What happened here?" he demanded.

Bobby stepped over Jack and grabbed Mitch by his shirtfront with both hands, giving him a hard shake. "How should I know? You were supposed to stay here and protect her!"

Mitch's feet actually came off the ground, but he did nothing to defend himself. "I had a call to a crime scene," he said. "I left Jack here."

Bobby pushed him away and watched Mitch struggle to keep from falling on the soggy ground. "You've got to be kidding me!"

Bobby put his hands on his hips and turned in a full circle, not even knowing where to go. He had her. Richmond Red had her. He knew on a deep instinctive level that time was not his friend right now. They needed to find them before drugs seeped through her veins and stopped her heart. He needed to find her before a violin string cut into the skin of her throat and cut off her air supply. He needed to find her now.

The wind continued to rage around them, bringing with it the occasional flash of blinding silver light as lightning warred above, sending rolling thunder to shake the earth. The very elements in the sky mimicked the emotions swirling through Bobby.

He needed to think. He looked at the house behind him, but knew that if he went back in there he might destroy some piece of evidence that could be used to find her. Instead, he turned his back on Mitch and marched across the lawn to his own house.

♫ ♫ ♫ ♫

AGONIZING pain squeezed Carol's head like a vise, strong enough to make her stomach roll. She tried to raise a hand to it, to rub her temples and ease some of the pain, but she couldn't. Something restrained her hands so that she couldn't move them.

With a moan she opened her eyes and blinked in the darkness. She lay on a hard floor. Her clothes were wet and muddy. Her hands were tied behind her back.

Then it came flooding back and she remembered. She remembered Jack's face above hers, the figure swinging something behind him. Her pulse fluttered and she tried to get her bearings. Why couldn't she move?

It was too dark. She couldn't see anything. Then lightning flashed outside a large picture window on the far wall and she spotted the outline of a piano in the dazzling glare. Bobby's piano.

With a sob she tried to sit up. She rolled until she could get to her knees, the movement causing the vise in her head to twist a little tighter and nausea to roll in her stomach. She bowed her head for a moment and tried to push the pain into the background. She'd done it before. She'd battled headaches most of her adult life and knew how to force them back.

When she felt like she could lift her head without it threatening to fall off, she looked around but still couldn't see anything. Then the flare of a match nearly blinded her.

"I fought him," Rhonda explained as she walked around the room and lit candles that had been placed on every surface. Carol recognized them as the candles she'd prepared at her house in case the power went out. Rhonda had carried them all to Bobby's house. How long had she been unconscious?

Why was she tied up?

"For weeks, now, I fought him. He's obsessed with you. Carol this and Carol that. Carol in the coffee shop and Carol here and Carol there and Carol on the news and Carol in the papers and Carol in the meeting with Maurice or the Governor or in open court. Carol, Carol, Carol! It was maddening."

Carol wasn't even aware that Rhonda knew Jack Gordon. How close were they? Were they related or in some kind of relationship? Or were they a team, partners in crime, a murderous pairing of beauty and the beast?

"Tonight was just the last straw. He just kept on and on until I actually wanted to kill him." Rhonda nodded exactly once, then finished lighting the next to last candle before she walked to stand directly in front of Carol.

Carol felt her eyebrows furrow. She remembered the tall figure swinging something heavy with great force. She wondered if, in fact, Jack Gordon was dead as a result of that blow.

"And then you and me, well… we worked that Kennedy case together. Hour after hour, meal after meal, all that time with you and he was like a caged animal who suddenly learned how to unlock the door."

"How…?" Carol swallowed. "How do you even know Jack?"

The candlelight gave the room an odd glow. Shadows of the flames danced on the walls and the black framed glasses Rhonda wore reflected the flickering candlelight. Carol couldn't see the woman's eyes, and wished she'd move so she could.

Rhonda lit the last candle, swished the matchstick out, and tossed it onto the saucer beside the now burning candle. Then she asked, "Jack who?"

Carol nervously licked her dry lips and began to work at the ropes binding her wrists. She did not understand this situation. Her head throbbed making it difficult to concentrate. She had no idea why she was tied up, why her candles were at Bobby's house, or what Rhonda was talking about. She needed more information. "Who, Rhonda? Who are you talking about?"

Rhonda tipped her head back and laughed. When she looked back down, the laughter vanished. She tapped the side of her head with a finger. "Rob, silly."

"Rob?" Carol's eyes filled with tears. "I don't understand, Rhonda. Who's Rob?"

Rhonda crouched down and lifted Carol's chin to look her in the eye. "My mother used to have this Christmas candle set with red candles that she set up in holly and pine branches. When I was seven, I was playing with the candles and knocked one over. The dried twigs caught fire quickly and in minutes, our whole house was engulfed. My dad died trying to save my brother, Rob. All I had left was my mom."

She pinched Carol's chin and moved her face slowly to the left, then back to the right. "That guy really got you good. Nothing a little makeup can't fix though."

Carol felt a sudden emptiness in the pit of her stomach. "Thank you for saving me, Rhonda. I don't know what would have happened if you hadn't come along."

Rhonda laughed. "I didn't save you. That was Rob. He was so angry that another man was touching you."

Carefully, slowly, she said, "I thought Rob died when you were little. You just said he died in the fire with your father."

Rhonda whispered, "I thought he died, too. But then he started talking to me the night after his funeral."

The full implications of what this woman had just said hit Carol. They had it all wrong. Everyone had it wrong. There wasn't a male serial killer with multiple personalities, one of which was a female personality. Rhonda was a female serial killer with multiple personalities, one of which was a male personality. Carol understood that she was mere hours or maybe bare minutes away from meeting her Maker. Carol never let Lisa down before, but she didn't know a way out of this one.

Lisa's life raced through Carol's mind. How tiny she was at birth, her first steps, the first time she sat on a horse, running into her father's arms for the first time in her life, singing in front of the church while Carol played in the orchestra, holding her grandfather's hand. It was as if she flipped through a stack of pictures, and the last one in the pile was Lisa lying in her bed, eyes filled with grief and worry when she asked Carol if she was going to die, too.

"Why are you doing this?" she asked in a near whisper.

Rhonda rose to her feet and walked in a circle around Carol while she spoke. "Every time I fall in love with someone, he kills her. The first few times I didn't know it was coming, but I started looking for signs and learned how to appease him with substitutes. It worked before, but the exposure to you was so constant, I could find no peace." She stepped back in front of her. "I tried to hide how I felt for you, but he knew. I can't hide anything from him."

She gripped her head with both of her hands and squeezed. "Shut up!

Shut up! Just shut up!" she growled, spittle flying out of her mouth.

When she looked at Carol again, the angle was just right so that she could see deep blue eyes shining in the candlelight. Rhonda had brown eyes. Was she wearing contacts? Carol could have sworn that just a moment ago her eyes were brown. But, in the dim flickering candlelight, she must have been mistaken.

Rhonda walked over to the piano and picked up a black wig and put it on. She expertly applied a fake mustache and goatee, then removed the glasses to complete the look. Carol started sobbing, knowing it was hopeless. She bowed her head. "Please don't do this to me, Rhonda. Oh, God, please don't let her do this to me." One of the knots tying her hands came loose, and Carol had to stop herself from giving it away. She began to work the next knot.

Rhonda knelt next to her and ran a hand down Carol's hair. She cupped her cheek with her hand. Her voice sounded deeper, like a male tenor voice. "Rhonda had to shut up for a while. I'm Rob. We've met before a few times, but I was wearing my sister, the puppet, so you probably don't recognize me."

"You don't have to do this, Rob. You can stop this right now." Carol tried to keep her voice calm and soothing.

Rob, speaking through Rhonda's body, said, "I don't *have* to do anything. I do whatever I want to do. You know what I want to do right now?"

Carol knew, but she had to stall him. It was lame, but she couldn't think of anything else. "I'm really thirsty. Do you want to share a cup of tea or some water with me?"

"I'm not thirsty. What I really, really want to do is watch you die, Carol Mabry. That's what I really want to do." The bloodthirsty look in Rhonda's eyes terrified Carol and she momentarily froze.

Finding her voice at last, she asked, "Why do you hate me?"

Rhonda laughed a little bark of laughter. "I don't hate you. You're less than nothing to me. But my sister thinks she's in love with you. She's sick, see. I keep trying to fix her and she keeps messing up and I have to come back and fix it. The bottom line is, you have to die. She doesn't deserve you."

The serial killer everyone knew as Richmond Red reached into the pocket of her black pants and pulled out a capped syringe. "This will make it all feel like a dream. You won't be scared anymore. In fact, some women die with smiles on their faces. It's really quite beautiful."

As she uncapped the syringe, the last knot on Carol's wrist came loose.

♫ ♫ ♫ ♫

BOBBY stood in the kitchen with his hands braced on the counter and his head bowed. Police cars, both marked and unmarked, slowly filled the street, but no one even knew where to start to try to find Carol.

He'd just found his life, and it was about to be ripped away from him.

He pushed himself away from the counter and walked to his living room. He sat in the dark and rubbed his face with his hands. Every cell in his body wanted to be doing something, but there was nothing he could do except wait. Wait until he got the phone call that they'd found her body.

He put his hands back down and leaned back in the chair, staring into the dark. It took several minutes for his exhausted mind to register what he was seeing, and he slowly sat up, feeling his heart rate increase as the adrenaline started to flow.

He'd left his house with the intention of not coming back for three days. He'd walked through the house, as he did whenever he was going out of town, and went through every room, making sure lights were out. His father had been a stickler for that, and the first time he'd come back from tour and found out that he'd left the light on in his bathroom, he'd kept looking over his shoulder, waiting for his father to tell him to cut himself a switch.

Now he was staring at the doorway to his music room, and coming through the crack in the bottom of the door was flickering light. Not the bright halogens he'd had installed in there, but a softer, yellow light. Light like a candle would make.

He very quietly got up from where he was sitting. Carol might still be alive. It's possible that he could still save her life. He didn't want to waste even one second of time to go outside and find Mitch so he headed straight for the doorway of the music room.

He put his ear to the door and heard voices. He understood a few words here and there, and then he heard the sound of Carol sobbing. He closed his eyes to the wave of relief that washed over him. She was still alive.

Trying to decide the best course of action to take, he finally settled on surprise. He had no weapon, and didn't want to take precious seconds to go upstairs and retrieve a weapon from his gun safe, so instead, he threw open the door hard enough that it bounced against the wall, and stepped into the room.

There were candles everywhere, giving the room a bright, eerie glow, the smell of the burning wax nearly overwhelming. In the center of the room, Carol knelt on her knees, her hands behind her back, while a dark haired woman who looked sort of like Rhonda Regalman but with a fake beard and mustache uncapped a syringe.

The sound of the door hitting the wall echoed through the room, causing both women to jump. Bobby watched Carol shake her hands and the rope that bound her wrists fell at her feet. As Bobby ran forward, Carol surged to her feet, hitting Rhonda square in the chest with her shoulder, knocking her backward.

She didn't fall to the floor, however, just stumbled until she regained her balance, then with a feral roar, turned and ran toward Bobby, her hands curled into claws. He stepped further into the room and braced himself for the onslaught. As soon as her body hit his, the force of her weight knocked him into the wall behind him.

"Get out of here, Carol! Go get Mitch. He's at your house," Bobby yelled, satisfied when she ran past him.

Rhonda was out of control. She bared her teeth and spittle flew out of her mouth while she screamed obscenities. She lashed out at him with fists and fingernails. Years of ingrained southern upbringing kept him from retaliating against a woman for about two seconds, then a baser instinct kicked in, and he began to fight back.

The first closed fisted blow knocked her backward. Before she could regain her balance, he landed another one on the side of her cheek, sending her to her knees. She supported herself with her hands and looked up at him like a rabid dog, growling deep in her throat. He was angry now, angry because she'd tried to hurt Carol.

Bobby saw the violin wire on the ground near where Carol had knelt. He assumed that she had planned to use it to squeeze the life out of the mother of his child. Snatching it up, he knelt and put his knee between Rhonda's shoulder blades, then lifted her wrists, intending to tie them together. She started to fight again, so he grabbed a handful of her hair, drew her head back, then slammed it forward onto the wooden floor. She kicked and screamed. He slammed her head into the floor again, harder.

She lay still now, and he neither knew nor cared about whether or not she was conscious. He wrapped the wire around her wrists over and over like a rodeo cowboy tying a roped calf. Satisfied that she wouldn't be able to get herself loose anytime soon, he sat down a few feet from her and wiped his mouth, seeing blood there from a wound he hadn't realized he'd sustained.

He heard the sound of them running through the house. Then Carol appeared at the doorway. He stood when he saw her, a need growing deep inside him to touch her, to make sure she was okay. She stopped just at the threshold, took in the scene within seconds, and hurled herself toward him before Mitch even made it into the room.

Nothing had ever felt so good in his life as when Carol's arms came around him. He held her so tightly that he briefly worried he'd smother her. But she laughed and cried and kissed him, then pulled back and looked at him, then kissed him again.

"I thought I was dead," she said, and pulled back again to look at his face. "Oh, Bobby," she said, the tears starting to flow again, "I thought she was going to kill me. All I could do was think of Lisa and pray that God wouldn't let her kill me."

Bobby squeezed her tighter, not able to speak because his throat was choked with the emotions that threatened to overwhelm him. He put an arm over her shoulder and walked her from the room, brushing past the innumerable police officers that suddenly filled his house, and headed outside.

Jack Gordon's body lay in the yard of her home, his corpse covered with a tarp like some old farm implement the farmer didn't want to rust in the rain. Carol averted her eyes and tucked her face into Bobby's shoulder, leaning on him and trusting him to guide her back to her house.

The rain had started falling again, but the wind had died down and the storm wasn't as violent, at least not in their vicinity. They walked across the lawn toward her porch and he took a seat. In seconds, he had Carol in his lap and they watched the police move between the two houses performing their duties.

He had started to calm down and think rationally again, and loosened his grip on her a bit. "Are you hurt?" he asked. "Do you need to go in an ambulance?"

Carol shook her head. "I'd rather not go in an ambulance. Can you drive me?"

"Of course, Darlin'. Let me check in with Mitch and make sure he doesn't need you."

"I'll go inside and clean up," she said.

He cupped her cheek with his hand and kissed her eyelids. "Why don't you call Henry and see if he can come here?"

Around a sniffle, she agreed. "That would be so much better than going there."

♫ ♫ ♫ ♫

CAROL sent Henry a text asking him to come over as soon as possible. Within seconds, he called and she briefly explained what happened. He told her it would take him a few minutes to get there.

She went inside to clean up. As she stared at her face in the mirror of her bathroom, she wanted to put makeup on, but she knew Henry would probably want to look at the bruises on her face. Instead, she went back downstairs without her usual shield. Her hip ached, and she didn't know if she'd hurt it while fighting Jack, or if Rhonda had done something when she lay there unconscious. There was no telling, really.

She headed for her kitchen, wanting a pot of tea.

From the black dust covering the counters, she could see the police had dusted for fingerprints. While the water came to a boil, she worked at cleaning it off. She wanted her life back in order, and might as well start in the kitchen.

She knew she was avoiding talking to Bobby. She didn't know how to tell him about Jack, but it was something she couldn't keep to herself. Or keep from him. She also knew she had to tell Mitch, and knew that telling him would hurt her more than anything.

She poured the steaming hot water over the tea leaves, then left the kitchen to find Bobby. He was on the front porch where she'd left him, talking to Mitch. She took his hand as she lowered herself into the chair next to him.

"Just heard word that she's regaining consciousness. I have a couple of uniforms taking her to the hospital." Mitch looked at Carol. "Our force lost a good detective tonight."

Carol frowned. "Lost?"

"Jack Gordon. The M.E. said his skull was crushed from behind. Looked like a struggle went on in your front yard there. He clearly died protecting you. Did you see what she hit him with?"

She didn't want to think about Jack or what he had done, but she felt like she might fall apart if she didn't say something. So she started speaking quietly.

"He didn't die protecting me. If he had been protecting me instead of trying to rape me, he might still be alive."

She barely recognized Mitch's voice when he demanded, "What?"

She told them everything. She told them about her cut battery cables and how Jack had thrown her against the brick wall beside her front door. She told them about how he had straddled her and hit her. She told them about stomping on his foot and spitting in his face. She told them everything, feeling Bobby's hand tense as she went on with her story, noticing both men and their excruciating silence as she neared the end. By the time she finished, tears streamed down her face. Suddenly overwhelmed by everything that had happened, she covered her face with her hands and fought back the urge to collapse into a sobbing heap.

Mitch stood up the second she finished her story, kicking the porch railing, then he stopped and ran his hands through his hair. "You tried to tell me, didn't you? I'm sorry, Carol. I'm so sorry."

He strode off the porch and walked next door. Bobby ran a hand down her back and she raised her head. He gently brushed the hair from her face and kissed her forehead. "I love you, Carol."

She nodded and pressed her lips together, trying to keep the tears back, and let him gather her into his arms.

♫ ♫ ♫ ♫

ABOUT five minutes after Mitch took their statements, Henry stepped onto the porch. Carol sat on the chair next to Bobby, her hand in his. She sat up straight. "Hi," she said. "Thank you for coming."

"Hi yourself." He sat in one of the vacant chairs, set his bag on the ground next to him, and stretched his legs out in front of him. "Well," he said with a deep sigh, "I've had quite a day. What's been going on around here?"

Carol laughed as she slowly stood. "Come inside, Henry. I need you to look at my head and my hip."

"I had a feeling," he said gently. "Though I'd have preferred you to get in an ambulance and come to me."

"Quit picking at me, Henry, I've had a rough night."

He stared at her, then nodded his head. "Go on inside. Put on a robe so I can look at your hip." He bent down to retrieve his bag and looked at Bobby. "What about you?"

"I'm fine."

"Good. We'll be right back out."

They went into the kitchen because that room had the most light, and Henry cleaned Carol's wounds while she told him the story. He asked no questions, just letting her speak. After he finished patching up her face, he poked and prodded at her hip until she thought she would scream at him, then shined a flashlight in her eyes until she was sure she would go blind.

"What about your shoulders? Did he hurt them when he was restraining you?" he asked, lifting one of her arms and rolling it around. She didn't realize they hurt until he pulled it behind her. She sucked in her breath and bit down on her lip.

He finally quit messing with her, then poured them each a fresh cup of tea. "Your hip's bruised. You have a moderate concussion. Your arms are going to be really sore for a few days while the muscles heal. Other than that, you're fine."

Bobby walked in during the middle of his diagnosis. "What do we do about the concussion?"

"If she gets dizzy or starts to feel nauseated, call me. Other than that, don't do anything." He drained his cup, and they watched as a wave of exhaustion wash over him and manifested in a tremendous yawn. "I'm going to go back to my apartment. I really did have a hard day." He re-packed his bag and stood, kissing Carol on the top of her head. "Call me if you need me."

"Thanks, Henry."

"I'll have my secretary send you my bill." He stopped in front of Bobby and held his hand out. "See you around, cowboy."

Bobby smiled and shook his hand. "Yeah, see you doc."

Carol put her head on the table. "I want Lisa," she said.

"She's probably already in bed. We'll go out and get her first thing in the morning," he said, sitting at the table next to her. Carol nodded and felt her eyes drift closed. "Go on up to bed, Carol. Mitch came back over and said he'll come by tomorrow with the statements for us to sign."

She sat up and ran her hands over her face. "Will you stay here tonight? I don't really want to be alone."

He grinned. "Thanks for the offer. I think I can find my normal guest room. Besides, I have no idea how much longer the police are going to be combing through my underwear drawer over there. "

"I'm going to take something for my headache. It will probably knock me out," she said. She stood and squeezed his shoulder as she walked past him.

"Okay, Darlin'," he said. "Call out if you need me."

♫ ♫ ♫ ♫

BOBBY Kent opened his eyes in an unfamiliar place and found a tall, lean man about his age and about his height standing at the foot of his bed. The man had a broad chest and shoulders and lean arms with lean muscles. He had faint scars on his chin and at his hairline. They were only visible because of his dark tan and close cropped hair. The man stood there holding a cup of tea, watching him, just watching him, with a perfectly blank expression.

The man spoke and said, "You're in a guest room at Carol Mabry's house."

"What?" Bobby asked, only because the statement was not the answer to the first question he would have asked and it jarred him.

He sat straight up and looked around, getting his bearings. The bright Virginia morning sunlight shone through the window. There was a humid smell in the air, though the storm had passed. The events of the previous night began to crowd his mind.

The man spoke again. "You looked disoriented. I wake up like that a lot. I'm Nick, by the way. We haven't met."

"Nick? What are you doing here?"

Nick Williams shrugged. "Apparently, nothing. I hear you did it already. Tea?"

Nick handed Bobby a cup of hot tea with a lemon wedge floating in it. Bobby asked, "No coffee?"

Nick shook his head. "Never touch the stuff. Want to tell me what went down last night?"

Bobby set the tea on the bedside table. Married to Carol's best friend or not, he hadn't decided whether he liked this man yet. "Nick, no offense, but you still haven't told me why you're here."

Nick nodded. "Carol and I go way back. Went to high school together if you can believe that. About a year ago, she did me a favor. It was kind of a big favor. I came because she asked me to. Got here as soon as I could."

"Did Carol let you in?"

Nick grinned. It was an ironic grin. "Carol's still sleeping. Must have taken one of her headache pills. Lisa's at your folk's ranch. That was a good move, by the way. Anyway, I thought just us boys could have a chat. So, Bobby... you go by Bobby?"

Bobby nodded.

"So what went down here last night Bobby?"

"You seem to already know what went down, Nick."

Nick nodded. "I don't know what you think went down."

Bobby Kent remembered Carol saying that a Roman Legion couldn't touch her once Nick Williams stood guarding her. Taking in this enigmatic man in these few waking minutes, Bobby suddenly understood what she meant and believed her. Something about the way he moved spoke volumes about years of training and combat experience. Nick moved like a male Jen Thorne. Bobby suddenly knew, without a doubt, that this man was armed to the teeth with concealed weaponry and could turn just as deadly as a viper if provoked to violence.

"Well, a crazy woman tried to kill Carol. She killed a cop right there in the front lawn and kidnapped her and had her tied up in my music room next door. She was about to drug her and strangle her when I got there."

Nick picked up the discarded tea and blew on it quietly, then took a sip. "How did 150 pound Rhonda Regalman get the drop on the 220 pound cop? I assume he was Carol's protection detail?"

Bobby found his jaw had clenched. "The cop was assaulting Carol."

Nick nodded and looked at Bobby. "How do you feel about the fact he's dead now, Bobby?"

That stopped him. He searched his heart and tried to put a name to his feelings. "I'm not exactly sad about it."

Nick nodded again. "That sounds about right. So how did you end up putting that 150 pound murdering serial killer in the hospital?"

Bobby closed his eyes. "I pounded her head into my hardwood floor until she stopped moving."

Nick sat down and met Bobby's eyes. "You should know that I've done far worse. It's taken me some time to come to terms with that. That's one of the reasons I wanted to talk to you alone this morning. I hope it isn't presumptuous of me."

Bobby could tell Nick spoke with deep sincerity. This wasn't some kind of stunt. This man wanted to help him in some way. Bobby said, "I'll let you know if it starts bothering me."

Nick grinned a toothless, tight-lipped grin. "Never been in a fight before, Bobby? Never put a woman in the hospital? Or anyone for that matter?"

"I was always tall coming up in school. Never got into a single fight. Later on I had security guards to keep overzealous fans back."

Nick nodded. "How do you feel about putting her in the hospital, Bobby?"

He really had to search his feelings. "She's crazy. She has a sickness."

Nick put his hand up in a halting motion. "We'll get there. I promise. That isn't the question yet. Tell me how you feel about the fact that you pounded a woman's head into your floor until she stopped moving. And I'll know if you lie to me, so don't bother."

Bobby stared at this strange man. "I'm not sorry."

Nick nodded sharply and exactly once. "Right. Okay, let's talk about her mental state. Hang on."

He reached into a cargo pocket and retrieved a dog-eared Soldier's Bible that had obviously seen better days. He opened it and flipped the pages carefully. Then he cleared his throat and said, "This is from the fifth book of Mark. 'And when He had come out of the boat, immediately there met Him out of the tombs a man with an unclean spirit, who had his dwelling among the tombs; and no one could bind him, not even with chains, because he had often been bound with shackles and chains. And the chains had been pulled apart by him, and the shackles broken in pieces; neither could anyone tame him. And always, night and day, he was in the mountains and in the tombs, crying out and cutting himself with stones.' You familiar with this passage?"

Bobby said, "It's the story of Christ casting out a legion of demons into a herd of pigs."

Nick closed his Bible. "Exactly. This guy cut himself and had a legion of voices in his head."

"Are you trying to tell me that the possibility that Rhonda Regalman might have been demon possessed should not escape my attention?"

Nick took a sip of tea. "I'm saying there are likely more things in heaven and earth, Bobby, than are dreamt of in your philosophies."

Bobby smiled, recognizing the paraphrase from Hamlet. "Don't take this the wrong way, Nick, but you're a bit of an odd duck."

Nick genuinely smiled for the first time since Bobby laid eyes on him. "Now you're catching on, Bobby."

Nick set his tea down and held his hand out. Bobby shook Nick's hand and the two communicated silently, in the way that men do, that they would be friends for now. When they dropped the hand shake, Nick said, "You did what you had to. In my opinion, you did what you were designed to do. You protected the life of the woman you love, the woman God made to be the mother of your child. Pretty soon, when the remorse comes and it feels like more than you can handle, try to remember that."

"Remorse, huh?"

Nick nodded with a very serious look on his face. "The inevitable remorse. I can't describe it, but you'll recognize it here in a few days. It's just horrible and appalling, but don't block it out or shut it away. Let yourself experience it. It's the only way you can heal. What you learn about yourself is going to surprise and sadden you."

Bobby shook his head. "I don't understand."

Nick nodded. "I know. But you will. Listen, Bobby, I know you don't know me very well – yet – but I want you to know that you can call me any time, night or day, day or night. You can talk to me about it. When you feel so depressed you feel like you can't deal with it, you need to remember that you can trust me to tell you the truth and not to judge you."

"Is that the message you felt called to deliver this morning, Nick?"

Nick put his hands in the pockets of his slacks. "Not at first. At first I was going to ask exactly when you intend to make an honest woman of my dear friend, Carol. And if you had no intentions of doing so, I intended to persuade you to change your mind."

Bobby smiled the same "star quality" sincere smile that had graced everything from billboards to magazine covers. "That can't happen soon enough, in my opinion."

Nick said, "See? You're still doing what God created you to do. How about you and I pray for a little while. You go first. Then we'll scare up some breakfast."

♫ ♫ ♫ ♫

Saturday, May 19th

CAROL stood at the end of her driveway and watched Lisa and Amy as they turned the corner. Lisa turned around and waved, then she and Amy took off at a run. Carol watched until she could no longer see them, then turned and started back up her driveway.

Her hip felt better, no longer causing a limp, and most of the bruises on her face had faded, leaving only one at the hairline of her forehead where Jack's head had smashed into hers. She'd taken the last week off work to heal, and felt rested, ready to get back to work and on with her life.

Things had begun to settle down around the city. The press had quit hounding her, and she hardly knew what to do without her cell phone ringing nonstop. She'd spoken with Maurice almost daily, getting current about the things going on at her office.

Mitch let her read the interview with Rhonda and the background report. She wondered, as she read all about what "Rob" had done over the years, how she could have missed working so closely with someone so malevolent.

Now she let her eyes drift to the pickup truck parked in the driveway next door. She cut across the yard, then rang the doorbell. There was no answer. She thought he must have earphones on so that he wasn't able to hear the doorbell.

Then she heard it. The soft sounds of a violin drifted through the spring air, the notes telling a poignant, sad story. They came from the back yard, so she walked around the house, stopping at the corner with her hands in her pockets and watched him.

He stood at the edge of his deck and played with his eyes closed. His fingers moved with absolute confidence over the strings of the instrument, bringing the song to life, making her heart ache, tightening her chest, and bringing tears to her eyes. The notes flowed around her, drawing her into the sorrow and grief, and she felt amazed that he could bring such emotion out of a simple song.

She stood there quietly when the song ended and watched him take the violin from under his chin and stare at it. He put it back in its case, laid the bow next to it, and closed it. She watched him look at his hands, then jumped back a little when he grabbed a chair next to him and with a yell, heaved it off the porch, where it hit the ground and bounced several feet from the force of the impact.

He whirled around and spotted her standing there and froze. They stared at each other for an eternity before he finally broke the spell.

"What?" he asked, his voice harsh with anger.

Confused, Carol closed the distance, stepping on the deck with him. She gestured at the chair. "What's wrong?"

His eyes were closed off from her, keeping her from being able to see what was going on in his mind. "I can't talk about it with you," he explained, sliding the glass door open and stepping inside.

"Well, I'd appreciate it if you would try."

She watched the life come back to his eyes and could see the banked fury there while he advanced on her. "I put a woman into the hospital because I beat her so badly, Carol," he snapped out. "I grabbed a handful of her hair and slammed her head onto a wooden floor hard enough to knock her out."

"So what?" she asked.

He stopped moving toward her and kicked the back of the couch. "So what?" His voice sounded quiet, strained, and very deep. "I'm not even sorry, is what. If I had to be completely honest, I wanted to kill her just as dead as a dinosaur. If I had it to do over again, that's exactly what I would have done!"

He turned his back on her. His hands closed into fists. "When I think about what almost happened..." He suddenly remembered waking up the next morning and having that strange conversation with Nick Williams. Nick had told him that a feeling of remorse was inevitable. He had told him that what he would learn about himself would both surprise and sadden him. Had he meant remorse for hurting the woman? Or had he meant remorse for not killing her?

When the realization hit Bobby, he felt himself instantly calm down. "I'm having a really hard time getting a grip on my feelings."

"Me, too," she admitted. "I'm jumpy and afraid." Her breath hitched.

He slipped an arm around her and pulled her to him. "I don't know what to do to let this go. I'm not the man I thought I was. I'm certainly not the man I want to be."

As she put her arms around his neck, she said, "I think we need to pray. Together. We need to pray for healing, but we also need to pray for Rhonda."

Pray for Rhonda? The woman he would rather had died by his hand?

The woman who had killed so many innocent people? Bobby let Carol go and shook his head. "How can you even say that?"

With a shrug, Carol replied, "Because Christ said to pray for our enemies. She's broken. Her mind is broken. I don't think she had any more control over what happened than we did."

He glared at her, his eyes narrowing. Was Rhonda's mind broken or was it her soul? Either way, she hadn't been fully in charge of her actions. "Good point," he relented, slipping his hands into his pockets and taking a deep breath. "I really don't know what it's like not to have control over my own faculties."

Carol walked over to him and reached up, cupping his cheek with her hand. "We have to forgive and release ourselves from any anger or hatred of her. We can't let what she did ruin our entire future."

She felt his smile a millisecond before she saw it. "I'm personally looking forward to our future," he said with a grin.

"So am I." She stepped back and gestured toward the couch. "Pray with me?"

CHAPTER 35

♫ ♫ ♫ ♫

Saturday, August 25

CAROL shook so badly that Aria Williams took the mascara wand from her hand and applied it to her lashes for her. She giggled with delight the entire time. Carol stared straight ahead, unable to see the humor, longing for this entire ordeal to end. "Tell me again how many people are out there," she whispered.

"Shush," Aria said, and tilted her face to the light. "It's only eight hundred."

She started to panic again and whispered a quiet prayer. "Dear God, help me, please."

"That's no big deal," Melody Montgomery said. "I've performed in front of sixty thousand before."

"Harmony's the one who has to sing in front of every Nashville star here. She's the one who should be nervous," Lori Bradford declared, putting a hand on the huge swell of her stomach.

Harmony Harper said, "All I have to do is face them and sing. Singing is my one for sure God given talent. Carol, on the other hand, has to turn her back to every last one of them and marry Bobby Kent."

Melody chuckled. "I'm so glad I eloped."

"It's times like this I remembered why I recommended Vegas," Jen Thorne said, adjusting her prosthetic arm under the sleeve of her dress.

"That's enough, girls," Carol's mother, Emily, chided from the corner of the room where she stood fastening a black and white polka dotted bow to Lisa's hair. "Carol, dear, this is a happy occasion, and long overdue I might add. You shouldn't be so nervous."

Carol leaned forward and looked in the mirror. "All I wanted was to get married, mom. I would have been happy doing it in my nice little church in Richmond. Not in this towering monstrosity in the heart of Nashville, where anyone with a name on a record label is sitting out there waiting to get a look at me."

Harriet Kent softly said, "Bobby just wants to show you off, dear." Carol looked over at Harriett who fastened a bow of the same design but opposite colors onto Amy's head. "You're beautiful. Let him enjoy it."

Lori said, "I say we hurry this thing up and get to the reception. I can't wait to get a bite of that cake!"

Carol's wedding cake could have qualified as one of the wonders of the modern world. Celebrity chef, Marcus Williams – who happened to be Nick's first cousin – had dodged a team of videographers for two weeks while constructing a monument to both music and law in icing and gum paste. The cake stood over 8 feet tall including the blown sugar music notes.

They heard a knock on the door a few seconds before Nick stuck his head through. "The photographer wants to come in here and take a few pictures. As soon as he's done, we're about ready for everyone to get in their places," he said. He sought Aria out of the crowd of women and gave her a wink, then shut the door.

Carol stood. The women oohed and ahhed over the dress she'd chosen. It was made from ivory satin with pearls sewn into an intricate design on the bodice. The sleeves came just off her shoulders and were long and tight, the skirt full, held out by the hoops she wore underneath it, with a long train that had pearls of the same design as the bodice sewn along it. She brushed at the skirt, knowing the pictures that would appear everywhere with her in it, and knew that even if she were dashing the hopes of millions of American women, as the gossip publications proclaimed, at least the dress helped her look good while doing it.

The photographer came in and made clucking noises while he snapped pictures of Emily putting the veil on her daughter's head, then of her wiping the tears from her eyes.

When the time came, Carol left the room, holding onto Lisa's hand, and found her father standing in the foyer of the church, nervously straightening his tie in the mirror there. She brushed his hands away and straightened it for him, then kissed his cheek, mindful of her lipstick. He wore a tuxedo like the other men in the groom's party instead of his uniform. He had insisted that he no longer wanted to put the uniform on since he had retired. At Carol's request, he wore tiny little ribbons on the lapel of his tuxedo in honor of the service he had rendered to his country. She thought he had never looked more heroic than in that moment.

"You ready, daddy?" she asked.

He squeezed her hand, then tucked it under his arm. "More than ready, love. You look so beautiful. You look like your mother on our wedding day."

Harmony elegantly glided down the side aisle to take her place at the front where she would sing. Melody walked down the center aisle first, beautiful in the russet colored dress, clutching a bouquet of lilies. Lori followed, then Jen, and finally Aria. Carol gave a small smile while she watched Lisa and Amy walk down the aisle hand-in-hand, then felt her stomach fall when she heard the music pause and the wedding march begin.

So many guests crowded inside that the huge church overflowed and people stood in the back. She felt a skitter of panic as she commenced down the aisle and stared into the sea of faces, few of whom she knew, most of whom she recognized. Then she got close enough to see Bobby, and saw the love in his eyes. By the time she made it to him, and her father placed her hand in his, she felt calm.

Harmony mesmerized the church with an original song she had written especially for this occasion. Carol barely heard the lyrics. She had lost herself in Bobby's eyes.

Her voice remained steady while she repeated her vows to him, and when his lips touched hers in a kiss that sealed the covenant, she knew the real meaning of true love.

The number of fans waiting outside the church surprised and touched her. They waved and smiled as the couple ran to the limo and, as soon as the door shut, they were in each other's arms. They had hardly seen each other in a month, and even with the lifetime ahead of them, they kissed until they made up for the lost time. The ride to Bobby's manager's house took about twenty minutes, and during the ride, they talked over each other, trying to catch up on lost time.

As they pulled through the gates of the property, he pulled her back into his arms and kissed her gently. "You are amazing," he said, then he set her away from him as the car came to a stop.

Carol stood in the corner of one of the rooms and watched hundreds of people milling about, enjoying delectable food among amazing and beautiful decorations. From another room came the sound of a fiddle, and one out of every three heads had a cowboy hat on it. She laughed at herself for the world that she'd gotten herself into. Then she watched as Melody approached and grabbed a *canapé* from a passing waiter and stood next to her.

"You're the talk of the town, Carol," she said, nibbling on the spinach and pastry.

"Much to my dismay," she said.

"Don't worry. James was too, two years ago. It dies down."

Harmony Harper brushed her long blonde hair off her shoulders and slipped an arm around Melody's waist, giving her a sideways hug. Smaller in stature even than Aria, the woman was so petite she looked like a little girl. "I remember when you married James. I always think of you two at Christmas."

Melody said, "You know what helps it die down is when some other big star gets married. Like you and Bobby. If nothing else, your wedding made James and my getting hitched yesterday's news."

Turning to stare directly at Harmony, Melody continued, "If only I could think of a big ticket singer who's still single. Who might be able to help with that? Harmony? Any ideas?"

While Harmony laughed, Aria came over and hugged Carol gently, careful of the intricate dress. "That was a beautiful wedding, Carol. It makes me want to do it all over again," she said.

Nick had carefully remained just two feet away while she spoke, but chose that moment to slip up behind her and wrap his arms around her to rest his hand on her middle. "With me, I hope," he said.

"When are you due, Aria?" Melody asked, studying Aria's perfectly flat stomach.

Aria leaned her head against her husband's chest. "Not until February."

Spotting James Montgomery strolling in her direction with one of his twin infants in each arm, Melody grinned and said, "Get ready, hon. It is going to change every part of your life."

James arrived with his precious cargo and a beautific look on his face. The babies in his arms had each started to root against his torso. "I hate to hand them over, but your son and daughter need their momma right now. I can't help them."

Melody took them with a smile and couldn't help but add, "Moooo!"

The band picked that moment to strike up a slow love song, and suddenly Bobby appeared at Carol's side, taking her hand in his, leading her to the dance floor.

Bobby pulled Carol close until they barely moved and placed a kiss on her waiting lips. "To a lifetime," he whispered in her ear.

"To forever," she whispered back.

THE END

♫ ♫ ♫ ♫

French words/phrases

au pair – Directly translated the phrase means "on even terms" but in common modern use refers to a domestic assistant from a foreign country working for, and living as part of, a host family. Typically, au pairs take on a share of the family's responsibility for childcare as well as some housework in return for the opportunity to learn the host family's language and usually also receive a small monetary allowance or stipend.

café au lait – Directly translated, this is the French term for "coffee with milk". The meaning of the term differs between Europe and these United States of America; in both cases it means some kind of coffee with hot milk added, in contrast to white coffee (*fr. café crème*), which is coffee with room temperature milk or other whitener added.

en route – while on the way, while traveling

Jargon or other terms

Came out with a bullet – A cliché insider term in the music industry that refers to song ratings. When a song debuts as a top 100 hit song it "comes out with a bullet." Etymology is murky, but likely has to do with the fact that only top 100 Billboard Chart songs had a "bullet" next to the printed song title when such ratings were printed on paper.

♫ ♫ ♫ ♫

Reader's Guide
Luncheon Menu

SUGGESTED luncheon menu to enjoy when hosting a group discussion surrounding *A Carol for Kent*, part 3 of the *Song of Suspense* series.

Those who follow my Hallee the Homemaker™ website know that one thing I am passionate about in life is selecting, cooking, and savoring good whole real food. A special luncheon just goes hand in hand with hospitality and ministry.

If you're planning a discussion group surrounding this book, I offer some humble suggestions to help your special luncheon talk come off as a success in this section.

The Entree:

Steak Kabobs

One of Bobby Kent's first purchases when he moves back to Richmond is his grill. Here is a wonderful steak kabob recipe to be cooked on a grill.

INGREDIENTS:

1 pound beef boneless top sirloin steak

1 medium bell pepper

16 baby bella mushrooms

16 grape tomatoes

1 TBS chopped fresh or 1 tsp dried dill weed

1 TBS lemon juice

1 TBS extra virgin olive oil

1 TBS honey mustard

$^{1}/_{4}$ tsp fresh ground pepper

SUPPLIES:

8 metal skewers

good sharp knife

2 cutting boards (1 for meat, 1 for veggies)

measuring cups/spoons

small bowl

whisk

pastry brush

PREPARATION:

Cut the beef into 24 each 1-inch cubes

Cut the green pepper into 16 each 1-inch pieces

Heat the grill.

DIRECTIONS:

Thread the metal skewers with the steak and vegetables, using 3 pieces of steak and 2 of each vegetable between cubes of steak per skewer.

Ensure that the vegetables separate the cubes of steak.

Example: Steak, pepper, mushroom, steak, tomato, pepper, etc.

(NOTE: Purple onion is an optional ingredient as well)

Whisk the remaining ingredients in the small bowl.

Place the skewers on the hot grill. Brush with the mixture.

Cover and grill the kabobs 4 to 6 inches from medium heat.

Grill for 15 to 18 minutes, turning and brushing kabobs 3 or 4 times with oil mixture, until beef is desired doneness and vegetables are tender.

The Side:

Rice Pilaf

Nothing goes as perfectly with grilled beef kabobs as rice pilaf.

INGREDIENTS:

1 cup water

1 cup white rice

1 cup chicken broth

$\frac{1}{4}$ cup minced onion

$\frac{1}{2}$ cup frozen peas & carrots

1 tsp salt (Kosher or sea salt is best)

$\frac{1}{4}$ tsp garlic powder

SUPPLIES:

good sharp knife

cutting board

measuring cups/spoons

colander

saucepan with lid

PREPARATION:

Mince the onion.

Rinse the carrots and peas.

DIRECTIONS:

Mix all ingredients in the saucepan.

Bring to a boil. Reduce heat to low.

Cover.

Simmer, covered, for 20 minutes.

The vegetable:

Herbed Corn on the Cob

I know corn is technically a grain but this corn is so perfect hot off the grill alongside grilled kabobs or a grilled steak.

INGREDIENTS:

4 ears of corn

$1/4$ cup olive oil

2 cloves garlic

1 tsp salt

$1/2$ tsp pepper

$1/2$ cup fresh parsley

SUPPLIES:

container of cold water large enough for the corn

sharp knife/cutting board

measuring cups/spoons

PREPARATION:

Carefully peel back the husks of a corn, but don't remove them. Remove the silks and wash. Put the husks back up over the corn and soak in cold water for at least an hour.

Mince the garlic.

Chop the parsley.

DIRECTIONS:

While the corn is soaking, mix the olive oil and the rest of the spices and let it sit for about an hour.

Remove the corn from the water and open back up. Pat the corn dry. Rub the flavored oil on the corn and put the husks back up over the corn. Place on the grill, turning regularly to keep from burning. Cook for several minutes, until the corn is heated through.

The dessert:

Lisa's PB and J Birthday Cake

This cake is SO good. It is peanut butter flavored with a jelly filling. Perfect for an 8-year-old's birthday.

 INGREDIENTS:

FOR THE CAKE:

2 cups plus 2 TBS whole wheat flour (I used fresh ground soft white wheat)

1 ½ cups sugar

1 TBS baking powder

1 tsp salt (Kosher or sea salt is best)

⅓ cup extra virgin coconut oil

⅓ cup natural peanut butter*

1 cup milk

2 eggs

FOR THE FILLING:

1 cup natural or homemade jam* flavor of your choice (I used strawberry)

3-ounce package flavored (preferably no-pork) gelatin (I used strawberry)

FOR THE ICING:

1 cup firmly packed brown sugar

½ cup butter

½ cup milk

1 cup sifted powdered sugar

1 tsp pure vanilla extract

 PREPARATION:

Preheat oven to 350° degrees F (120° degrees C)

Grease and flour cake pans.

SUPPLIES:

large bowl/stand mixer

measuring cups/spoons

spatula/whisk

small saucepan

2-quart saucepan

2 each 8 inch round cake pans

wire cooling rack

DIRECTIONS:

Sift together flour, sugar, baking powder, and salt. Put in large mixer bowl. Add the coconut oil, peanut butter, and milk. Beat for two minutes on medium speed. Add the eggs, one at a time. Beat for an additional two minutes.

Pour into prepared pans and bake for 25-30 minutes at 350° degrees F (120° degrees C), or until toothpick inserted into the center of the cake comes out clean.

FOR THE FILLING:

While the cake is baking, prepare the filling so that it is cooled and ready to spread. In a small saucepan, combine the jam and the gelatin. Cook over low heat until the jam is melted and the gelatin is dissolved. Remove from heat and let cool.

When the cake is cooled, place one cake round on the serving plate. Spread the filling on the top, almost to the edge. You likely won't use all of the filling. Place the other round on top of the filling.

FOR THE ICING:

Don't make the icing until the cake is ready to be iced. You need to work fast because it hardens as it cools.

In the 2-quart saucepan, bring brown sugar, butter, and milk to a boil over medium heat, whisking constantly. Boil for one minute.

Remove from heat. Whisk in powdered sugar and vanilla until smooth. Stir gently for three to five minutes or until smooth.

Immediately ice the cake.

Readers' Guide
Discussion Questions

SUGGESTED questions for a discussion group surrounding *A Carol for Kent*, part 3 of the *Song of Suspense* series.

In bringing those He ministered to into an understanding of the truth, Our Lord used fiction in the form of parables to illustrate very real truths. In the same way, we can minister to one another by the use of fictional characters and situations to help us to reach logical, valid, cogent, and very sound conclusions about our real lives here on earth.

While the characters and situations in the *Song of Suspense* series are fictional, I pray that these extended parables can help readers come to a better understanding of truth. Please prayerfully consider the questions that follow, consult scripture, and pray upon your conclusions. May the Lord of the universe richly bless you.

♫ ♫ ♫ ♫

Carol relied on Bobby's parents to tell him about her pregnancy and the birth of Lisa.

> 1. Do you think Carol should have followed up on her own? Was she wrong to just accept what she considered child support and continue to raise Lisa on her own?

> 2. Carol and the Kents did not tell Lisa who her dad was because they wanted to protect her from the constant exposure and scrutiny she would suffer due to his fame. Do you believe this was a wise decision?

> 3. Do you think Carol sinned in any way by withholding that information from her daughter?

♫ ♫ ♫ ♫

Bobby discovers that his parents didn't tell him about Lisa because they wanted his income from his country music career.

1 Timothy 6:10 says: *For the love of money is a root of all kinds of evil, for which some have strayed from the faith in their greediness, and pierced themselves through with many sorrows.*

4. Do you believe that what the Kents did was evil?

5. How hard was it for you to accept that Bobby had no choice but to forgive his parents?

6. Do you believe Bobby would have been justified in not forgiving his parents?

7. The Bible says we are to forgive those who wronged us not once, not twice, but seven times seventy times. Search your heart. Are you harboring unforgiveness that might be coming between you and God?

♫ ♫ ♫ ♫

Carol is very quick and very ready to release any negative feelings about Bobby. She knows that he didn't know about Lisa and guesses that her past would be completely different if he had known.

8. Do you think you would still continue to harbor ill feelings toward him, almost out of habit instead of logic and fairness?

9. Even though she knew he didn't know about Lisa, she still used his absenteeism during an argument. As human as that may be, what could she have done differently, in her mind and heart, so that nothing like that ever comes in between their relationship again?

♫ ♫ ♫ ♫

After Bobby rescues Carol, Nick tells him that there will be remorse for his actions – and other things.

> 10. Do you think Bobby's actions during the rescue of Carol were justified?

> 11. How might Bobby better cope with his feelings about what he did and how he feels?

♫ ♫ ♫ ♫

Nick suggests that the killer might be possessed by a demon.

> 12. How realistic do you think that might be?

> 13. Is there any indication given to us, Biblically, that possession is just "a thing of the past"?

> 14. When Judas was preparing to betray Jesus, the Bible tells us that a spirit entered him.

Luke 22:3-6 says: *Then Satan entered Judas, surnamed Iscariot, who was numbered among the twelve. So he went his way and conferred with the chief priests and captains, how he might betray Him to them. And they were glad, and agreed to give him money. So he promised and sought opportunity to betray Him to them in the absence of the multitude.*

> Do you think Judas was still responsible for his actions?

♫ ♫ ♫ ♫

The *Song of Suspense* Series...

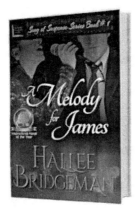

A MELODY FOR JAMES

MELODY Mason and James Montgomery lead separate lives of discord until an unexpected meeting brings them to a sinister realization. Unbeknownst to them, dark forces have directed their lives from the shadows, orchestrating movements that keep them in disharmony. Fire, loss, and bloodshed can't shake their faith in God to see them through as they face a percussive climax that will leave lives forever changed.

♫ ♫ ♫ ♫

AN ARIA FOR NICK

ARIA Suarez remembers her first real kiss and Nick Williams, the blue eyed boy who passionately delivered it before heading off to combat. The news of his death is just a footnote in a long war and her lifelong dream to become a world class pianist is shattered along with her wrist on the day of his funeral.

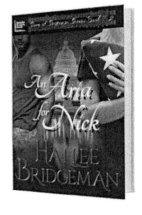

Years later, Aria inadvertently uncovers a sinister plot that threatens the very foundations of a nation. Now, stalked by assassins and on the run, her only hope of survival is in trusting her very life to a man who has been dead for years.

♫ ♫ ♫ ♫

A CAROL FOR KENT

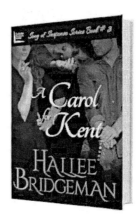

BOBBY Kent's name is synonymous with modern Country Music and he is no stranger to running from overzealous fans and paparazzo. But he has no idea how to protect his daughter and Carol, the mother of his only child, from a vicious and ruthless serial killer bent on their destruction.

♫ ♫ ♫ ♫

A HARMONY FOR STEVE

CHRISTIAN contemporary singing sensation, Harmony Harper, seeks solitude after winning her umpteenth award. She finds herself in the midst of the kind of spiritual crisis that only prayer and fasting can cure. Steve Slayer, the world renowned satanic acid rock icon, who has a reputation for trashing women as well as hotel rooms, stumbles into her private retreat on the very edge of death.

In ministering to Steve, Harmony finds that the Holy Spirit is ministering to her aching soul. The two leave the wilderness sharing a special bond and their hearts are changed forever.

They expect rejection back in their professional worlds. What neither of them could foresee is the chain of ominous events that threaten their very lives.

♫ ♫ ♫ ♫

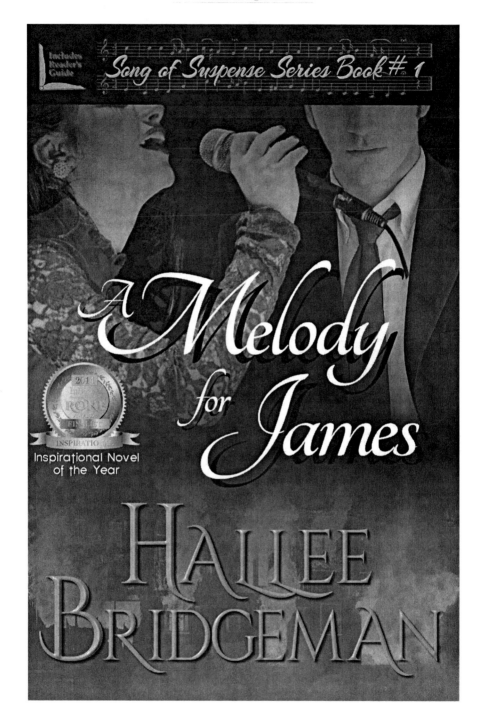

A Melody for James was voted the July *Clash of the Titles* <u>WINNER</u> in 2013, voted **The Book Club Network's** 1st runner up for <u>Book of the Year</u>, RONE Awards finalist for <u>Inspirational Novel of the Year</u>, and IRC finalist for <u>Book of the Year</u>. If you missed *A Melody for James*, buy it now in Paperback or eBook wherever fine books are sold. Please enjoy this special excerpt from the full length Christian suspense novel, *A Melody for James*, part one in the *Song of Suspense* series.

♪ ♪ ♪ ♪

ANGELA Montgomery nearly missed it. She had lost herself in memories of her recent birthday celebration marking the passing of her 30th year on earth. Her husband, James, her junior by 2 short years, had gone all out. Being "much" younger, he had decorated the entire house with black balloons and held a surprise "wake" for the passing of her late youth. Daydreaming and lost in feelings of love and adoration for her beloved groom, Angela nearly failed to recognize the moment when it happened.

When her consciousness shifted from her reverie back to the present, for several breaths she simply stared at the smart board in front of her and ran through the calculations again. Then she tried to ignore the little shivers of nervous excitement that danced up her spine.

"Heeyyyyy ..." Donald Andrews clicked a few keys on the laptop in front of him, magnifying the image on the smart board screen so that it covered the entire wall. "Did we just ..."

Angela rose, her legs feeling uncharacteristically stiff, and walked forward while staring at the screen. "You know what, I'm cautiously going to say yes. Yes, we did."

Alvin Berry let out a loud, "Whoop!" He removed the ever present knit cap from the top of his head and tossed it into the air. The group collectively looked at each other and grinned. Years of work, and the breakthrough sat right there on that smart board, staring back at them.

"We should celebrate," Lorie Frazier announced. She pulled her glasses from her nose and casually tossed them onto the stack of papers in front of her. "We need to celebrate, then we need to call a press conference. But only after we get to the patent office."

Angela looked back at the screen. "We have to be sure."

"We're sure," Alvin said. "Look at that beauty. It is so simple yet so elegant."

"Call James," Lorie said. "Tell him to make us a reservation in the most ridiculously expensive restaurant Atlanta has to offer. Tell him we're going to celebrate."

Despite her naturally conservative nature, Angela started to let the feeling of giddy excitement take over. She laughed and hugged Don as she pulled her cell phone from her pocket.

Her husband would probably jump up and down or do a little dance of celebration. She felt like she might just as easily be making a call to announce that she was expecting their first child instead of the conclusion of this long project.

For five years, she and this amazing team of engineers had worked to perfect this revolutionary data storage solution. For five years, usually working six days a week, usually not less than twelve hours a day, they'd toiled in this basement lab in her inherited home. While she'd hoped and prayed for all that time, now that the reality of what they'd accomplished actually shone back at her from that beautiful smart screen, she realized she hadn't ever really been certain they'd succeed.

But they had.

She got James' voice mail. "Darling," she purred, knowing he'd hear the smile in her voice, "We did it. We're done. I cannot wait to show you. Come home. Come see. We need to celebrate."

As soon as Angela hung up, she gave Lorie a hug and said, "I vote for cheesecake."

"Copious amounts," the nearsighted genius agreed. "Oh! With strawberries! And really good coffee."

Angela felt her heart skip when the red security light started flashing. Her eyebrows crowded together in confusion. Why was the intruder alarm going off now?

Angela had inherited the farmhouse from her late uncle at the age of 17 and lived there throughout her lengthy matriculation at Georgia Tech. For a brief time when this venture was just beginning, she and her brand new husband, James, as well as their business partner and his best friend, Kurt, had all lived there under the same roof.

During the initial months and years, Kurt and James had renovated the basement entirely; installing a T1, a two post rack of networking gear, a four post rack of high performance servers; and most importantly, a state-of-the-art security system, designed and built by her brilliant husband himself. For the last five years, they had hardened the basement into a panic room with steel reinforced doors, magnetic locks, and pinhole security cameras. It took two-factor authentication to even get into the room.

When the magnitude of the fact that the security alarm was still sounding sunk in, Angela whirled around until her eyes met with Don. When she spoke, she hated the shrill edge of panic she detected in her voice. "Back it up to the Snap."

His fingers clicked on the keys with the speed of machine gun fire as spoke. "There's no time. We didn't do an incremental yesterday because the waffle was running a defrag."

"Right. Execute a differential and encrypt it." She waited a few heartbeats while Don's fingers played out a staccato percussion on his laptop.

With confusion clouding his eyes, he looked up and announced, "Our hard line is down."

Alvin pressed a series of keys on his computer and several small screens appeared on the smart board, all showing different angles of her home. Men in masks moved through the empty house with military precision, high powered and very deadly looking carbine rifles tucked tightly into their shoulders at the ready. They stared around every corner through the sights on the short rifles.

Lorie gasped and said, "What is going on? Who are they?"

Fear and panic tried to take over. Her stomach turned into ice and Angela felt like her breathing wasn't productive, like she could never get a deep enough breath. Focus, she said to herself. You will have time to be scared when it's over.

"Can you remember how we got here since the last backup?" Angela asked Alvin, her hand pointing in his direction like a knife blade. If she'd ever met anyone whose memory rivaled her husband's, it was Alvin.

His voice sounded flat, emotionless. "Yes. Of course I can."

She watched a crouched figure outside the entrance to the lab tape two liter plastic bottles filled with water to the hinges of the security door. The security that James and Kurt had installed was tight, state-of-the-art even, and the door was sealed. But no seal in 100 miles would withstand the blast of a shaped charge pushing water ahead of a supersonic shock wave. It would slice through the steel door faster than the world's most powerful cutting torch.

Whomever these people were, they had known the defenses they would have to overcome. They were prepared. They had planned. They had obviously even rehearsed as was apparent in their staged and perfectly timed precision movements. And the most dangerous thing Angela and her team had for protection once that door came down were a few custom computer viruses.

She'd known the risks. The success of their project was potentially worth upward of a hundred billion dollars in the first year alone, and that was on the conservative side. The long term applications of the soon to be patented technology could not even be calculated. The reason they worked out of her home instead of in some downtown lab was for the secrecy of the project, a vain hope of security by obscurity.

They'd taken additional precautions which Angela belatedly realized she had characterized as "paranoid." A commercial exothermic incendiary device much like a military grade thermite grenade perched atop each server array that would, when detonated, melt their way through the machines at over 4 thousand degrees Fahrenheit, effectively destroying everything in a completely unrecoverable fashion. They would burn 3 times hotter than molten lava and the crew would have to be careful not to look at them since the radiant energy was bright enough to blind them without a welding visor.

"Then destroy it. Destroy it all."

Lorie's finger hovered over a steel pin. "You're sure?"

The explosion above them shook the room. Alvin rushed to the inner door and made sure the panic room door remained bolted on all four corners. Angela closed the lid on her laptop and slid it into the 2 inch air gap between network switches. Then she draped her hand on Lorie's shoulder and whispered, "Do it."

She closed her eyes and started to pray as the room around her grew suddenly very hot and smoke started billowing up to the ceiling. "Lord Jesus, if I live through this, let me remain in Your will. But if I come home to you, sweet Jesus, please watch over my husband. Let him feel your comforting love and let him find the destiny you have in mind for him."

Smoke alarms went off and the lights flickered. Then she felt herself being picked up and thrown aside, riding on the wave of a perfectly timed blast. As she flew backward from the shock of the multiple explosions blowing open her steel door she prayed even harder – she prayed for courage, for protection, for strength.

As she landed and fell against the tower of computer drives, she watched the thermite spill and splatter like lava, setting the entire area on fire. Her last thought was of pain as a spray of burning powder fell on her chest.

♫ ♫ ♫ ♫

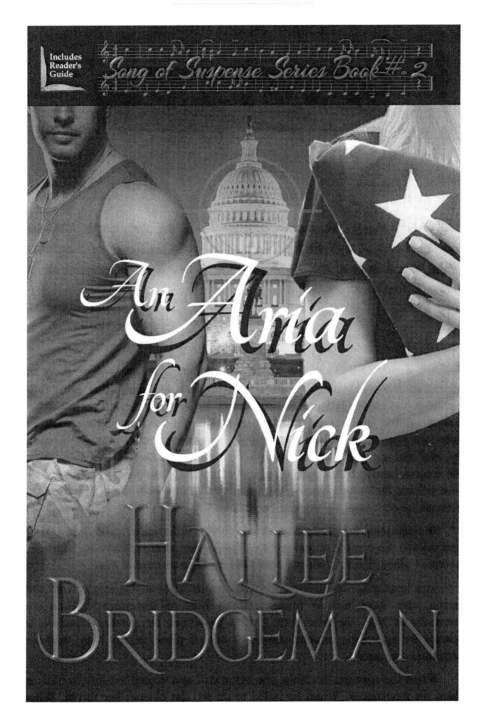

PLEASE enjoy this special excerpt from the full length Christian suspense novel, *An Aria for Nick*, part two in the *Song of Suspense* series. If you missed *An Aria for Nick*, buy it in paperbck or ebook wherever fine books are sold.

♫ ♫ ♫ ♫

ARIA Suarez stood on the corner of the patio at the coffee shop on Macadam Avenue observing the man wearing the dark blue shirt who occupied the corner table of the outdoor cafe. Sunlight glinted on his brown hair, revealing highlighted streaks that nearly glowed, lending his visage a halo-like appearance. He'd flirted with the waitress each time she'd come by, and had even grinned at a small child making a mess at a nearby table. He looked harmless enough, though she couldn't completely make out his face behind the sunglasses he wore and the Monday edition of the Portland Tribune he continuously ducked behind.

She clenched the purse strap in her hand a little tighter. She kept a sharp eye toward the crowd, scanning faces for anyone who looked either familiar or out of place. Finally, she mustered the courage to step forward.

Aria hesitantly began her approach, unsure of how this might work and trying very hard not to reveal even a hint of uncertainty. Then she remembered that she also didn't want to attract any undue attention to herself by appearing uncomfortable or out of place in any way, and she smoothed her stride.

When she reached his table, she stood still and waited for him to look up from his newspaper. When he failed to do so, she cleared her throat. When that didn't work, she said, "Excuse me."

He shifted the newspaper downward enough to peer over the top of it in her direction, staring at her through the dark lenses of his sunglasses, but she still couldn't see his eyes. All she could see was her own reflection in the tinted lenses. "Are you waiting for me?"

The man glanced downward, very purposefully and very carefully folding the newspaper which he set on the table at right angles to his silverware directly next to his cup. That accomplished, he gestured with his left hand in the direction of the chair across from him, silently inviting her to join him without raising his eyes. As she perched herself on the wrought iron chair, she thought to herself that this man looked familiar.

All those weeks when she had felt such apprehension, glancing over her shoulder in foreboding, she had checked all the shadows and every corner, certain someone was always following her. Had her trepidation been well-founded after all? Had this man been following her? Had she seen him somewhere before? Or was her nervousness and disquiet simply getting the best of her? Did this man just have one of those faces that you felt sure you recognized?

Aria started to feel some very deep, very real anxiety and did her best to quell it. She waited for him to speak, assuming if everything was on the up-and-up that he had done this kind of thing before, and would take the lead to get them to the next level, whatever that was.

The waitress came back to the table to refill the man's lemonade and Aria ordered a cup of decaf with cream, no sugar, then folded her hands and waited. The man across from her sat up a bit straighter then took a deep breath and finally spoke.

"Hello, Aria." His voice flowed over her like a warm baritone blanket. It was deep and comforting and frighteningly familiar. He removed his sunglasses. Ice blue eyes, almost silver in color, calmly met her glance. Already tense muscles contracted in her stomach and around her heart, stealing the breath from her body and sending a surge of adrenaline that made her palms sweat even though her fingers felt ice cold. Her throat let out a startled gasp as recognition dawned.

It can't be! her mind screamed. *It's not possible!*

"How've you been?" he asked. "You look even more beautiful than I remember."

Aria didn't know what to say, literally shocked speechless. She had never spoken to a ghost. Her mouth felt so dry that the air coursing in and out of her lungs scorched her throat. Finally, she made an attempt. "What? ... How? ..."

Nicholas "Nick" Williams leaned forward and spoke very quietly but with great urgency, his low voice pitched for her ears alone. "It's okay, Aria. It's a long story, and I'll be happy to share it with you. But I have to call my superiors in less than twenty minutes, so right now, just show me what you have. We can stroll down memory lane later on, okay?"

Aria finally felt able to speak. She gripped the wrought iron chair handles beneath her fingers until her muscles ached. "You aren't Nick Williams," she announced as she stood. "Nice try, but I buried Nick ten years ago."

♪ ♪ ♪ ♪

Includes Reader's Guide

Song of Suspense Series Book # 4

A Harmony for Steve

HALLEE BRIDGEMAN

PLEASE enjoy this special excerpt from the upcoming full length Christian suspense novel, *A Harmony for Steve*, part four in the *Song of Suspense* series.

♫ ♫ ♫ ♫

HARMONY Harper stood on the deck of the cabin. The crisp air provided a sharpness to the late morning drizzle. Through the mist, she could see the bone white car climbing the curving road below her. She estimated that she had about three minutes before he arrived. She'd anticipated her brother arriving yesterday and wondered what took so long for the news of her recent nuptials to reach him. With a nervous twist in her stomach, she turned and went through the glass door and back into the great room.

Steve Slayer, her husband of less than two months, added another log to the fire. He'd changed into slacks and a dark brown sweater. Her heart gave a little leap of love and excitement when she saw him. He fit so perfectly in this room. He fit so perfectly into her life. They'd had six weeks of peace and restoration in this secluded little environment. However, the real world rapidly approached in the form of a bone colored Mercedes.

He turned as she slid the door closed, smiling at her. She couldn't believe how much he'd changed over the last several weeks. He'd gained weight, his hair had grown back, and his green eyes shown bright with the passion for God that had so recently taken over in his life. His features looked relaxed, happy – no longer strained by the addictions and hate that had poisoned his life for so long.

While she had no desire to see the relaxed and content look leave her husband's face, they both knew that this day would eventually come. "Franklin's on his way up. I just saw his car."

There was a hesitation to his smile before Steve stepped forward and offered his hand to her. "You're not scared, are you?"

Scared? With half a laugh she said, "Maybe a little."

"I'll be right here beside you." She stepped down into the room and took his hand, letting him pull her into his arms. "We knew this would come."

"He's not going to be happy."

He framed her face with his hands and looked down into her eyes. "Of course not. I'm a wasted drug addict who sings very worldly songs. What's there to be happy about? He'll either accept me or not. We knew this going into it."

With a sense of urgency she put both of her hands on his chest. "Don't let him discourage you or bring you down. He's very good at verbal play."

His smile set her at ease. "Princess, I got this. Don't worry. What is it you would say to me? 'Fear is not of the Lord?'"

Standing on tiptoe, she gave his mouth a quick peck with her own just as she heard the crunch of tires on the gravel outside. "*Touché.*"

Hand in hand, they walked to the front door and stepped out onto the porch. Harmony felt her stomach twist when she saw her mother sitting in the front seat of the car. Alice Harper did not wait for Franklin to come around to open the door for her. For the first time in Harmony's memory, her mother opened the door herself and got out of the car. Harmony had prepared herself for Franklin, not Alice.

"Mama," she said, smiling, praying, hoping.

"Darling," Alice greeted as Franklin exited the driver's seat.

"Harmony," he began, but Alice held her hand up and stopped him.

Her mother walked up the steps and onto the porch until she stood in front of Harmony and Steve. "This is Steven Slayer?"

He didn't seem phased by Alice Harper, international best-selling author and radio personality. "Yes, ma'am," Steve confirmed, holding out his right hand, keeping Harmony's secure in his left. "It's a pleasure to meet you."

She took his hand and looked him up and down, clearly taking in the holes in his ear lobes and the tattoo snaking out from beneath his right sleeve. "Is it? What makes you say that?"

"Because Harmony loves you, and I love her. That's enough to make it a pleasure for me."

Alice raised an eyebrow. "Do you have any idea what the media is saying?"

Her mother still held his hand. Harmony wondered about that. She looked away from her mother and glanced briefly over at Franklin, who scowled at her with cold, steely gray eyes.

Steve answered her mother. "I imagine they're all about little Harmony here and her break away from the message of Christ to shack up with a drug addict rocker. I'm sure I'm not doing them justice at the way they'd word things."

"Do you find it amusing?" Franklin bit out.

Steve pulled his hand from Alice's and slipped it into his pocket, as if knowing Franklin would not return an offer of a hand shake. "Nothing that would hurt Harmony would amuse me. However, I stand here with the grace of God, sanctified and redeemed. I don't answer to man, but to Him. They are going to crucify me and, because I love your sister she'll hang on the cross next to mine. All we can do is stay steadfast and strong, and we'll be old news one day."

Alice tilted her head, sizing him up once again, then she gestured at the door. "Let's go inside. Harmony, dear, make us some tea. Franklin, get my bag. Steven, we have some rather urgent things we must discuss."

As Franklin carried Alice's bag into one of the guest rooms, and Harmony put together a tea tray, Alice and Steve sat on the big sectional couch. From the kitchen counter she watched as Alice drew out a stack of envelopes and handed them to Steve. Whatever he saw when he opened the first one darkened his face in a way that made her worry. He looked up at her but was too far away for her to read anything on his face but a flash of anger.

Harmony quickly sliced a lemon and tossed it into a bowl, then poured boiling water over the tea leaves in the tea pot. She picked up the tray and carried it down to the living room, setting it on the table in front of the couch.

"What are those?" She gestured to the stack of envelopes as she perched on the couch next to Steve.

He handed them to her. "I don't know yet."

"They began arriving about three days after your marriage announcement," Franklin said, coming down the stairway. "I have no idea if your people have received the same kinds of things, Steven. They won't return my calls."

Harmony opened the first envelope as Alice poured the tea. She pulled out an index card that had a pentagram burned onto it. In what looked like dried blood, someone had written "DIE" across the burned image. She frowned and looked up at Franklin. "What does this mean?"

"Well, sis, I'm no expert but I reckon it means someone wants you to die. They were addressed to you, after all." His gray eyes cut to Steve. "Addressed to Harmony Slayer." His tone carried an accusatory sound.

Steve's lips thinned. "Have you contacted the police?"

"I told Franklin that was your decision. They were addressed to Harmony, after all." Alice handed him a cup and saucer. Despite his strong dislike of the brew, Steve accepted it automatically which made Harmony love him all over again.

Harmony tossed the envelopes onto the table and took Steven's free hand in both of hers. "I guess it's time to go back to Nashville."

"You need to contact the police," Franklin began, but Harmony cut him off and looked at Steve.

"What's your impression?"

He rubbed his face with his hands and leaned back against the couch. With a nervous finger, he tapped his knee, something that she knew he did when he wanted to be smoking a cigarette. "I have some odd fans. I'm sure it's a juvenile prank, but I don't want to risk it being something more."

"More?" Harmony picked up her cup and saucer, her hand trembling enough to make the china rattle. "Like what?"

"Like true danger. Like a true threat. This is absolutely something that should not be ignored." He reached over and took her hand. "I'm sure it's nothing, though."

Despite his comforting words, she could see the worry in his eyes. She could feel his tension in the way he gripped her hand. Her heart gave a nervous flutter at the thought that someone might actually want to harm her.

♫ ♫ ♫ ♫

The Virtues and Valor series
The battle begins in 2014 ...

SEVEN women from different backgrounds and social classes come together on the common ground of a shared faith during the second World War. Each will earn a code name of a heavenly virtue. Each will risk discovery and persevere in the face of terrible odds. One will be called upon to make the ultimate sacrifice.

Introduction	Heavenly Heroines
Part 1	Temperance's Trial
Part 2	Homeland's Hope
Part 3	Charity's Code
Part 4	A Parcel for Prudence
Part 5	Grace's Ground War
Part 6	Mission of Mercy
Part 7	Flight of Faith

INSPIRED by real events, these are stories of Virtues and Valor.

EXCERPT: TEMPERANCE'S TRIAL

PLEASE enjoy this special preview prerelease excerpt from the upcoming Christian historical novella, Temperance's Trial, part of the exciting upcoming Virtues and Valor series.

THE pounding on the door surprised Marie and she let out a startled cry. The pounding came again, even louder and more insistent, and the scissors she held in her hand clattered to the table as she covered her heart with her hand.

She looked around the little room. The single bed was neatly made. The trifold screen in the corner had no undergarments draped over the top of it. Her sewing machine in the center of the room stood ready. Most importantly, the ceiling beams above the screen were in place and did not look like they had been moved at all.

The visual inspection took place instantly and concluded within seconds. She had to check because in reality she was not a seamstress. The one thing she had learned about sewing over the course of the last few months that overshadowed everything else was that she never wanted to be a seamstress. Additionally, she no longer called herself Marie Gilbert, but rather Marie Perrin. Lastly, she had a code name, now; Temperance. Since accepting that code name and her mission, nothing in her life was exactly as it appeared.

Running suddenly damp palms over her skirt, she went to the door and opened it. The sight of a German officer, a Second Leutenant, made her heart freeze in her chest. Had they finally discovered her?

"You are the seamstress, are you not?" he demanded by way of introduction. He stood tall, a couple inches over six feet, and looked young for an officer. He had hair the color of straw and piercing dark blue eyes – the very caricature of an Arian in Hitler's army. His French accent sounded different than the accent she had heard from other Germans, though she couldn't place the discrepancy.

Trying not to sound as nervous as she felt, Marie answered, "Yes, *Leutnant*. I am a seamstress." She looked him up and down. "Perhaps you need a dress?"

He opened his mouth, closed it, then barked a laughed. "A dress? I like that, *Fräulein*. Very amusing." The smile completely transformed his face and made him look less formidable. Putting a hand over his heart, he gave her a stiff and short bow. "I am *Leutnant* Leopold Schäfer and I have an emergency."

"What kind of emergency?"

"An unexpected uniform malfunction. It seems I have lost a button." As his face flooded with color, he gestured toward the fly of his trousers.

Looking over his shoulder and seeing he was alone, she said, "Well, I can't sew it on while you're still wearing your pants. Bring them back anytime today. It won't take a minute to mend."

"No time for that. I have my promotion ceremony to *Oberleutnant* in twenty minutes. I cannot go to that ceremony with a button missing from my fly." He put his hands together like a child begging for a cookie. "Please, *Fräulein*. I am at your mercy. I beg you to help me. I am a desperate man."

Torn, not wanting to offend a German officer but very much not wanting to help Germany either, she looked around again. "I'm very sorry, *Leutnant*, but men aren't allowed into my room."

"I am aware. I sought and obtained permission from your landlady before knocking on your door."

Marie raised an eyebrow. "How did you manage that?"

He smirked. "Must you ask?"

Of course. This man was a German officer, a conqueror. He represented the military might of the entire Third Reich, of Adolf Hitler himself. And her landlady was merely a lowly French woman, a commoner. If she didn't want any trouble, she couldn't refuse. Likewise, how could Marie refuse to sew on his button right this very instant?

Fresh anger surged through her heart, but she did not let it show on her face. Instead, she stepped back and held the door wider. "Please come in, *Leutnant* Schäfer. Leave the door open, if you please."

He raised an eyebrow but pushed the door back fully open instead of shutting it behind him as he had automatically begun to do. Marie continued. "There is a dressing screen just there. Remove your trousers and pass them over to me but do not come out from behind the screen in a state of undress."

With the door wide open and the privacy screen in place, she could hope for some decency or humility in this situation. Not that any kind of modesty would protect her from a German officer who might have other intentions. Nonetheless, nearly two decades of social etiquette drilled into her by her father could not go ignored, even in a war zone.

While the German went behind the screen and began to disrobe, Marie looked through her jar of buttons and found a few that should work on his uniform. In a matter of seconds, he flipped his pants over the top of the dressing screen. As she reached for them, she couldn't help but glance up at the ceiling. Above the German's head, the case containing her wireless lay hidden in the ceiling.

"I am very happy that you were in this afternoon," he announced from behind the screen.

"I'm sure you would have been resourceful if I hadn't been," Marie answered, threading a needle with dark gray thread.

"Are you curious to know how I lost a button on my trousers?"

"Dare I ask?" Uninvited images raced through her imagination.

He laughed. "I wish I knew myself. I left my room this morning in a perfect state of dress. Now, right before this important ceremony, I find myself out of uniform."

"One hopes this is the only time you lose your fly button before a military ceremony. I'm not going to be around all the time after all," Marie said, deftly sewing on the button that most closely matched the others on his uniform. He laughed again while she sewed. It took her less than a minute. With small scissors, she snipped the thread and lay the trousers over the screen again. "All done. Here you go, *Leutnant*."

"*Bitte*," he said enthusiastically.

"Please, don't mention it." She crossed her arms over her chest and waited, listening to the rustle of clothing as he put the trousers back on. When he came from around the screen, he carried his boots. She gestured toward the chair facing her sewing machine.

"I will be out of your hair in just a moment," he said, sitting down. "I can't be late, after all."

"After he made the trains run on time, I imagine the *Führer* looks down on any officers who are less than punctual." Her voice remained very monotone.

He looked up at her sharply, staring at her with very serious eyes for a moment, his jaw set to speak something in anger before he apparently reconsidered and quietly said, "Yes, I imagine he does." He finished fastening his boot strap and stood. "How much do I owe you, *Fräulein*?"

Marie waved her hand dismissively. "Nothing. I'm happy to help, *Leutnant*."

"I insist on paying you for your work."

"I'm afraid I must insist on accepting nothing from you, *Leutnant*." She walked to the open door and gripped the handle. "Congratulations on your promotion, First Lieutenant. I hope I have not delayed you too long and that you make it to your ceremony on time."

He stopped at the door and looked down at her. "At least accept my gratitude. Thank you, *Fräulein*, from the bottom of my heart."

She felt her cheeks flush with color as he rushed from the room. When she was certain he was gone, she shut the door and locked it, pressing a shaking hand to her suddenly nauseated stomach. She stared at the ceiling, where the wireless machine sat hidden.

"Dear God," she prayed in a whisper, thankful for whatever protection He'd just granted her. "Thank You, God. Thank You."

U U U U

MARIE pushed the headphones tighter against her ears. "Come on," she whispered urgently.

After several seconds of silence, she retransmitted the message and waited. A bead of perspiration trickled down her forehead and she closed her eyes and prayed. It was taking so long. The longer she transmitted, the more time the Germans had to do the arithmetic. They would intercept her signal, intersect her frequency, triangulate the origin from more than one angle, and resect her exact location. The computations could be made within minutes. Say what you wanted about the German Army but no one could criticize their math skills.

Suddenly, a reply sounded in her ear. "That a girl," she uttered, guessing the identity of the operator on the other end.

Marie wrote as fast as she could then quickly dashed off a confirmation. With nimble fingers, she packed everything up into the bag, hid the equipment in the false bottom, then stacked seamstress supplies on top of everything.

When she stood, her stomach rumbled and she looked at the barn next to her, wondering if Marcel, the owner of the farm, would mind much if she just took an egg or two. Before she could even devise a way to ask him, his wife, Armelle, came around the corner.

"I don't want you here," she said without preamble. "You are placing my husband and I in danger."

"Marcel said —"

With the wave of her hand, the older, stockier woman cut her off. "I do not care what that man said, *Mademoiselle*. It was fine when it was another man. We could easily pass him off as a farm hand or a neighbor come by to help. But you have no business here. Do I look like someone wanting a new dress?"

Marie pressed her lips together, and kept from replying that a new dress might make her feel better. She understood the woman's point. "Very well, *Madame*. After today, I won't be back."

"See that you don't."

Armelle glared at her while she strapped her bag to her bike and got on it. She could feel the stare right in the middle of her shoulder blades as she pedaled down the lane.

Nerves danced in her stomach. She hated confrontation. She hated anger. Suppose the farmer's wife decided to turn her in to the Gestapo. How had it all come to this?

She pedaled along the country road and scooted closer to the road's edge when she heard the sound of a motor behind her. Instead of passing her, though, it pulled up along side her.

"Excuse me, *Fräulein*!"

Startled, she looked over and saw an armored *Kübelwagen* driven by First Lieutenant Schäfer. Her heart started pounding frantically in her chest and the front tire of her bike wobbled. She hit the brakes and put both feet on the ground, unconsciously laying a hand over her heart. She darted a glance all around, fearfully searching every dark corner and copse for German soldiers or Gestapo laying in wait, but it appeared they were alone on the road. "You startled me, *Oberleutnant*."

He stopped the *Kübelwagen*, killing the engine and setting the parking brakes in the same motion. He hopped out and jogged around the front of it to where she stood straddling the bike. He moved in a very precise manner, efficiently and with a total economy of motion. It was as if all of his movements were staged and well scripted in advance or he had rehearsed them for hours before executing.

"I am so sorry to startle you, *Fräulein* Perrin." His voice rang out in the cool air, confident and baritone, and a little bit self-satisfied.

A man so precise was bound to notice any mistake. All she could think of was the wireless in the bag strapped to the back of the bike. Her hands went cold and she felt perspiration bead on her upper lip. "How do you know my name, *Oberleutnant*?"

His smile was handsome, despite his German Army uniform. Marie couldn't believe she even entertained the thought. "I made an inquiry of your landlady. She was generous to give me your name."

What was she supposed to do? Shake his hand? How did she handle this? "It's nice to see you again, *Oberleutnant*," she said, trying to appear calm. Had they triangulated the position of her last broadcast? Was he just a decoy until a larger arrest unit arrived? "Did you make it to your ceremony on time last week?"

He held his hand out, and she felt inclined to take it. His palm felt warm, his fingers strong. "Yes, thanks to you." He smiled with even white teeth, his eyes crinkling up with laugh lines. "You are very beautiful, *Fräulein* Perrin."

Despite her circumstance, she felt her cheeks fuse with color. She felt her fingers tighten against his grip. "*Oberleutnant* Schäfer, I hardly think that is appropriate."

He finally released her hand and bowed stiffly. "You are correct, *Fräulein*. I apologize."

She gave him a slight nod but suddenly felt afraid that she'd offended him. Him, a German officer. "Thank you. I hope you don't –"

He cut off her panicked apology. "Of course not. I should have kept that thought to myself even though it is a fact."

He stood close enough that she could smell the earthy wool smell of his uniform. Marie felt her eyes lower as her cheeks grew hot. She noticed the mirror-bright shine on his boots before she heard her heartbeat thundering in her ears. Was this fear or something else?

He cleared his throat. "I have been searching for you, *Fräulein*."

Marie tasted bitter bile in the back of her throat and kept her gaze downcast. Had she gone too far taunting him about Hitler in their first meeting? Had a careless glance revealed the hiding place of her wireless? Had he sent a team of Gestapo to search her quarters while she had been away? Had she transmitted too long and been discovered? She relied upon her training and forced her voice to remain even as she prompted, "You've been searching for me?"

"Yes. I want to ask you. Would you like to go see a show with me?"

Was this some new euphemism for imprisonment and torture? Confused, she raised an eyebrow. "A show?"

"Yes. Next week, Virginia Benoit will be here to perform for our *Oberst*, our Colonel. *Herr Oberst* is her biggest fan and we are all invited to see the show … to lift the morale of the troops, you see. Tell me, *Fräulein*, do you know Virginia Benoit?"

Marie swallowed. Hard. How was she supposed to handle this situation? Never, in all of her training, was this brought up. "Of course I have heard of her," *and laughed with her and prayed with her*, though she kept that part to herself.

"She is from America, like me," he proclaimed, almost proudly.

She knew his accent had sounded wrong somehow. "American? Why are you here in France, then?"

He gestured in the air. "The call of the Fatherland I'm afraid. My father insisted I return a few years ago."

With wide eyes, she let that digest. "Do you know Virginia Benoit?"

"No." He chuckled, perhaps at her *naïveté*. "America is enormous. She's from a state called Louisiana in the deep south near the Gulf coast. I'm from Oregon a few thousand kilometers away on the north of the Pacific coast. Also, I understand the lady is a Negro. Perhaps you've heard that Negros and Arians hardly ever socialize in America. Still, it will be nice to hear an American accent again, I think."

His casual remark establishing his racial beliefs disgusted Marie and she tried very hard to conceal her loathing. She knew with an unshakable faith that God made all men and all nations of just one blood. Everyone on earth was a son or daughter of Adam and Eve. The bloody Nazi campaign of terror relied on faith in a lie – a form of Darwinian evolution establishing separate races coupled with the notion Friedrich Nietzsche proposed, that some races were inferior while other races were superior. Hitler aimed to create a "master race," a race of supermen, by practicing enforced eugenics that either sterilized or eliminated the races Hitler deemed inferior.

In practically the same breath, Schäfer had mentioned his father. Thoughts of her own father rushed through her mind, and she once more remembered that First Lieutenant Schäfer was her sworn enemy. How had she forgotten that for even half a second? She could not let her thoughts travel too far down that road or else her expression would betray her. She had to lighten the conversation somehow. "I imagine you must feel very homesick at times, *Oberleutnant*."

"I am homesick." He put a hand to his heart. "It would do me a great deal of good to attend the performance with the most beautiful woman in the village on my arm."

"*Oberleutnant* Schäfer, I don't think –"

He held up a hand to halt her speech. "Please, don't say no, *Fräulein*. At least let me have a little hope by telling me you'll consider the offer. Besides, I still owe you for sewing on my button."

She would have to clear any action with headquarters. It was possible that she could collect valuable intelligence by accompanying the junior German officer. It was even possible that Marie, code named Temperance, could pass intelligence to Virginia Benoit, code named Hope, in person. Pressing her lips together, desperate to find a way to end this conversation, she nodded. "Very well, *Oberleutnant*. As you say, I will think about it."

His eyebrow cocked, "You give me your word?"

After perhaps a half second of hesitation, she nodded. "You have my word."

He clicked his heels again. "*Wunderbar*! I will seek you out in two days time to learn your final decision." He leaned closer and whispered as if conspiring with her. She could smell his musky aftershave. "I hope you say yes."

Then he took her hand again and kissed the backs of her fingers. She struggled not to snatch her hand back from his grasp before his lips touched her skin. He smiled and said, "I look forward to speaking with you again, *Fräulein* Perrin."

"Good day, *Oberleutnant* Schäfer." She stayed put while he got back into his *Kübelwagen* and drove away. As soon as he was out of sight, Marie let the shaking overwhelm her. Carefully lying her bike on its side, she sat down on the side of the road and wrapped her arms around her knees while tremors shook her entire body. Out of nowhere, she felt very sick and crawled into the grass.

While heaves clutched her body, tears raced down her face. Spent and terrified, she lay back and covered her eyes with her hands. She felt so afraid all the time. What did she think she was doing here?

She silently prayed, desperate for God to reach out to her and physically reassure her that He hadn't abandoned her. But, of course, He did not and she eventually remembered not to test her Creator.

Rolling to her feet, she stumbled to her bike and climbed back on. Her legs felt so weak that she wobbled a bit while she pedaled back to town, but eventually her strength returned.

THE JEWEL SERIES

More Great Christian Fiction...

The Jewel Anthology
by Hallee Bridgeman

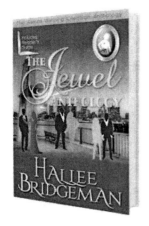

Hallee Bridgeman's critically acclaimed best selling award winning Christian anthology, together in one book. The complete novel *Sapphire Ice*. Inspired by *The Jewel Series*, the all new novella *Greater Than Rubies*. The second full length novel *Emerald Fire*, and the final novel *Topaz Heat*. All works complete, uncut, and unabridged.

Sapphire Ice

Robin's heart is as cold as her deep blue eyes. After a terrifying childhood, she trusts neither God nor men. With kindness and faith, Tony prays for the opportunity to shatter the wall of ice around her heart.

Greater Than Rubies

2014 EPIC eBook Awards™ Finalist: Robin plans her wedding but anxiety arises when she starts to realize the magnitude of change this marriage will bring. Forgotten nightmares resurface bringing reminders of past horrors. She gives in to her insecurities and cancels Boston's "Royal Wedding." With God's guidance, will her bridegroom convince her of her true worth?

Emerald Fire

Inspirational Novel of the Year RONE Award Finalist 2013: Maxine fights daily to extinguish the embers of her fiery youth. Barry's faith is deeply shaken when he is suddenly widowed. Just as they begin to live the "happily ever after" love story that neither of them ever dreamed could come true, a sudden catastrophe could wreck everything. Will her husband find peace and strength enough to carry them through the flames?

Topaz Heat

Inspirational Novel of the Year RONE Award Nominee 2013: Honey eyed Sarah remembers absolutely nothing from her bloodcurdling younger years. Derrick fled a young life of crime to become a billionaire's successful protégé. After years of ignoring the heat between them they surrender to love, but must truly live their faith to see them through.

Available in eBook or Paperback wherever fine books are sold.

EXCERPT: SAPPHIRE ICE

Sapphire Ice was voted **The Book Club Network's** July <u>Book of the Month</u> and nominated for <u>Book of the Year</u> in 2013. If you missed *Sapphire Ice*, part 1 of *The Jewel Series*, buy it now in Paperback or eBook wherever fine books are sold.

Enjoy this special excerpt from the critically acclaimed full length novel *Sapphire Ice*.

ROBIN stopped near him to grab a carafe of coffee. "How did we manage to get the early shift, Clarence?"

He winked and whispered conspiratorially. "Tell me about it. I have my lunch patrons' whole lives memorized, but I only know half the people out there." He looked over her head to the head table. "Boston's royalty is here."

Robin was too tired to even be intrigued by Clarence's abnormal awe. "Maybe we can get Stanley a jester's hat," she whispered back, then pushed open the door to the dining room and forced a serious expression onto her face. The door swinging shut cut off his choking laughter.

The dining room was packed with people, seated at tables of eight. The restaurant was closed for the meeting, and it surprised her to see so many people there. But then, most of the customers weren't members and wouldn't get many opportunities to dine at Benedict's, especially for free.

She was given the head table to serve, and knew some of them as regular lunch patrons. She addressed those she knew by name, and tried to discretely read the name tags of those she didn't. Methodically, she worked her way down the long table, pausing to chat when it was required, fetching drinks as they were needed.

"Mr. Riley, it's good to see you again. I think it's been several weeks," she said, speaking to the president of the Chamber.

"I've been on vacation, Robin. Have you ever been to Greece?"

She smiled and filled his coffee cup. "Not yet, but I want to go someday."

"Beautiful country, dear. If you ever get the opportunity, don't pass it up."

"If a trip to Greece ever falls into my lap, I'll remember your advice." She moved to the next person while Riley continued to speak.

"Tony, if you've never had Robin here serve you, you've been missing out on the best that Benedict's has to offer."

"Yes. I think I've heard something similar about her before."

The smooth voice seemed familiar, but she couldn't quite place it. She took her attention from the cup and lifted her head, her eyes crashing into a pair of black eyes that seemed to look all the way inside of her, instantly learning all her secrets. "I didn't expect to see you here," he said.

Tony felt deep shock when he'd seen Robin enter the dining room. He'd had time to recover as she worked her way to him, and had nearly gained back enough self control to not show any outward reaction as she leaned in from behind him to pour his coffee. He had already had his normal morning quota of two cups, but allowing her to serve it gave him a chance to have her stop at his shoulder. As she completed her task, he caught her scent, something exotic and spicy, entirely feminine. Then she met his eyes and he thought that his heart would beat itself out of his chest.

When she looked away, it broke the spell, but a tremor in his hand that he neither liked nor appreciated remained. He was better prepared when she looked directly at him again, and concentrated fully on keeping his brain functioning.

"Do I know you?" She asked, her voice soft so as not to carry.

He kept his voice as soft as hers. "Not officially."

"I'm sorry, I don't … " her eyes skimmed his name tag, "I don't recall meeting you, Mr. Viscolli."

His teeth flashed white against his olive skin. "I unofficially met you last night."

Panic skirted up her spine and she looked around the room. Lowering her voice even farther, she leaned closer so that he could hear her. "Please, don't say anything. I … we can't … I mean, another job … "

He placed a hand on her wrist, startling her. His hand felt rough, but warm. Warm enough that it sent heat up her arm, causing her to flush. "So, what you're saying is that your job may be in my hands."

The flush that covered her cheeks was no longer from heat, but from the anger he saw flash in her eyes. "Release me, sir." She bit out.

He didn't think he could. "What would you do to keep your job, I wonder?"

She could never take him on in a game of cards. Every cruel thought in her imagination seared right through her sapphire eyes and bored into his, which he struggled to keep impassive. Still, she maintained her cool façade, something he deeply admired amidst his mirth. Tony carefully bit down on the inside of his lip to keep himself from laughing at her next words. "I don't play those games, Mr. Viscolli. Remove your hand, or else I'll remove it."

He shifted his grip until his fingers encircled her wrist. They overlapped on the thin bones, and this time he did chuckle. "You think you could?"

In a panic, knowing how long she was taking with this customer, she glanced up and spotted Clarence watching her. Baring her teeth, she leaned close to this man's ear and whispered. "I can and I have, on men bigger than you. Are you willing to test me?"

With a grin, he reluctantly let her go. It was that or drag her into his lap, and he didn't think anyone in the room would appreciate that too much. "Perhaps another time I'll take you up on your challenge."

Unable to stand the thought of leaving him with the last word, she leaned forward again, barely speaking above a whisper. "If the thought of seeing you again didn't repulse me, Mr. Viscolli, I'd almost look forward to it."

With that she moved on down the table, ignoring his chuckle that followed her parting shot. She found it especially challenging to keep a polite smile on her face and make inane chatter with the other patrons as she continued to serve while seething inside. How dare he?

She headed back into the kitchen to get more coffee and Clarence immediately intercepted her. "Did you have a problem with that man, Robin?"

Out of earshot of the customers, she was able to slam things around, surprised that she didn't break the glass coffee carafe. "Nothing I couldn't handle," she said, slamming the top back on her serving container.

He gripped her elbow and kept her from reentering the room. "I know that sometimes customers might get a little – well – fresh with some of our girls, but I wouldn't want to think that you might have – albeit unintentionally – insulted one of them."

She bared her teeth at him. "Did he look insulted?"

"No, but you looked insulting, and I'm concerned because I've never seen you act that way before."

She slammed the coffee onto a counter and stepped closer, until she could poke his bony chest with her finger. "I didn't like the way he looked at me, I didn't like the way he touched me, and I didn't like what he implied when he spoke to me." When he flinched, she realized what she was doing and stepped away from him, drawing in a deep breath to calm down. "Now, you've had your little 'chat' with me. Do you intend to speak with him?"

Clarence's face fused with color. "Robin, do you have any idea who that is out there?"

"I don't quite have the approbation for most of our patrons as you do, because I truly don't care." She grabbed the pot of coffee and pushed open the door.

He took insult at her words, as was her intent, though she regretted it the second his face fell. She paused and went back into the kitchen. As she opened her mouth to retract it, he straightened, stiff as a board, and put a regal tone in his voice. "That is Mr. Antonio Viscolli. He is one of the stockholders of this club, and is hosting this morning's breakfast. If you would like to lodge a formal, written complaint, I will entertain reviewing it, but in the meantime, you are here to serve, so I suggest you return to your post." He looked her up and down, his expression hinting that he didn't much care for what he saw. "Unless, of course, you'd like me to have someone else wait the head table. I'm sure that any server out there would be happy to trade places with you."

Oh, what a tempting notion. She considered it, very seriously, for several breaths. Ultimately, she decided that trading tables would most certainly give Viscolli a great deal of satisfaction, a game point. No, she'd serve him, and do a heck of a good job at it. "That won't be necessary, sir. I'm fully capable of performing all of my duties."

His face softened, momentarily. "I know. Now, get back to work."

Not wanting to leave things tense with someone she considered a friend, she paused to make one of her normal parting remarks. "Purple and green," she said. At his confused look, she continued, "with bells. For Stan's hat."

His mouth twitched as he fought the smile and waved her away.

Greater Than Rubies is a 2014 EPIC™ Awards <u>Finalist</u> in the Spiritual category. If you missed this wonderful novella inspired by *The Jewel Series*, buy it in Paperback or find the **FREE** eBook anywhere fine books are sold.

Enjoy this special excerpt from the critically acclaimed novella *Greater Than Rubies*.

ROBIN nervously fiddled with her ring while she waited for the Inside Boston magazine reporter to arrive. She sat in the conference room adjacent to the office of Tony's public relations manager, Linda Cross. She still wore the clothes and makeup from the photo shoot that had taken place in a room just down the hall. She'd hoped Tony could be there for the photos, but the magazine had specifically requested only her.

The door opened and Robin's heart lurched, but Linda entered alone. She was short and stocky, with a thick waist and jet black hair. Thick glasses with square black frames dominated her face. "Don will be in momentarily," she said. "He's signing some papers for me right now." She raised an eyebrow behind her glasses. "No worries, Miss Bartlett. I'll be here the whole time."

"I've just never done this before." She licked her lips.

"A year from now, it will be old hat," Linda assured. Robin wondered if she meant that to intimidate her or make her feel more at ease, because, honestly, she wasn't feeling better in the wake of that remark.

A tap at the door preceded the entrance of Don Roberts. He was younger than Robin, tall, boy-next-door good looking with straight brown hair and a fake tan. Nothing about him made her feel at ease about this interview.

He shook her hand - again - then sat in the chair adjacent to her. He took a phone out of his pocket, pressed a series of buttons on it, then set it on the table in front of her. She could only assume he'd activated some sort of recording device. "Miss Bartlett, Robin, thank you for giving me this opportunity."

"It's my pleasure," she said around a suddenly too-dry mouth.

"Let's go ahead and cover the basics. Tell us how you met Tony."

This was the first person outside of church to address Tony as Tony and not Mr. Viscolli. It intrigued Robin. "He, ah, bought a restaurant where I worked." She cleared her throat. "We met then."

"When was that?"

"Last fall."

"And, to add a spice of romance to our story, how did he propose?"

Robin smiled and relaxed, thinking back. "Christmas Eve, on the beach in the Florida Keys."

"That's really nice," Don said. He smiled. "Tony Viscolli is a powerful force in the business world, and not just in the Boston area. He has businesses all over the country and thousands of employees. What do you think drew him to you in particular?"

Uncomfortable, Robin shrugged. "I really couldn't tell you. You'd have to ask him."

"But we can probably guess what drew you to him, right?"

Robin put her hands in her lap and laced her fingers, squeezing them tightly. "If you knew his heart, or anything about him personally, you'd not have to ask that question. He is amazing and generous and loving, and I feel so incredibly blessed."

"Is he?"

"I beg your pardon?"

"Is he really all those things? Or simply uninformed?"

Robin felt her eyebrows crease under the thick makeup from the photo shoot. "What?"

"Does he know all there is to know about you?"

Robin shifted her eyes to Linda, who frowned but did not speak. "I beg your pardon?"

Don sat forward and tapped the top of the table with every question. He looked like an anaconda eyeing a mouse. "He knows you were a waitress moonlighting as a bartender. Does he know your father went to prison for drug smuggling and now faces double murder charges? Does he know your mother was an addict who was murdered in a drug deal? Does he know you, yourself, stabbed your foster parent in the back with a buck knife? Does he know you were a fugitive until you turned eighteen and your juvenile crimes were sealed? Does he know about the improprietary manner in which you had your former employer pull strings with city hall to clear your record so you could obtain custody of one of your sisters? How did you convince that retired sailor to help you pull those strings, Miss Bartlett?"

Panic swirled in her brain, freezing her ability to form cohesive thoughts. "I don't – what are you –?" Robin gasped and looked from Don to Linda. Her heart pounded and she felt sweat break out on her forehead.

Linda pressed a button on the table next to her before standing. "Mr. Roberts? This interview is over. Our attorneys at the Anderson firm will be in contact with your editor in light of the NDA you signed and this particular line of questioning."

"You can't hide her. Believe me if I know, the tabloids know, too. This is the kind of rags to riches story that everyone will be clamoring after. You need to let her – "

As he spoke the door opened and two uniformed security officers marched into the room. They walked straight up to Don. "You need to come with us, sir," one of them said.

"Now." The other one said, picking up the reporter's phone from the table.

"Hey! You can't have that!"

"We'll return your property when you're safely outside the building, sir." The guard stepped aside, placing his body between Roberts and the two women, and gestured with his hand. "Right this way, sir."

Roberts stood but quickly bent around the guard toward Robin. "You might as well figure out the best thing to do is embrace your story and tell it, or else others will do it with their own spin and you won't be able to influence what they say."

The second guard grabbed his arm at the elbow and said, "You've already outstayed your welcome, sir. Time to go."

Roberts jerked himself free. "Don't touch me. I'm leaving."

"Leave now," the guard warned, "Without another word, or I will use force." His finger stabbed in the direction of the door.

Robin stared at the closed door long after it shut behind them. Linda sat where Don had been and touched her hand. "I'm so sorry. All of his credentials checked out."

With a shaking hand, Robin brushed the hair off her forehead. "I'm not doing something like this again."

Linda nodded. "I understand." She pressed some buttons on her phone. "Margaret? I need to talk to Mr. V. This isn't good."

Without waiting for Linda to hang up the phone or Tony to come gallantly into the room, Robin gathered her bag and her coat and left. Linda tried to call her back, but she was stuck on hold with Tony's office. Escape. Flee. Hide.

The elevator arrived. Thankful to find it empty, she slipped inside and pressed the lobby button, then the door close button in rapid succession. As soon as it started moving, she went to the back corner of the elevator and pressed back against the wall. She used to be good at hiding. Hide way in the back of the closet. Protect her sisters. Make the monsters forget you're there.

But she couldn't hide from her past, could she? What did she think she was doing, becoming Mrs. Antonio Viscolli? Inadequate didn't begin to describe her. Her cell phone started ringing, but she turned it off as she stepped off the elevator and into the lobby of the hotel. As she walked out of the doors, the valet lifted his hand in greeting, grabbed her keys, and rushed to get her car. With no choice but to wait, she slipped her coat on and shoved her hands into the pockets, lifting her shoulders against the wind. Before her car arrived, she felt Tony at her elbow.

"I'm sorry."

"I'm not doing that again."

"It will never happen again."

Robin turned her head and looked him straight in the eye. "Oh, I know it won't."

Her car pulled up in front of them. Tony touched her elbow. "Robin, please."

"It's okay. I have to go now. But I'll see you when you get back from

California." He looked so worried and a frown marred his forehead. Putting a hand on his cheek, loving him, needing him, she pressed her lips to his. "I love you. Have a safe trip."

Emerald Fire was a 2012 RONE Award <u>Finalist</u> for ***Inspirational Novel of the Year***. If you missed *Emerald Fire*, part 2 of *The Jewel Series*, buy it now in Paperback or eBook wherever fine books are sold.

Enjoy this special excerpt from the critically acclaimed full length novel *Emerald Fire*.

MAXINE rolled over in the bed. As the blankets slipped off, she felt cool air on her shoulders. While her partially asleep brain pondered that, she tugged the sheets back up to cover herself and her ring caught a thread on the blanket.

Her ring?

Maxine's eyes flew open as memories of the night before flooded her mind. She whipped her head around. The bed next to her was empty, the pillow indented from where her husband's head had recently lain.

Her husband!

Alone in the bedroom, she lifted her left hand and stared. There sat the ridiculously enormous, preposterously expensive platinum ring, encrusted with emeralds and diamonds, that the man with whom she had been engaged for less than two hours before their wedding ceremony had picked out for her. When he slipped it onto her finger, he'd said something about the color of her eyes. Seconds later, he'd kissed her.

After a cursory glance around the room to be certain she was actually alone and the bedroom door was shut, she threw the covers off and rushed to the closet, looking for anything to wear. She grabbed a pair of jeans and a sweater and dashed to the bathroom, shutting and locking the door behind her. She leaned against the closed door for a moment while her heart raced and her mind reeled.

What in the name of all things holy had they done? Rather, what had she done?

With a few flicks of her wrist, she turned the water on for a shower and stopped to look at herself in the mirror. She lifted her fingers to her mouth and traced lips swollen from his kisses. Her green eyes sparkled like the emeralds on her finger. Normally, her olive complexion needed the help of cosmetics to bring out any kind of rosy flush. This morning, however, her cheeks looked rosy, flushed. She felt warm inside despite the morning chill.

In her entire adult life, no other man had ever even so much as kissed her. Not once. Many men had tried to taste her mouth, but whenever they'd gotten close enough, panic would rise up and make her push them away. That typically ended the relationship. The ones who suffered that humiliation soon learned that it wasn't a onetime thing and very quickly gave up trying. As she stepped under the warm spray of water, she thought back to the night before and to her complete lack of fear.

Her husband of less than twelve hours – her husband didn't frighten her at all. When he kissed her, it occurred to her that she felt absolutely none of her normal panic. Instead what she felt was warmth, excitement, attraction. He made her feel safe. He made her feel … loved.

"Husband and wife," the Elvis impersonator had proclaimed with a shimmy and a shake. Then her husband had slowly leaned in close and taken her lips with his strong, masculine mouth as if they were the most delicate rose petals. Her knees had vanished and she felt his arm around her waist holding her up, lifting her, supporting her as she kissed his heavenly mouth.

Then, here, in this hotel suite last night on the very top floor of the Las Vegas casino, her husband had let her lead the way. It was as if he sensed that she needed to be able to control all of the activity. She never had to say anything to him or explain her fear. He just accepted her hesitations or kissed her through them. He slowly coaxed and guided and offered until she accepted. It had been so wonderful, so beautiful, that he had held her to him with her head cradled against his broad, thick chest and his strong arms around her while she wept at the beauty of it.

Her sister was going to kill her.

Reflecting on that for a moment, Maxine realized she didn't much care.

She was excited, thrilled. Married!

She quickly finished showering and got dressed. After brushing her teeth and running a comb through her long straight black hair, compliments of her Native American father, she left the bathroom, again comforted by the solitude. Little nervous butterflies woke up in her stomach while she slipped into her shoes, the sight of the enormous ring on her finger distracting her with every motion of her hand.

Stalling, she straightened the bed. As she pulled the coverlet up, her ring caught the light. Running her hand over his pillow she smiled and felt a warm rush of love flow through her heart, quelling the nervous butterflies.

When she could think of nothing else to do, she opened the bedroom door and stepped out into the living room. Seeing him standing there staring out into the sunrise brought back visions of every time she had seen his face in the last three years. She thought of every time she had sketched his face. She could not believe how much had happened in the last three weeks.

The thought stopped her. Three weeks? Had it only been that long since they put her brand new husband's first wife in the ground?

Without turning to look at her, his smooth, baritone voice reached her ears. "Obviously, we need to talk."

EXCERPT: TOPAZ HEAT

Topaz Heat was a 2012 RONE Award <u>Nominee</u> for ***Inspirational Novel of the Year***. If you missed *Topaz Heat*, part 3 of *The Jewel Series*, buy it now in Paperback or eBook wherever fine books are sold.

Enjoy this special excerpt from the critically acclaimed full length novel *Topaz Heat*.

SARAH heard another clang. She quietly set her purse down but held onto the umbrella, holding it just above the handle like a baseball bat. Running lightly on her toes, she crossed the room quickly and stood by the door of the dining room. There were a few more sounds, then the sound of a man whistling that got louder as he got closer.

Taking a deep breath, she raised the umbrella over her head and waited, focused on the door. She let it swing open, watched the figure of the man come out of the dining room, and brought the umbrella down. Hard.

He must have sensed the movement because he ducked and the umbrella hit him across the back of his shoulders. "Ow! Hey!"

In the next second, and utterly without warning, he rolled to the floor and used one of his legs to sweep hers out from under her. She flailed her arms as she landed on her backside, finding herself under his weight. She started struggling, but he threw one of his legs over hers and grabbed her arms in a bone-lock, pinning them up by her head.

"Sarah?"

She realized her eyes were closed. At the sound of his voice they flew open. Immediate recognition prefaced the heat that rushed her face from total embarrassment. "Derrick? What are you doing here?"

"I was about to ask you the same question."

She hadn't seen him in at least five years. No, it was six. He left town right after his mother's funeral. He'd not been back. She got updates from Maxine or Robin each time they'd seen him in New York. She hadn't been to New York and hadn't seen him at all in that space of time. He'd filled out, she thought. His face looked more mature, almost tougher, his shoulders wider.

Derrick was thinking that Sarah hadn't changed at all. She still looked like a teenager. Her hair had come out of its clip and lay spread out around her head on the carpet, the red highlights caught in the curls, catching the light. She still had the spray of freckles across her nose, and her eyes, behind their glasses, still looked exactly like the color of the richest topaz.

Realizing he was staring, he released her instantly, pushed away, and sat next to her. "What in the world did you hit me with?" He reached behind him and gingerly touched the back of his shoulders, wincing when his hand came away smeared in blood.

The only thing he had on was a pair of sweat pants. "My, um, umbrella."

He saw it next to her and grabbed it. It was snapped in half. Irritated anger burned through him. "This? You think there's an intruder and this is what you use to defend yourself?"

She ripped it out of his hands and stood. "It was all I had."

"It never occurred to you to call security?"

Her cheeks flushed bright red. No, it had not occurred to her. She waved her hand as if to dismiss his last statement. "Let me see," she said, moving behind him.

He jerked to his feet. "No, thank you. Don't touch it."

"Don't be such a baby. Let me see."

He held a hand up to ward her off. "Really. Don't worry about it."

"I promise I won't hurt you, Derrick. I won't even touch it." She put her hands on her hips. "I am a nurse, you know."

She almost withdrew the offer. Then he glared at her before moving to one of the oversized chairs, sitting sideways so she could see his back. The skin across his shoulders was already starting to purple with a bruise, and it looked like something had caught the skin and ripped it. He had a gash about three inches long diagonally across his right shoulder. "Ouch, Derrick. Sorry about that."

Over his left shoulder, just shy of the bruise, was a tattoo of a dragon, done in brilliant colors – turquoise, fuchsia, purple, bright green. She was surprised that it was there, intrigued. He had done everything to get rid of his past, and she wondered why he still had the tattoo. Before she realized it, her fingers were hovering over it, about to touch it.

He looked at her over his shoulder and glared. She bit her lip and gingerly touched the bruise. "You'll want to put some ice on it, and you should let me clean and dress the cut."

She turned to leave. "What are you doing?" he asked.

She was halfway down the hallway before she answered him. "I'll be right back." Moving quickly, she went to the master bathroom and pulled open the medicine cabinet, finding the supplies she needed. She slipped the roll of tape and the package of bandages into her scrubs pocket, then pulled a washcloth out of the linen closet and wet it.

When she returned to the front room, he stared at the brown bottle in her hand suspiciously. "What's that?"

"Hydrogen peroxide."

"Uh huh. And what do you think you're going to do with it?"

With a sigh, she poured some on the cloth and stepped closer. "I'm going to clean the cut."

He hissed the breath between his teeth and cringed away as the cloth came in contact with his skin. "Ouch. That hurts."

"Good Lord, Derrick, quit being such a baby."

He clenched his teeth and swallowed a retort. Then he felt her warm breath blowing on the wound. He imagined her lips puckered as she blew against his fevered skin.

"There, is that better?"

"It's great. Kind of like a carnival ride but without the cotton candy. Thank you."

He heard her moving behind him, heard the sound of the cap going back on the bottle. He felt her fingers graze his skin as she placed a bandage over the cut and taped it to his skin. He tried desperately not to react to her touch in any way, to pretend she was some platonic stranger tending his wound. "You need to ice it. I'll go get some."

While she was gone, he closed his eyes and took a deep breath, seeking some inner steadiness. Why was she here? She quickly returned and gently set a plastic bag filled with ice across his shoulders, then sat on the couch that angled with the chair so that she faced him.

"You never answered my question," he said, staring at her with those brown eyes that always made her uncomfortable. "What are you doing here?"

"They're painting my brownstone today and tomorrow. My furniture is under sheets in the middle of the rooms. Robin never told me that you were going to be here." She looked down at her shoes. "I really am sorry, Derrick."

"I guess I forgot to tell her where I was staying. I thought Tony might've let her know." He reached behind him and shifted the bag of ice. "You would have had to park next to my car in the garage though."

"I walked."

He narrowed his eyes. "From where?"

She gestured at her pastel pink pants, the matching top, and the white jacket with the pastel slashes of color. "Hello? From the hospital."

"Are you out of your mind?" She opened her mouth to argue with him, but he cut her off. "That's easily four or five blocks. Downtown. On a Friday night."

"It's not like the streets were deserted or anything."

"What possessed you to walk?"

She bared her teeth. "It might have something to do with the fact that my car wouldn't start."

"Why didn't you call someone?"

She'd had enough. She was really sorry that she'd whacked him with her umbrella, but the truth was she really couldn't stand the man and never had been able to stomach him. "I've been an adult for a long time, Derrick, and I don't answer to anyone, most especially you. If you'll excuse me, I've had a really long day and I'm going to bed."

"Sarah ..."

She stood. "No. I'm done. Good night."

As she brushed by him, his hand came out of nowhere and grabbed her arm. She froze, stared down at him, waiting. "I apologize," he offered with his most velvet voice.

"I'm not going to fall for the smooth charm, Derrick. Now let me go.

I'm tired."

His jaw clenched as he released her. When he heard the click of her bedroom door shutting, he ripped the ice pack off his back and threw it across the room. He turned and carefully leaned back until his back touched the chair. Then he closed his eyes and sighed.

Six years later. Six years and he was still completely in love with her.

He'd hoped it had been a crush, kind of like what he had for Robin, even a touch for Maxine. The sisters had charmed him the second he laid eyes on them, and he loved them for their beauty and their love of life. Except it was more, much more, with Sarah.

And she couldn't stand him.

She would never look at him and see anything but the teenager in the ripped leather jacket with the I-dare-you scowl. He'd changed, though, in every way he possibly could. He had cleaned his clothes, cleaned his act, found Christ, and followed God. Like his water baptism cleansed his soul and made him a new person, he shed his past and created a new person. It didn't matter. She still looked down her perky little befreckled nose at him.

He rubbed his face with his hands and surged to his feet. He thought about her traipsing through the heart of the city alone at this hour with only a purse and an umbrella and thought about all of the terrible things that could have been waiting for her during that five block walk. He whispered a prayer of thanksgiving for God's protection over her in those early morning hours, and retired to his own bedroom, sorry that their reunion had not gone well at all.

Any secret, unacknowledged hope he had of winning her over with a smoothly executed reunion meeting was now gone forever.

ABOUT THE AUTHOR

HALLEE BRIDGEMAN is a best-selling Christian author who writes action-packed romantic suspense focusing on true to life characters facing real world problems. Her work has been described as everything from refreshing to heart-stopping exciting.

An Army brat turned Floridian, Hallee finally settled in central Kentucky with her family so she could enjoy the beautiful changing seasons. She enjoys the roller- coaster ride thrills that life with a National Guard husband, a teenage daughter, and two elementary age sons delivers.

When not penning novels, she blogs about all things cooking and homemaking at Hallee the Homemaker™ (www.halleethehomemaker.com). Her passion for cooking spurred her to launch a whole food, real food "Parody" cookbook series. In addition to nutritious, Biblically grounded recipes, readers will find that each cookbook also confronts some controversial aspect of secular pop culture.

Hallee loves coffee, campy action movies, and regular date nights with her husband. Above all else, she loves God with all her heart, soul, mind, and strength; has been redeemed by the blood of Christ; and relies on the presence of the Holy Spirit. She prays her work here on earth is a blessing to you and would love to hear from you. Contact information is on her website.

FICTION BOOKS BY HALLEE:

Sapphire Ice, book 1 of the Jewel Series

Greater Than Rubies (a novella inspired by the Jewel Series)

Emerald Fire, book 2 of the Jewel Series

Topaz Heat, book 3 of the Jewel Series

Christmas Diamond (a novella inspired by the Jewel Series)

A Melody for James, book 1 of the Song of Suspense Series

An Aria for Nicholas, book 2 of the Song of Suspense Series

A Carol for Kent, book 3 of the Song of Suspense Series

A Harmony for Steven, book 4 of the Song of Suspense Series (upcoming)

Hallee the Homemaker blog
www.halleethehomemaker.com/

Hallee Bridgeman, Novelist blog
www.bridgemanfamily.com/hallee/

Ask your local library to stock fine Olivia Kimbrell Press titles. Consider purchasing a copy of this book for your church library or as a gift. This book and upcoming releases from Hallee Bridgeman are available in e-Book format and trade paperback wherever fine books are sold. For more information, visit us on the web:

www.bridgemanfamily.com/hallee/book-samples/

www.oliviakimbrellpress.com

Hallee News Letter

http://tinyurl.com/HalleeNews/

Never miss updates about upcoming releases, book signings, appearances, or other events. Sign up for Hallee's monthly newsletter.

♫ ♫ ♫ ♫